MW00785439

THE ANNOTATED GREAT GATSBY

*Celestial Eyes* by Spanish American painter and graphic designer Francis Cugat
(1893–1981), cover art for the dust jacket for the first edition of *The Great Gatsby*.
Gouache on board. See also Cugat's preliminary sketches on p. 197.

# THE ANNOTATED GREAT GATSBY

F. SCOTT FITZGERALD

## 100TH ANNIVERSARY DELUXE EDITION

Edited by James L. W. West III
Introduction by Amor Towles

LIBRARY OF AMERICA

THE ANNOTATED GREAT GATSBY

100th Anniversary Deluxe Edition

is published with support from

THE GIORGI FAMILY FOUNDATION

# CONTENTS

# PREFACE

## BY JAMES L. W. WEST III

The first edition of F. Scott Fitzgerald's *The Great Gatsby* was published on April 10, 1925, by Charles Scribner's Sons. Fitzgerald's novel was very much of its moment: it was filled with references to prohibition, World War I, and jazz; to popular movies and songs of the period; to amateur sports, fast automobiles, and Broadway stars; to ocean liners, wealthy industrialists, and scandal magazines. Readers of the first edition would have recognized most of these references; today's readers do not. Much has changed in American society in the one hundred years since the novel first appeared. The value of a dollar, for example, has diminished. The rent for Nick Carraway's shabby bungalow in West Egg was "eighty a month" in 1922, the year in which the novel is set. Robert Keable's semi-scandalous novel *Simon Called Peter*, which Nick finds on a table in Tom and Myrtle's love nest, has been forgotten; and no contemporary reader has seen a copy of *Town Topics*, the gossip magazine that Myrtle enjoys paging through (Fitzgerald alludes to it as *Town Tattle*). *The New York Tribune*, a thoroughly conservative newspaper, ceased publication many years ago, as did the *New York Evening Journal*, a racy sheet with sensationalist reporting and celebrity news. Gilda Gray and Joe Frisco, Broadway headliners in the 1920s, are now known only to students of theater history. The Plaza Hotel still stands, but the original Murray Hill Hotel on Park Avenue was torn down in 1947, and Penn Station was demolished in 1963. Sports-car owners no longer wear "dusters" to protect their clothes from automobile exhaust, and only a retro entertainer would style his hair in a pompadour. Aficionados of African American music might recognize the "Beale Street Blues," but almost no one will remember "The Sheik of Araby," a popular tune of 1921, or "The Rosary," the sentimental ditty that Wolfshiem whistles off-key in his office.

Contemporary readers can certainly understand *The Great Gatsby* without knowing these names, songs, events, and titles. Annotations and glosses, however, add much to the reading experience. This Library of America edition, with marginal notes and illustrations throughout, is the most extensively annotated edition of *The Great Gatsby* yet published. The identifications and explanations supplied here will transport readers back to the 1920s and to the world that Fitzgerald knew and sought to capture. These annotations emphasize the enduring themes and concerns that have placed the book on so many "best of" lists and have made it a frequent candidate for consideration as one of the Great American Novels. References to World War I are identified; the role of Prohibition is explained; books and movies are glossed; song lyrics are given; stage and movie stars are named. These annotations also provide a running commentary on the text—on its composition and publication, on earlier versions of the narrative, and on the interpretation of key passages. It would be impossible to represent the breadth of scholarship on *The Great Gatsby* in a single annotated volume of this kind. The editor makes no claim to have done so. He has, however, brought into the margins a selection of diverse voices of novelists, journalists, and critics, with priority given to the work of public-facing writers.

## COMPOSITION, REVISION, AND PUBLICATION

Three versions of *The Great Gatsby* survive—a handwritten manuscript, a set of revised galley proofs, and the first edition. These versions differ considerably from one another. Also extant is Fitzgerald's personal copy of the novel into which he marked, by hand, post-publication corrections and revisions. These materials are among the F. Scott Fitzgerald Papers at Princeton University Library. The correspondence between Fitzgerald and Maxwell Perkins, his editor, is also preserved at Princeton, in the Scribner Archive. We have other letters and writings by Fitzgerald in which he describes the inception, composition, and revision of his book. This material allows us to look over his shoulder as he sat at his writing desk and composed his most famous novel.

Fitzgerald began working on the book that became *The Great Gatsby* in the late spring of 1922. In a letter of June 10, 1922, to Perkins, he gave a few hints about the material he wanted to use. His idea was to write a novel with a "catholic element" and to set it in "the middle west and New York of 1885." Fitzgerald worked on this version during 1922 and 1923 but was dissatisfied with the results. He salvaged one of his best short stories from the drafts ("Absolution," published in *The American Mercury* in June 1924), but he scrapped the rest of the writing. In the spring of 1924 he reconceived the novel, setting it now in a fictional version of Great Neck,

Long Island, where he and his wife and daughter were living. He produced three chapters of this version; then he and his family left for France, on the ocean liner *Minnewaska*, in April 1924. By June they had settled in Valescure, St. Raphaël, on the French Riviera. Fitzgerald continued to labor on the novel through the summer months and into the fall, working with stenographers and putting the text through two and perhaps three additional drafts. By the end of October he had a completed typescript in hand; this he sent to Perkins, via transatlantic mail, on the twenty-seventh of that month.

Perkins read the book and responded immediately with high praise. "I think the novel is a wonder," he wrote to the author on November 18, 1924. The story has "vitality to an extraordinary degree" and "a kind of mystic atmosphere. . . ." Perkins continued: "It is a marvelous fusion, into a unity of presentation, of the extraordinary incongruities of life today. And as for sheer writing, it's astonishing." Two days later Perkins wrote a second and longer letter to Fitzgerald in which he reiterated his admiration for the novel but made several suggestions. "Gatsby is somewhat vague," he said. "The reader's eyes can never quite focus upon him, his outlines are dim." Perhaps Fitzgerald might undertake some revisions? "You might here and there interpolate some phrases, and possibly incidents, little touches of various kinds, that would suggest that he was in some active way mysteriously engaged." Clues about Gatsby's origins might "come out bit by bit in the course of actual narrative," this to satisfy the curiosity of readers. As the novel then stood, most of the revelations about Gatsby's past appeared in the final two chapters of the book.

Fitzgerald responded with a thorough revision of the galley proofs, sent to him by Scribner's in two batches in late December 1924. These galleys—long sheets of freshly set type with the equivalent of two or three pages of the novel printed on each galley—survive among his papers at Princeton. Many of the galleys are covered with handwritten revisions; other galleys have freshly typed passages affixed to them; still other pages bear a mixture of handwritten and typed text. These galley proofs show evidence of Fitzgerald's intense engagement with the text and his desire to bring it as close to perfection as he could. He shifted material about, changed the order of chapters, cut long blocks of text, and composed new passages of description and exposition. He sharpened the dialogue and polished the prose throughout. With these revisions he created a new round of labor for Perkins and his assistants at Scribner's, who had to see these changes into print. Fitzgerald's alterations in the galleys went far beyond the limit usually allowed, but Perkins was determined to let Fitzgerald have his way. The editor oversaw the transfer of the revisions into the text, and the novel was published on schedule in an edition that, apart from a few typos, was free of significant error.

## TITLE AND DUST JACKET

The typescript that Fitzgerald submitted to Perkins in October was titled "Trimalchio in West Egg." Trimalchio is a character in the *Satyricon* of the Roman author Petronius (c. 27–66 CE). He is a freed slave who has grown wealthy; he gives lavish parties for guests who come, partake of his food and drink, and depart without bothering to ask his name. Fitzgerald was dissatisfied with this allusive title, in part because it would have required an explanation, probably printed on the dust jacket. He had considered several other titles during composition; these included "Gold-Hatted Gatsby," "The High-Bouncing Lover," "Among the Ash Heaps and Millionaires," "On the Road to West Egg," "Trimalchio," and "Gatsby." On December 16 Fitzgerald sent a cable to Perkins changing the title to "The Great Gatsby," but he was not entirely happy with that title either. On March 19, 1925, three weeks before publication, he attempted another change. In a cable sent to Perkins on that day he wrote: "CRAZY ABOUT TITLE 'UNDER THE RED WHITE AND BLUE' STOP WHART WOULD DELAY BE." The following day, Perkins replied: "Advertised and sold for April tenth publication. Change suggested would mean some weeks delay, very great psychological damage. Think irony is far more effective under less leading title. Everyone likes present title. Urge we keep it." Fitzgerald conceded in a March 22 reply: "YOURE RIGHT." The book was published on Friday, April 10, under the title *The Great Gatsby*, but it is useful to think about which elements of the novel Fitzgerald was attempting to highlight with the rejected titles—Jay Gatsby as a kind of circus performer, millionaires as denizens of a moral wasteland, an ironic portrayal of the American Dream.

Before departing for France in April 1924, Fitzgerald had visited the Scribner's offices and had seen a painting—or perhaps preliminary sketches—by the Spanish American artist Francis Cugat, contracted by the publisher for possible use on a dust jacket. The jacket artwork had not been assigned to a book. Cugat's painting, a gouache on board, depicts a woman's face floating over an amusement-park scene, the whole set against a dark blue background. A single tear falls down the woman's face. Reflected in her eyes is a naked figure. The painting caught Fitzgerald's attention; he asked that it be reserved for his novel in progress. In a letter to Perkins written on or about August 25, 1924, from Saint-Raphaël, Fitzgerald reminded the editor about Cugat's painting: "For Christs sake don't give anyone that jacket you're saving for me. I've written it into the book." Fitzgerald probably took the inspiration for the eyes of Doctor T. J. Eckleburg in Chapter II from the painting. The front panel of the original dust jacket for *The Great Gatsby* has since become one of the best known and most widely reproduced book jackets in the history of American book design.

## RECEPTION, SALES, AND SUBSEQUENT REPUTATION

Ten days after publication of *The Great Gatsby*, on April 10, 1925, Maxwell Perkins sent a cable to Fitzgerald: "SALES SITUATION DOUBTFUL. EXCELLENT REVIEWS." Perkins was exaggerating a bit: most of the major notices were indeed favorable, but there was disagreement among reviewers about how to assess this new novel by the author of *This Side of Paradise* and *The Beautiful and Damned*—an author best known for publishing entertaining stories in *The Saturday Evening Post* and *Metropolitan Magazine*. Some of the praise was lukewarm. Laurence Stallings, writing in the *New York World* (April 22), mentioned the "development of character" and the "color and sweep of prose" but found a "lack of breadth" in the portrait of Jay Gatsby. Fanny Butcher, reviewing for the *Chicago Tribune* (April 18), had this to offer: "It is the story of an almost undreamed of love, of a sordid affair which is a background and a contrast to that love, of a group of that class of America's 'nobility' who take all of the privileges of the European ruling class and assume none of its responsibilities." Writing in *The Evening World* (April 15), Ruth Snyder described the style as "painfully forced." An anonymous reviewer for *The New Yorker* (May 23) found "a new maturity" side by side with "any amount of flash and go." William Rose Benét, in the *Saturday Review of Literature* (May 9), called *The Great Gatsby* "a disillusioned novel, and a mature novel . . . a novel of admirable control." H. L. Mencken, reviewing for the *Baltimore Evening Sun* (May 2), thought the plot of *The Great Gatsby* to be "no more than a glorified anecdote" but called attention to a "fine texture, a careful and brilliant finish." The most laudatory of the reviews was by Gilbert Seldes in the August issue of *The Dial*. Seldes praised *The Great Gatsby* as "one of the finest of contemporary novels," with an admirable "artistic structure." The least complimentary notices were typified by an anonymous assessment in the *New York World* (April 12), published under the headline "F. Scott Fitzgerald's Latest a Dud."*

Sales were disappointing, at least to Fitzgerald. The first printing of 20,870 copies lasted through the spring and summer; Scribner's issued a reprint in August 1925, but in an impression of only 3,000 copies. This supply lasted for the next sixteen years. *The Great Gatsby* became a backlist title with a small readership and almost no continuing sale. By 1940, the year of Fitzgerald's death, its sales had all but ceased. The last royalty statement sent to the author during his lifetime, dated August 1, 1940, records the sale of only seven copies of *The Great Gatsby* during the preceding twelve months.

Fitzgerald died on December 21, 1940, at the age of forty-four. In October 1941 Scribner's published an edition of the unfinished text of *The Last Tycoon*, the novel that Fitzgerald had been working on when he died, together with a new edition of *The Great Gatsby* and five of the author's best short stories. This volume was edited by Fitzgerald's friend and fellow Princetonian Edmund Wilson, a leading literary and social critic of the time. Much new attention came to Fitzgerald and to *The Great Gatsby* from this 1941 edition. Fitzgerald's reputation grew during the 1950s and 1960s and in the decades after that. *The Great Gatsby* won a devoted following among critics and teachers: it has been taught to many generations of American high-school students and read by hundreds of thousands of people. The characters are sharply drawn, the writing pitch-perfect, and the themes readily grasped. Over time the novel has become a classic work, perhaps a national scripture.

*Some forty-seven reviews of the novel are reprinted in Jackson R. Bryer, ed., *F. Scott Fitzgerald: The Critical Reception* (New York: Burt Franklin, 1978): 194–250.

# INTRODUCTION

## BY AMOR TOWLES

### THE KALEIDOSCOPE

In the 1980s, I managed to attain both a bachelor's and a master's degree in English and American Literature without having read a word of F. Scott Fitzgerald. At the time, I didn't mourn the omission. As a contrarian, I took some pleasure in being able to report I had not read this author so commonly assigned in high school, so lauded by critics, and so omnipresent in the cultural conversation. A Freudian might have observed I probably also enjoyed the omission because of my father's deep admiration for Fitzgerald—an admiration reinforced by the fact that he, like Fitzgerald, had been raised in the Midwest and attended Princeton without the benefit of family wealth or social status.

But in my late twenties when I moved to New York City with the aim of writing fiction, I figured it was time to acquaint myself with some of the American literary classics I had foregone. At the Strand Book Store, I purchased used copies of Twain, James, Welty, Wharton, Hemingway, and yes, Fitzgerald, then began working my way systematically through their works. It ended up being one of the most rewarding years of reading in my life. And *The Great Gatsby* was a pinnacle.

I think I knew within ten pages that I was reading something extraordinary. As soon as I finished the book, I turned back to the beginning and started again. What was it about *Gatsby* that struck me so? For starters, it's an ingeniously plotted story with vivid characters interacting against a glamorous backdrop. And I was captivated by the narrative point of view: Nick Carraway is by turns an observer, voyeur, and detective who looks at the world in a manner at once shrewd and wistful. Mostly though, I was enamored with Fitzgerald's prose. It was so deceptively accessible. Eschewing the stylistic obscurity characterized by some of the most revered works of the era, Fitzgerald had written a seemingly transparent narrative that could support a hundred different interpretations. It struck me that with *Gatsby* Fitzgerald had created a thematic kaleidoscope. All the elements of craft he was employing—the images and motifs, allusions and allegories, similes and metaphors—were like the

A page from one of Fitzgerald's scrapbooks, including newspaper clippings and the front panel of the original dust jacket for *The Great Gatsby*. The cover art by Francis Cugat has become an iconic image in American book design. Fitzgerald carefully documented his and Zelda's public life in a series of scrapbooks, now held at the Princeton University Library. He employed a clipping service for that purpose.

shards of brightly colored glass at the bottom of the tubular device. Though distinct and disconnected, the shards would allow each reader with the turn of the wrist to create a unique and cohesive pattern for their own consideration and delight.

Within the Western canon *Gatsby* stands out for achieving its thematic abundance with an unusual economy. When we consider many of the great nineteenth-century novels that have survived—George Eliot's *Middlemarch*, Charles Dickens's *David Copperfield*, Leo Tolstoy's *War & Peace*—they are sprawling works in which the narration follows a reasonably large cast of characters over an extended period of time. By comparison, *Gatsby* is fairly limited in scope.

The book has only five principal characters—the narrator, Nick Carraway; his cousin Daisy; Daisy's husband, Tom Buchanan; Jordan Baker; and Jay Gatsby. Beyond the principals there are only two secondary characters of real significance: Tom's mistress, Myrtle Wilson, and her husband, George. In terms of age, all seven appear to be in their late twenties or thirties. The sole reference in the book to a younger generation is the one-page visit by the Buchanans' three-year-old daughter, while the primary representatives of the older generation—Meyer Wolfshiem and Gatsby's father—each make only brief appearances.

In terms of settings, the action of the novel occurs in just a handful of locations: three houses on the north shore of Long Island; an apartment, restaurant, and hotel in New York City; and the roadway that connects them. In terms of duration, the events unfold over the course of the single summer of 1922. Almost half of the book is dedicated to the description of six social engagements: two grand affairs at Gatsby's mansion; a drinking party at Tom and Myrtle's illicit retreat; a small tea at Nick's; a small dinner at the Buchanans'; and an afternoon gathering of the principal characters that travels from the Buchanans' to the Plaza Hotel. In all, the book is composed of less than fifty thousand words—just a fraction of *War & Peace*'s five hundred thousand, *Copperfield*'s three hundred and fifty thousand, and *Middlemarch*'s three hundred thousand. In this short novel with its small ensemble of hopeful yet deeply flawed characters, Fitzgerald gives us through the poetry of his language a glimpse of the human condition that is both timeless and universal.

## The Elusiveness of Identity

For me, one of the most important themes in *Gatsby* is the elusiveness of identity. Throughout the story, Fitzgerald explores the intrinsic challenges we face in knowing another person. Gatsby, of course, is the centerpiece of this meditation. At the start of the novel, Gatsby's background is murky. It's unclear to Nick and society at large where he is from, whether he was educated, and how he came by his money. Complicating Nick's effort to know Gatsby are rumors that have filled the vacuum: that he was a bootlegger, that he killed a man once, that he was a German spy during the war. As Nick observes, "It was testimony to the romantic speculation he inspired that there were whispers about him from those who had found little that it was necessary to whisper about in this world."

Over the course of the novel, Nick progresses from being a distant observer of Gatsby, to an acquaintance, and finally to a position of confidant. As Nick draws closer, he learns more and more about Gatsby's past. Despite this, he continues to find Gatsby's identity elusive because, in essence, Gatsby is the product of self-invention. He is a man who has adapted and changed significantly from his poor beginnings as James Gatz to the glamorous, wealthy, and urbane Jay Gatsby. So, Nick can never quite pin down his identity with full assurance. Is "Gatsby" an aspirational but inauthentic invention of the young Gatz? Is "Gatsby" a persona he has adopted in order to win over Daisy and thus reclaim the romance of his youth? Or is "Gatsby" the true version of the self the young Gatz was destined to become despite his poor beginnings? Nick can never say with full assurance where the real Gatsby ends and the imagined one begins—perhaps any more than Gatsby could himself.

When Nick ultimately receives from Gatsby the details of his life, this is how he sums up his impression:

> Through all he said . . . I was reminded of something—an elusive rhythm, a fragment of lost words, that I had heard somewhere a long time ago. For a moment a phrase tried to take shape in my mouth and my lips parted like a dumb man's, as though there was more struggling upon them than a wisp of startled air. But they made no sound, and what I had almost remembered was uncommunicable forever.

When Nick finally hears Gatsby's biography directly from the source, all it conjures up for him is an elusive idea from the distant past expressed in a fragment of words that disappear into thin air just as they are about to materialize.

If we consider the other principal characters in the story, incomplete biographies, rumors, misinterpretations, and acts of self-invention abound—making them almost as hard to pin down as Gatsby. Like Gatsby they are all transplants to New York: Daisy and Jordan from Louisville, Tom from Chicago, and Nick from an unnamed spot in the Middle West. When a person in their twenties or early thirties moves from one part of the country to another, it almost always involves some act of reinvention—the leaving behind of one sense of self and the adoption of another. While Nick is Daisy's cousin and an old acquaintance of Tom's, he admits they are "two old friends whom I scarcely knew at all." In terms of Nick's own past, all that we know is that he came from the Midwest, went to Yale, fought in the Great War, had a romance that failed, then migrated to New York where he has a barely described Wall Street job. In other words, what little we know of Nick's background is surprisingly similar to what we first learn of Gatsby's.

Like Gatsby, the other principal characters have stories trailing behind them. In the first chapter when Nick is having lunch at the Buchanans' with Jordan Baker, Jordan shushes Nick in order to listen to the "subdued impassioned murmur" of the Buchanans arguing in another room—because she has heard the rumor that "Tom's got some woman in New York." And the mystery as to why the Buchanans suddenly left Chicago, where they had planned to settle down, is eventually tied to Tom's philandering with a different woman. "I'm surprised that they didn't treat you to the story of that little spree," Daisy later tells Nick. At the same luncheon in the first chapter, Nick remembers of Jordan, "I had heard some story of her too, a critical, unpleasant story, but what it was I had forgotten long ago." Later, when Nick catches Jordan in a lie, he remembers the forgotten story—that she had been accused of cheating in a golf tournament, which Nick takes as evidence of her fundamental untrustworthiness. Nick has his own stories that he's running away from. At the end of the Buchanan lunch, when Nick starts the engine of his car, Daisy suddenly calls out: "Wait! I forgot to ask you something, and it's important. We heard you

Portrait of F. Scott Fitzgerald by Gordon Bryant, 1921. Matthew Bruccoli offers this insight about Fitzgerald's view of the rich and the author's relationship to money: "Fitzgerald's judgements on the rich were complicated by his attitudes toward his own money, which he could never manage. He knew what money could buy—even more than luxury, a fuller life with time to write. . . . Yet it is not entirely paradoxical that he threw his money away. His carelessness with money expressed his superiority to it. If he could waste it, then it didn't own him. The inevitable result was that he was in bondage to it after all because he had to earn the money he was squandering." See Bruccoli's *Some Sort of Epic Grandeur: The Life of F. Scott Fitzgerald* (University of South Carolina Press, 2002), p. 230.

were engaged to a girl out West." When Nick denies the engagement as libel, Daisy says, "We heard it from three people, so it must be true." Nick offers Daisy no further words of explanation, but he confides in us that, while he had been involved with an unnamed woman, he left the Midwest because he had "no intention of being rumored into marriage."

Gossip and rumor can spring from misinformation, but also from sensationalism, maliciousness, and jealousy. In social circles rife with gossip and rumor, one inevitably struggles to separate the real from the manufactured or imagined. Fitzgerald emphasizes this notion in *Gatsby* through his frequent use of the verbs *murmur* and *whisper*. Both appear more than fifteen times in this short novel. In the first chapter alone Nick murmurs to Jordan, Daisy to Nick, the butler to Tom, and, as noted above, Tom and Daisy murmur together in the adjoining room. Nick says Daisy's voice owes its seductiveness to its whispering quality, and she whispers a good deal. In the course of the novel, Jordan whispers to Nick, Tom to Nick, Gatsby to Nick, and Daisy and Gatsby whisper together. In this bright, glamorous, and highly social milieu, communication is often muted to the point of indiscernibility.

Having established the essential elusiveness of his principal characters, Fitzgerald uses the motif of the silhouette—the visual equivalent of a whisper—to suggest that the trait is universal. At one of Gatsby's parties, Nick looks up at a second-story window and observes: "Sometimes a shadow moved against a dressing-room blind above, gave way to another shadow, an indefinite procession of shadows, who rouged and powdered in an invisible glass." Earlier, while at the party in Tom's illicit apartment, Nick reflects, "high over the city our line of yellow windows must have contributed their share of human secrecy to the casual watcher in the darkening streets, and I was him too, looking up and wondering." Of course, the recurrence of these windowed silhouettes recalls Plato's allegory of the cave in which the philosopher equates our limited perception of reality to the watching of shadows on a wall. Fitzgerald is suggesting that like Nick we all stand in a similar position. As observers, we are trying to make sense of the fleeting incomplete images cast by others; but we are also part of the "indefinite procession of shadows," casting our silhouettes against window shades in a manner that displays our "share of human secrecy" to the rest of the world.

## RESTLESSNESS AND RISK

A second central theme in the book is the struggle of the principal characters to find serenity in their lives. Fitzgerald intimates this struggle through a shared trait of restlessness. As noted above, all of the principal characters are transplants to New York, but most have been moving from place to place in the years preceding the novel's action. Having been raised in North Dakota, Gatsby spent time traveling on a yacht, trained as an officer in Kentucky, fought in the Great War, and may have attended a program at Oxford before ending up in New York. Having been married in Louisville, the Buchanans had a three-month honeymoon in the South Seas, then "drifted here and there unrestfully," moving to Santa Barbara, then France for a year, then to Chicago "to settle down" before finally coming to New York. After finishing at Yale in New Haven, Nick has also fought in the war, then returned to the Middle West before coming to the city.

In the novel's opening chapter, Nick tells us, "I enjoyed the counter-raid [in the war] so thoroughly that I came back restless." In the same chapter, when he pays his first visit to the Buchanans, he describes Tom "hovering restlessly about the room" with eyes that are "flashing about restlessly." As Jordan sits on the couch, "her body asserted itself with a restless movement of her knee . . ." And in describing Gatsby later, Nick observes that his sportsman-like grace "was continually breaking through his punctilious manner in the shape of restlessness."

Fitzgerald emphasizes the restless state of the ensemble by describing them at key moments in their lives, in various modes of transportation. When Gatsby was seventeen and frustrated with his lot, he saw a multimillionaire's yacht moored on a dangerous stretch of Lake Superior. So he borrowed a boat, rowed out to warn the yacht's owner, and ingratiated himself so successfully that he was invited on board—indefinitely. As Nick observes, it was thanks to this brief rowboat ride that Gatz became Gatsby. The first time Jordan saw Daisy and Gatsby together in Louisville, they were seated in a car. The first time Tom meets his mistress, Myrtle, they are seated together on a train. The first time Nick has an extended conversation with Gatsby, they're driving into the city for lunch. And when Nick learns about Gatsby and Daisy's history, he is riding with Jordan in a hired carriage in Central Park. Whether in boats, trains, cars, or carriages the lives of the principals are defined by motion. In fact, Jordan Baker's name was derived by Fitzgerald from the combination of two early automobile brands.

The backdrop of the novel is the postwar boom when America was experiencing a period of unusual peace and prosperity, especially relative to Europe, which was still recovering from the war's devastation. Over the eight years ending in 1922, the S&P 500 was up almost 100 percent. Most of the central characters either come from money or have earned enough that they lead lives of luxury and leisure. They attend parties, dine, and pursue sports, all the while being catered to by servants. And yet, they are all restless in each other's company, suggesting that something unnamed but essential is missing from their lives. Daisy sums up their collective malaise when she observes, "I think everything's terrible anyhow . . . Everybody thinks so—the most advanced people. And I *know*. I've been everywhere and seen everything and done everything." In other words, the movement to new places, which would seem like the natural antidote to restlessness, leads to a jadedness that results in more restlessness.

One of the recurring artistic achievements of *Gatsby* is how Fitzgerald transitions from a detailed description of his characters interacting in a specific moment to a poetic passage that gives us a glimpse of the universal. One of the most beautiful examples is his description of Nick's bittersweet wanderings through the city, a passage that is in perfect harmony with the lonely paintings of Edward Hopper.

> I liked to walk up Fifth Avenue and pick out romantic women from the crowd and imagine that in a few minutes I was going to enter into their lives, and no one would ever know or disapprove. Sometimes, in my mind, I followed them to their apartments on the corners of hidden streets, and they turned and smiled back at me before they faded through a door into warm darkness. At the enchanted metropolitan twilight I felt a haunting loneliness sometimes, and felt it in others—poor young clerks who loitered in front of windows waiting until it was time for a solitary restaurant dinner—young clerks in the dusk, wasting the most poignant moments of night and life.

Having described for us the existential restlessness of his principal characters, through Nick's bittersweet reverie Fitzgerald points to a loneliness that is being experienced not only by Nick, but by many others, like the poor young clerks, or the young women disappearing behind doors on hidden streets. And as with the "procession of shadows" passage, Fitzgerald draws us into the lonely community to which Nick pays witness. The anonymity of the figures, the poignancy of the sentiments, and the beauty of Fitzgerald's language lure us as readers so effectively into

## An Admirable Novel

THE GREAT GATSBY. By F. Scott Fitz-
GERALD. New York: Charles Scribner's Sons.
1925. $2.

Reviewed by WILLIAM ROSE BENÉT

THE book finished, we find again, at the top
of page three, the introductory remark:
No—Gatsby turned out all right at the end;
it was what preyed on Gatsby, what foul dust floated in
the wake of his dreams that temporarily closed out my
interest in the abortive sorrows and short-winded elations
of men.

Scott Fitzgerald's new novel is a remarkable
analysis of this "foul dust." And his analysis leads
him, at the end of the book, to the conclusion that
all of us "beat on, boats against the current, borne
back ceaselessly into the past." There is depth of
philosophy in this.

The writer—for the story is told in the first
person, but in a first person who is not exactly the
author, but rather one of the number of personali-
ties that compose the actual author,—the hypothe-
cated chronicler of Gatsby is one in whose tolerance
all sorts and conditions of men confided. So he
came to Gatsby, and the history of Gatsby, obscured
by the "foul dust" aforementioned, "fair sickened"
him of human nature.

"The Great Gatsby" is a disillusioned novel, and
a mature novel. It is a novel with pace, from the
first word to the last, and also a novel of admirable
"control." Scott Fitzgerald started his literary career with enormous facility. His high spirits were
infectious. The queer charm, color, wonder, and
drama of a young and reckless world beat constantly
upon his senses, stimulated a young and intensely
romantic mind to a mixture of realism and extravaganza shaken up like a cocktail. Some people are
born with a knack, whether for cutting figure eights,
curving an in-sheet,. picking out tunes on the piano,
or revealing some peculiar charm of their intelligence on the typewritten page. Scott Fitzgerald
was born with a knack for writing. What they call
"a natural gift." And another gift of the fairies
at his christening was a reckless confidence in himself. And he was quite intoxicated with the joy of
life and rather engagingly savage toward an elder
world. He was out "to get the world by the neck"
and put words on paper in the patterns his exuberant
fancy suggested. He didn't worry much about what
had gone before Fitzgerald in literature. He
dreamed gorgeously of what there was in Fitzgerald to "tell the world."

And all these elements contributed to the amazing
performance of "This Side of Paradise," amazing
in its excitement and gusto, amazing in phrase and
epithet, amazing no less for all sorts of thoroughly
bad writing pitched in with the good, for preposterous carelessness, and amazing as well as for the
sheer pace of the narrative and the fresh quality of
its oddly pervasive poetry. Short stories of flappers
and philosophers displayed the same vitality and
flourished much the same faults. "Tales of the
Jazz Age" inhabited the same glamour. "The
Beautiful and Damned," while still in the mirage,

---

ALEXANDER WOOLLCOTT

All citizens in mourning
who have moved to Hyères, France, for
3 yrs. where Mr. Fitzgerald expects to
do a whole lot of work. He says it
pretty near impossible to work in
Great Neck. I wished he would show
the some place where it ain't.

May 15

Dear Scott,

This is a line to report
that I read "The Great Gatsby"
with the deepest interest.
It is, I think, your best job by
a long jump. I have the
profoundest respect for the
man who could write it./ A. Woollcott

---

THE AMERICAN MERCURY
730 FIFTH AVENUE
NEW YORK

OFFICE OF THE EDITORS        George Jean Nathan and H. L. Mencken

Dear Scott: A thousand congratulations!
"The Great Gatsby" is an excellent
job. It is leagues in advance of
anything you have ever done.

As ever,

George Jean Nathan

---

The Scott Fitzgeralds are now dem-
iciled in Paris with their small
daughter Patricia. . . . Having
got "The Great Gatsby" off his hands,
Mr. Fitzgerald is contemplating a
new novel. . . . Also a volume
of his short stories will be published
under the title "All the Sad Young
Men." . . . Well, if that's positively all of them. . . . This
once. . . .

It's many a moon since F. Scott
Fitzgerald glorified the horizon with
a rising new novel. The Great
Gatsby is announced for publication
in March.

To
most people, irony is poison. They cannot
assimilate it, and don't intend to try. To
a minority, it is as necessary and zestful
as salt in porridge; but minorities don't
make best sellers. Scott Fitzgerald's
"The Great Gatsby" has a similar handi-
cap to overcome. It is not all in the satiric
mood, but mostly; and the art of the writing and construction is so artfully concealed, only a writer can quite appreciate it.

F. SCOTT FITZGERALD
In "The Great Gatsby" Mr.
Fitzgerald abandons the rôle
of the *enfant terrible* of contemporary letters

SCOTT Fitzgerald's *The Great Gatsby*
(Scribner) has "arrived," but without any
of those adventitious aids to immortality which
were acceptable in his early work, but which
could not be prolonged indefinitely. There is
more maturity here and none of the "smart-
ness" which he himself came to deplore; the
author has grown up and his friends—and also,
I imagine, his admirers—have cheered up at
the immense stride he has taken. In a letter
from Rome he tells me that he is "$99,000.00
short of the $100,000.00" which he went into
exile in order to save. *The Great Gatsby* looks
as if it might do something towards bringing
about that consummation, so creditable to the
ambition of the author. I hope that, by the
time he gets home, the supply of Mr. Buck-
ner's padlocks will have run out. Meanwhile,
one can get the book, and it is "real stuff."

---

From Fitzgerald's scrapbooks, early reviews of *The Great Gatsby*. The novel was widely reviewed,
but notices were mixed. Only a handful of the book critics recognized the cultural resonance of
the novel. The letters are from Alexander Woollcott, a drama critic and journalist, and George
Jean Nathan, co-editor of *The American Mercury*. The review is by William Rose Benét, a prominent poet, critic, and editor.

the moment that we are bound to recall our own experiences of isolation in languid hours.

For Fitzgerald, malaise may best be evoked through idle afternoons and muted twilights, but it's a mood that can have dangerous consequences. For when we are restless, we are less likely to think through our actions and more likely to do something rash. Fitzgerald dramatizes the connection between restlessness and risk through the recurring image of incidental car accidents—long before we reach the book's fateful collision. The first party that Nick attends at Gatsby's concludes with a drunken man driving his coupé into a ditch. At another of Gatsby's parties, we're told Mrs. Ulysses Swett ran over the hand of Ripley Snell. Not long after Tom married Daisy, he drove into a wagon, ripping the front wheel off his car and breaking the arm of the hotel chambermaid who happened to be in the passenger seat. Nick is a passenger in Jordan's car when she nearly causes an accident. When Nick protests she doesn't drive carefully enough, she glibly observes that she needn't drive carefully because others will. Fundamentally dissatisfied and without a sense of serenity, the five principal characters are to some degree careening through their lives, and thus constantly at the risk of crashing into others in a careless and self-involved manner.

## The Crescendo

Structurally, *The Great Gatsby* is a novel of tragic convergence. Over the course of the story, the principal characters with their elusive histories and conflicting aspirations are moving slowly but surely toward one another. When they finally gather in a "stifling" room of the Plaza Hotel on a sweltering August afternoon, their troubled interrelationships boil over into a full-scale confrontation, setting in motion the book's disastrous conclusion. This denouement—a thirty-hour period that takes up most of the book's final third—is a masterstroke of artistic crescendo. It represents the culmination not simply of the characters' fates but of an array of thematic elements all reinforced by the reappearance of central motifs.

The first component of the crescendo is the gathering of the principal characters for a lunch at the Buchanan house. These five individuals are interlinked through multiple relationships. Nick is Daisy's cousin, an old college acquaintance of Tom's, Jordan's boyfriend, and Gatsby's neighbor/confidant; Daisy is Nick's cousin, Tom's wife, an old friend of Jordan's, and lover of Gatsby's; and so on. The entire book has been dedicated to following their various interactions across a series of social engagements. Yet, up until this moment, the five characters have never been in the same room at the same time. Fitzgerald reinforces this crescendo by having virtually every other combination occur earlier in the novel: Nick with Daisy, Tom, and Jordan; Nick with Gatsby and Jordan; Nick with Tom; Nick with Gatsby and Daisy. With each variation, our anticipation is building for when they will all convene.

The gathering finally occurs on "almost the last" day of summer and "certainly the warmest"—a day that is "broiling" with a "relentless beating heat." The characters drink gin rickeys before lunch, then ale with their meal, with everybody smoking. The restlessness that has beleaguered the characters since the beginning of the novel resurfaces in the heat. "What'll we do with ourselves this afternoon?" says Daisy. "And the day after that, and the next thirty years?" Naturally, the answer is to move. With no clear aim, they decide to drive into the city. Stepping out onto "the blazing gravel," they pile into separate cars, and shoot off "into the oppressive heat," stopping briefly for gas at Wilson's garage.

While still at the Buchanans', Daisy is convinced (mistakenly) that Tom is speaking on the phone to his mistress, Myrtle. Partly as a result, she becomes so indiscreet about her feelings for Gatsby that Tom realizes for the first time they are having an affair. At the gas station, Wilson implies that he's just discovered his wife is cheating, while Myrtle, looking out her window in distress, mistakenly assumes that Jordan is Tom's wife, her rival. By the time the principals take a suite in the Plaza Hotel to have another round of drinks, the collective mood is simmering with unexpressed suspicion, jealousy, and hostility. So, it takes only a few moments for their emotions to boil over.

As the five finally face each other, whispers and murmurings are cast aside in favor of direct confrontation. Gatsby is challenged by Tom on the details of his past and profession. Tom is challenged by Daisy for his infidelities. Daisy is challenged by Gatsby to abandon her husband and challenged by Tom to confirm her marital loyalty. When the five finally pile back into their cars—those high-powered symbols of their restless and reckless ways—it seems inevitable that they are hurtling irrevocably toward someone's destruction.

## The Final Tally

At the very end of the novel, Gatsby's poor father shares with Nick something he's discovered: a daily schedule with a list of "General Resolves" that the young Jimmy

Gatz had written down on the last page of a Western. Recalling the adolescent Benjamin Franklin's scheme of self-improvement in his *Autobiography*, this itemization includes self-imposed resolutions to wake up early, practice poise and elocution, and generally improve through exercise and reading. Readers have debated the meaning of this artifact from Jimmy's youth as it can be interpreted in contradictory ways. We could view it as evidence of Gatsby's sincere and long-standing pursuit of a dream that he'd had the unusual persistence to see through—placing him firmly in the lauded American tradition of the self-made man. Alternatively, we could view the list as further evidence of Gatsby's inauthenticity, a playbook designed so that he could represent himself to the world as someone he was not. But as with so many of Fitzgerald's symbols, in order to understand its larger meaning, we must consider it in the context of the book as a whole. For this list does not stand alone in the text. It is, in fact, the fifth to appear.

The first list in the book is Myrtle's. At the drunken party in Tom's illicit apartment she tells Nick that she's "going to make a list of all the things I've got to get. A massage and a wave, and a collar for the dog, and one of those cute little ash trays . . . and a wreath with a black silk bow for mother's grave . . . I got to write down a list so I won't forget all the things I got to do." The second list is the one that Nick once "wrote down on the empty spaces of a time-table [recording] the names of those who came to Gatsby's house that summer." The third is the list the motorcycle policeman makes in Wilson's garage, "taking down names" of witnesses to the vehicular manslaughter of Myrtle. Finally, Nick tells us that the day after the accident while back in his office, "I tried for a while to list the quotations on an interminable amount of stock, then I fell asleep in my swivel chair."

What these lists seem to share is a suggestion of overwhelming inadequacy. Nick's party list purports to be comprehensive but could never capture the essence of the glamorous crowded parties that Gatsby threw. The policeman's list will not lead to an accurate re-creation of the collision, or to justice on Myrtle's behalf. In fact, we later learn that the official record will be clouded by three misleading witnesses: Myrtle's sister will provide a false account, and both Tom and Nick will withhold implicating facts from the authorities. All the lists seem pathetic in the context of how events eventually unfold. Nick's listing of stock quotations is transparently purposeless in the immediate aftermath of the tragedy. And Myrtle's aspirational list is rendered meaningless by her death, just as the policeman's and Gatsby's lists are rendered meaningless by his.

When we consider these lists together, I think Fitzgerald is pointing to the challenge of capturing the essence of life in direct language. There are few instances of language more direct than a list. It itemizes the relevant details in an orderly fashion without embellishment or digression. But in so doing, it leaves out the quintessence of what it may be trying to capture. For Fitzgerald, in order to truly capture a story, an experience, or a life, whether it's Gatsby's or our own, what is required is nothing less than a language that is rich, nuanced, evocative, and open to interpretation. In other words, the language of this novel.

P. & A.
MR. F. SCOTT FITZGERALD AND HIS SMALL DAUGHTER
Motoring in Rome, where the young author has just completed his latest novel, "The Great Gatsby,"
which is being published by Scribner's about the end of March

Page from Fitzgerald's scrapbook. Prior to the publication of *The Great Gatsby* in April 1925, the Fitzgeralds vacationed in Rome.

THE ANNOTATED GREAT GATSBY

**1** Fitzgerald had difficulty settling on a title for his novel: He was never convinced that he had chosen the right one. In a letter to his editor, Maxwell Perkins, written shortly after the novel was published, Fitzgerald was fretful: "The title is only fair, rather bad than good." (*Dear Scott/Dear Max*, p. 101). Among the many titles he considered were "Among the Ash Heaps and Millionaires," "Trimalchio in West Egg," "Gold-Hatted Gatsby," "The High-Bouncing Lover," and "Under the Red, White, and Blue." See also pp. xix–xv in this volume for other possibilities entertained by Fitzgerald and further discussion of his challenges in titling his novel.

**2** Epigraph composed by Fitzgerald. D'Invilliers is not a real person but a fictional character who appears in *This Side of Paradise*—a literary man and one of protagonist Amory Blaine's best friends at Princeton. Fitzgerald, however, based D'Invilliers on his own Princeton friend John Peale Bishop (1892–1944). Maureen Corrigan speculates that Fitzgerald's "literary gag" was inspired by T. S. Eliot's phony footnotes in *The Waste Land*: "There's something fizzy and irreverent about that fake poem at the threshold of *Gatsby*. Nowadays, when *The Great Gatsby* has ascended to the Great Books Pantheon, it helps to decalcify the novel by remembering that Fitzgerald was quite young when he wrote it." See Maureen Corrigan's *So We Read On: How* The Great Gatsby *Came to Be and Why It Endures* (Little, Brown, 2014), p. 79.

# THE GREAT GATSBY[1]

---

*Then wear the gold hat, if that will move her;*
*If you can bounce high, bounce for her too,*
*Till she cry "Lover, gold-hatted, high-bouncing lover,*
*I must have you!"[2]*
—THOMAS PARKE D'INVILLIERS.

Alabama belle Zelda Sayre, in February 1920, just before her marriage to Fitzgerald. They met in July 1918, when Fitzgerald was stationed at Camp Sheridan near Montgomery. While courting Zelda, a brokenhearted Scott was still in touch with former flame Ginevra King back in Chicago. Three days after King married William H. Mitchell, an investment broker, on September 4, 1918, Fitzgerald recorded in his ledger: "Fell in love on the 7th."

ONCE AGAIN
TO
ZELDA[3]

**3** Fitzgerald had dedicated his second book, *Flappers and Philosophers* (1920), to his wife, Zelda Sayre Fitzgerald. Less than a year after Fitzgerald's death in December 1940, Scribner's published a new edition of *The Great Gatsby*, edited by the critic Edmund Wilson, a friend of Fitzgerald's from his Princeton years. Wilson neglected to include the dedication to Zelda in his edition. Some twenty-five subsequent editions of the novel, all of which derive from the 1941 Scribner's typesetting, also omit the dedication. See *The Great Gatsby: A Variorum Edition*, ed. James L. W. West III (Cambridge, 2019), pp. xxxvi–xxxvii.

Photograph of Scott and Zelda taken for the May 1923 cover of *Hearst's International*. They married on April 3, 1920, and became one of the first celebrity glamour couples, tastemakers and icons of the Jazz Age—emblems of youth, freedom, and excess. For a time, the gossip columns followed their every move.

# CHAPTER I

In my younger and more vulnerable years my father gave me some advice that I've been turning over in my mind ever since.

"Whenever you feel like criticizing anyone," he told me, "just remember that all the people in this world haven't had the advantages that you've had."

He didn't say any more, but we've always been unusually communicative in a reserved way, and I understood that he meant a great deal more than that. In consequence, I'm inclined to reserve all judgments,[1] a habit that has opened up many curious natures to me and also made me the victim of not a few veteran bores. The abnormal mind is quick to detect and attach itself to this quality when it appears in a normal person, and so it came about that in college I was unjustly accused of being a politician, because I was privy to the secret griefs of wild, unknown men. Most of the confidences were unsought—frequently I have feigned sleep, preoccupation, or a hostile levity when I realized by some unmistakable sign that an intimate revelation was quivering on the horizon; for the intimate revelations of young men, or at least the terms in which they express them, are usually plagiaristic and marred by obvious suppressions. Reserving judgments is a matter of infinite hope. I am still a little afraid of missing something if I forget that, as my father snobbishly suggested, and I snobbishly repeat, a sense of the fundamental decencies is parcelled out unequally at birth.

And, after boasting this way of my tolerance, I come to the admission that it has a limit. Conduct may be founded on the hard rock or the wet marshes, but after a certain point I don't

---

1 In a letter of November 20, 1924, to Fitzgerald, Maxwell Perkins offers this high praise for Fitzgerald's narrative technique in *Gatsby*: "You adopted exactly the right method of telling it, that of employing a narrator who is more of a spectator than an actor: this puts the reader upon a point of observation on a higher level than that on which the characters stand and at a distance that gives perspective. In no other way could your irony have been so immensely effective, nor the reader have been enabled so strongly to feel at times the strangeness of human circumstance in a vast heedless universe." See Perkins's full letter on pages 202–5 in this volume.

FIFTEEN CENTS

# TIME
*The Weekly News-Magazine*

VOL. I. NO. 6     JOSEPH CONRAD     APRIL 7, 1923

Polish-born English writer Joseph Conrad (1857–1924) on the cover of *Time* magazine, April 7, 1923, at the time of the author's first and only trip to the United States. About Conrad's influence on his work, Fitzgerald states in a letter of 1925 to H. L. Mencken: "God! I've learned a lot from him." What Fitzgerald learned from Conrad he learned by studying the character Charles Marlow, the narrator in several Conrad novels, including *Heart of Darkness* and *Lord Jim*. This mode of narration allows the meaning-seeker and tale-teller to be both involved in and detached from the story. See *The Letters of F. Scott Fitzgerald*, ed. Andrew Turnbull (Scribner's, 1963), p. 482.

**2** Harold Bloom counts himself among the many critics who see narrator Nick Carraway as a version of Joseph Conrad's Marlow, "somewhat sentimentalized but still an authentic secret sharer in Gatsby's fate." Bloom argues that *Gatsby*'s singular achievement is its combination of "the lyrical sensibility of Keats and the fictive

care what it's founded on. When I came back from the East last autumn I felt that I wanted the world to be in uniform and at a sort of moral attention forever; I wanted no more riotous excursions with privileged glimpses into the human heart. Only Gatsby, the man who gives his name to this book, was exempt from my reaction—Gatsby, who represented everything for which I have an unaffected scorn. If personality is an unbroken series of successful gestures, then there was something gorgeous about him, some heightened sensitivity to the promises of life, as if he were related to one of those intricate machines that register earthquakes ten thousand miles away. This responsiveness had nothing to do with that flabby impressionability which is dignified under the name of the "creative temperament"—it was an extraordinary gift for hope, a romantic readiness such as I have never found in any other person and which it is not likely I shall ever find again. No— Gatsby turned out all right at the end; it is what preyed on Gatsby, what foul dust floated in the wake of his dreams that temporarily closed out my interest in the abortive sorrows and short-winded elations of men.[2]

My family have been prominent, well-to-do people in this Middle Western city for three generations. The Carraways are something of a clan, and we have a tradition that we're descended from the Dukes of Buccleuch,[3] but the actual founder of my line was my grandfather's brother, who came here in fifty-one, sent a substitute to the Civil War,[4] and started the wholesale hardware business that my father carries on today.

I never saw this great-uncle, but I'm supposed to look like him—with special reference to the rather hard-boiled painting that hangs in father's office. I graduated from New Haven[5] in 1915, just a quarter of a century after my father, and a little later I participated in that delayed Teutonic migration known as the Great War.[6] I enjoyed the counter-raid so thoroughly that I came back restless. Instead of being the warm center of the world, the Middle West now seemed like the ragged edge of the universe—so I decided to go East and learn the bond business. Everybody I knew was in the bond business, so I supposed it could support one more single man. All my aunts and uncles talked it over as if they were choosing a prep school for me, and finally said, "Why—ye-es," with very grave, hesitant faces. Father agreed to finance me for a year, and after various delays I came East, permanently, I thought, in the spring of twenty-two.[7]

The practical thing was to find rooms in the city, but it was a warm season, and I had just left a country of wide lawns and friendly trees, so when a young man at the office suggested that we take a house together in a commuting town, it sounded like a great idea. He found the house, a weather-beaten cardboard bungalow at eighty a month,[8] but at the last minute the firm ordered him to Washington, and I went out to the country alone. I had a dog—at least I had him for a few days until he ran away—and an old Dodge[9] and a Finnish woman, who made my bed and cooked breakfast and muttered Finnish wisdom to herself over the electric stove.

It was lonely for a day or so until one morning some man, more recently arrived than I, stopped me on the road.

"How do you get to West Egg Village?" he asked helplessly.

I told him. And as I walked on I was lonely no longer. I was a guide, a pathfinder, an original settler. He had casually conferred on me the freedom of the neighborhood.

And so with the sunshine and the great bursts of leaves growing on the trees, just as things grow in fast movies, I had that familiar conviction that life was beginning over again with the summer.

There was so much to read, for one thing, and so much fine health to be pulled down out of the young breath-giving air. I bought a dozen volumes on banking and credit and investment securities, and they stood on my shelf in red and gold like new

mode of Conrad," which "makes of so odd a blending a uniquely American story, certainly a candidate for *the* American story of its time." Jessica Martell and Zachary Vernon suggest that Fitzgerald's title is in fact his acknowledgment of Conrad's influence, containing an "allusion to a passage in *Lord Jim* (1899) in which a businessman with a thick Swiss German accent tells the narrator Charles Marlow that Jim is 'of great gabasidy [capacity].'" See Harold Bloom's *The American Canon* (Library of America, 2019), pp. 235–37; and Jessica Martell and Zackary Vernon's "'Of Great Gabasidy': Joseph Conrad's *Lord Jim* and F. Scott Fitzgerald's *The Great Gatsby*," in *Journal of Modern Literature* 38, no. 3 (2015), pp. 56–70.

3 Ducal house of the Scotts of Buccleuch, granted land by King James II of Scotland in the fifteenth century. The title "Duke of Buccleuch" was created for James Scott, Duke of Monmouth (1649–1685).

4 The Enrollment Act of 1863 allowed men in the Northern states who were eligible for conscription to avoid service in the Civil War by hiring a substitute.

5 Yale University, located in New Haven, Connecticut.

6 Fitzgerald, along with most of the other members of his Princeton class, enlisted in the U.S. Army in the spring of 1917. He was accepted as an officer candidate in late October of that year and reported to Fort Leavenworth, Kansas, in November to begin his training. Fitzgerald spent the war in stateside training camps. He was about to embark for Europe when the Armistice was signed in November 1918. Because he had no firsthand experience of warfare, he often glossed over the war in his writings, as he does in this passage. Both Nick and

Gatsby served in France, an experience that draws them together initially and contributes to their friendship later in the novel. No mention is made of Tom Buchanan's service in the war, something that readers would have speculated about in 1925. Perhaps Tom, aided by the wealth and influence of his family, had connections that kept him out of the armed forces or provided him with a safe assignment.

7 Nick is writing his account in 1924, two years after the events in the novel have occurred. The action opens two weeks before the summer solstice, in June 1922. Initially, in the manuscript, Fitzgerald had set the novel in 1923; later he changed his mind, adjusting the year to 1922 in the typescript drafts that followed. Sarah Churchwell, in her book *Careless People*, considers Fitzgerald's decision to set the novel in 1922: "A conventional answer has been that Fitzgerald wanted to signal his allegiance to the annus mirabilis of literary modernism, the year that began with the publication of James Joyce's *Ulysses* and ended with the publication of T. S. Eliot's *The Waste Land*. But while that may be part of the answer, the meanings of 1922 in relation to *The Great Gatsby* are far more expansive than that. . . . In his 1931 essay 'Echoes of the Jazz Age,' Fitzgerald would 'offer in exhibit the year 1922!' for anyone hoping to understand the roaring twenties: 'it was an age of miracles, it was an age of art, it was an age of excess, and it was an age of satire.'" See Sarah Churchwell's *Careless People: Murder, Mayhem and the Invention of The Great Gatsby* (Penguin Press, 2014), pp. xvi–xvii.

8 In 1922, eighty dollars would have had the approximate buying power of fifteen hundred dollars in 2025.

1915 Dodge Brothers Touring Car. Dodge cars began to roll off the assembly line in 1914. Nick, in 1922, drives an "old Dodge."

money from the mint, promising to unfold the shining secrets that only Midas and Morgan and Mæcenas[10] knew. And I had the high intention of reading many other books besides. I was rather literary in college—one year I wrote a series of very solemn and obvious editorials for the Yale News—and now I was going to bring back all such things into my life and become again that most limited of all specialists, the "well-rounded man." This isn't just an epigram—life is much more successfully looked at from a single window, after all.

It was a matter of chance that I should have rented a house in one of the strangest communities in North America. It was on that slender riotous island which extends itself due east of New York—and where there are, among other natural curiosities, two unusual formations of land. Twenty miles from the city a pair of enormous eggs, identical in contour and separated only by a courtesy bay, jut out into the most domesticated body of salt water in the Western hemisphere, the great wet barnyard of Long Island Sound. They are not perfect ovals—like the egg in the Columbus story,[11] they are both crushed flat

Fitzgerald in his Brooks Brothers uniform (1917) before heading to officers' training camp at Fort Leavenworth, Kansas. Expecting to be killed on the battlefield, the aspiring author hastily completed a novel manuscript called "The Romantic Egotist" on nights and weekends but never saw military action in World War I, the defining event of his generation. This lack of war experience would gnaw at him for the remainder of his life.

**9** The Dodge Brothers Company of Hamtramck, Michigan, began making motorcars in 1914. Their Model 30, a four-cylinder passenger vehicle, was a modestly priced machine, meant to compete with the Ford Model T. "The characters are visibly represented by the cars they drive," the writer and critic Malcolm Cowley comments. "Nick has a conservative old Dodge, the Buchanans, too rich for ostentation, have an 'easygoing blue coupé' and Gatsby's car is 'a rich cream color, bright with nickel, swollen here and there in its monstrous length with triumphant hat-boxes and supper-boxes and tool-boxes, and terraced with a labyrinth of wind-shields that mirrored a dozen suns'—it is West Egg on wheels." See Malcolm Cowley's *A Second Flowering: Works and Days of the Lost Generation* (Penguin Press, 1980), p. 46.

**10** Fitzgerald is being playful with these references: Midas, in Greek and Roman mythology, a king of Phrygia, who was granted his wish that everything he touched be turned to gold; John Pierpont Morgan (1837–1913), American financier and banker of the Gilded Age; and Gaius Maecenas (c. 70–8 B.C.E.), Roman statesman, friend and confidant of Augustus, and great literary patron of the "golden"

at the contact end—but their physical resemblance must be a source of perpetual confusion to the gulls that fly overhead. To the wingless a more arresting phenomenon is their dissimilarity in every particular except shape and size.

I lived at West Egg,[12] the—well, the less fashionable of the two, though this is a most superficial tag to express the bizarre and not a little sinister contrast between them. My house was at the very tip of the egg, only fifty yards from the Sound, and squeezed between two huge places that rented for twelve or fifteen thousand a season. The one on my right was a colossal affair by any standard—it was a factual imitation of some Hôtel de Ville in Normandy, with a tower on one side, spanking new under a thin beard of raw ivy, and a marble swimming pool, and more than forty acres of lawn and garden. It

Augustan era who fostered the careers of both Horace and Vergil.

**11** Apocryphal story concerning Christopher Columbus. Columbus is said to have challenged detractors of his discovery of the "New World" to stand an egg on its end. After his doubters had failed in the attempt, Columbus smashed one end of the egg against a table and left it standing upright.

**12** East Egg and West Egg suggest, respectively, Manhasset Neck (old money) and Great Neck (new money) on Long Island. In the manuscript version of the novel, Jordan gives Tom this description of West Egg: "Most expensive town on Long Island. Full of moving picture people, playrites, singers and cartoonists and kept women. You'd love it." From October 1922 until April 1924, Fitzgerald and his wife and daughter lived in rented quarters on Great Neck. See Katherine Park's "A Historical Tour from Great Neck to West Egg," *F. Scott Fitzgerald Review* 21 (2023), pp. 1–26.

Sketch of F. Scott Fitzgerald, circa 1920, by American illustrator James Montgomery Flagg (1877–1960), creator of the 1917 Army recruiting poster "I want YOU for the U.S. Army," depicting Uncle Sam pointing at the viewer.

was Gatsby's mansion. Or, rather, as I didn't know Mr. Gatsby, it was a mansion inhabited by a gentleman of that name. My own house was an eyesore, but it was a small eyesore, and it had been overlooked, so I had a view of the water, a partial view of my neighbor's lawn, and the consoling proximity of millionaires—all for eighty dollars a month.

Across the courtesy bay the white palaces of fashionable East Egg glittered along the water, and the history of the summer really begins on the evening I drove over there to have dinner with the Tom Buchanans. Daisy was my second cousin once removed, and I'd known Tom in college. And just after the war I spent two days with them in Chicago.

Her husband, among various physical accomplishments, had been one of the most powerful ends that ever played football at New Haven—a national figure in a way, one of those men who reach such an acute limited excellence at twenty-one that everything afterward savors of anti-climax. His family were enormously wealthy—even in college his freedom with money was a matter for reproach—but now he'd left Chicago and come East in a fashion that rather took your breath away: for instance, he'd brought down a string of polo ponies from Lake Forest.[13] It was hard to realize that a man in my own generation was wealthy enough to do that.

Why they came East I don't know. They had spent a year in France for no particular reason, and then drifted here and there unrestfully wherever people played polo and were rich together. This was a permanent move, said Daisy over the telephone,[14] but I didn't believe it—I had no sight into Daisy's heart, but I felt that Tom would drift on forever seeking, a little wistfully, for the dramatic turbulence of some irrecoverable football game.

And so it happened that on a warm windy evening I drove over to East Egg to see two old friends whom I scarcely knew at all. Their house was even more elaborate than I expected, a cheerful red-and-white Georgian Colonial mansion, overlooking the bay. The lawn started at the beach and ran toward the front door for a quarter of a mile, jumping over sun-dials and brick walks and burning gardens—finally when it reached the house drifting up the side in bright vines as though from the momentum of its run. The front was broken by a line of French windows, glowing now with reflected gold and wide open to the warm windy afternoon, and Tom Buchanan in riding clothes was standing with his legs apart on the front porch.[15]

He had changed since his New Haven years. Now he was a sturdy straw-haired man of thirty with a rather hard mouth and a supercilious manner. Two shining arrogant eyes had established dominance over his face and gave him the

**13** A suburb of Chicago on the North Shore of Lake Michigan. Ginevra King, Fitzgerald's first serious romantic interest, lived in Lake Forest for much of the summer season. Her father, Charles Garfield King, was a successful stockbroker; he kept a string of polo ponies and played in matches at Onwentsia, a country club for the wealthy near Lake Forest. When Fitzgerald visited her in Lake Forest in 1916, he overheard someone (perhaps her father) say: "Poor boys shouldn't think of marrying rich girls." See James L. W. West III, *The Perfect Hour: The Romance of F. Scott Fitzgerald and Ginevra King, His First Love* (Random House, 2005), pp. 4–5.

**14** The telephone was still a relatively new device in 1922. Many commercial businesses and financial institutions had telephones then, but most private residences did not. A telling amount of communication in *The Great Gatsby* takes place on the telephone: Myrtle calls Tom; Jordan calls Nick; Wilson calls Tom; Nick calls Daisy; Klipspringer calls Nick; and Gatsby's colleagues in crime call him at all hours, often from distant cities. The telephone was a convenient but intrusive new instrument of communication. Hugh Kenner refers to T. S. Eliot's *The Waste Land*, published in 1922, as "a telephone poem," noting "how the numerous voices of the poem have no locality and observe no occasion." See Hugh Kenner's *The Mechanic Muse* (Oxford University Press, 1987), p. 36.

**15** Hugh Kenner observes: "The too-elaborate house is not 'setting,' it is a first adumbration of the values by which the Buchanans live, just as the first house the Bovarys inhabit adumbrates, with its too-large clock on the exiguous mantel and its plaster curé in the miserable back garden, a former wife's thwarted yearning after elegance. Fitzgerald's acute sensitivity to the things people did with their money afforded him an economical way of delineating their values, summing up, in an inventory of purchases, a hundred things they have done before they did what they are doing now." See Kenner's *A Homemade World: The American Modernist Writers.* (Morrow, 1975), p. 131.

*Town & Country*

SOCIETY · AND · COUNTRY · LIFE · ART · LITERATURE · RECREATION · TRAVEL

MISS GINEVRA KING

Photograph of twenty-year-old Ginevra King, taken for the cover of the July 1918 issue of *Town & Country*. She was one of the inspirations for Daisy Buchanan. Fitzgerald met the beautiful Chicago debutante when was a sophomore at Princeton. "Because she's the one who got away, Ginevra—even more than Zelda—is the love who lodged like an irritant in Fitzgerald's imagination," Maureen Corrigan writes. See Corrigan's *So We Read On*, p. 58.

appearance of always leaning aggressively forward. Not even the effeminate swank of his riding clothes could hide the enormous power of that body—he seemed to fill those glistening boots until he strained the top lacing, and you could see a great pack of muscle shifting when his shoulder moved under his thin coat. It was a body capable of enormous leverage—a cruel body.

His speaking voice, a gruff husky tenor, added to the impression of fractiousness he conveyed. There was a touch of paternal contempt in it, even toward people he liked—and there were men at New Haven who had hated his guts.

"Now, don't think my opinion on these matters is final," he seemed to say, "just because I'm stronger and more of a man than you are." We were in the same senior society, and while we were never intimate I always had the impression that he approved of me and wanted me to like him with some harsh, defiant wistfulness of his own.

We talked for a few minutes on the sunny porch.

"I've got a nice place here," he said, his eyes flashing about restlessly.

Turning me around by one arm, he moved a broad flat hand along the front vista, including in its sweep a sunken Italian garden, a half acre of deep, pungent roses, and a snub-nosed motor-boat that bumped the tide offshore.

"It belonged to Demaine, the oil man." He turned me around again, politely and abruptly. "We'll go inside."

We walked through a high hallway into a bright rosy-colored space, fragilely bound into the house by French windows at either end. The windows were ajar and gleaming white against the fresh grass outside that seemed to grow a little way into the house. A breeze blew through the room, blew curtains in at one end and out the other like pale flags, twisting them up toward the frosted wedding-cake of the ceiling, and then rippled over the wine-colored rug, making a shadow on it as wind does on the sea.

The only completely stationary object in the room was an enormous couch on which two young women were buoyed up as though upon an anchored balloon. They were both in white, and their dresses were rippling and fluttering as if they had just been blown back in after a short flight around the house. I must have stood for a few moments listening to the whip and snap of the curtains and the groan of a picture on the wall. Then there was a boom as Tom Buchanan shut the rear windows and the caught wind died out about the room, and the curtains and the rugs and the two young women ballooned slowly to the floor.

The younger of the two was a stranger to me. She was extended full length at her end of the divan, completely motionless, and with her chin raised a little, as if she were balancing something on it which was quite likely to fall.[16] If she saw me out of the corner of her eyes she gave no hint of it—indeed, I was almost surprised into murmuring an apology for having disturbed her by coming in.

The other girl, Daisy, made an attempt to rise—she leaned slightly forward with a conscientious expression—then she laughed, an absurd, charming little laugh, and I laughed too and came forward into the room.

"I'm p-paralyzed with happiness."

She laughed again, as if she said something very witty, and held my hand for a moment, looking up into my face, promising that there was no one in the world she so much wanted to see. That was a way she had. She hinted in a murmur that the surname of the balancing girl was Baker. (I've heard it said that Daisy's murmur was only to make people lean toward her; an irrelevant criticism that made it no less charming.)

At any rate, Miss Baker's[17] lips fluttered, she nodded at me almost imperceptibly, and then quickly tipped her head back again—the object she was balancing had obviously tottered a little and given her something of a fright. Again a sort of apology arose to my lips. Almost any exhibition of complete self-sufficiency draws a stunned tribute from me.

[16] The critic and journalist Wesley Morris reminds us that Nick, the Buchanans, and Jordan Baker represent not just a privileged class but a privileged white class. Jordan, he remarks, holds her chin as if balancing on it "the precarious purity of their monotonous little empire." As the reader discovers a few pages later, Tom Buchanan subscribes to the theories of the scientific racist Lothrop Stoddard. See Wesley Morris's introduction to the Modern Library edition of *The Great Gatsby* (Modern Library, 2021), p. xii. See also the relevant note on p. 19 in this volume.

[17] Before World War I, young men and women of the haute bourgeoisie addressed each other as "Mr." and "Miss"—at least until they became friends. These customs began to fade after the war, but Nick still observes them in the novel. (In Chapter II, in which Nick relates the events of the party at Tom and Myrtle's New York love nest, he tells us that "after the first drink Mrs. Wilson and I called each other by our first names.")

18 The Buchanans were married in June 1919; according to Daisy's friend Jordan, the Buchanans' daughter was born ten months later, in April 1920. The child must therefore be two years old when this scene takes place in June 1922. The reading "three years old" originates in Fitzgerald's manuscript, in which the action of the novel takes place in 1923. Fitzgerald neglected to adjust the child's age when he shifted the year to 1922.

I looked back at my cousin, who began to ask me questions in her low, thrilling voice. It was the kind of voice that the ear follows up and down, as if each speech is an arrangement of notes that will never be played again. Her face was sad and lovely with bright things in it, bright eyes and a bright passionate mouth, but there was an excitement in her voice that men who had cared for her found difficult to forget: a singing compulsion, a whispered "Listen," a promise that she had done gay, exciting things just a while since and that there were gay, exciting things hovering in the next hour.

I told her how I had stopped off in Chicago for a day on my way East, and how a dozen people had sent their love through me.

"Do they miss me?" she cried ecstatically.

"The whole town is desolate. All the cars have the left rear wheel painted black as a mourning wreath, and there's a persistent wail all night along the North Shore."

"How gorgeous! Let's go back, Tom. Tomorrow!" Then she added irrelevantly: "You ought to see the baby."

"I'd like to."

"She's asleep. She's three years old.[18] Haven't you ever seen her?"

"Never."

"Well, you ought to see her. She's——"

Tom Buchanan, who had been hovering restlessly about the room, stopped and rested his hand on my shoulder.

"What you doing, Nick?"

"I'm a bond man."

"Who with?"

I told him.

"Never heard of them," he remarked decisively.

This annoyed me.

"You will," I answered shortly. "You will if you stay in the East."

"Oh, I'll stay in the East, don't you worry," he said, glancing at Daisy and then back at me, as if he were alert for something more. "I'd be a God Damn fool to live anywhere else."

At this point Miss Baker said: "Absolutely!" with such suddenness that I started—it was the first word she had uttered since I came into the room. Evidently it surprised her as much as it did me, for she yawned and with a series of rapid, deft movements stood up into the room.

"I'm stiff," she complained. "I've been lying on that sofa for as long as I can remember."

"Don't look at me," Daisy retorted. "I've been trying to get you to New York all afternoon."

"No, thanks," said Miss Baker to the four cocktails just in from the pantry. "I'm absolutely in training."

Her host looked at her incredulously.

"You are!" He took down his drink as if it were a drop in the bottom of a glass. "How you ever get anything done is beyond me."

I looked at Miss Baker, wondering what it was she "got done." I enjoyed looking at her. She was a slender, small-breasted girl, with an erect carriage, which she accentuated by throwing her body backward at the shoulders like a young cadet. Her gray sun-strained eyes looked back at me with polite reciprocal curiosity out of a wan, charming, discontented face. It occurred to me now that I had seen her, or a picture of her, somewhere before.

"You live in West Egg," she remarked contemptuously. "I know somebody there."

"I don't know a single——"

"You must know Gatsby."

"Gatsby?" demanded Daisy. "What Gatsby?"

Before I could reply that he was my neighbor dinner was announced; wedging his tense arm imperatively under mine, Tom Buchanan compelled me from the room as though he were moving a checker to another square.

Slenderly, languidly, their hands set lightly on their hips, the two young women preceded us out onto a rosy-colored porch,

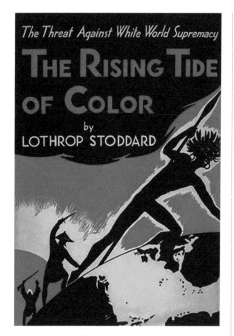

Lothrop Stoddard's *The Rising Tide of Color against White World-Supremacy* was published by Scribner's, Fitzgerald's own publisher, in 1920, the same year as *This Side of Paradise*.

open toward the sunset, where four candles flickered on the table in the diminished wind.

"Why *candles?*" objected Daisy, frowning. She snapped them out with her fingers. "In two weeks it'll be the longest day in the year." She looked at us all radiantly. "Do you always watch for the longest day of the year and then miss it? I always watch for the longest day in the year and then miss it."

"We ought to plan something," yawned Miss Baker, sitting down at the table as if she were getting into bed.

"All right," said Daisy. "What'll we plan?" She turned to me helplessly: "What do people plan?"

Before I could answer her eyes fastened with an awed expression on her little finger.

"Look!" she complained. "I hurt it."

We all looked—the knuckle was black and blue.

"You did it, Tom," she said accusingly. "I know you didn't mean to, but you *did* do it. That's what I get for marrying a brute of a man, a great, big, hulking physical specimen of a——"

"I hate that word hulking," objected Tom crossly, "even in kidding."

"Hulking," insisted Daisy.

Sometimes she and Miss Baker talked at once, unobtrusively and with a bantering inconsequence that was never quite chatter, that was as cool as their white dresses and their impersonal eyes in the absence of all desire. They were here, and they accepted Tom and me, making only a polite pleasant effort to entertain or to be entertained. They knew that presently dinner would be over and a little later the evening too would be over and casually put away. It was sharply different from the West, where an evening was hurried from phase to phase toward its close, in a continually disappointed anticipation or else in sheer nervous dread of the moment itself.

"You make me feel uncivilized, Daisy," I confessed on my second glass of corky but rather impressive claret. "Can't you talk about crops or something?"

I meant nothing in particular by this remark, but it was taken up in an unexpected way.

"Civilization's going to pieces," broke out Tom violently. "I've gotten to be a terrible pessimist about things. Have you read 'The Rise of the Colored Empires'[19] by this man Goddard?"

"Why, no," I answered, rather surprised by his tone.

"Well, it's a fine book, and everybody ought to read it. The idea is if we don't look out the white race will be—will be utterly submerged. It's all scientific stuff; it's been proved."

"Tom's getting very profound," said Daisy, with an expression of unthoughtful sadness. "He reads deep books with long words in them. What was that word we——"

"Well, these books are all scientific," insisted Tom, glancing at her impatiently. "This fellow has worked out the whole thing. It's up to us, who are the dominant race, to watch out or these other races will have control of things."

"We've got to beat them down," whispered Daisy, winking ferociously toward the fervent sun.

"You ought to live in California—" began Miss Baker, but Tom interrupted her by shifting heavily in his chair.

"This idea is that we're Nordics. I am, and you are, and you are, and—" After an infinitesimal hesitation he included Daisy with a slight nod, and she winked at me again. "—And we've produced all the things that go to make civilization—oh, science and art, and all that. Do you see?"

There was something pathetic in his concentration, as if his complacency, more acute than of old, was not enough to him any more. When, almost immediately, the telephone rang inside and the butler left the porch Daisy seized upon the momentary interruption and leaned toward me.

"I'll tell you a family secret," she whispered enthusiastically. "It's about the butler's nose. Do you want to hear about the butler's nose?"

"That's why I came over tonight."

"Well, he wasn't always a butler; he used to be the silver polisher for some people in New York that had a silver service

19 Tom misremembers both the title and author of the book: *The Rising Tide of Color against White World-Supremacy* (1920), by the American historian and white supremacist Lothrop Stoddard (1883–1950). According to Stoddard's thesis, a racial world war was inevitable if Africans and Asians were not prevented from migrating to Western nations: "The grim truth of the matter is this: The whole white race is exposed, immediately or ultimately, to the possibility of social sterilization and final replacement or absorption by the teeming colored races" (*The Rising Tide of Color against White World-Supremacy*, p. 298). Stoddard divides the white races into three groups (Nordic, Alpine, and Mediterranean), with the Nordic group representing the superior stock. Jews he classifies as partly Yellow/Asiatic. Tom Buchanan is portrayed by Fitzgerald as a buffoon; however, with white anxieties about non-Nordic immigrants running high in the 1920s, Stoddard's ideas found traction with many readers. *The New York Times*, for example, published a positive review of Stoddard's book, concluding that the author's arguments merit "respectful consideration."

for two hundred people. He had to polish it from morning till night, until finally it began to affect his nose——"

"Things went from bad to worse," suggested Miss Baker.

"Yes. Things went from bad to worse, until finally he had to give up his position."

For a moment the last sunshine fell with romantic affection upon her glowing face; her voice compelled me forward breathlessly as I listened—then the glow faded, each light deserting her with lingering regret, like children leaving a pleasant street at dusk.

The butler came back and murmured something close to Tom's ear, whereupon Tom frowned, pushed back his chair, and without a word went inside. As if his absence quickened something within her, Daisy leaned forward again, her voice glowing and singing.

"I love to see you at my table, Nick. You remind me of a—of a rose, an absolute rose. Doesn't he?" She turned to Miss Baker for confirmation: "An absolute rose?"

This was untrue. I am not even faintly like a rose. She was only extemporizing, but a stirring warmth flowed from her, as if her heart was trying to come out to you concealed in one of those breathless, thrilling words. Then suddenly she threw her napkin on the table and excused herself and went into the house.

Miss Baker and I exchanged a short glance consciously devoid of meaning. I was about to speak when she sat up alertly and said "Sh!" in a warning voice. A subdued impassioned murmur was audible in the room beyond, and Miss Baker leaned forward unashamed, trying to hear. The murmur trembled on the verge of coherence, sank down, mounted excitedly, and then ceased altogether.

"This Mr. Gatsby you spoke of is my neighbor—" I said.

"Don't talk. I want to hear what happens."

"Is something happening?" I inquired innocently.

"You mean to say you don't know?" said Miss Baker, honestly surprised. "I thought everybody knew."

"I don't."

"Why—" she said hesitantly, "Tom's got some woman in New York."

"Got some woman?" I repeated blankly.

Miss Baker nodded.

"She might have the decency not to telephone him at dinner-time. Don't you think?"

Almost before I had grasped her meaning there was the flutter of a dress and the crunch of leather boots, and Tom and Daisy were back at the table.

"It couldn't be helped!" cried Daisy with tense gayety.

She sat down, glanced searchingly at Miss Baker and then at me, and continued: "I looked outdoors for a minute, and it's very romantic outdoors. There's a bird on the lawn that I think must be a nightingale come over on the Cunard or White Star Line.[20] He's singing away—" Her voice sang: "It's romantic, isn't it, Tom?"

**20** The two major British transatlantic passenger lines of Fitzgerald's era. (In 1934, the two rivals merged to form the Cunard–White Star Line.) The Cunard liners included the *Mauretania*, the *Aquitania*, and the *Berengaria*; the White Star liners, which were known for their black-topped funnels, included the *Olympic*, the *Britannic*, and the ill-fated *Titanic*.

T.S.S. *Aquitania*

Length, 901 ft.
Width, 97 ft.
Tonnage, 47,000.
Speed, 23 Knots.

Ocean liner RMS *Aquitania*, Cunard Line, launched in 1913. On their first trip abroad in May 1921, Scott and Zelda traveled first-class to Europe aboard the *Aquitania*. Zelda was pregnant, and Scott had just completed his second novel, *The Beautiful and Damned* (1922).

"Very romantic," he said, and then miserably to me: "If it's light enough after dinner, I want to take you down to the stables."

The telephone rang inside, startlingly, and as Daisy shook her head decisively at Tom the subject of the stables, in fact all subjects, vanished into air. Among the broken fragments of the last five minutes at table I remember the candles being lit again, pointlessly, and I was conscious of wanting to look squarely at everyone, and yet to avoid all eyes. I couldn't guess what Daisy and Tom were thinking, but I doubt if even Miss Baker, who seemed to have mastered a certain hardy skepticism, was able utterly to put this fifth guest's shrill metallic urgency out of mind. To a certain temperament the situation might have seemed intriguing—my own instinct was to telephone immediately for the police.

The horses, needless to say, were not mentioned again. Tom and Miss Baker, with several feet of twilight between them, strolled back into the library, as if to a vigil beside a perfectly tangible body, while, trying to look pleasantly interested and a little deaf, I followed Daisy around a chain of connecting verandas to the porch in front. In its deep gloom we sat down side by side on a wicker settee.

Daisy took her face in her hands as if feeling its lovely shape, and her eyes moved gradually out into the velvet dusk. I saw that turbulent emotions possessed her, so I asked what I thought would be some sedative questions about her little girl.

"We don't know each other very well, Nick," she said suddenly. "Even if we are cousins. You didn't come to my wedding."

"I wasn't back from the war."

"That's true." She hesitated. "Well, I've had a very bad time, Nick, and I'm pretty cynical about everything."

Evidently she had reason to be. I waited but she didn't say any more, and after a moment I returned rather feebly to the subject of her daughter.

"I suppose she talks, and—eats, and everything."

"Oh, yes." She looked at me absently. "Listen, Nick; let me

tell you what I said when she was born. Would you like to hear?"

"Very much."

"It'll show you how I've gotten to feel about—things. Well, she was less than an hour old and Tom was God knows where. I woke up out of the ether[21] with an utterly abandoned feeling, and asked the nurse right away if it was a boy or a girl. She told me it was a girl, and so I turned my head away and wept. 'All right,' I said, 'I'm glad it's a girl. And I hope she'll be a fool—that's the best thing a girl can be in this world, a beautiful little fool.'[22]

"You see I think everything's terrible anyhow," she went on in a convinced way. "Everybody thinks so—the most advanced people. And I *know*. I've been everywhere and seen everything and done everything." Her eyes flashed around her in a defiant way, rather like Tom's, and she laughed with thrilling scorn. "Sophisticated—God, I'm sophisticated!"

The instant her voice broke off, ceasing to compel my attention, my belief, I felt the basic insincerity of what she had said. It made me uneasy, as though the whole evening had been a trick of some sort to exact a contributary emotion from me. I waited, and sure enough, in a moment she looked at me with an absolute smirk on her lovely face, as if she had asserted her membership in a rather distinguished secret society to which she and Tom belonged.

Inside, the crimson room bloomed with light. Tom and Miss Baker sat at either end of the long couch and she read aloud to him from the Saturday Evening Post[23]— the words, murmurous and uninflected, running together in a soothing tune. The lamp-light, bright on his boots and dull on the autumn-leaf yellow of her hair, glinted along the paper as she turned a page with a flutter of slender muscles in her arms.

21 During the 1920s, halogenated ether was a commonly used anesthetic. Daisy would have been unconscious during childbirth.

22 After the birth of their daughter, Scottie, on October 26, 1921, Fitzgerald recorded in his ledger Zelda's wandering remarks while she was still under the influence of anesthesia: "Oh God, goofo I'm drunk. Mark Twain. Isn't she smart—she has the hiccups. I hope its beautiful and a fool—a beautiful little fool." *F. Scott Fitzgerald's Ledger: A Facsimile*, ed. Matthew J. Bruccoli (NCR/Microcard Editions, 1972), p. 176.

23 *The Saturday Evening Post* was the most popular middle-class magazine of the period, with a circulation of almost three million in the 1920s. During Fitzgerald's peak earning years, the *Post* was the most dependable venue for his short fiction. Some of his best stories appeared in its pages, including "The Ice Palace" (1920), "Jacob's Ladder" (1927), the Basil Duke Lee stories (1928–1929), and "Babylon Revisited" (1931). *The Red Book Magazine*, *Woman's Home Companion*, and *Metropolitan Magazine* were other popular glossy magazines (the "slicks") in which his work appeared. The greater part of Fitzgerald's literary income came not from his books but from his magazine publications, and through them he reached his largest readership. Fitzgerald came to think of his work as divided between serious writing and commercial magazine fiction, but the line between artistic respectability and commercial success was never an absolute one in the author's mind. See *As Ever, Scott Fitz—Letters between F. Scott Fitzerald and His Literary Agent Harold Ober, 1919–1940*, ed. Matthew J. Bruccoli (Lippincott, 1972), pp. 190–93.

**24** Fitzgerald's 1925 readers would have recognized that "Jordan Baker" combines the names of two early automobile manufacturers. Both produced vehicles aimed at female buyers. The Jordan Motor Car Company (1916–1931) in Cleveland was known for its stylish runabouts; the Baker Motor Vehicle Company (1899–1914), also based in Cleveland, specialized in electric two-seaters, ideal for use in town.

Wallace Irwin — Hugh Wiley — F. Scott Fitzgerald — Harrison Rhodes
Oscar Graeve — Henry C. Rowland — Thomas Joyce — Hal G. Evarts

The May 1, 1920, issue of *The Saturday Evening Post*, with Fitzgerald's name for the first time on the cover. In 1932, for tax purposes, Fitzgerald attempted to have himself declared "virtually an employee" of the *Post*. More than sixty of his stories would appear in the magazine.

When we came in she held us silent for a moment with a lifted hand.

"To be continued," she said, tossing the magazine on the table, "in our very next issue."

Her body asserted itself with a restless movement of her knee, and she stood up.

"Ten o'clock," she remarked, apparently finding the time on the ceiling. "Time for this good girl to go to bed."

"Jordan's going to play in the tournament tomorrow," explained Daisy, "over at Westchester."

"Oh—you're *Jor*dan Baker."[24]

I knew now why her face was familiar—its pleasing contemptuous expression had looked out at me from many rotogravure pictures[25] of the sporting life at Asheville and Hot Springs and Palm Beach.[26] I had heard some story of her too, a critical, unpleasant story, but what it was I had forgotten long ago.

"Good night," she said softly. "Wake me at eight, won't you."

"If you'll get up."

"I will. Good night, Mr. Carraway. See you anon."

"Of course you will," confirmed Daisy. "In fact I think I'll arrange a marriage. Come over often, Nick, and I'll sort of—oh—fling you together. You know—lock you up accidentally in linen closets and push you out to sea in a boat, and all that sort of thing——"

"Good night," called Miss Baker from the stairs. "I haven't heard a word."

"She's a nice girl," said Tom after a moment. "They oughtn't to let her run around the country this way."

"Who oughtn't to?" inquired Daisy coldly.

"Her family."

"Her family is one aunt about a thousand years old. Besides, Nick's going to look after her, aren't you, Nick? She's going to spend lots of weekends out here this summer. I think the home influence will be very good for her."

Daisy and Tom looked at each other for a moment in silence.

"Is she from New York?" I asked quickly.

"From Louisville. Our white girlhood was passed together there. Our beautiful white——"

"Did you give Nick a little heart-to-heart talk on the veranda?" demanded Tom suddenly.

"Did I?" She looked at me. "I can't seem to remember, but I think we talked about the Nordic race. Yes, I'm sure we did. It sort of crept up on us and first thing you know——"

"Don't believe everything you hear, Nick," he advised me.

I said lightly that I had heard nothing at all, and a few

Golfer Edith Cummings, known as the "Fairway Flapper," circa 1918, at the Onwentsia Club, in Lake Forest, Illinois. Cummings, whom Fitzgerald met through her close friend Ginevra King, served as the inspiration for Jordan Baker. A talented golfer and one of the first female sports celebrities, she won the U.S. Women's Amateur tournament in 1923.

25 Rotogravure was a printing process using intaglio cylinders on a rotary press. Here, "rotogravure" refers to the illustrated supplement found in most Sunday newspapers of the day, featuring printed images of celebrities, society people, stage and movie stars, and sports figures.

26 Luxury resorts, known for their golf courses, in North Carolina, Arkansas, and Florida. Fitzgerald lived in Asheville off and on during the 1930s so that he could be near Zelda, who was being treated at Highland Hospital, a sanitarium near the city.

**27** Fitzgerald almost surely has in mind here his courtship of Zelda Sayre in the months following the conclusion of World War I. Zelda broke off their engagement, believing that Fitzgerald would never be able to support her with the slender emoluments of authorship. Fitzgerald's prospects were much improved when Scribner's accepted *This Side of Paradise* for publication in September 1919. He was able to renew the engagement, and he and Zelda were married on April 3, 1920, at St. Patrick's Cathedral in New York City. Fitzgerald never forgot the experience of having to prove himself to Zelda before she would accept his proposal of marriage. The poor boy/rich girl theme appears repeatedly in his stories and novels.

*This Side of Paradise* (1920), Fitzgerald's debut novel. The novel was an immediate success, selling some 50,000 copies and making its author famous. Its acceptance for publication influenced Zelda's decision to marry Scott. Writing in *The New Republic* on February 17, 1941, shortly after Fitzgerald's death, the novelist Glenway Wescott recalls: "*This Side of Paradise* haunted the decade like a song, popular but perfect. It hung over an entire youth-movement like a banner."

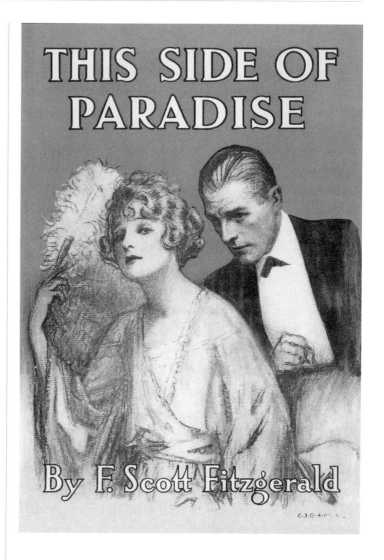

minutes later I got up to go home. They came to the door with me and stood side by side in a cheerful square of light. As I started my motor Daisy peremptorily called: "Wait!

"I forgot to ask you something, and it's important. We heard you were engaged to a girl out West."[27]

"That's right," corroborated Tom kindly. "We heard that you were engaged."

"It's a libel. I'm too poor."

"But we heard it," insisted Daisy, surprising me by open-

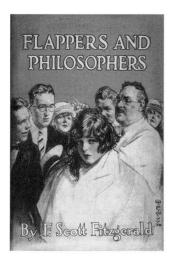 

Flappers and Philosophers (1920),
Fitzgerald's first story collection, appeared
the same year as This Side of Paradise.
Fitzgerald did not invent the flapper, but he
can be credited with creating the American
flapper as a fictional type—a strong-willed,
free-spirited young woman.

Front panel of the original dust cover for
Tales of the Jazz Age (1922), Fitzgerald's
second story collection. "The word jazz
in its progress toward respectability has
meant first sex, then dancing, then music,"
Fitzgerald explains in "Echoes of the Jazz
Age." By yoking the word to the twenties
(he coined the term "the Jazz Age"), he
also meant to convey "a state of nervous
stimulation" that gripped Americans
following World War I and the influenza
pandemic of 1918–19.

ing up again in a flower-like way. "We heard it from three people, so it must be true."

Of course I knew what they were referring to, but I wasn't
even vaguely engaged. The fact that gossip had published the
banns was one of the reasons I had come East. You can't stop
going with an old friend on account of rumors, and on the
other hand I had no intention of being rumored into marriage.

Their interest rather touched me and made them less
remotely rich—nevertheless, I was confused and a little dis-
gusted as I drove away. It seemed to me that the thing for
Daisy to do was to rush out of the house, child in arms—but
apparently there were no such intentions in her head. As for
Tom, the fact that he "had some woman in New York" was
really less surprising than that he had been depressed by a
book. Something was making him nibble at the edge of stale
ideas as if his sturdy physical egotism no longer nourished his
peremptory heart.

Already it was deep summer on roadhouse roofs and in
front of wayside garages, where new red gas-pumps sat out
in pools of light, and when I reached my estate at West Egg
I ran the car under its shed and sat for a while on an abandoned grass roller in the yard. The wind had blown off, leaving a loud, bright night, with wings beating in the trees and a

Zelda's sketch for the proposed cover art for *The Beautiful and Damned*: not Venus emerging from the sea on a half shell but an unclothed Zelda, "the first American flapper," climbing from a champagne glass.

Front panel of the original dust jacket for *The Beautiful and Damned* (1922), Fitzgerald's second novel. "The girl is excellent of course—it looks somewhat like Zelda," Fitzgerald wrote to Perkins. "But the man, I suspect, is a sort of debauched edition of me." FSF to Perkins, ca. Jan. 31, 1922, in *Dear Scott/Dear Max: The Fitzgerald-Perkins Correspondence*, ed. John Kuehl and Jackson R. Bryer (Scribner's, 1971), p. 52.

**28** Fitzgerald did not immediately seize upon the "single green light" as the symbol of Gatsby's desire but perfected it in revision, before the novel was set in type. In the surviving manuscript of *Gatsby*, there are "two green lights" at the end of Daisy's dock; and, in the final two paragraphs of the manuscript, the narrator refers to a "green glimmer" instead of "a single green light." The Great Gatsby: *An Edition of the Manuscript*, ed. James L. W. West III and Don C. Skemer (Cambridge University Press, 2018), pp. 76, 157.

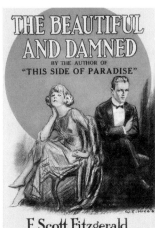

persistent organ sound as the full bellows of the earth blew the frogs full of life. The silhouette of a moving cat wavered across the moonlight, and turning my head to watch it, I saw that I was not alone—fifty feet away a figure had emerged from the shadow of my neighbor's mansion and was standing with his hands in his pockets regarding the silver pepper of the stars. Something in his leisurely movements and the secure position of his feet upon the lawn suggested that it was Mr. Gatsby himself, come out to determine what share was his of our local heavens.

I decided to call to him. Miss Baker had mentioned him at dinner, and that would do for an introduction. But I didn't call to him, for he gave a sudden intimation that he was content to be alone—he stretched out his arms toward the dark water in a curious way, and, far as I was from him, I could have sworn he was trembling. Involuntarily I glanced seaward—and distinguished nothing except a single green light,[28] minute and far away, that might have been at the end of a dock.[29] When I looked once more for Gatsby he had vanished, and I was alone again in the unquiet darkness.

**29** Glossing the final two paragraphs of Chapter I, Jonathan Bate reflects on Fitzgerald's indebtedness to John Keats's great sonnet "Bright Star," addressed to the poet's beloved Fanny Brawne: "Gatsby first appears on his lawn in moonlight, watching 'the silver pepper of the stars,'" Bate writes. "Below those bright stars, he stretches his arms outwards towards the dark water. Across the Sound, Nick sees 'a single green light, minute and far away, that might have been at the end of a dock'. . . . The bright star, denoting Fanny Brawne, has become the green light on Daisy's dock." See Jonathan Bate's *Bright Star, Green Light* (Yale University Press, 2021), p. 277.

Bright Star, would I were stedfast as thou art—
    Not in lone splendour hung aloft the night,
And watching, with eternal lids apart,
    Like nature's patient sleepless Eremite,
The moving waters at their priestlike task
    Of pure ablution round earth's human shores,
Or gazing on the new soft fallen mask
    Of snow upon the mountains and the moors—
No—yet still stedfast, still unchangeable,
    Pillow'd upon my fair love's ripening breast,
To feel for ever its soft fall and swell,
    Awake for ever in a sweet unrest,
Still, still to hear her tender-taken breath,
    And so live ever—or else swoon to death.

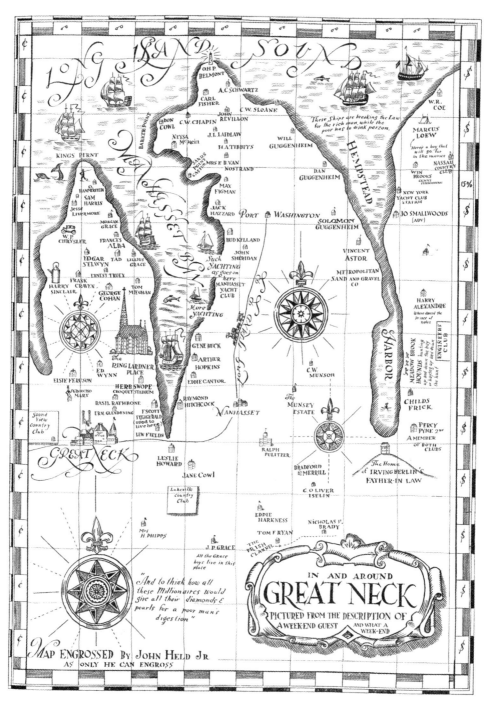

Map of Great Neck, from *The New Yorker*, July 16, 1927. Fitzgerald's former place of residence and his friend Ring Lardner's home are identified.

# CHAPTER II

About half way between West Egg and New York the motor-road hastily joins the railroad and runs beside it for a quarter of a mile, so as to shrink away from a certain desolate area of land. This is a valley of ashes[1]— a fantastic farm where ashes grow like wheat into ridges and hills and grotesque gardens; where ashes take the forms of houses and chimneys and rising smoke and, finally, with a transcendent effort, of men who move dimly and already crumbling through the powdery air. Occasionally a line of gray cars crawls along an invisible track, gives out a ghastly creak, and comes to rest, and immediately the ash-gray men swarm up with leaden spades and stir up an impenetrable cloud, which screens their obscure operations from your sight.

But above the gray land and the spasms of bleak dust which drift endlessly over it, you perceive, after a moment, the eyes of Doctor T. J. Eckleburg.[2] The eyes of Doctor T. J. Eckleburg are blue and gigantic—their retinas are one yard high. They look out of no face, but, instead, from a pair of enormous yellow spectacles which pass over a non-existent nose. Evidently some wild wag of an oculist set them there to fatten his practice in the borough of Queens, and then sank down himself into eternal blindness, or forgot them and moved away. But his eyes, dimmed a little by many paintless days under sun and rain, brood on over the solemn dumping ground.

The valley of ashes is bounded on one side by a small foul river, and, when the drawbridge is up to let barges through, the passengers on waiting trains can stare at the dismal scene for as long as half an hour. There is always a halt there of at

1 Critics have long recognized the influence of T. S. Eliot's *The Waste Land* (1922) on *The Great Gatsby*, notably on the symbols of waste and emptiness in the novel. (One of Fitzgerald's working titles was "Among the Ash Heaps and Millionaires.") More literally, the "valley of ashes" refers to the Corona Ash Dump in the northern part of the borough of Queens, once pristine salt marshes that were transformed in the 1910s into a vast dumping-ground for Brooklyn's coal ash, garbage, street sweepings, and animal waste. This was a breeding area for mosquitoes and a source of airborne diseases—a health hazard for the poor living in the adjacent areas of Corona and Flushing. For commuters on the Long Island Rail Road it was merely an eyesore. While living in Great Neck, 1922–24, Fitzgerald would have passed the dumps when going to and coming from Manhattan. Leo Marx, writing of Fitzgerald's valley of ashes, has this to say: "This hideous, man-made wilderness is a product of the technological power that also makes possible Gatsby's wealth, his parties, his car. . . . The car and the garden of ashes belong to a world, like Ahab's [in *Moby-Dick*], where natural objects are of no value in themselves." See Marx's *The Machine in the Garden: Technology and the Pastoral Ideal in America* (Oxford University Press, 1964), p. 358.

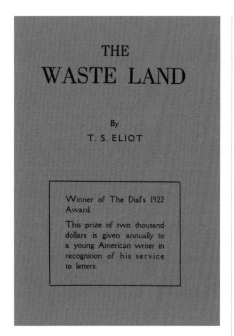

# THE
# WASTE LAND

By
T. S. ELIOT

Winner of The Dial's 1922
Award.

This prize of two thousand
dollars is given annually to
a young American writer in
recognition of his service
to letters.

T. S. Eliot's *The Waste Land*, published in 1922. Eliot was an admirer of Fitzgerald's novel. He called it "the first step that American fiction has taken since Henry James."

**2** Sarah Churchwell, writing about the eyes on the billboard, offers these remarks: "Dr. Eckleburg's eyes symbolize not only what Fitzgerald viewed as America's short-sightedness, but the way such myopia suggests a nation buying into its own myths, and the financially asymmetrical society that these self-advertisements have always shielded and protected. What is being sold so aggressively doesn't exist: Eckleburg is a defunct billboard, after all, selling services that are no longer available, an apt image for a nation selling itself a dream that increasingly seems to many like just so much snake oil." See Churchwell's "Dr. Eckleburg's Myopia," in *The Junket* (January 24, 2013).

least a minute, and it was because of this that I first met Tom Buchanan's mistress.

The fact that he had one was insisted upon wherever he was known. His acquaintances resented the fact that he turned up in popular restaurants with her and, leaving her at a table, sauntered about, chatting with whomsoever he knew. Though I was curious to see her, I had no desire to meet her—but I did. I went up to New York with Tom on the train one afternoon, and when we stopped by the ashheaps he jumped to his feet and, taking hold of my elbow, literally forced me from the car.

"We're getting off," he insisted. "I want you to meet my girl."

I think he'd tanked up a good deal at luncheon, and his determination to have my company bordered on violence. The supercilious assumption was that on Sunday afternoon I had nothing better to do.

I followed him over a low whitewashed railroad fence, and we walked back a hundred yards along the road under Doctor Eckleburg's persistent stare. The only building in sight was a small block of yellow brick sitting on the edge of the waste land, a sort of compact Main Street ministering to it, and contiguous to absolutely nothing. One of the three shops it contained was for rent and another was an all-night restaurant, approached by a trail of ashes; the third was a garage—*Repairs*. GEORGE B. WILSON. *Cars bought and sold.*—and I followed Tom inside.

The interior was unprosperous and bare; the only car visible was the dust-covered wreck of a Ford which crouched in a dim corner. It had occurred to me that this shadow of a garage must be a blind, and that sumptuous and romantic apartments were concealed overhead, when the proprietor himself appeared in the door of an office, wiping his hands on a piece of waste. He was a blond, spiritless man, anæmic, and faintly handsome. When he saw us a damp gleam of hope sprang into his light blue eyes.

"Hello, Wilson, old man," said Tom, slapping him jovially on the shoulder. "How's business?"

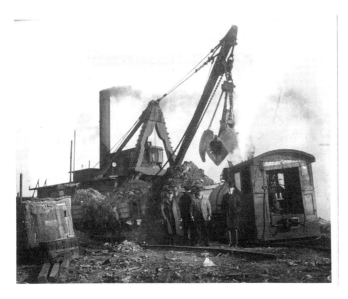

The Corona Ash Dump in Queens, the real-life "valley of ashes." Brooklyn's coal ash and street sweepings were transported to the site by the Long Island Rail Road on freight trains not so affectionately known as the "Talcum Powder Express." Sanitation workers are posing.

"I can't complain," answered Wilson unconvincingly. "When are you going to sell me that car?"

"Next week; I've got my man working on it now."

"Works pretty slow, don't he?"

"No, he doesn't," said Tom coldly. "And if you feel that way about it, maybe I'd better sell it somewhere else after all."

"I don't mean that," explained Wilson quickly. "I just meant——"

His voice faded off and Tom glanced impatiently around the garage. Then I heard footsteps on a stairs, and in a moment the thickish figure of a woman blocked out the light from the office door. She was in the middle thirties, and faintly stout, but she carried her surplus flesh sensuously as some women can. Her face, above a spotted dress of dark blue crêpe-de-chine, contained no facet or gleam of beauty, but there was an immediately perceptible vitality about her as if the nerves of her body were continually smouldering. She smiled slowly and, walking through her husband as if he were a ghost, shook hands with Tom, looking him flush in the eye. Then she wet her lips, and without turning around spoke to her husband in a soft, coarse voice:

3 A fictional magazine. Cf. *Town Topics: The Journal of Society*, a New York gossip rag known for printing scandalous stories about the rich and celebrated, published from 1885 to 1937. A person of wealth could often bury a report of improper behavior by purchasing "advertising space" in the magazine. Scott and Zelda were frequently mentioned in its pages. Later in this chapter, a copy of *Town Tattle* is used to protect Myrtle Wilson's upholstered couch from the blood that is flowing from her nose.

"Get some chairs, why don't you, so somebody can sit down."

"Oh, sure," agreed Wilson hurriedly, and went toward the little office, mingling immediately with the cement color of the walls. A white ashen dust veiled his dark suit and his pale hair as it veiled everything in the vicinity—except his wife, who moved close to Tom.

"I want to see you," said Tom intently. "Get on the next train."

"All right."

"I'll meet you by the newsstand on the lower level."

She nodded and moved away from him just as George Wilson emerged with two chairs from his office door.

We waited for her down the road and out of sight. It was a few days before the Fourth of July, and a gray, scrawny Italian child was setting torpedoes in a row along the railroad track.

"Terrible place, isn't it," said Tom, exchanging a frown with Doctor Eckleburg.

"Awful."

"It does her good to get away."

"Doesn't her husband object?"

"Wilson? He thinks she goes to see her sister in New York. He's so dumb he doesn't know he's alive."

So Tom Buchanan and his girl and I went up together to New York—or not quite together, for Mrs. Wilson sat discreetly in another car. Tom deferred that much to the sensibilities of those East Eggers who might be on the train.

She had changed her dress to a brown figured muslin, which stretched tight over her rather wide hips as Tom helped her to the platform in New York. At the newsstand she bought a copy of Town Tattle[3] and a moving-picture magazine, and in the station drug-store some cold cream and a small flask of perfume. Upstairs in the solemn echoing drive she let four taxi cabs drive away before she selected a new one, lavender-colored with gray upholstery, and in this we slid out from the mass of the station into the glowing sunshine. But immediately she turned sharply from the window and, leaning forward, tapped on the front glass.

"I want to get one of those dogs," she said earnestly. "I want to get one for the apartment. They're nice to have—a dog."

We backed up to a gray old man who bore an absurd resemblance to John D. Rockefeller.[4] In a basket swung from his neck cowered a dozen very recent puppies of an indeterminate breed.

"What kind are they?" asked Mrs. Wilson eagerly, as he came to the taxi window.

"All kinds. What kind do you want, lady?"

"I'd like to get one of those police dogs; I don't suppose you got that kind?"

The man peered doubtfully into the basket, plunged in his hand and drew one up, wriggling, by the back of the neck.

"That's no police dog," said Tom.

"No, it's not exactly a pol*ice* dog," said the man with disappointment in his voice. "It's more of an Airedale." He passed his hand over the brown wash-rag of a back. "Look at that coat. Some coat. That's a dog that'll never bother you with catching cold."

"I think it's cute," said Mrs. Wilson enthusiastically. "How much is it?"

"That dog?" He looked at it admiringly. "That dog will cost you ten dollars."

The Airedale—undoubtedly there was an Airedale concerned in it somewhere, though its feet were startlingly white—changed hands and settled down into Mrs. Wilson's lap, where she fondled the weather-proof coat with rapture.

"Is it a boy or a girl?" she asked delicately.

"That dog? That dog's a boy."

"It's a bitch," said Tom decisively. "Here's your money. Go and buy ten more dogs with it."

We drove over to Fifth Avenue, so warm and soft, almost pastoral, on the summer Sunday afternoon that I wouldn't

John D. Rockefeller, founder of the Standard Oil Company, as he appeared in 1922.

[4] American business magnate and wealthiest American of the twentieth century (1839–1937), known for his philanthropy and for his Social Darwinist beliefs. He founded the Standard Oil Company in 1870.

**5** Semi-scandalous best-selling novel of 1921 by British author Robert Keable (1887–1927). The protagonist is an army chaplain who loses his morals and ideals while serving on the front during World War I, and begins an affair with a young French nurse. From the Dutton edition: "Almost the next second Julie appeared in the doorway. She was still half-wet from the water, and her sole dress was a rosebud which she had just tucked into her hair" (p. 287). Fitzgerald was nervous about including a reference to Keable's novel in this scene. In a letter to Perkins written in early December 1924, he asked: "[I]n Chap. II of my book when Tom + Myrte go into the bedroom while Carraway reads Simon called Peter—is that raw? Let me know. I think its pretty nessessary." See page 207 in this volume.

have been surprised to see a great flock of white sheep turn the corner.

"Hold on," I said. "I have to leave you here."

"No, you don't," interposed Tom quickly. "Myrtle'll be hurt if you don't come up to the apartment. Won't you, Myrtle?"

"Come on," she urged. "I'll telephone my sister Catherine. She's said to be very beautiful by people who ought to know."

"Well, I'd like to, but——"

We went on, cutting back again over the Park toward the West Hundreds. At 158th Street the cab stopped at one slice in a long white cake of apartment-houses. Throwing a regal homecoming glance around the neighborhood, Mrs. Wilson gathered up her dog and her other purchases, and went haughtily in.

"I'm going to have the McKees come up," she announced as we rose in the elevator. "And, of course, I got to call up my sister, too."

The apartment was on the top floor—a small living-room, a small dining-room, a small bedroom, and a bath. The living-room was crowded to the doors with a set of tapestried furniture entirely too large for it, so that to move about was to stumble continually over scenes of ladies swinging in the gardens of Versailles. The only picture was an over-enlarged photograph, apparently a hen sitting on a blurred rock. Looked at from a distance, however, the hen resolved itself into a bonnet, and the countenance of a stout old lady beamed down into the room. Several old copies of Town Tattle lay on the table together with a copy of "Simon Called Peter,"[5] and some of the small scandal magazines of Broadway. Mrs. Wilson was first concerned with the dog. A reluctant elevator-boy went for a box full of straw and some milk, to which he added on his own initiative a tin of large, hard dog-biscuits—one of which decomposed apathetically in the saucer of milk all afternoon. Meanwhile Tom brought out a bottle of whiskey from a locked bureau door.

I have been drunk just twice in my life, and the second time was that afternoon; so everything that happened has a dim, hazy cast over it, although until after eight o'clock the apartment was full of cheerful sun. Sitting on Tom's lap Mrs. Wilson called up several people on the telephone; then there were no cigarettes, and I went out to buy some at the drug-store on the corner. When I came back they had disappeared, so I sat down discreetly in the living-room and read a chapter of "Simon Called Peter"—either it was terrible stuff or the whiskey distorted things, because it didn't make any sense to me.

Just as Tom and Myrtle (after the first drink Mrs. Wilson and I called each other by our first names) reappeared, company commenced to arrive at the apartment-door.

The sister, Catherine, was a slender, worldly girl of about thirty, with a solid, sticky bob of red hair, and a complexion powdered milky white. Her eyebrows had been plucked and then drawn on again at a more rakish angle, but the efforts of nature toward the restoration of the old alignment gave a blurred air to her face. When she moved about there was an incessant clicking as innumerable pottery bracelets jingled up and down upon her arms. She came in with such a proprietary haste and looked around so possessively at the furniture that I wondered if she lived here. But when I asked her she laughed immoderately, repeated my question aloud, and told me she lived with a girl friend at a hotel.

Mr. McKee was a pale, feminine man from the flat below. He had just shaved, for there was a white spot of lather on his cheekbone, and he was most respectful in his greeting to everyone in the room. He informed me that he was in the "artistic game," and I gathered later that he was a photographer and had made the dim enlargement of Mrs. Wilson's mother which hovered like an ectoplasm on the wall. His wife was shrill, languid, handsome, and horrible. She told me with pride that her husband had photographed her a hundred and twenty-seven times since they had been married.

Mrs. Wilson had changed her costume sometime before, and was now attired in an elaborate afternoon dress of

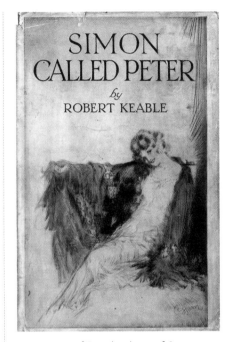

Front cover of British edition of *Simon Called Peter* (1921). In a 1923 review of another novel, Fitzgerald disparagingly refers to Keable's blockbuster: "There is a recent piece of trash entitled *Simon Called Peter*, which seems to me utterly immoral, because the characters move in a continual labyrinth of mild sexual stimulation. Over this stimulation play the colored lights of romantic Christianity." See "Sherwood Anderson on the Marriage Question," *New York Herald*, March 4, 1923, Sec. 9, p. 5.

cream-colored chiffon, which gave out a continual rustle as she swept about the room. With the influence of the dress her personality had also undergone a change. The intense vitality that had been so remarkable in the garage was converted into impressive hauteur. Her laughter, her gestures, her assertions became more violently affected moment by moment, and as she expanded the room grew smaller around her, until she seemed to be revolving on a noisy, creaking pivot through the smoky air.

"My dear," she told her sister in a high, mincing shout, "most of these fellas will cheat you every time. All they think of is money. I had a woman up here last week to look at my feet, and when she gave me the bill you'd of thought she had my appendicitus out."

"What was the name of the woman?" asked Mrs. McKee.

"Mrs. Eberhardt. She goes around looking at people's feet in their own homes."

"I like your dress," remarked Mrs. McKee. "I think it's adorable."

Mrs. Wilson rejected the compliment by raising her eyebrow in disdain.

"It's just a crazy old thing," she said. "I just slip it on sometimes when I don't care what I look like."

"But it looks wonderful on you, if you know what I mean," pursued Mrs. McKee. "If Chester could only get you in that pose I think he could make something of it."

We all looked in silence at Mrs. Wilson, who removed a strand of hair from over her eyes and looked back at us with a brilliant smile. Mr. McKee regarded her intently with his head on one side, and then moved his hand back and forth slowly in front of his face.

"I should change the light," he said after a moment. "I'd like to bring out the modelling of the features. And I'd try to get hold of all the back hair."

"I wouldn't think of changing the light," cried Mrs. McKee. "I think it's——"

Her husband said "*Sh!*" and we all looked at the subject again, whereupon Tom Buchanan yawned audibly and got to his feet.

"You McKees have something to drink," he said. "Get some more ice and mineral water, Myrtle, before everybody goes to sleep."

"I told that boy about the ice." Myrtle raised her eyebrows in despair at the shiftlessness of the lower orders. "These people! You have to keep after them all the time."

She looked at me and laughed pointlessly. Then she flounced over to the dog, kissed it with ecstasy, and swept into the kitchen, implying that a dozen chefs awaited her orders there.

"I've done some nice things out on Long Island," asserted Mr. McKee.

Tom looked at him blankly.

"Two of them we have framed downstairs."

"Two what?" demanded Tom.

"Two studies. One of them I call 'Montauk Point—The Gulls,' and the other I call 'Montauk Point—The Sea.'"

The sister Catherine sat down beside me on the couch.

"Do you live down on Long Island, too," she inquired.

"I live at West Egg."

"Really? I was down there at a party about a month ago. At a man named Gatsby's. Do you know him?"

"I live next door to him."

"Well, they say he's a nephew or a cousin of Kaiser Wilhelm's.[6] That's where all his money comes from."

"Really?"

She nodded.

"I'm scared of him. I'd hate to have him get anything on me."

This absorbing information about my neighbor was interrupted by Mrs. McKee's pointing suddenly at Catherine:

"Chester, I think you could do something with *her*," she broke out, but Mr. McKee only nodded in a bored way, and turned his attention to Tom.

6 Kaiser Wilhelm II (1859–1941), the last German emperor, who abdicated in November 1918 at the end of World War I after losing the support of the German army. He spent the rest of his life in exile in the Netherlands. Owing to intermarriage among the royal families of Europe and Russia, Wilhelm II was a first cousin to George V, who was king of England during the war. Perhaps in jest, many people in the U.K. and U.S. claimed kinship with "Kaiser Bill," as he was known in the press.

"America was going on the greatest, gaudiest spree in history, and there was going to be plenty to tell about it." From "Early Success," in *The Crack-Up*, ed. Edmund Wilson (New Directions, 1945), p. 87. Publicity photograph of Fitzgerald posing at desk.

"I'd like to do more work on Long Island, if I could get the entry. All I ask is that they should give me a start."

"Ask Myrtle," said Tom, breaking into a short shout of laughter as Mrs. Wilson entered with a tray. "She'll give you a letter of introduction, won't you, Myrtle?"

"Do what?" she asked, startled.

"You'll give McKee a letter of introduction to your husband, so he can do some studies of him." His lips moved silently for a moment as he invented. "'George B. Wilson at the Gasoline Pump,' or something like that."

Catherine leaned close to me and whispered in my ear:

"Neither of them can stand the person they're married to."

"Can't they?"

"Can't *stand* them." She looked at Myrtle and then at Tom. "What I say is, why go on living with them if they can't stand them? If I was them I'd get a divorce and get married to each other right away."

"Doesn't she like Wilson either?"

The answer to this was unexpected. It came from Myrtle, who had overheard the question, and it was violent and obscene.

"You see?" cried Catherine triumphantly. She lowered her voice again. "It's really his wife that's keeping them apart. She's a Catholic, and they don't believe in divorce."

Daisy was not a Catholic, and I was a little shocked at the elaborateness of the lie.

"When they do get married," continued Catherine, "they're going West to live for a while until it blows over."

"It'd be more discreet to go to Europe."

"Oh, do you like Europe?" she exclaimed surprisingly. "I just got back from Monte Carlo."

"Really."

"Just last year. I went over there with another girl."

"Stay long?"

"No, we just went to Monte Carlo and back. We went by way of Marseilles. We had over twelve hundred dollars when we started, but we got gypped out of it all in two days in the private rooms. We had an awful time getting back, I can tell you. God, how I hated that town!"

The late afternoon sky bloomed in the window for a moment like the blue honey of the Mediterranean—then the shrill voice of Mrs. McKee called me back into the room.

"I almost made a mistake, too," she declared vigorously. "I almost married a little kyke who'd been after me for years. I knew he was below me. Everybody kept saying to me: 'Lucille, that man's way below you!' But if I hadn't met Chester, he'd of got me sure."

"Yes, but listen," said Myrtle Wilson, nodding her head up and down. "At least you didn't marry him."

"I know I didn't."

"Well, I married him," said Myrtle, ambiguously. "And that's the difference between your case and mine."

"Why did you, Myrtle?" demanded Catherine. "Nobody forced you to."

Myrtle considered.

"I married him because I thought he was a gentleman," she said finally. "I thought he knew something about breeding, but he wasn't fit to lick my shoe."

"You were crazy about him for a while," said Catherine.

"Crazy about him!" cried Myrtle incredulously. "Who said I was crazy about him? I never was any more crazy about him than I was about that man there."

She pointed suddenly at me, and everyone looked at me accusingly. I tried to show by my expression that I had played no part in her past.

"The only *crazy* I was was when I married him. I knew right away I made a mistake. He borrowed somebody's best suit to get married in, and never even told me about it, and the man came after it one day when he was out." She looked to see who was listening. "'Oh, is that your suit?' I said. 'This is the first I ever heard about it.' But I gave it to him and then I lay down and cried to beat the band all afternoon."

"She really ought to get away from him," resumed Catherine to me. "They've been living over that garage for eleven years. And Tom's the first sweetie she ever had."

The bottle of whiskey—a second one—was now in constant demand by all present, excepting Catherine, who "felt just as good on nothing at all." Tom rang for the janitor and sent him for some celebrated sandwiches which were a complete supper in themselves. I wanted to get out and walk eastward toward the Park through the soft twilight, but each time I tried to go I became entangled in some wild, strident argument which pulled me back, as if with ropes, into my chair. Yet high over

the city our line of yellow windows must have contributed their share of human secrecy to the casual watcher in the darkening streets, and I was him too, looking up and wondering. I was within and without, simultaneously enchanted and repelled by the inexhaustible variety of life.

Myrtle pulled her chair close to mine, and suddenly her warm breath poured over me the story of her first meeting with Tom.

"It was on the two little seats facing each other that are always the last ones left on the train. I was going up to New York to see my sister and spend the night. He had on a dress suit and patent leather shoes, and I couldn't keep my eyes off him, but every time he looked at me I had to pretend to be looking at the advertisement over his head. When we came into the station he was next to me, and his white shirt front

Scott and Zelda on the French Riviera. The celebrity couple went to France in April 1924 to escape the scrutiny of gossip journalists and the hectic party life on Long Island. And there, for a while, they managed to make a clean break, as Fitzgerald completed his masterpiece, *The Great Gatsby.*

7 Myrtle Wilson is the "mirror image" of
Gatsby, Sarah Churchwell observes. Myrtle
wants what Daisy has, while Gatsby wants
what Tom has. "They are both upstarts,"
Churchwell writes, "trying to foist themselves upon high society, poseurs who lead
double lives. But Myrtle, according to the
code of the novel, lacks Gatsby's greatness,
while her party, although cheaper than
Gatsby's, shares (and foreshadows) the
crassness and violence that will come at the
end of his." See Churchwell's *Careless People: Murder, Mayhem, and the Invention of
The Great Gatsby* (Penguin Press, 2014),
p. 67.

pressed against my arm, and so I told him I'd have to call a
policeman, but he knew I lied. I was so excited that when I got
into a taxi with him I didn't hardly know I wasn't getting into
a subway train. All I kept thinking about, over and over, was
'You can't live forever, you can't live forever.'"

She turned to Mrs. McKee and the room rang full of her
artificial laughter.

"My dear," she cried, "I'm going to give you this dress as soon
as I'm through with it. I've got to get another one tomorrow.
I'm going to make a list of all the things I've got to get. A massage and a wave, and a collar for the dog, and one of those cute
little ash trays where you touch a spring, and a wreath with a
black silk bow for mother's grave that'll last all summer. I got
to write down a list so I won't forget all the things I got to do."

It was nine o'clock—almost immediately afterward I
looked at my watch and found it was ten. Mr. McKee was
asleep on a chair with his fists clenched in his lap, like a photograph of a man of action. Taking out my handkerchief I
wiped from his cheek the spot of dried lather that had worried me all the afternoon.

The little dog was sitting on the table looking with blind
eyes through the smoke, and from time to time groaning
faintly. People disappeared, reappeared, made plans to go
somewhere, and then lost each other, searched for each other,
found each other a few feet away. Some time toward midnight
Tom Buchanan and Mrs. Wilson stood face to face discussing,
in impassioned voices, whether Mrs. Wilson had any right to
mention Daisy's name.

"Daisy! Daisy! Daisy!" shouted Mrs. Wilson. "I'll say it
whenever I want to! Daisy! Dai——"[7]

Making a short deft movement, Tom Buchanan broke her
nose with his open hand.

Then there were bloody towels upon the bathroom floor,
and women's voices scolding, and high over the confusion a
long broken wail of pain. Mr. McKee awoke from his doze
and started in a daze toward the door. When he had gone half

way he turned around and stared at the scene—his wife and Catherine scolding and consoling as they stumbled here and there among the crowded furniture with articles of aid, and the despairing figure on the couch, bleeding fluently, and trying to spread a copy of Town Tattle over the tapestry scenes of Versailles. Then Mr. McKee turned and continued on out the door. Taking my hat from the chandelier, I followed.

"Come to lunch some day," he suggested, as we groaned down in the elevator.

"Where?"

"Anywhere."

"Keep your hands off the lever," snapped the elevator boy.

"I beg your pardon," said Mr. McKee with dignity. "I didn't know I was touching it."

"All right," I agreed, "I'll be glad to."

. . . I was standing beside his bed and he was sitting up between the sheets, clad in his underwear,[8] with a great portfolio in his hands.

"Beauty and the Beast . . . Loneliness . . . Old Grocery Horse . . . Brook'n Bridge . . ."

Then I was lying half asleep in the cold lower level of the Pennsylvania Station, staring at the morning Tribune,[9] and waiting for the four o'clock train.

8 All queer readings of The Great Gatsby posit that Nick's interest in Gatsby is at least partly homoerotic. Most focus on this post-party scene, with the conspicuous gaps in Nick's account of it. The ellipses indicate not drunken lapses in Nick's memory, queer readings contend, but rather suggest that a sexual encounter has taken place between Nick and the "feminine" (Nick's word) McKee. Further, Nick's attraction to Jordan Baker, who stands erect "like a young cadet" (p. 17), has been adduced as a coded allusion to Nick's homoerotic feelings, as has his squeamishness about such physical details as the "faint mustache of perspiration" on the upper lip of his girlfriend back home (p. 66). While evidence that Nick is a closeted gay man is sparse, it is true that homosexual relations could only be represented in coded language, by necessity, throughout the publishing industry in 1925. See Keath Fraser's "Another Reading of The Great Gatsby," in ESC: English Studies in Canada 5.3 (Fall 1979), pp. 33–43; Edward Wasiolek's "The Sexual Drama of Nick and Gatsby," in The International Fiction Review 19.1 (1992), pp. 14–22; and Maggie Gordon Froehlich's "Gatsby's Mentors: Queer Relations between Love and Money in The Great Gatsby," in Journal of Men's Studies 19.3 (October 2011), pp. 209–26.

9 The New-York Tribune, founded by Horace Greeley in 1841, the leading Republican newspaper in the country and the chief rival of The New York Times. The Tribune was conservative in its outlook; it would have been the logical paper for Nick—a bond salesman from the Midwest, with old-fashioned ideas—to read. It merged with the New York Herald in 1924 to form the New York Herald-Tribune.

# CHAPTER III

There was music from my neighbor's house through the summer nights. In his blue gardens men and girls came and went like moths among the whisperings and the champagne and the stars. At high tide in the afternoon I watched his guests diving from the tower of his raft, or taking the sun on the hot sand of his beach while his two motor-boats slit the waters of the Sound, drawing aquaplanes[1] over cataracts of foam. On weekends his Rolls-Royce became an omnibus, bearing parties to and from the city between nine in the morning and long past midnight, while his station wagon scampered like a brisk yellow bug to meet all trains. And on Mondays eight servants, including an extra gardener, toiled all day with mops and scrubbing-brushes and hammers and garden shears, repairing the ravages of the night before.[2]

Every Friday five crates of oranges and lemons arrived from a fruiterer in New York—every Monday these same oranges and lemons left his back door in a pyramid of pulpless halves. There was a machine in the kitchen which could extract the juice of two hundred oranges in half an hour if a little button was pressed two hundred times by a butler's thumb.

At least once a fortnight a corps of caterers came down with several hundred feet of canvas and enough colored lights to make a Christmas tree of Gatsby's enormous garden. On buffet tables, garnished with glistening hors-d'œuvre, spiced baked hams crowded against salads of harlequin designs and pastry pigs and turkeys bewitched to a dark gold. In the main hall a bar with a real brass rail was set up, and stocked with

1 Aquaplaning was a water sport popular before the advent of waterskiing. The participant, either standing or kneeling, rode a flat board towed behind a motorboat.

2 In his essay "Early Success" (1937), Fitzgerald looks back on the Jazz Age and his role as its preeminent chronicler: "The uncertainties of 1919 were over—there seemed little doubt about what was going to happen—America was going on the greatest, gaudiest spree in history and there was going to be plenty to tell about it. The whole golden boom was in the air—its splendid generosities, its outrageous corruptions and the tortuous death struggle of the old America in prohibition. All the stories that came into my head had a touch of disaster in them—the lovely young creatures in my novels went to ruin, the diamond mountains of my short stories blew up, my millionaires were as beautiful and damned as Thomas Hardy's peasants." From "Early Success," in *The Crack-Up*, p. 87.

**3** In the dancing style of Joe Frisco (1889–1958), a comedian popular during the 1920s. Frisco was famous for a soft-shoe shuffle, of his own invention, called the "Frisco Dance." Beginning in 1918, he was featured in *The Midnight Frolic*, a late-night floor show staged by the impresario Florenz Ziegfeld (1867–1932) on the rooftop of the New Amsterdam Theatre, on West 42nd Street. He performed also in *Vanities*, a Broadway girly-leggy variety show produced by Earl Carroll (1893–1948).

American vaudeville performer Joe Frisco doing the "Frisco Dance."

gins and liquors and with cordials so long forgotten that most of his female guests were too young to know one from another.

By seven o'clock the orchestra has arrived, no thin five-piece affair, but a whole pitful of oboes and trombones and saxophones and viols and cornets and piccolos, and low and high drums. The last swimmers have come in from the beach now and are dressing upstairs; the cars from New York are parked five deep in the drive, and already the halls and salons and verandas are gaudy with primary colors, and hair shorn in strange new ways, and shawls beyond the dreams of Castile. The bar is in full swing, and floating rounds of cocktails permeate the garden outside, until the air is alive with chatter and laughter, and casual innuendo and introductions forgotten on the spot, and enthusiastic meetings between women who never knew each other's names.

The lights grow brighter as the earth lurches away from the sun, and now the orchestra is playing yellow cocktail music, and the opera of voices pitches a key higher. Laughter is easier minute by minute, spilled with prodigality, tipped out at a cheerful word. The groups change more swiftly, swell with new arrivals, dissolve and form in the same breath; already there are wanderers, confident girls who weave here and there among the stouter and more stable, become for a sharp, joyous moment the center of a group, and then, excited with triumph, glide on through the sea-change of faces and voices and color under the constantly changing light.

Suddenly one of these gypsies, in trembling opal, seizes a cocktail out of the air, dumps it down for courage and, moving her hands like Frisco,[3] dances out alone on the canvas platform. A momentary hush; the orchestra leader varies his rhythm obligingly for her, and there is a burst of chatter as the erroneous news goes around that she is Gilda Gray's understudy from the Follies.[4] The party has begun.

I believe that on the first night I went to Gatsby's house I was one of the few guests who had actually been invited. People were not invited—they went there.[5] They got into automobiles which bore them out to Long Island, and somehow they ended up at Gatsby's door. Once there they were introduced by somebody who knew Gatsby, and after that they conducted themselves according to the rules of behavior associated with amusement parks. Sometimes they came and went without having met Gatsby at all, came for the party with a simplicity of heart that was its own ticket of admission.

I had been actually invited. A chauffeur in a uniform of robin's-egg blue crossed my lawn early that Saturday morning with a surprisingly formal note from his employer: the honor would be entirely Gatsby's, it said, if I would attend his "little party" that night. He had seen me several times, and had intended to call on me long before, but a peculiar combination of circumstances had prevented it—signed Jay Gatsby, in a majestic hand.

Dressed up in white flannels I went over to his lawn a little after seven, and wandered around rather ill at ease among swirls and eddies of people I didn't know—though here and there was a face I had noticed on the commuting train. I was immediately struck by the number of young Englishmen dotted about; all well-dressed, all looking a little hungry, and all talking in low, earnest voices to solid and prosperous Americans. I was sure that they were selling something: bonds or insurance or automobiles. They were at least agonizingly aware of the easy money in the vicinity and convinced that it was theirs for a few words in the right key.

As soon as I arrived I made an attempt to find my host, but the two or three people of whom I asked his whereabouts stared at me in such an amazed way, and denied so vehemently any knowledge of his movements, that I slunk off in the direction of the cocktail table—the only place in the garden where a single man could linger without looking purposeless and alone.

I was on my way to get roaring drunk from sheer embarrassment when Jordan Baker came out of the house and stood at the head of the marble steps, leaning a little backward and looking with contemptuous interest down into the garden.

**4** Gilda Gray (1901–1959), born Marianna Michalska, was a Polish American dancer and cabaret singer who popularized the "shimmy" in the 1920s. She performed the dance in the *Ziegfeld Follies*, a Broadway revue with revealing costumery and elaborate sets. The shimmy was characterized by suggestive movements of the shoulders and hips ("I'm shaking my shimmy, that's what I'm doing," Gray explained).

Theatrical poster of Gilda Gray, 1925.

**5** Gatsby wants to belong to a more elevated social class but does not understand that the important thing, among the *haute bourgeoise*, is not who *is* invited but who is *not* invited.

Welcome or not, I found it necessary to attach myself to someone before I should begin to address cordial remarks to the passers-by.

"Hello!" I roared, advancing toward her. My voice seemed unnaturally loud across the garden.

"I thought you might be here," she responded absently as I came up. "I remembered you lived next door to——"

She held my hand impersonally, as a promise that she'd take care of me in a minute, and gave ear to two girls in twin yellow dresses, who stopped at the foot of the steps.

"Hello!" they cried together. "Sorry you didn't win."

That was for the golf tournament. She had lost in the finals the week before.

"You don't know who we are," said one of the girls in yellow, "but we met you here about a month ago."

"You've dyed your hair since then," remarked Jordan, and I started, but the girls had moved casually on and her remark was addressed to the premature moon, produced like the supper, no doubt, out of a caterer's basket. With Jordan's slender golden arm resting in mine, we descended the steps and sauntered about the garden. A tray of cocktails floated at us through the twilight, and we sat down at a table with the two girls in yellow and three men, each one introduced to us as Mr. Mumble.

"Do you come to these parties often?" inquired Jordan of the girl beside her.

"The last one was the one I met you at," answered the girl, in an alert confident voice. She turned to her companion: "Wasn't it for you, Lucille?"

It was for Lucille, too.

"I like to come," Lucille said. "I never care what I do, so I always have a good time. When I was here last I tore my gown on a chair, and he asked me my name and address—inside of a week I got a package from Croirier's with a new evening gown in it."

"Did you keep it?" asked Jordan.

"Sure I did. I was going to wear it tonight, but it was too big

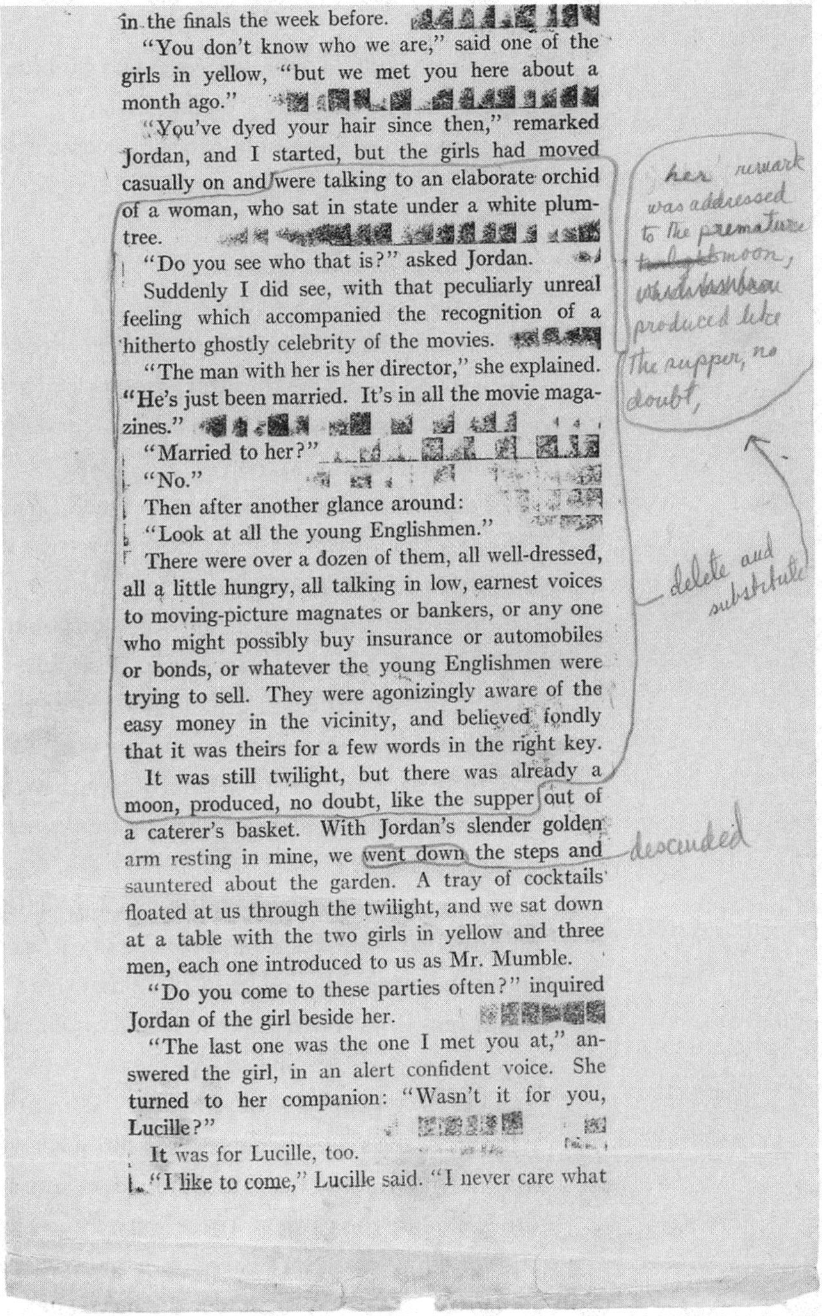

in the finals the week before.

"You don't know who we are," said one of the girls in yellow, "but we met you here about a month ago."

"You've dyed your hair since then," remarked Jordan, and I started, but the girls had moved casually on and were talking to an elaborate orchid of a woman, who sat in state under a white plum-tree.

"Do you see who that is?" asked Jordan.

Suddenly I did see, with that peculiarly unreal feeling which accompanied the recognition of a hitherto ghostly celebrity of the movies.

"The man with her is her director," she explained. "He's just been married. It's in all the movie magazines."

"Married to her?"

"No."

Then after another glance around:

"Look at all the young Englishmen."

There were over a dozen of them, all well-dressed, all a little hungry, all talking in low, earnest voices to moving-picture magnates or bankers, or any one who might possibly buy insurance or automobiles or bonds, or whatever the young Englishmen were trying to sell. They were agonizingly aware of the easy money in the vicinity, and believed fondly that it was theirs for a few words in the right key.

It was still twilight, but there was already a moon, produced, no doubt, like the supper out of a caterer's basket. With Jordan's slender golden arm resting in mine, we went down the steps and sauntered about the garden. A tray of cocktails floated at us through the twilight, and we sat down at a table with the two girls in yellow and three men, each one introduced to us as Mr. Mumble.

"Do you come to these parties often?" inquired Jordan of the girl beside her.

"The last one was the one I met you at," answered the girl, in an alert confident voice. She turned to her companion: "Wasn't it for you, Lucille?"

It was for Lucille, too.

"I like to come," Lucille said. "I never care what

her remark was addressed to the premature ~~twilight~~ moon, ~~[illegible]~~ produced like the supper, no doubt,

delete and substitute

descended

Detail from galley 13 of *Trimalchio*. Fitzgerald condenses the action at Gatsby's first party. Princeton University Library.

in the bust and had to be altered. It was gas blue with lavender beads. Two hundred and sixty-five dollars."

"There's something funny about a fellow that'll do a thing like that," said the other girl eagerly. "He doesn't want any trouble with *anybody*."

"Who doesn't?" I inquired.

"Gatsby. Somebody told me——"

The two girls and Jordan leaned together confidentially.

"Somebody told me they thought he killed a man once."

A thrill passed over all of us. The three Mr. Mumbles bent forward and listened eagerly.

"I don't think it's so much *that*," argued Lucille skeptically; "it's more that he was a German spy during the war."

One of the men nodded in confirmation.

"I heard that from a man who knew all about him, grew up with him in Germany," he assured us positively.

"Oh, no," said the first girl, "it couldn't be that, because he was in the American army during the war." As our credulity switched back to her she leaned forward with enthusiasm. "You look at him sometime when he thinks nobody's looking at him. I'll bet he killed a man."

She narrowed her eyes and shivered. Lucille shivered. We all turned and looked around for Gatsby. It was testimony to the romantic speculation he inspired that there were whispers about him from those who had found little that it was necessary to whisper about in this world.

The first supper—there would be another one after midnight—was now being served, and Jordan invited me to join her own party, who were spread around a table on the other side of the garden. There were three married couples and Jordan's escort, a persistent undergraduate given to violent innuendo, and obviously under the impression that sooner or later Jordan was going to yield him up her person to a greater or lesser degree. Instead of rambling this party had preserved a dignified homogeneity, and assumed to itself the function of representing the staid nobility of the country-side—East Egg condescending to West Egg, and carefully on guard against its spectroscopic gayety.

"Let's get out," whispered Jordan, after a somehow wasteful and inappropriate half hour; "this is much too polite for me."

We got up, and she explained that we were going to find the host: I had never met him, she said, and it was making me uneasy. The undergraduate nodded in a cynical, melancholy way.

The bar, where we glanced first, was crowded, but Gatsby was not there. She couldn't find him from the top of the steps, and he wasn't on the veranda. On a chance we tried an important-looking door, and walked into a high Gothic library, panelled with carved English oak, and probably transported complete from some ruin overseas.

A stout, middle-aged man, with enormous owl-eyed spectacles, was sitting somewhat drunk on the edge of a great table, staring with unsteady concentration at the shelves of books. As we entered he wheeled excitedly around and examined Jordan from head to foot.

"What do you think?" he demanded impetuously.

"About what?"

He waved his hand toward the bookshelves.

"About that. As a matter of fact you needn't bother to ascertain. I ascertained. They're real."

"The books?"

He nodded.

"Absolutely real—have pages and everything. I thought they'd be a nice durable cardboard. Matter of fact, they're absolutely real. Pages and— Here! Lemme show you."

Taking our skepticism for granted, he rushed to the bookcases and returned with Volume One of the "Stoddard Lectures."[6]

"See!" he cried triumphantly. "It's a bona-fide piece of printed matter. It fooled me. This fella's a regular Belasco.[7] It's

---

**6** John L. Stoddard (1850–1931), an American author and popular performer on the lecture circuit. He was among the first to use the stereopticon, a slide projector, in his presentations. His travelogues, comprising ten volumes and five supplements, were published in a uniform edition beginning in 1897. The series, in identical bindings, would have been the kind of matched set chosen by a book supplier for Gatsby's library.

**7** David Belasco (1853–1931), a Broadway dramatist and producer, was known for creating lifelike illusions onstage. Among his best-known productions were *Lord Chumley* in 1888 and *The Girl of the Golden West* in 1905. Hugh Kenner observes: "Owl Eyes supposes that the intention of Gatsby was to create an effect. But Gatsby, save when he is being (understandably) misleading about his past, is innocent of the lust after effects. For life is infinite. Someday he may read those books, much as one night, having turned on all the lights in his house ('the whole corner of the peninsula was blazing with light'), he occupies himself with 'glancing into some of the rooms.'" See Kenner's *A Homemade World*, p. 31.

**8** In the early twentieth century, some books were still issued with untrimmed edges. Progressing through the book, the reader separated the leaves from one another with a paper-knife or letter-opener.

a triumph. What thoroughness! What realism! Knew when to stop, too—didn't cut the pages.[8] But what do you want? What do you expect?"

He snatched the book from me and replaced it hastily on its shelf, muttering that if one brick was removed the whole library was liable to collapse.

"Who brought you?" he demanded. "Or did you just come? I was brought. Most people were brought."

Jordan looked at him alertly, cheerfully, without answering.

"I was brought by a woman named Roosevelt," he continued. "Mrs. Claud Roosevelt. Do you know her? I met her somewhere last night. I've been drunk for about a week now, and I thought it might sober me up to sit in a library."

"Has it?"

"A little bit, I think. I can't tell yet. I've only been here an hour. Did I tell you about the books? They're real. They're——"

"You told us."

We shook hands with him gravely and went back outdoors.

There was dancing now on the canvas in the garden; old men pushing young girls backward in eternal graceless circles, superior couples holding each other tortuously, fashionably, and keeping in the corners—and a great number of single girls dancing individualistically or relieving the orchestra for a moment of the burden of the banjo or the traps. By midnight the hilarity had increased. A celebrated tenor had sung in Italian, and a notorious contralto had sung in jazz, and between the numbers people were doing "stunts" all over the garden, while happy, vacuous bursts of laughter rose toward the summer sky. A pair of stage twins, who turned out to be the girls in yellow, did a baby act in costume, and champagne was served in glasses bigger than finger-bowls. The moon had risen higher, and floating in the Sound was a triangle of silver scales, trembling a little to the stiff, tinny drip of the banjoes on the lawn.

I was still with Jordan Baker. We were sitting at a table with a man of about my age and a rowdy little girl, who gave way upon the slightest provocation to uncontrollable laughter.

I was enjoying myself now. I had taken two finger-bowls of champagne, and the scene had changed before my eyes into something significant, elemental, and profound.

At a lull in the entertainment the man looked at me and smiled.

"Your face is familiar," he said, politely. "Weren't you in the Third Division during the war?"

"Why, yes. I was in the Ninth Machine-Gun Battalion."

"I was in the Seventh Infantry until June nineteen-eighteen. I knew I'd seen you somewhere before."

We talked for a moment about some wet, gray little villages in France. Evidently he lived in this vicinity, for he told me that he had just bought a hydroplane,[9] and was going to try it out in the morning.

"Want to go with me, old sport? Just near the shore along the Sound."

"What time?"

"Any time that suits you best."

It was on the tip of my tongue to ask his name when Jordan looked around and smiled.

"Having a gay time now?" she inquired.

"Much better." I turned again to my new acquaintance. "This is an unusual party for me. I haven't even seen the host. I live over there—" I waved my hand at the invisible hedge in the distance, "and this man Gatsby sent over his chauffeur with an invitation."

For a moment he looked at me as if he failed to understand.

"I'm Gatsby," he said suddenly.

"What!" I exclaimed. "Oh, I beg your pardon."

"I thought you knew, old sport. I'm afraid I'm not a very good host."

He smiled understandingly—much more than understandingly. It was one of those rare smiles with a quality of eternal reassurance in it, that you may come across four or five times in life. It faced—or seemed to face—the whole external world for an instant, and then concentrated on *you* with an irresistible

[9] Here, a fixed-wing aircraft that could take off and land on water. The term was also used for a high-speed motorboat that rode on the surface of the water.

prejudice in your favor. It understood you just so far as you wanted to be understood, believed in you as you would like to believe in yourself, and assured you that it had precisely the impression of you that, at your best, you hoped to convey. Precisely at that point it vanished—and I was looking at an elegant young rough-neck, a year or two over thirty, whose elaborate formality of speech just missed being absurd. Sometime before he introduced himself I'd got a strong impression that he was picking his words with care.

Almost at the moment when Mr. Gatsby identified himself a butler hurried toward him with the information that Chicago was calling him on the wire. He excused himself with a small bow that included each of us in turn.

"If you want anything just ask for it, old sport," he urged me. "Excuse me. I will rejoin you later."

When he was gone I turned immediately to Jordan—constrained to assure her of my surprise. I had expected that Mr. Gatsby would be a florid and corpulent person in his middle years.

"Who is he?" I demanded. "Do you know?"

"He's just a man named Gatsby."

"Where is he from, I mean? And what does he do?"

"Now *you're* started on the subject," she answered with a wan smile. "Well, he told me once he was an Oxford man."

A dim background started to take shape behind him, but at her next remark it faded away.

"However, I don't believe it."

"Why not?"

"I don't know," she insisted. "I just don't think he went there."

Something in her tone reminded me of the other girl's "I think he killed a man," and had the effect of stimulating my curiosity. I would have accepted without question the information that Gatsby sprang from the swamps of Louisiana or from the Lower East Side of New York. That was comprehensible. But young men didn't—at least in my provincial inexperience

I believed they didn't—drift coolly out of nowhere and buy a palace on Long Island Sound.

"Anyhow, he gives large parties," said Jordan, changing the subject with an urban distaste for the concrete. "And I like large parties. They're so intimate. At small parties there isn't any privacy."

There was the boom of a bass drum, and the voice of the orchestra leader rang out suddenly above the echolalia of the garden.

"Ladies and gentlemen," he cried. "At the request of Mr. Gatsby we are going to play for you Mr. Vladimir Tostoff's[10] latest work, which attracted so much attention at Carnegie Hall last May. If you read the papers you know there was a big sensation." He smiled with jovial condescension, and added: "Some sensation!" Whereupon everybody laughed.

"The piece is known," he concluded lustily, "as 'Vladimir Tostoff's Jazz History of the World.'"

The nature of Mr. Tostoff's composition eluded me, because just as it began my eyes fell on Gatsby, standing alone on the marble steps and looking from one group to another with approving eyes. His tanned skin was drawn attractively tight on his face and his short hair looked as though it were trimmed every day. I could see nothing sinister about him. I wondered if the fact that he was not drinking helped to set him off from his guests, for it seemed to me that he grew more correct as the fraternal hilarity increased. When the "Jazz History of the World" was over, girls were putting their heads on men's shoulders in a puppyish, convivial way, girls were swooning backward playfully into men's arms, even into groups, knowing that someone would arrest their falls—but no one swooned backward on Gatsby, and no French bob touched Gatsby's shoulder, and no singing quartets were formed with Gatsby's head for one link.

"I beg your pardon."

Gatsby's butler was suddenly standing beside us.

10 The Russian jazz musician Vladimir Tostoff is a fictional invention. His name playfully alludes to the improvisational nature of jazz ("tossed-off"). George Gershwin's *Rhapsody in Blue* (1923) and other works of serious jazz had world premieres in New York at Carnegie Hall.

"Miss Baker?" he inquired. "I beg your pardon, but Mr. Gatsby would like to speak to you alone."

"With me?" she exclaimed in surprise.

"Yes, madame."

She got up slowly, raising her eyebrows at me in astonishment, and followed the butler toward the house. I noticed that she wore her evening-dress, all her dresses, like sports clothes—there was a jauntiness about her movements as if she had first learned to walk upon golf courses on clean, crisp mornings.

I was alone and it was almost two. For some time confused and intriguing sounds had issued from a long, many-windowed room which overhung the terrace. Eluding Jordan's undergraduate, who was now engaged in an obstetrical conversation with two chorus girls, and who implored me to join him, I went inside.

The large room was full of people. One of the girls in yellow was playing the piano, and beside her stood a tall, red-haired young lady from a famous chorus, engaged in song. She had drunk a quantity of champagne, and during the course of her song she had decided, inaptly, that everything was very, very sad—she was not only singing, she was weeping too. Whenever there was a pause in the song she filled it with gasping, broken sobs, and then took up the lyric again in a quavering soprano. The tears coursed down her cheeks—not freely, however, for when they came into contact with her heavily beaded eyelashes they assumed an inky color, and pursued the rest of their way in slow black rivulets. A humorous suggestion was made that she sing the notes on her face, whereupon she threw up her hands, sank into a chair, and went off into a deep vinous sleep.

"She had a fight with a man who says he's her husband," explained a girl at my elbow.

I looked around. Most of the remaining women were now having fights with men said to be their husbands. Even Jordan's party, the quartet from East Egg, were rent asunder by dissension. One of the men was talking with curious intensity to a young actress, and his wife, after attempting to laugh at the situation in a dignified and indifferent way, broke down entirely and resorted to flank attacks—at intervals she appeared suddenly at his side like an angry diamond, and hissed: "You promised!" into his ear.

The reluctance to go home was not confined to wayward men. The hall was at present occupied by two deplorably sober men and their highly indignant wives. The wives were sympathizing with each other in slightly raised voices.

"Whenever he sees I'm having a good time he wants to go home."

"Never heard anything so selfish in my life."

"We're always the first ones to leave."

"So are we."

"Well, we're almost the last tonight," said one of the men sheepishly. "The orchestra left half an hour ago."

In spite of the wives' agreement that such malevolence was beyond credibility, the dispute ended in a short struggle, and both wives were lifted, kicking, into the night.

As I waited for my hat in the hall the door of the library opened and Jordan Baker and Gatsby came out together. He was saying some last word to her, but the eagerness in his manner tightened abruptly into formality as several people approached him to say good-by.

Jordan's party were calling impatiently to her from the porch, but she lingered for a moment to shake hands.

"I've just heard the most amazing thing," she whispered. "How long were we in there?"

"Why, about an hour."

"It was . . . simply amazing," she repeated abstractedly. "But I swore I wouldn't tell it and here I am tantalizing you." She yawned gracefully in my face. "Please come and see me. . . . Phone book. . . . Under the name of Mrs. Sigourney Howard. . . . My aunt. . . ." She was hurrying off as she talked—her

11 A lightweight overcoat worn by drivers and passengers for protection against engine exhaust and dirt from the roads.

brown hand waved a jaunty salute as she melted into her party at the door.

Rather ashamed that on my first appearance I had stayed so late, I joined the last of Gatsby's guests, who were clustered around him. I wanted to explain that I'd hunted for him early in the evening and to apologize for not having known him in the garden.

"Don't mention it," he enjoined me eagerly. "Don't give it another thought, old sport." The familiar expression held no more familiarity than the hand which reassuringly brushed my shoulder. "And don't forget we're going up in the hydroplane tomorrow morning, at nine o'clock."

Then the butler, behind his shoulder:

"Philadelphia wants you on the phone, sir."

"All right, in a minute. Tell them I'll be right there. . . . Good night."

"Good night."

"Good night." He smiled—and suddenly there seemed to be a pleasant significance in having been among the last to go, as if he had desired it all the time. "Good night, old sport. . . . Good night."

But as I walked down the steps I saw that the evening was not quite over. Fifty feet from the door a dozen headlights illuminated a bizarre and tumultuous scene. In the ditch beside the road, right side up, but violently shorn of one wheel, rested a new coupé which had left Gatsby's drive not two minutes before. The sharp jut of a wall accounted for the detachment of the wheel, which was now getting considerable attention from half a dozen curious chauffeurs. However, as they had left their cars blocking the road, a harsh, discordant din from those in the rear had been audible for some time, and added to the already violent confusion of the scene.

A man in a long duster[11] had dismounted from the wreck and now stood in the middle of the road, looking from the car to the tire and from the tire to the observers in a pleasant, puzzled way.

"See!" he explained. "It went in the ditch."

The fact was infinitely astonishing to him, and I recognized first the unusual quality of wonder, and then the man—it was the late patron of Gatsby's library.

"How'd it happen?"

He shrugged his shoulders.

"I know nothing whatever about mechanics," he said decisively.

"But how did it happen? Did you run into the wall?"

"Don't ask me," said Owl Eyes, washing his hands of the whole matter. "I know very little about driving—next to nothing. It happened, and that's all I know."

"Well, if you're a poor driver you oughtn't to try driving at night."

*Suggested Bookplates*

"Be Your Age," by cartoonist Herb Roth (1887–1953) in the September 26, 1925, issue of *The New Yorker*. It was one in a series of "Suggested Bookplates" for American and British authors that Roth drew for the magazine that year. Anne Margaret Daniels notes that the cartoon "shows how fully the magazine at the pulse of the Jazz Age registered both Fitzgerald's personification of the decade as well as the dangers he had foretold in *The Beautiful and Damned*, and again in *Gatsby*, of decadence and of the coming Crash. It's a very double-edged image of festivity and fatality, just like so many of the images of people at parties that end in disasters in Fitzgerald's best-known, and best-loved, novel." Fitzgerald pasted a clipping of the cartoon in his scrapbook. See Daniel's "F. Scott Fitzgerald, American Beauty, Gets a Bookplate in the *New Yorker*, 1925," in *The Huffington Post*, May 1, 2013.

"But I wasn't even trying," he explained indignantly. "I wasn't even trying."

An awed hush fell upon the bystanders.

"Do you want to commit suicide?"

"You're lucky it was just a wheel! A bad driver and not even *trying*!"

"You don't understand," explained the criminal. "I wasn't driving. There's another man in the car."

The shock that followed this declaration found voice in a sustained "Ah-h-h!" as the door of the coupé swung slowly open. The crowd—it was now a crowd—stepped back involuntarily, and when the door had opened wide there was a ghostly pause. Then, very gradually, part by part, a pale, dangling individual stepped out of the wreck, pawing tentatively at the ground with a large uncertain dancing shoe.

Blinded by the glare of the headlights and confused by the incessant groaning of the horns, the apparition stood swaying for a moment before he perceived the man in the duster.

"Wha's matter?" he inquired calmly. "Did we run outa gas?"

"Look!"

Half a dozen fingers pointed at the amputated wheel—he stared at it for a moment, and then looked upward as though he suspected that it had dropped from the sky.

"It came off," someone explained.

He nodded.

"At first I din' notice we'd stopped."

A pause. Then, taking a long breath and straightening his shoulders, he remarked in a determined voice:

"Wonder 'ff tell me where there's a gas'line station?"

At least a dozen men, some of them little better off than he was, explained to him that wheel and car were no longer joined by any physical bond.

"Back out," he suggested after a moment. "Put her in reverse."

"But the *wheel's* off!"

He hesitated.

"No harm in trying," he said.

The caterwauling horns had reached a crescendo and I turned away and cut across the lawn toward home. I glanced back once. A wafer of a moon was shining over Gatsby's house, making the night fine as before, and surviving the laughter and the sound of his still glowing garden. A sudden emptiness seemed to flow now from the windows and the great doors, endowing with complete isolation the figure of the host, who stood on the porch, his hand up in a formal gesture of farewell.

Reading over what I have written so far, I see I have given the impression that the events of three nights several weeks apart were all that absorbed me. On the contrary, they were merely casual events in a crowded summer, and, until much later, they absorbed me infinitely less than my personal affairs.

Most of the time I worked. In the early morning the sun threw my shadow westward as I hurried down the white chasms of lower New York to the Probity Trust. I knew the other clerks and young bond-salesmen by their first names, and lunched with them in dark, crowded restaurants on little pig sausages and mashed potatoes and coffee. I even had a short affair with a girl who lived in Jersey City and worked in the accounting department, but her brother began throwing mean looks in my direction, so when she went on her vacation in July I let it blow quietly away.

I took dinner usually at the Yale Club[12]—for some reason it was the gloomiest event of my day—and then I went upstairs to the library and studied investments and securities for a conscientious hour. There were generally a few rioters around, but they never came into the library, so it was a good place to work. After that, if the night was mellow, I strolled down Madison Avenue past the old Murray Hill Hotel,[13] and over Thirty-third Street to the Pennsylvania Station.

I began to like New York, the racy, adventurous feel of it at night, and the satisfaction that the constant flicker of men

12 A private New York club for graduates and faculty of Yale University. It is located at the corner of Vanderbilt and East 44th Street. Fitzgerald was likely familiar with the Yale Club: just after World War I, when he was working for an advertising agency in New York City, the Yale Club was open to alumni of Princeton while the new Princeton Club was being built at Park Avenue and 39th Street.

13 Late Victorian New York hotel that was razed in 1947. The Murray Hill Hotel had one entrance on Park Avenue opposite Grand Central Station and another entrance on 40th Street. According to one 1920s guidebook, the atmosphere inside was "heavily gracious."

and women and machines gives to the restless eye. I liked to walk up Fifth Avenue and pick out romantic women from the crowd and imagine that in a few minutes I was going to enter into their lives, and no one would ever know or disapprove. Sometimes, in my mind, I followed them to their apartments on the corners of hidden streets, and they turned and smiled back at me before they faded through a door into warm darkness. At the enchanted metropolitan twilight I felt a haunting loneliness sometimes, and felt it in others—poor young clerks who loitered in front of windows waiting until it was time for a solitary restaurant dinner—young clerks in the dusk, wasting the most poignant moments of night and life.

Again at eight o'clock, when the dark lanes of the Forties were five deep with throbbing taxi cabs, bound for the theatre district, I felt a sinking in my heart. Forms leaned together in the taxis as they waited, and voices sang, and there was laughter from unheard jokes, and lighted cigarettes outlined unintelligible gestures inside. Imagining that I, too, was hurrying toward gayety and sharing their intimate excitement, I wished them well.

For a while I lost sight of Jordan Baker, and then in midsummer I found her again. At first I was flattered to go places with her, because she was a golf champion, and everyone knew her name. Then it was something more. I wasn't actually in love, but I felt a sort of tender curiosity. The bored haughty face that she turned to the world concealed something—most affectations conceal something eventually, even though they don't in the beginning—and one day I found what it was. When we were on a house-party together up in Warwick, she left a borrowed car out in the rain with the top down, and then lied about it—and suddenly I remembered the story about her that had eluded me that night at Daisy's. At her first big golf tournament there was a row that nearly reached the newspapers—a suggestion that she had moved her ball from a bad lie in the semi-final round. The thing approached the proportions of a scandal—then died away. A caddy retracted his

Interior of Murray Hill Hotel. Fitzgerald stayed there in February 1920, prior to the publication of *This Side of Paradise*.

statement, and the only other witness admitted that he might have been mistaken. The incident and the name had remained together in my mind.

Jordan Baker instinctively avoided clever, shrewd men, and now I saw that this was because she felt safer on a plane where any divergence from a code would be thought impossible. She was incurably dishonest. She wasn't able to endure being at a disadvantage and, given this unwillingness, I suppose she had begun dealing in subterfuges when she was very young in order to keep that cool, insolent smile turned to the world and yet satisfy the demands of her hard, jaunty body.

It made no difference to me. Dishonesty in a woman is a thing you never blame deeply—I was casually sorry, and then I forgot. It was on that same house-party that we had a curious conversation about driving a car. It started because she passed so close to some workmen that our fender flicked a button on one man's coat.

"You're a rotten driver," I protested. "Either you ought to be more careful, or you oughtn't to drive at all."

"I am careful."

"No, you're not."

"Well, other people are," she said lightly.

"What's that got to do with it?"

"They'll keep out of my way," she insisted. "It takes two to make an accident."

"Suppose you met somebody just as careless as yourself."

"I hope I never will," she answered. "I hate careless people. That's why I like you."

Her gray, sun-strained eyes stared straight ahead, but she had deliberately shifted our relations, and for a moment I thought I loved her. But I am slow-thinking and full of interior rules that act as brakes on my desires, and I knew that first I had to get myself definitely out of that tangle back home. I'd been writing letters once a week and signing them: "Love, Nick," and all I could think of was how, when that certain girl played tennis, a faint mustache of perspiration appeared on her upper lip. Nevertheless there was a vague understanding that had to be tactfully broken off before I was free.

Everyone suspects himself of at least one of the cardinal virtues, and this is mine: I am one of the few honest people that I have ever known.

# CHAPTER IV

On Sunday morning while church bells rang in the villages alongshore, the world and its mistress returned to Gatsby's house and twinkled hilariously on his lawn.

"He's a bootlegger," said the young ladies, moving somewhere between his cocktails and his flowers. "One time he killed a man who had found out that he was nephew to Von Hindenburg[1] and second cousin to the devil. Reach me a rose, honey, and pour me a last drop into that there crystal glass."

Once I wrote down on the empty spaces of a time-table the names of those who came to Gatsby's house that summer. It is an old time-table now, disintegrating at its folds, and headed "This schedule in effect July 5th, 1922." But I can still read the gray names, and they will give you a better impression than my generalities of those who accepted Gatsby's hospitality and paid him the subtle tribute of knowing nothing whatever about him.[2]

From East Egg, then, came the Chester Beckers and the Leeches, and a man named Bunsen, whom I knew at Yale, and Doctor Webster Civet, who was drowned last summer up in Maine. And the Hornbeams and the Willie Voltaires, and a whole clan named Blackbuck, who always gathered in a corner and flipped up their noses like goats at whosoever came near. And the Ismays and the Chrysties (or rather Hubert Auerbach and Mr. Chrystie's wife), and Edgar Beaver, whose hair, they say, turned cotton-white one winter afternoon for no good reason at all.

Clarence Endive was from East Egg, as I remember. He came only once, in white knickerbockers, and had a fight with a bum

[1] Paul von Hindenburg (1847–1934), field marshal of the German armed forces during World War I. After the war he served as president of the Weimar Republic (1925–1934).

[2] Hugh Kenner calls attention in this paragraph to its *trompe l'oeil* aesthetic: "a genuine timetable, authenticated by its dateline, now 'disintegrating at its folds,' but filled, to authenticate this work of fiction, with names we are assured we will recognize, as we nearly persuade ourselves we do, though they are extraordinary names." Concerning the many names that come in the paragraphs that follow, Kenner continues: "Dickens is behind this characterization by naming, and so is J. Alfred Prufrock, whose surname came from a St. Louis furniture house. . . . But Dickens' people live in a fabricated world, and Eliot's Prufrocks and Krumpackers in a world of the dream-grotesque. Fitzgerald is engaged in something subtler: he is weaving the grotesque so firmly into the real that their textures, however improbable the *Gestalt*, are thread by thread indistinguishable." Hugh Kenner, *A Homemade World*, pp. 40–41.

named Etty in the garden. From farther out on the Island came the Cheadles and the O. R. P. Schraeders, and the Stonewall Jackson Abrams of Georgia, and the Fishguards and the Ripley Snells. Snell was there three days before he went to the penitentiary, so drunk out on the gravel drive that Mrs. Ulysses Swett's automobile ran over his right hand. The Dancies came, too, and S. B. Whitebait, who was well over sixty, and Maurice A. Flink, and the Hammerheads, and Beluga the tobacco importer, and Beluga's girls.

From West Egg came the Poles and the Mulreadys and Cecil Roebuck and Cecil Schoen and Gulick the state senator and Newton Orchid, who controlled Films Par Excellence, and Eckhaust and Clyde Cohen and Don S. Schwartze (the son) and Arthur McCarty, all connected with the movies in one way or another. And the Catlips and the Bembergs and G. Earl Muldoon, brother to that Muldoon who afterward strangled his wife. Da Fontano the promoter came there, and Ed Legros and James B. ("Rot-Gut") Ferret and the De Jongs and Ernest Lilly—they came to gamble, and when Ferret wandered into the garden it meant he was cleaned out and Associated Traction would have to fluctuate profitably next day.

A man named Klipspringer was there so often and so long that he became known as "the boarder"—I doubt if he had any other home. Of theatrical people there were Gus Waize and Horace O'Donavan and Lester Myer and George Duckweed and Francis Bull. Also from New York were the Chromes and the Backhyssons and the Dennickers and Russel Betty and the Corrigans and the Kellehers and the Dewars and the Scullys and S. W. Belcher and the Smirkes and the young Quinns, divorced now, and Henry L. Palmetto, who killed himself by jumping in front of a subway train in Times Square.

Benny McClenahan arrived always with four girls. They were never quite the same ones in physical person, but they were so identical one with another that it inevitably seemed they had been there before. I have forgotten their names— Jaqueline, I think, or else Consuela, or Gloria or Judy or June, and their last names were either the melodious names of flowers and months or the sterner ones of the great American capitalists whose cousins, if pressed, they would confess themselves to be.

In addition to all these I can remember that Faustina O'Brien came there at least once and the Baedeker girls and young Brewer, who had his nose shot off in the war, and Mr. Albrucksburger and Miss Haag, his fiancée, and Ardita Fitz-Peters and Mr. P. Jewett, once head of the American Legion, and Miss Claudia Hip, with a man reputed to be her chauffeur, and a prince of something, whom we called Duke, and whose name, if I ever knew it, I have forgotten.

All these people came to Gatsby's house in the summer.[3]

At nine o'clock, one morning late in July, Gatsby's gorgeous car lurched up the rocky drive to my door and gave out a burst of melody from its three-noted horn. It was the first time he had called on me, though I had gone to two of his parties, mounted in his hydroplane, and, at his urgent invitation, made frequent use of his beach.

"Good morning, old sport. You're having lunch with me today and I thought we'd ride up together."

He was balancing himself on the dashboard[4] of his car with that resourcefulness of movement that is so peculiarly American—that comes, I suppose, with the absence of lifting work or rigid sitting in youth and, even more, with the formless grace of our nervous, sporadic games. This quality was continually breaking through his punctilious manner in the shape of restlessness. He was never quite still; there was always a tapping foot somewhere or the impatient opening and closing of a hand.

He saw me looking with admiration at his car.

"It's pretty, isn't it, old sport?" He jumped off to give me a better view. "Haven't you ever seen it before?"

3 In his letter of November 20, 1924, to Fitzgerald, Maxwell Perkins writes: "The description of the valley of ashes adjacent to the lovely country, the conversation and the action in Myrtle's apartment, the marvelous catalogue of those who came to Gatsby's house,—these are such things as make a man famous." See pp. 202–5 in this volume.

4 Narrow platform fixed beneath each car door. Later called a "running-board."

5 Gatsby's supposition that San Francisco is in the Middle West, Hugh Kenner writes, is a way of establishing "for the hasty reader of novels the fact that Gatsby is not quite what he seems to be." *A Homemade World*, p. 41.

6 Wooded area of over two thousand acres, lying just west of Paris, originally designated by Napoleon III in the 1850s as a recreational space for the upper classes. By the early 1900s "Le Bois" had been transformed into a public park for the bourgeoisie, with areas for rowing, riding, and picnicking.

I'd seen it. Everybody had seen it. It was a rich cream color, bright with nickel, swollen here and there in its monstrous length with triumphant hat-boxes and supper-boxes and tool-boxes, and terraced with a labyrinth of wind-shields that mirrored a dozen suns. Sitting down behind many layers of glass in a sort of green leather conservatory, we started to town.

I had talked with him perhaps half a dozen times in the past month and found, to my disappointment, that he had little to say. So my first impression, that he was a person of some undefined consequence, had gradually faded and he had become simply the proprietor of an elaborate roadhouse next door.

And then came that disconcerting ride. We hadn't reached West Egg Village before Gatsby began leaving his elegant sentences unfinished and slapping himself indecisively on the knee of his caramel-colored suit.

"Look here, old sport," he broke out surprisingly. "What's your opinion of me, anyhow?"

A little overwhelmed, I began the generalized evasions which that question deserves.

"Well, I'm going to tell you something about my life," he interrupted. "I don't want you to get a wrong idea of me from all these stories you hear."

So he was aware of the bizarre accusations that flavored conversation in his halls.

"I'll tell you God's truth." His right hand suddenly ordered divine retribution to stand by. "I am the son of some wealthy people in the Middle West—all dead now. I was brought up in America but educated at Oxford, because all my ancestors have been educated there for many years. It is a family tradition."

He looked at me sideways—and I knew why Jordan Baker had believed he was lying. He hurried the phrase "educated at Oxford," or swallowed it, or choked on it, as though it had bothered him before. And with this doubt, his whole statement fell to pieces, and I wondered if there wasn't something a little sinister about him, after all.

"What part of the Middle West?" I inquired casually.

"San Francisco."[5]

"I see."

"My family all died and I came into a good deal of money."

His voice was solemn, as if the memory of that sudden extinction of a clan still haunted him. For a moment I suspected that he was pulling my leg, but a glance at him convinced me otherwise.

"After that I lived like a young rajah in all the capitals of Europe—Paris, Venice, Rome—collecting jewels, chiefly rubies, hunting big game, painting a little, things for myself only, and trying to forget something very sad that had happened to me long ago."

With an effort I managed to restrain my incredulous laughter. The very phrases were worn so threadbare that they evoked no image except that of a turbaned "character" leaking sawdust at every pore as he pursued a tiger through the Bois de Boulogne.[6]

"Then came the war, old sport. It was a great relief, and I tried very hard to die, but I seemed to bear an enchanted life. I accepted a commission as first lieutenant when it began. In the Argonne Forest[7] I took two machine-gun detachments so far forward that there was a half mile gap on either side of us where the infantry couldn't advance. We stayed there two days and two nights, a hundred and thirty men with sixteen Lewis guns, and when the infantry came up at last they found the insignia of three German divisions among the piles of dead. I was promoted to be a major, and every Allied government gave me a decoration—even Montenegro, little Montenegro down on the Adriatic Sea!"[8]

Little Montenegro! He lifted up the words and nodded at them—with his smile. The smile comprehended Montenegro's troubled history[9] and sympathized with the brave struggles of the Montenegrin people. It appreciated fully the

7 Wooded area in northeastern France, 135 miles east of Paris, through which American troops pushed in the final offensive of World War I, known as the Meuse-Argonne Offensive, which lasted from September 26, 1918, until the Armistice on November 11, 1918. American troops sustained more than 110,000 casualties.

8 Gatsby's exploits are based on the story of "The Lost Battalion," a force of some 550 men from the 77th Division of the U.S. infantry who, in early October 1918, advanced beyond their flank support and were surrounded by German units in the Argonne Forest. Led by Major Charles W. Whittlesey, they held out for six days until relief troops could push through to rescue them. They communicated with their rescuers via carrier pigeon. The battalion suffered heavy losses; only 194 men survived the action. Whittlesey was treated as a war hero and received the Congressional Medal of Honor. He felt intense guilt for his role in the action, however, and took his own life on November 26, 1921. Gatsby's medal from "little Montenegro" may well be genuine, but it is possible he purchased a blank medal and had his name engraved on the back. See Thomas M. Johnson and Fletcher Pratt's *The Lost Battalion* (University of Nebraska Press, 2000).

9 Montenegro was among the Allied Powers during World War I. After the Treaty of Versailles, it was absorbed by Yugoslavia as part of a newly unified Montenegro and Serbia; however, the unification was contested by the exiled king of Montenegro and his supporters.

— a toast to Kultur

Drawn by
Louis Raemaekers
for The Century Magazine

Barron Collier Series of Patriotic Cartoons

Part of Barron Collier Series of Patriotic Cartoons, this World War I poster (1916) depicts a German skeleton guzzling blood from a goblet. After the Armistice, Fitzgerald worked briefly in Manhattan as an adman for the Barron Collier agency.

10 Trinity College, Oxford, founded in 1555, is one of the constituent colleges of the University of Oxford. On his first trip to Europe, during the spring of 1921, Fitzgerald and his wife, Zelda, visited Trinity.

chain of national circumstances which had elicited this tribute from Montenegro's warm little heart. My incredulity was submerged in fascination now; it was like skimming hastily through a dozen magazines.

He reached in his pocket, and a piece of metal, slung on a ribbon, fell into my palm.

"That's the one from Montenegro."

To my astonishment, the thing had an authentic look. "Orderi di Danilo," ran the circular legend, "Montenegro, Nicolas Rex."

"Turn it."

"Major Jay Gatsby," I read. "For Valour Extraordinary."

"Here's another thing I always carry. A souvenir of Oxford days. It was taken in Trinity Quad[10]—the man on my left is now the Earl of Doncaster."

It was a photograph of half a dozen young men in blazers loafing in an archway through which were visible a host of spires. There was Gatsby, looking a little, not much, younger—with a cricket bat in his hand.

Then it was all true. I saw the skins of tigers flaming in his palace on the Grand Canal;[11] I saw him opening a chest of rubies to ease, with their crimson-lighted depths, the gnawings of his broken heart.

"I'm going to make a big request of you today," he said, pocketing his souvenirs with satisfaction, "so I thought you ought to know something about me. I didn't want you to think I was just some nobody. You see, I usually find myself among strangers because I drift here and there trying to forget the sad thing that happened to me." He hesitated. "You'll hear about it this afternoon."

"At lunch?"

"No, this afternoon. I happened to find out that you're taking Miss Baker to tea."

"Do you mean you're in love with Miss Baker?"

"No, old sport, I'm not. But Miss Baker has kindly consented to speak to you about this matter."

I hadn't the faintest idea what "this matter" was, but I was more annoyed than interested. I hadn't asked Jordan to tea in order to discuss Mr. Jay Gatsby. I was sure the request would be something utterly fantastic, and for a moment I was sorry I'd ever set foot upon his overpopulated lawn.

He wouldn't say another word. His correctness grew on him as we neared the city. We passed Port Roosevelt, where there was a glimpse of red-belted ocean-going ships, and sped along a cobbled slum lined with the dark, undeserted saloons of the faded-gilt nineteen-hundreds. Then the valley of ashes opened out on both sides of us, and I had a glimpse of Mrs. Wilson straining at the garage pump with panting vitality as we went by.

With fenders spread like wings we scattered light through half Astoria—only half, for as we twisted among the pillars of the elevated I heard the familiar "jug-jug-*spat*!" of a motorcycle, and a frantic policeman rode alongside.

"All right, old sport," called Gatsby. We slowed down. Taking a white card from his wallet, he waved it before the man's eyes.

Gatsby's medal, the Orderi di Danilo.

11 A major waterway that winds through Venice. The canal takes the shape of an inverted letter "S" on a map of the city. Known to Venetians as the *Canalazzo*, it is lined with opulent palaces belonging to the wealthiest Venetian families.

12 The skyline of New York was then, and is now, best viewed by entering the city via the Queensboro Bridge. Fitzgerald's relationship with New York was complicated—and changed as he grew older. As a young man, he says, he was able "only to stare at the show." It had for him in those boom years after the war "all the iridescence of the beginning of the world." See "My Lost City," in *The Crack-Up*, pp. 24–25.

13 Wesley Morris comments on the irony of this passage: "This is a world where 'anything can happen'—like the fancy car full of Black people that Nick spies on the road ('two bucks and a girl,' in his parlance) being driven by a white chauffeur. Anything can happen, 'even Gatsby.' (Especially, I'd say.) Except there's so much nothing. Here is a book whose magnificence culminates in an exposé of waste—of time, of money, of space, of devotion, of life." Introduction by Wesley Morris to the Modern Library edition of *The Great Gatsby*, p. xii.

"Right you are," agreed the policeman, tipping his cap. "Know you next time, Mr. Gatsby. Excuse *me!*"

"What was that?" I inquired. "The picture of Oxford?"

"I was able to do the commissioner a favor once, and he sends me a Christmas card every year."

Over the great bridge, with the sunlight through the girders making a constant flicker upon the moving cars, with the city rising up across the river in white heaps and sugar lumps all built with a wish out of non-olfactory money. The city seen from the Queensboro Bridge is always the city seen for the first time, in its first wild promise of all the mystery and the beauty in the world.[12]

A dead man passed us in a hearse heaped with blooms, followed by two carriages with drawn blinds, and by more cheerful carriages for friends. The friends looked out at us with the tragic eyes and short upper lips of southeastern Europe, and I was glad that the sight of Gatsby's splendid car was included in their somber holiday. As we crossed Blackwell's Island a limousine passed us, driven by a white chauffeur, in which sat three modish negroes, two bucks and a girl. I laughed aloud as the yolks of their eyeballs rolled toward us in haughty rivalry.

"Anything can happen now that we've slid over this bridge," I thought; "anything at all. . . ."[13]

Even Gatsby could happen, without any particular wonder.

⸺

Roaring noon. In a well-fanned Forty-second Street cellar I met Gatsby for lunch. Blinking away the brightness of the street outside, my eyes picked him out obscurely in the anteroom, talking to another man.

"Mr. Carraway, this is my friend Mr. Wolfshiem."

A small, flat-nosed Jew raised his large head and regarded me with two fine growths of hair which luxuriated in either nostril.[14] After a moment I discovered his tiny eyes in the half darkness.

View of Midtown Manhattan skyline from Queensboro Bridge, circa 1930. "The city seen from the Queensboro Bridge is always the city seen for the first time, in its first wild promise of all the mystery and the beauty in the world."

**14** Frances Kroll Ring, Fitzgerald's secretary in Hollywood during the last period of his life, writes that Fitzgerald was "stung" by criticisms leveled at him in the thirties for his negative portrait of Wolfshiem. "He was a gangster who happened to be Jewish," Fitzgerald told her. It is true that Wolfshiem is a thinly veiled stand-in for Arnold Rothstein, kingpin of the Jewish Mob in New York City; it is also true, however, that Fitzgerald makes use of racial stereotypes in his portrait of Wolfshiem. "*Gatsby* is at once timeless and timebound," Maureen Corrigan observes. "But view the novel in its entirety rather than in isolated passages, and its politics get more complicated. The novel clearly relishes more than it fears the modernity and mixing of New York City." See Frances Kroll Ring's *Against the Current: As I Remember F. Scott Fitzgerald* (Figueroa Press, 2005), pp. 46–47; and Maureen Corrigan's *So We Read On*, p. 97.

"—So I took one look at him," said Mr. Wolfshiem, shaking my hand earnestly, "and what do you think I did?"

"What?" I inquired politely.

But evidently he was not addressing me, for he dropped my hand and covered Gatsby with his expressive nose.

"I handed the money to Katspaugh and I sid: 'All right, Katspaugh, don't pay him a penny till he shuts his mouth.' He shut it then and there."

Gatsby took an arm of each of us and moved forward into the restaurant, whereupon Mr. Wolfshiem swallowed a new sentence he was starting and lapsed into a somnambulatory abstraction.

15 A whiskey drink, usually mixed with soda water or ginger ale, and served with ice in a tall glass. Prohibition had gone into effect in 1920, but it was not difficult to get a drink at most New York restaurants in the summer of 1922. In practice prohibition laws were winked at or ignored, especially in large cities and among the wealthy. Prohibition ended in 1933 with the ratification of the Twenty-first Amendment.

16 Fitzgerald based Wolfshiem's recollections on the murder of the gangster and bookmaker Herman Rosenthal. The shooting took place on July 16, 1912, in New York, at the Metropole Hotel, 147 West 43rd Street, near Times Square. Accounts of the killing stayed on the front pages of metropolitan newspapers for the rest of the summer.

"Highballs?"[15] asked the head waiter.

"This is a nice restaurant here," said Mr. Wolfshiem, looking at the Presbyterian nymphs on the ceiling. "But I like across the street better!"

"Yes, highballs," agreed Gatsby, and then to Mr. Wolfshiem: "It's too hot over there."

"Hot and small—yes," said Mr. Wolfshiem, "but full of memories."

"What place is that?" I asked Gatsby.

"The old Metropole."

"The old Metropole," brooded Mr. Wolfshiem gloomily. "Filled with faces dead and gone. Filled with friends gone now forever. I can't forget so long as I live the night they shot Rosy Rosenthal there.[16] It was six of us at the table, and Rosy had eat and drunk a lot all evening. When it was almost morning the waiter came up to him with a funny look and says somebody wants to speak to him outside. 'All right,' says Rosy, and begins to get up, and I pulled him down in his chair.

"'Let the bastards come in here if they want you, Rosy, but don't you, so help me, move outside this room.'

"It was four o'clock in the morning then, and if we'd of raised the blinds we'd of seen daylight."

"Did he go?" I asked innocently.

"Sure he went." Mr. Wolfshiem's nose flashed at me indignantly. "He turned around in the door and says: 'Don't let that waiter take away my coffee!' Then he went out on the sidewalk, and they shot him three times in his full belly and drove away."

"Four of them were electrocuted," I said, remembering.

"Five, with Becker." His nostrils turned to me in an interested way. "I understand you're looking for a business gonnegtion."

The juxtaposition of these two remarks was startling. Gatsby answered for me:

"Oh, no," he exclaimed, "this isn't the man."

"No?" Mr. Wolfshiem seemed disappointed.

"This is just a friend. I told you we'd talk about that some other time."

"I beg your pardon," said Mr. Wolfshiem. "I had a wrong man."

A succulent hash arrived, and Mr. Wolfshiem, forgetting the more sentimental atmosphere of the old Metropole, began to eat with ferocious delicacy. His eyes, meanwhile, roved very slowly all around the room—he completed the arc by turning to inspect the people directly behind. I think that, except for my presence, he would have taken one short glance beneath our own table.

"Look here, old sport," said Gatsby, leaning toward me, "I'm afraid I made you a little angry this morning in the car."

There was the smile again, but this time I held out against it.

Rathskeller in the Metropole, where Wolfshiem would have dined with Rosy Rosenthal the night he was murdered.

In the front row: Harry Horowitz ("Gyp the Blood") and "Lefty Louie" Rosenberg, two of the four members of the Lenox Avenue Gang who gunned down Herman Rosenthal on July 16, 1912, after the bookmaker left the Metropole. The murder was allegedly ordered by Lieutenant Charles Becker of the NYPD. All five men, including Becker, were convicted and sentenced to death.

"I don't like mysteries," I answered, "and I don't understand why you won't come out frankly and tell me what you want. Why has it all got to come through Miss Baker?"

"Oh, it's nothing underhand," he assured me. "Miss Baker's a great sportswoman, you know, and she'd never do anything that wasn't all right."

Suddenly he looked at his watch, jumped up, and hurried from the room, leaving me with Mr. Wolfshiem at the table.

"He has to telephone," said Mr. Wolfshiem, following him with his eyes. "Fine fellow, isn't he? Handsome to look at and a perfect gentleman."

"Yes."

"He's an Oggsford man."

"Oh!"

"He went to Oggsford College in England. You know Oggsford College?"

"I've heard of it."

"It's one of the most famous colleges in the world."

"Have you known Gatsby for a long time?" I inquired.

"Several years," he answered in a gratified way. "I made the pleasure of his acquaintance just after the war. But I knew I had discovered a man of fine breeding after I talked with him an hour. I said to myself: 'There's the kind of man you'd like to take home and introduce to your mother and sister.'" He paused. "I see you're looking at my cuff buttons."

I hadn't been looking at them, but I did now. They were composed of oddly familiar pieces of ivory.

"Finest specimens of human molars," he informed me.

"Well!" I inspected them. "That's a very interesting idea."

"Yeah." He flipped his sleeves up under his coat. "Yeah, Gatsby's very careful about women. He would never so much as look at a friend's wife."

When the subject of this instinctive trust returned to the table and sat down Mr. Wolfshiem drank his coffee with a jerk and got to his feet.

"I have enjoyed my lunch," he said, "and I'm going to run off from you two young men before I outstay my welcome."

"Don't hurry, Meyer," said Gatsby, without enthusiasm. Mr. Wolfshiem raised his hand in a sort of benediction.

"You're very polite, but I belong to another generation," he announced solemnly. "You sit here and discuss your sports and your young ladies and your—" He supplied an imaginary noun with another wave of his hand. "As for me, I am fifty years old, and I won't impose myself on you any longer."

As he shook hands and turned away his tragic nose was trembling. I wondered if I had said anything to offend him.

"He becomes very sentimental sometimes," explained Gatsby. "This is one of his sentimental days. He's quite a character around New York—a denizen of Broadway."

"Who is he, anyhow, an actor?"

"No."

"A dentist?"

"Meyer Wolfshiem? No, he's a gambler." Gatsby hesitated, then added coolly: "He's the man who fixed the World's Series back in 1919."[17]

"Fixed the World's Series?" I repeated.

The idea staggered me. I remembered, of course, that the World's Series had been fixed in 1919, but if I had thought of

[17] Racketeer Arnold Rothstein (1882–1928), on whom Wolfshiem is modeled, is said to have fixed the 1919 World's Series in the infamous "Black Sox" scandal. Rothstein got wind of a plan by several players on the Chicago White Sox team to throw the series; he therefore bet heavily on the Cincinnati Reds, their opponents. The White Sox lost the series, and Rothstein won more than $300,000. Rothstein was never formally charged with involvement in the swindle, but eight members of the Chicago White Sox, including star outfielder "Shoeless Joe" Jackson and pitcher Eddie Cicotte, were banned for lifetime from baseball for their participation.

Racketeer and crime boss Arnold Rothstein in 1919, the year of the infamous "Black Sox" scandal.

it at all I would have thought of it as a thing that merely *happened*, the end of some inevitable chain. It never occurred to me that one man could start to play with the faith of fifty million people—with the single-mindedness of a burglar blowing a safe.

"How did he happen to do that?" I asked after a minute.

"He just saw the opportunity."

"Why isn't he in jail?"

"They can't get him, old sport. He's a smart man."

I insisted on paying the check. As the waiter brought my change I caught sight of Tom Buchanan across the crowded room.

"Come along with me for a minute," I said; "I've got to say hello to someone."

When he saw us Tom jumped up and took half a dozen steps in our direction.

"Where've you been?" he demanded eagerly. "Daisy's furious because you haven't called up."

"This is Mr. Gatsby, Mr. Buchanan."

They shook hands briefly, and a strained, unfamiliar look of embarrassment came over Gatsby's face.

"How've you been, anyhow?" demanded Tom of me. "How'd you happen to come up this far to eat?"

"I've been having lunch with Mr. Gatsby."

I turned toward Mr. Gatsby, but he was no longer there.

⌐───────⌐

18 The Plaza, among the most fashionable of the New York caravansaries, stands across from the southeast corner of Central Park at Fifth Avenue and 59th Street. Later, in Chapter VII, the Plaza is the setting for Gatsby's confrontation with Tom Buchanan. "Scott Fitzgerald from St. Paul remains the only Proust of luxurious upper-middle class landmarks in New York like the Plaza Hotel," Alfred

One October day in nineteen-seventeen——

(said Jordan Baker that afternoon, sitting up very straight on a straight chair in the tea-garden at the Plaza Hotel)[18]

—I was walking along from one place to another, half on the sidewalks and half on the lawns. I was happier on the lawns because I had on shoes from England with rubber knobs on the soles that bit into the soft ground. I had on a new plaid skirt also that blew a little in the wind, and whenever this happened the red, white, and blue banners in front of all the houses stretched out stiff and said *tut-tut-tut-tut*, in a disapproving way.

The largest of the banners and the largest of the lawns belonged to Daisy Fay's house. She was just eighteen, two years older than me, and by far the most popular of all the young girls in Louisville. She dressed in white, and had a little white roadster, and all day long the telephone rang in her house and excited young officers from Camp Taylor demanded the privilege of monopolizing her that night. "Anyways, for an hour!"

When I came opposite her house that morning her white roadster was beside the curb, and she was sitting in it with a lieutenant I had never seen before. They were so engrossed in each other that she didn't see me until I was five feet away.

Kazin writes. "New York was dreamland to Fitzgerald. It represented his imagination of what is forever charming, touched by the glamour of money, romantically tender, and gay. . . . New York was much more beautiful to Fitzgerald than was Paris. But by the same token it was as unreal as Gatsby's too-glamorous life on Long Island, as subtly corrupt and even canniballike as Meyer Wolfshiem's cuff links of molars. . . . The name of the American dream was New York." See Alfred Kazin's *An American Procession: The Major American Writers from 1830 to 1930—the Crucial Century* (Knopf, 1984), pp. 390–91.

1919 Chicago White Sox team photograph. Eight members of the White Sox were accused of throwing the 1919 World Series against the Cincinnati Reds.

**19** The agreement that ended hostilities between the Allies and Germany in World War I specified that fighting should cease on November 11, 1918, at 11:00 A.M.—the eleventh hour of the eleventh day of the eleventh month (Matthew 20:1–16). Artillery shelling continued in some sectors until the final moments. Here, "after the armistice" means "after the war."

**20** A grand hotel in downtown Louisville, designed in the opulent European style. The establishment was operated by immigrant brothers from Bavaria named Louis and Otto Seelbach. Fitzgerald would have known the hotel, which opened in 1903: he was stationed at Fort Zachary Taylor, near Louisville, in March 1918 during his officer training.

"Hello, Jordan," she called unexpectedly. "Please come here."

I was flattered that she wanted to speak to me, because of all the older girls I admired her most. She asked me if I was going to the Red Cross and make bandages. I was. Well, then, would I tell them that she couldn't come that day? The officer looked at Daisy while she was speaking, in a way that every young girl wants to be looked at sometime, and because it seemed romantic to me I have remembered the incident ever since. His name was Jay Gatsby, and I didn't lay eyes on him again for over four years—even after I'd met him on Long Island I didn't realize it was the same man.

That was nineteen-seventeen. By the next year I had a few beaux myself, and I began to play in tournaments, so I didn't see Daisy very often. She went with a slightly older crowd—when she went with anyone at all. Wild rumors were circulating about her—how her mother had found her packing her bag one winter night to go to New York and say good-by to a soldier who was going overseas. She was effectually prevented, but she wasn't on speaking terms with her family for several weeks. After that she didn't play around with the soldiers any more, but only with a few flat-footed, short-sighted young men in town, who couldn't get into the army at all.

By the next autumn she was gay again, gay as ever. She had a début after the armistice,[19] and in February she was presumably engaged to a man from New Orleans. In June she married Tom Buchanan of Chicago, with more pomp and circumstance than Louisville ever knew before. He came down with a hundred people in four private cars, and hired a whole floor of the Seelbach Hotel,[20] and the day before the wedding he gave her a string of pearls valued at three hundred and fifty thousand dollars.

I was a bridesmaid. I came into her room half an hour before the bridal dinner, and found her lying on her bed as lovely as the June night in her flowered dress—and as drunk as a monkey. She had a bottle of Sauterne in one hand and a letter in the other.

Plaza Hotel, Fifth Avenue, New York City, circa 1927. Fitzgerald, in conversation with the critic Van Wyck Brooks, described an evening dip into the Pulitzer fountain that stands in front of the Plaza Hotel: "I looked up and saw that great creamy palace all blazing with green and gold lights, and the taxis and the limousines streaming up and down the Avenue—why I jumped into the Pulitzer fountain just out of sheer joy!" See Brooks's *Days of the Phoenix: The Nineteen-Twenties I Remember* (Dutton, 1953), p. 109.

"'Gratulate me," she muttered. "Never had a drink before, but oh how I do enjoy it."

"What's the matter, Daisy?"

I was scared, I can tell you; I'd never seen a girl like that before.

"Here, deares'." She groped around in a wastebasket she had with her on the bed and pulled out the string of pearls. "Take 'em downstairs and give 'em back to whoever they belong to. Tell 'em all Daisy's change' her mine. Say: 'Daisy's change' her mine!'"

She began to cry—she cried and cried. I rushed out and found her mother's maid, and we locked the door and got her into a cold bath. She wouldn't let go of the letter. She took it into the tub with her and squeezed it up into a wet ball, and only let me leave it in the soap dish when she saw that it was coming to pieces like snow.

But she didn't say another word. We gave her spirits of ammonia and put ice on her forehead and hooked her back into her dress, and half an hour later, when we walked out of the room, the pearls were around her neck and the incident was over. Next day at five o'clock she married Tom Buchanan without so much as a shiver, and started off on a three months' trip to the South Seas.

I saw them in Santa Barbara when they came back, and I thought I'd never seen a girl so mad about her husband. If he left the room for a minute she'd look around uneasily, and say: "Where's Tom gone?" and wear the most abstracted expression until she saw him coming in the door. She used to sit on the sand with his head in her lap by the hour, rubbing her fingers over his eyes and looking at him with unfathomable delight. It was touching to see them together—it made you laugh in a hushed, fascinated way. That was in August. A week after I left Santa Barbara Tom ran into a wagon on the Ventura road one night, and ripped a front wheel off his car. The girl who was with him got into the papers, too, because her arm was broken—she was one of the chambermaids in the Santa Barbara Hotel.

The next April Daisy had her little girl, and they went to France for a year. I saw them one spring in Cannes, and later in Deauville, and then they came back to Chicago to settle down. Daisy was popular in Chicago, as you know. They moved with a fast crowd, all of them young and rich and wild, but she came out with an absolutely perfect reputation. Perhaps because she doesn't drink. It's a great advantage not to drink among hard-drinking people. You can hold your tongue, and, moreover, you can time any little irregularity of your own so that everybody else is so blind that they don't see or care. Perhaps Daisy never went in for amour at all—and yet there's something in that voice of hers.…

Well, about six weeks ago, she heard the name Gatsby for the first time in years. It was when I asked you—do you remember?—if you knew Gatsby in West Egg. After you had gone home she came into my room and woke me up, and said: "What Gatsby?" and when I described him—I was half asleep—she said in the strangest voice that it must be the man she used to know. It wasn't until then that I connected this Gatsby with the officer in her white car.

✦

When Jordan Baker had finished telling all this we had left the Plaza for half an hour and were driving in a Victoria[21] through Central Park. The sun had gone down behind the tall apartments of the movie stars in the West Fifties, and the clear voices of children, already gathered like crickets on the grass, rose through the hot twilight:

> "I'm the Sheik of Araby.
> Your love belongs to me.
> At night when you're asleep
> Into your tent I'll creep——"[22]

"It was a strange coincidence," I said.

"But it wasn't a coincidence at all."

"Why not?"

"Gatsby bought that house so that Daisy would be just across the bay."[23]

Then it had not been merely the stars to which he had aspired on that June night. He came alive to me, delivered suddenly from the womb of his purposeless splendor.

"He wants to know," continued Jordan, "if you'll invite Daisy to your house some afternoon and then let him come over."

21 A low, light, horse-drawn carriage that had a calash top and, in front, a perch for the driver. Then as now, one could take a ride through Central Park in a horse-drawn vehicle.

22 Lyrics from "The Sheik of Araby," a hit tune in 1921, with lyrics by Harry B. Smith and Francis Wheeler and music by Ted Snyder. Readers in 1925 might also have been reminded of *The Sheik*, a silent movie of 1921 starring Rudolph Valentino (1895–1926), Hollywood's original "Latin Lover" screen idol. During the early 1920s, romantic young men were often called "sheiks"— the male counterpart to the flapper.

23 Many readers have observed that the only real coincidence is that Nick Carraway, Daisy's cousin, has rented a cottage adjacent to Gatsby's mansion.

Movie still from *The Sheik* (1921), a Paramount Pictures silent film starring Rudolph Valentino and Agnes Ayres. The movie was based on the 1919 novel of the same title by British novelist Edith Maude Hull. The role of the Sheik made Valentino a matinee idol and a modern-day Don Juan.

The modesty of the demand shook me. He had waited five years and bought a mansion where he dispensed starlight to casual moths—so that he could "come over" some afternoon to a stranger's garden.

"Did I have to know all this before he could ask such a little thing?"

"He's afraid. He's waited so long. He thought you might be offended. You see, he's a regular tough underneath it all."

Something worried me.

"Why didn't he ask you to arrange a meeting?"

"He wants her to see his house," she explained. "And your house is right next door."

"Oh!"

"I think he half expected her to wander into one of his parties, some night," went on Jordan, "but she never did. Then he began asking people casually if they knew her, and I was the first one he found. It was that night he sent for me at his dance, and you should have heard the elaborate way he worked up to it. Of course, I immediately suggested a luncheon in New York—and I thought he'd go mad:

"'I don't want to do anything out of the way!' he kept saying. 'I want to see her right next door.'

"When I said you were a particular friend of Tom's, he started to abandon the whole idea. He doesn't know very much about Tom, though he says he's read a Chicago paper for years just on the chance of catching a glimpse of Daisy's name."

It was dark now, and as we dipped under a little bridge I put my arm around Jordan's golden shoulder and drew her toward me and asked her to dinner. Suddenly I wasn't thinking of Daisy and Gatsby any more, but of this clean, hard, limited person, who dealt in universal skepticism, and who leaned back jauntily just within the circle of my arm. A phrase began to beat in my ears with a sort of heady excitement: "There are only the pursued, the pursuing, the busy and the tired."

"And Daisy ought to have something in her life," murmured Jordan to me.

"Does she want to see Gatsby?"

"She's not to know about it. Gatsby doesn't want her to know. You're just supposed to invite her to tea."

We passed a barrier of dark trees, and then the façade of Fifty-ninth Street, a block of delicate pale light, beamed down into the Park. Unlike Gatsby and Tom Buchanan, I had no girl whose disembodied face floated along the dark cornices and blinding signs, and so I drew up the girl beside me, tightening my arms. Her wan, scornful mouth smiled, and so I drew her up again closer, this time to my face.

# Somewhere West of Laramie

SOMEWHERE west of Laramie there's a broncho-busting, steer-roping girl who knows what I'm talking about.

She can tell what a sassy pony, that's a cross between greased lightning and the place where it hits, can do with eleven hundred pounds of steel and action when he's going high, wide and handsome.

The truth is—the Playboy was built for her.

Built for the lass whose face is brown with the sun when the day is done of revel and romp and race.

She loves the cross of the wild and the tame.

There's a savor of links about that car—of laughter and lilt and light—a hint of old loves—and saddle and quirt. It's a brawny thing—yet a graceful thing for the sweep o' the Avenue.

Step into the Playboy when the hour grows dull with things gone dead and stale.

Then start for the land of real living with the spirit of the lass who rides, lean and rangy, into the red horizon of a Wyoming twilight.

# JORDAN

JORDAN MOTOR CAR COMPANY, Inc., Cleveland, Ohio

Jordan Motor Car Company advertisement for the Jordan Playboy, in *The Saturday Evening Post*, 1923. "Somewhere west of Laramie," the ad reads, "there's a broncho-busting, steer-roping girl who knows what I'm talking about. She can tell what a sassy pony, that's a cross between greased lightning and the place where it hits, can do with eleven hundred pounds of steel and action when he's going high, wide and handsome. The truth is—the Playboy was built for her."

# CHAPTER V

When I came home to West Egg that night I was afraid for a moment that my house was on fire. Two o'clock and the whole corner of the peninsula was blazing with light, which fell unreal on the shrubbery and made thin elongating glints upon the roadside wires. Turning a corner, I saw that it was Gatsby's house, lit from tower to cellar.

At first I thought it was another party, a wild rout that had resolved itself into "hide-and-go-seek" or "sardines-in-the-box" with all the house thrown open to the game. But there wasn't a sound. Only wind in the trees, which blew the wires and made the lights go off and on again as if the house had winked into the darkness. As my taxi groaned away I saw Gatsby walking toward me across his lawn.

"Your place looks like the World's Fair," I said.

"Does it?" He turned his eyes toward it absently. "I have been glancing into some of the rooms. Let's go to Coney Island, old sport. In my car."

"It's too late."

"Well, suppose we take a plunge in the swimming pool? I haven't made use of it all summer."

"I've got to go to bed."

"All right."

He waited, looking at me with suppressed eagerness.

"I talked with Miss Baker," I said after a moment. "I'm going to call up Daisy tomorrow and invite her over here to tea."

"Oh, that's all right," he said carelessly. "I don't want to put you to any trouble."

"What day would suit you?"

"What day would suit *you?*" he corrected me quickly. "I don't want to put you to any trouble, you see."

"How about the day after tomorrow?"

He considered for a moment. Then, with reluctance:

"I want to get the grass cut," he said.

We both looked at the grass—there was a sharp line where my ragged lawn ended and the darker, well-kept expanse of his began. I suspected that he meant my grass.

"There's another little thing," he said uncertainly, and hesitated.

"Would you rather put it off for a few days?" I asked.

"Oh, it isn't about that. At least—" He fumbled with a series of beginnings. "Why, I thought—why, look here, old sport, you don't make much money, do you?"

"Not very much."

This seemed to reassure him and he continued more confidently.

"I thought you didn't, if you'll pardon my—you see, I carry on a little business on the side, a sort of sideline, you understand. And I thought that if you don't make very much—You're selling bonds, aren't you, old sport?"

"Trying to."

"Well, this would interest you. It wouldn't take up much of your time and you might pick up a nice bit of money. It happens to be a rather confidential sort of thing."

I realize now that under different circumstances that conversation might have been one of the crises of my life. But, because the offer was obviously and tactlessly for a service to be rendered, I had no choice except to cut him off there.

"I've got my hands full," I said. "I'm much obliged but I couldn't take on any more work."

"You wouldn't have to do any business with Wolfshiem." Evidently he thought that I was shying away from the "gonnegtion" mentioned at lunch, but I assured him he was wrong. He waited a moment longer, hoping I'd begin a conversation, but

I was too absorbed to be responsive, so he went unwillingly home.

The evening had made me light-headed and happy; I think I walked into a deep sleep as I entered my front door. So I don't know whether or not Gatsby went to Coney Island, or for how many hours he "glanced into rooms" while his house blazed gaudily on. I called up Daisy from the office next morning, and invited her to come to tea.

"Don't bring Tom," I warned her.

"What?"

"Don't bring Tom."

"Who is 'Tom'?" she asked innocently.

The day agreed upon was pouring rain. At eleven o'clock a man in a raincoat, dragging a lawn-mower, tapped at my front door and said that Mr. Gatsby had sent him over to cut my grass. This reminded me that I had forgotten to tell my Finn to come back, so I drove into West Egg Village to search for her among soggy whitewashed alleys and to buy some cups and lemons and flowers.

The flowers were unnecessary, for at two o'clock a greenhouse arrived from Gatsby's, with innumerable receptacles to contain it. An hour later the front door opened nervously, and Gatsby, in a white flannel suit, silver shirt, and gold-colored tie, hurried in. He was pale, and there were dark signs of sleeplessness beneath his eyes.

"Is everything all right?" he asked immediately.

"The grass looks fine, if that's what you mean."

"What grass?" he inquired blankly. "Oh, the grass in the yard." He looked out the window at it, but, judging from his expression, I don't believe he saw a thing.

"Looks very good," he remarked vaguely. "One of the papers said they thought the rain would stop about four. I think it was The Journal.[1] Have you got everything you need in the shape of—of tea?"

I took him into the pantry, where he looked a little

[1] The *New York Evening Journal*, a Hearst newspaper known for its racy, sensationalist reporting. It carried a daily comic-strip page and sold for one cent in 1922. Columnists included O. O. McIntyre and Nellie Bly, with society news provided by Maury Henry Biddle Paul (a.k.a. "Cholly Knickerbocker"). Contemporary readers would have noted that Gatsby favors this newspaper, while Nick reads the much more conservative *Tribune*. (See also note 9 on p. 45 in this volume.)

**2** *Economics: An Introduction for the General Reader* (1916) by British economist and lecturer Henry Clay (1883–1954). Among Clay's concerns was the redistribution of wealth for the public good. This is an ironic reference here, suggested by the detail that Gatsby skims through the book with "vacant eyes."

reproachfully at the Finn. Together we scrutinized the twelve lemon cakes from the delicatessen shop.

"Will they do?" I asked.

"Of course, of course! They're fine!" and he added hollowly, ". . . old sport."

The rain cooled about half-past three to a damp mist, through which occasional thin drops swam like dew. Gatsby looked with vacant eyes through a copy of Clay's "Economics,"[2] starting at the Finnish tread that shook the kitchen floor, and peering toward the bleared windows from time to time as if a series of invisible but alarming happenings were taking place outside. Finally he got up and informed me, in an uncertain voice, that he was going home.

"Why's that?"

"Nobody's coming to tea. It's too late!" He looked at his watch as if there was some pressing demand on his time elsewhere. "I can't wait all day."

"Don't be silly; it's just two minutes to four."

He sat down miserably, as if I had pushed him, and simultaneously there was the sound of a motor turning into my lane. We both jumped up, and, a little harrowed myself, I went out into the yard.

Under the dripping bare lilac trees a large open car was coming up the drive. It stopped. Daisy's face, tipped sideways beneath a three-cornered lavender hat, looked out at me with a bright ecstatic smile.

"Is this absolutely where you live, my dearest one?"

The exhilarating ripple of her voice was a wild tonic in the rain. I had to follow the sound of it for a moment, up and down, with my ear alone, before any words came through. A damp streak of hair lay like a dash of blue paint across her cheek, and her hand was wet with glistening drops as I took it to help her from the car.

"Are you in love with me," she said low in my ear, "or why did I have to come alone?"

"That's the secret of Castle Rackrent.[3] Tell your chauffeur to go far away and spend an hour."

"Come back in an hour, Ferdie." Then in a grave murmur: "His name is Ferdie."

"Does the gasoline affect his nose?"

"I don't think so," she said innocently. "Why?"

We went in. To my overwhelming surprise the living-room was deserted.

"Well, that's funny!" I exclaimed.

"What's funny?"

She turned her head as there was a light dignified knocking at the front door. I went out and opened it. Gatsby, pale as death, with his hands plunged like weights in his coat pockets, was standing in a puddle of water glaring tragically into my eyes.

With his hands still in his coat pockets he stalked by me into the hall, turned sharply as if he were on a wire, and disappeared into the living-room. It wasn't a bit funny. Aware of the loud beating of my own heart I pulled the door to against the increasing rain.

For half a minute there wasn't a sound. Then from the living-room I heard a sort of choking murmur and part of a laugh, followed by Daisy's voice on a clear artificial note:

"I certainly am awfully glad to see you again."

A pause; it endured horribly. I had nothing to do in the hall, so I went into the room.

Gatsby, his hands still in his pockets, was reclining against the mantelpiece in a strained counterfeit of perfect ease, even of boredom. His head leaned back so far that it rested against the face of a defunct mantelpiece clock, and from this position his distraught eyes stared down at Daisy, who was sitting, frightened but graceful, on the edge of a stiff chair.

"We've met before," muttered Gatsby. His eyes glanced momentarily at me, and his lips parted with an abortive attempt at a laugh. Luckily the clock took this moment to tilt

3 The ancestral home of the Irish Rackrent family in the novel of the same name by Anglo-Irish novelist Maria Edgeworth (1767–1849). *Castle Rackrent* recounts the adventures of three generations of Rackrents. They squander their wealth and eventually lose their tumbledown castle.

4 The German philosopher Immanuel Kant (1724–1804) was said to gaze at the steeple of Löbenicht Church, visible from the window of his writing room in Königsberg. As Horst Kruse notes, "[L]ike Kant gazing at the steeple," Nick gazes at Gatsby's mansion, ignoring it "as a physical presence" to meditate on time and space. More particularly, Nick considers "the futility of the previous owner's [the brewer's] high ambitions and the folly of his attempt to assert himself against time," namely, his efforts to establish a kind of feudal dynasty on Long Island. The brewer's story underscores the grandeur and futility of Gatsby's own quest to recapture the past. See Horst Kruse's "*The Great Gatsby*: A View from Kant's Window," in *F. Scott Fitzgerald Review* 2 (2003), pp. 76–77.

dangerously at the pressure of his head, whereupon he turned and caught it with trembling fingers and set it back in place. Then he sat down, rigidly, his elbow on the arm of the sofa and his chin in his hand.

"I'm sorry about the clock," he said.

My own face had now assumed a deep tropical burn. I couldn't muster up a single commonplace out of the thousand in my head.

"It's an old clock," I told them idiotically.

I think we all believed for a moment that it had smashed in pieces on the floor.

"We haven't met for many years," said Daisy, her voice as matter-of-fact as it could ever be.

"Five years next November."

The automatic quality of Gatsby's answer set us all back at least another minute. I had them both on their feet with the desperate suggestion that they help me make tea in the kitchen when the demoniac Finn brought it in on a tray.

Amid the welcome confusion of cups and cakes a certain physical decency established itself. Gatsby got himself into a shadow and, while Daisy and I talked, looked conscientiously from one to the other of us with tense, unhappy eyes. However, as calmness wasn't an end in itself, I made an excuse at the first possible moment, and got to my feet.

"Where are you going?" demanded Gatsby in immediate alarm.

"I'll be back."

"I've got to speak to you about something before you go."

He followed me wildly into the kitchen, closed the door, and whispered: "Oh, God!" in a miserable way.

"What's the matter?"

"This is a terrible mistake," he said, shaking his head from side to side, "a terrible, terrible mistake."

"You're just embarrassed, that's all," and luckily I added: "Daisy's embarrassed too."

"She's embarrassed?" he repeated incredulously.

"Just as much as you are."

"Don't talk so loud."

"You're acting like a little boy," I broke out impatiently. "Not only that, but you're rude. Daisy's sitting in there all alone."

He raised his hand to stop my words, looked at me with unforgettable reproach, and, opening the door cautiously, went back into the other room.

I walked out the back way—just as Gatsby had when he had made his nervous circuit of the house half an hour before—and ran for a huge black knotted tree, whose massed leaves made a fabric against the rain. Once more it was pouring, and my irregular lawn, well-shaved by Gatsby's gardener, abounded in small muddy swamps and prehistoric marshes. There was nothing to look at from under the tree except Gatsby's enormous house, so I stared at it, like Kant[4] at his church steeple, for half an hour. A brewer had built it early in the "period" craze, a decade before, and there was a story that he'd agreed to pay five years' taxes on all the neighboring cottages if the owners would have their roofs thatched with straw.[5] Perhaps their refusal took the heart out of his plan to Found a Family—he went into an immediate decline. His children sold his house with the black wreath still on the door. Americans, while occasionally willing to be serfs, have always been obstinate about being peasantry.

After half an hour, the sun shone again, and the grocer's automobile rounded Gatsby's drive with the raw material

5 The brewer's architectural plans and his ambitions to have his neighbors' cottages thatched with straw might have been suggested to Fitzgerald by the outlandish example of William Waldorf Astor (1848–1919). A scion of the wealthy Astor family of New York City, Astor moved to England in 1891 to indulge his interests in art and architecture and to pursue a title. In 1903, he purchased Hever Castle in Kent, some thirty miles to the south of London; he restored the castle and had a thatched-roof imitation Tudor village constructed for his staff and servants. Several years earlier, he had built a mansion, with gothic arches and crenellations, on Victoria Embankment in London. These activities were widely reported in the press.

AUSSICHT VON KANT'S FENSTER

Löbenicht Church, as it would have appeared from Kant's window. Text below drawing reads "View from Kant's window."

for his servants' dinner—I felt sure he wouldn't eat a spoon-ful. A maid began opening the upper windows of his house, appeared momentarily in each, and, leaning from a large cen-tral bay, spat meditatively into the garden. It was time I went back. While the rain continued it had seemed like the murmur of their voices, rising and swelling a little now and then with gusts of emotion. But in the new silence I felt that silence had fallen within the house too.

I went in—after making every possible noise in the kitchen, short of pushing over the stove—but I don't believe they heard a sound. They were sitting at either end of the couch, looking at each other as if some question had been asked, or was in the air, and every vestige of embarrassment was gone.

Daisy's face was smeared with tears, and when I came in she jumped up and began wiping at it with her handkerchief before a mirror. But there was a change in Gatsby that was simply confounding. He literally glowed; without a word or a gesture of exultation a new well-being radiated from him and filled the little room.

"Oh, hello, old sport," he said, as if he hadn't seen me for years. I thought for a moment he was going to shake hands.

"It's stopped raining."

"Has it?" When he realized what I was talking about, that there were twinkle-bells of sunshine in the room, he smiled like a weather man, like an ecstatic patron of recurrent light, and repeated the news to Daisy. "What do you think of that? It's stopped raining."

"I'm glad, Jay." Her throat, full of aching, grieving beauty, told only of her unexpected joy.

"I want you and Daisy to come over to my house," he said. "I'd like to show her around."

"You're sure you want me to come?"

"Absolutely, old sport."

Daisy went upstairs to wash her face—too late I thought with humiliation of my towels—while Gatsby and I waited on the lawn.

"My house looks well, doesn't it?" he demanded. "See how the whole front of it catches the light."

I agreed that it was splendid.

"Yes." His eyes went over it, every arched door and square tower. "It took me just three years to earn the money that bought it."

"I thought you inherited your money."

"I did, old sport," he said automatically, "but I lost most of it in the big panic—the panic of the war."

I think he hardly knew what he was saying, for when I asked him what business he was in he answered: "That's my affair," before he realized that it wasn't an appropriate reply.

"Oh, I've been in several things," he corrected himself. "I was in the drug business and then I was in the oil business. But I'm not in either one now." He looked at me with more attention. "Do you mean you've been thinking over what I proposed the other night?"

Before I could answer, Daisy came out of the house and two rows of brass buttons on her dress gleamed in the sunlight.

"That huge place *there*?" she cried pointing.

"Do you like it?"

"I love it, but I don't see how you live there all alone."

"I keep it always full of interesting people, night and day. People who do interesting things. Celebrated people."

Instead of taking the short-cut along the Sound we went down to the road and entered by the big postern. With enchanting murmurs Daisy admired this aspect or that of the feudal silhouette against the sky, admired the gardens, the sparkling odor of jonquils and the frothy odor of hawthorn and plum blossoms and the pale gold odor of kiss-me-at-the-gate. It was strange to reach the marble steps and find no stir of bright dresses in and out the door, and hear no sound but bird voices in the trees.

And inside, as we wandered through Marie Antoinette music-rooms and Restoration salons, I felt that there were guests concealed behind every couch and table, under orders to

6 Merton College, which dates from 1264, was among the first colleges to be founded at Oxford. Its library is considered one of the most beautiful college libraries in Oxford. The library at Cottage Club (Fitzgerald's club at Princeton) is modeled on the Merton College Library.

7 The "Adam style" was a neoclassical furniture style developed by the Scottish brothers Robert and James Adam, an ornate choice for a man of Gatsby's age during the 1920s. The implication is that the study is for show and the pieces of furniture are reproductions.

be breathlessly silent until we had passed through. As Gatsby closed the door of "the Merton College Library"[6] I could have sworn I heard the owl-eyed man break into ghostly laughter.

We went upstairs, through period bedrooms swathed in rose and lavender silk and vivid with new flowers, through dressing-rooms and poolrooms, and bathrooms with sunken baths—intruding into one chamber where a dishevelled man in pajamas was doing liver exercises on the floor. It was Mr. Klipspringer, the "boarder." I had seen him wandering hungrily about the beach that morning. Finally we came to Gatsby's own apartment, a bedroom and a bath, and an Adam study,[7] where we sat down and drank a glass of some Chartreuse he took from a cupboard in the wall.

He hadn't once ceased looking at Daisy, and I think he revalued everything in his house according to the measure of response it drew from her well-loved eyes. Sometimes, too, he stared around at his possessions in a dazed way, as though in her actual and astounding presence none of it was any longer real. Once he nearly toppled down a flight of stairs.

His bedroom was the simplest room of all—except where the dresser was garnished with a toilet set of pure dull gold. Daisy took the brush with delight, and smoothed her hair, whereupon Gatsby sat down and shaded his eyes and began to laugh.

"It's the funniest thing, old sport," he said hilariously. "I can't— When I try to——"

He had passed visibly through two states and was entering upon a third. After his embarrassment and his unreasoning joy he was consumed with wonder at her presence. He had been full of the idea so long, dreamed it right through to the end, waited with his teeth set, so to speak, at an inconceivable pitch of intensity. Now, in the reaction, he was running down like an overwound clock.

Recovering himself in a minute he opened for us two hulking patent cabinets which held his massed suits and dressing gowns and ties, and his shirts, piled like bricks in stacks a dozen high.

"I've got a man in England who buys me clothes. He sends over a selection of things at the beginning of each season, spring and fall."

He took out a pile of shirts and began throwing them, one by one, before us, shirts of sheer linen and thick silk and fine flannel, which lost their folds as they fell and covered the table in many-colored disarray.[8] While we admired he brought more and the soft rich heap mounted higher—shirts with stripes and scrolls and plaids in coral and apple-green and lavender and faint orange, with monograms of Indian blue. Suddenly, with a strained sound, Daisy bent her head into the shirts and began to cry stormily.

"They're such beautiful shirts," she sobbed, her voice muffled in the thick folds. "It makes me sad because I've never seen such—such beautiful shirts before."

After the house, we were to see the grounds and the swimming pool, and the hydroplane and the midsummer flowers—but outside Gatsby's window it began to rain again, so we stood in a row looking at the corrugated surface of the Sound.

"If it wasn't for the mist we could see your home across the bay," said Gatsby. "You always have a green light that burns all night at the end of your dock."

Daisy put her arm through his abruptly, but he seemed absorbed in what he had just said. Possibly it had occurred to him that the colossal significance of that light had now vanished forever. Compared to the great distance that had separated him from Daisy it had seemed very near to her, almost touching her. It had seemed as close as a star to the moon. Now it was again a green light on a dock. His count of enchanted objects had diminished by one.

8 Gatsby's shirts, among his "enchanted objects," seem never to have been worn—or perhaps were never intended to be worn. In Fitzgerald's other great novel, *Tender Is the Night* (1934), the protagonist Dick Diver, though married to a wealthy woman, gets a second day's wear out of his shirts by hanging them up immediately when he comes home—a small economy retained from his student days, when he was on limited funds. Dick, in contrast to Gatsby, is flesh and blood—a man who soils his shirts. The novelist Amor Towles offers this writerly observation: "*The Great Gatsby* is fundamentally a novel of imagination—a tidy parable that has been crafted with great care and economy. By contrast, *Tender Is the Night* is a novel of experience." See Amor Towles's introduction to *Tender Is the Night* (Scribner's, 2019), p. xviii.

Scene from the 1926 Broadway stage production of *The Great Gatsby*. The playwright Owen Davis adapted the novel for the stage, reducing the novel to a prologue and three acts. A young George Cukor was the director. Cut from Davis's script are the valley of ashes, Doctor T. J. Eckleburg's eyes, Gatsby's car, and his pink suit. Fortunately, the glittering parties and jazz music survive, along with the green light across the bay. Gatsby uses the expression "old sport" several times. The play ran on Broadway for 112 performances before traveling to other cities. Scott and Zelda, in Europe during 1926, never saw the production. *Gatsby* has since been adapted to the stage numerous other times, including a ballet, an opera, a seven-hour Off-Broadway production by Elevator Repair Service in which every word of the book was recited or read aloud, and, in a 2024 return to Broadway, a musical directed by Marc Bruni.

I began to walk about the room, examining various indefinite objects in the half darkness. A large photograph of an elderly man in yachting costume attracted me, hung on the wall over his desk.

"Who's this?"

"That? That's Mr. Dan Cody, old sport."

The name sounded faintly familiar.

"He's dead now. He used to be my best friend years ago."

There was a small picture of Gatsby, also in yachting costume, on the bureau—Gatsby with his head thrown back defiantly—taken apparently when he was about eighteen.

"I adore it," exclaimed Daisy. "The pompadour![9] You never told me you had a pompadour—or a yacht."

"Look at this," said Gatsby quickly. "Here's a lot of clippings—about you."

They stood side by side examining it. I was going to ask to see the rubies when the phone rang, and Gatsby took up the receiver.

"Yes. . . . Well, I can't talk now. . . . I can't talk now, old sport. . . . I said a *small* town. . . . He must know what a small town is. . . . Well, he's no use to us if Detroit is his idea of a small town. . . ."

He rang off.

"Come here *quick*!" cried Daisy at the window.

The rain was still falling, but the darkness had parted in the west, and there was a pink and golden billow of foamy clouds above the sea.

"Look at that," she whispered, and then after a moment: "I'd like to just get one of those pink clouds and put you in it and push you around."

I tried to go then, but they wouldn't hear of it; perhaps my presence made them feel more satisfactorily alone.

"I know what we'll do," said Gatsby. "We'll have Klip-springer play the piano."

He went out of the room calling "Ewing!" and returned in a few minutes accompanied by an embarrassed, slightly worn

**9** A hairstyle in which the hair is swept upward from the sides and forehead and fixed in place with hair oil or gel. The pompadour was popular during the 1910s but would have been passé by 1922.

**10** Popular song from the 1920 Broadway musical comedy *Mary*, with music by Louis A. Hirsch (1887–1924) and lyrics by Otto Harbach (1873–1963). The lyrics read in part: "Just a love nest / Cozy and warm / Like a dove rest / Down on a farm / A veranda with some sort of clinging vine / Then a kitchen where some rambler roses twine / Then a small room / Tea set of blue / Best of all room / Dream room for two / Better than a palace with gilded dome / Is a love nest / You can call home."

young man, with shell-rimmed glasses and scanty blond hair. He was now decently clothed in a "sport-shirt," open at the neck, sneakers, and duck trousers of a nebulous hue.

"Did we interrupt your exercises?" inquired Daisy politely.

"I was asleep," cried Mr. Klipspringer, in a spasm of embarrassment. "That is, I'd *been* asleep. Then I got up . . ."

"Klipspringer plays the piano," said Gatsby, cutting him off. "Don't you, Ewing, old sport?"

"I don't play well. I don't—I hardly play at all. I'm all out of prac——"

"We'll go downstairs," interrupted Gatsby. He flipped a switch. The gray windows disappeared as the house glowed full of light.

In the music-room Gatsby turned on a solitary lamp beside the piano. He lit Daisy's cigarette from a trembling match, and sat down with her on a couch far across the room, where there was no light save what the gleaming floor bounced in from the hall.

When Klipspringer had played "The Love Nest"[10] he turned around on the bench and searched unhappily for Gatsby in the gloom.

"I'm all out of practice, you see. I told you I couldn't play. I'm all out of prac——"

"Don't talk so much, old sport," commanded Gatsby. "Play!"

> "In the morning,
> In the evening,
> Ain't we got fun——"

Outside the wind was loud and there was a faint flow of thunder along the Sound. All the lights were going on in West Egg now; the electric trains, men-carrying, were plunging home through the rain from New York. It was the hour of a profound human change, and excitement was generating on the air.

> "One thing's sure and nothing's surer
> The rich get richer and the poor get—children.
>    In the meantime,
>    In between time——"[11]

As I went over to say good-by I saw that the expression of bewilderment had come back into Gatsby's face, as though a faint doubt had occurred to him as to the quality of his present happiness. Almost five years! There must have been moments even that afternoon when Daisy tumbled short of his dreams—not through her own fault, but because of the colossal vitality of his illusion. It had gone beyond her, beyond everything. He had thrown himself into it with a creative passion, adding to it all the time, decking it out with every bright feather that drifted his way. No amount of fire or freshness can challenge what a man will store up in his ghostly heart.

As I watched him he adjusted himself a little, visibly. His hand took hold of hers, and as she said something low in his ear he turned toward her with a rush of emotion. I think that voice held him most, with its fluctuating, feverish warmth, because it couldn't be over-dreamed—that voice was a deathless song.

They had forgotten me, but Daisy glanced up and held out her hand; Gatsby didn't know me now at all. I looked once more at them and they looked back at me, remotely, possessed by intense life. Then I went out of the room and down the marble steps into the rain, leaving them there together.

[11] The seven lines are from "Ain't We Got Fun?" (1921), with music by Richard A. Whiting (1891–1938) and lyrics by Gus Kahn (1886–1941) and Raymond B. Egan (1890–1952). In the third-from-last line, Klipspringer sings the variant "children" for "poorer."

# GREAT GATSBY LEAVES BOOK FOR STAGE

### BY PLAYGOER.

NEW YORK—By those who have read the much talked of novel by Scott Fitzgerald on which the play of the same name is based, The Great Gatsby may be remembered as entertaining, well written and something above the ordinary in characterization. Scott Fitzgerald drew an impressive picture of a modern soldier of fortune against the background of the higher life of Long Island, a rough diamond polished only by his own determination, and the victim, finally, of a collapse of luck as freakish as his sudden rise had been.

Now Owen Davis has come along to transfer to the stage this interesting study of American opportunities, and William A. Brady has given it a well-rounded cast and two amazingly good leads.

James Rennie, as Gatsby, reveals alarmingly Gatsby's lack of humor (something one somehow misses in the book) but adds to the hero's stature by his dignity and quiet force. Not for nothing did Fitzgerald put into his character's mouth speeches that might have come straight out of the highbrow novel of 10 years ago. Rennie delivers them with the pomp of a Fourth of July oration, getting to the full every bit of unconscious humor there is in them.

Florence Eldridge as Daisy is charming, and ample explanation of Gatsby's idealization of their brief love affair. The play gives her less chance for explanation than the novel did; her husband's philandering is less to the fore and consequently his final plea that after all they belong to a different class sounds less effective than as Fitzgerald wrote the scene.

But it is a genuine transfer, nevertheless, of what was a much talked of book, and one likely to be popular with theatergoers. Certainly it is far and away the best role Mr. Rennie has had for several seasons.

## "The Great Gatsby" Subject of Dramatic Reading in Millburn

Nearly 100 persons attended the presentation of "The Great Gatsby," by F. Scott Fitzgerald, at the Millburn High School last evening by Miss Elsie West Quaife, dramatic reader. The reading was under the auspices of the Parent-Teacher Association of Millburn Township.

Miss Quaife, in her introduction, said the book was superior to the play and she followed the book rather than the dramatization of the story.

## THE FINAL POT SHOT AT THE GREAT GATSBY

How Owen Davis makes Drama out of Scott Fitzgerald's romantic vulgarian, the great bootlegger and the near-great lover, at the Ambassador Theatre. Here depicted are James Rennie writhing in the noble agonies of his small catastrophe and Florence Eldridge whooping large whoops in an effort to get away without too much Long Island mud on her reputation.

So liquid is the stage business in "The Great Gatsby," which brought Long Island's guzzling set to the Ambassador last night, that the producer is said to have let long term contracts for the ginger ale, mineral waters and cigarettes consumed in wholesale quantities by the players. In this respect it is considered the most aquatic exhibition outside the Hippodrome tank, and at the present estimate of ninety-two cigarettes a performance it is probable that somebody will have to stand in front of the theatre every night to shoo the fire trucks away. Observing the cost of buying the necessary properties at retail, Mr. Brady is said to have contracted for a supply of everything on an optimistic six months' basis.

WHETHER is it a mere coincidence or due to the fact that "The Great Gatsby" is a play dealing with bootlegging, three speakeasies have opened in West 49th Street since the play had its first performance at the Ambassador Theatre.

### To Observe "The Great Gatsby."

STUDENT artists of the Chicago Laboratory theater — the entire company—will visit "The Great Gatsby" at the Studebaker theater next Friday night as a part of the observation course planned for them by Ivan Lazareff, director.

GUEST — "DID YOU CRASH THE GATE AT THIS GREAT PARTY OF MR GATSBY'S?"

JAMES RENNIE — "NO — I'M MR. GATSBY."

From Fitzgerald's scrapbooks, reviews of the 1926 Broadway production of *The Great Gatsby*.

# CHAPTER VI

About this time an ambitious young reporter from New York arrived one morning at Gatsby's door and asked him if he had anything to say.

"Anything to say about what?" inquired Gatsby politely.

"Why—any statement to give out."

It transpired after a confused five minutes that the man had heard Gatsby's name around his office in a connection which he either wouldn't reveal or didn't fully understand. This was his day off and with laudable initiative he had hurried out "to see."

It was a random shot, and yet the reporter's instinct was right. Gatsby's notoriety, spread about by the hundreds who had accepted his hospitality and so become authorities upon his past, had increased all summer until he fell just short of being news. Contemporary legends such as the "underground pipe-line to Canada"[1] attached themselves to him, and there was one persistent story that he didn't live in a house at all, but in a boat that looked like a house and was moved secretly up and down the Long Island shore. Just why these inventions were a source of satisfaction to James Gatz of North Dakota isn't easy to say.

James Gatz—that was really, or at least legally, his name. He had changed it at the age of seventeen and at the specific moment that witnessed the beginning of his career—when he saw Dan Cody's yacht drop anchor over the most insidious flat on Lake Superior. It was James Gatz who had been loafing along the beach that afternoon in a torn green jersey and a pair of canvas pants, but it was already Jay Gatsby who borrowed a

[1] Illegal alcohol entered the U.S. from Canada in automobiles and trucks; but a popular myth of the Prohibition era, 1920–33, held that liquor flowed southward across the border through an underground pipeline.

**2** See Luke 2:49. "[W]ist ye not that I must be about my Father's business?" is the young Christ's reply to his distressed parents when, after searching for their missing son, they find him conversing in the Temple court.

**3** Lionel Trilling glosses this sentence: "Clearly it is Fitzgerald's intention that our mind should turn to the thought of the nation that has sprung from its 'Platonic conception' of itself. To the world it is anomalous in America, just as in the novel it is anomalous in Gatsby, that so much power should be haunted by envisioned romance. Yet in that anomaly lies, for good or bad, much of the truth of our national life, as, at the present moment, we think about it." See Trilling's *The Liberal Imagination* (Viking, 1950), pp. 251–52.

**4** St. Olaf College in Northfield, Minnesota, founded in 1874 by Norwegian Lutherans—a small, sectarian institution at which Jimmy Gatz, as like as not, would have felt uncomfortable.

rowboat, pulled out to the *Tuolomee*, and informed Cody that a wind might catch him and break him up in half an hour.

I suppose he'd had the name ready for a long time, even then. His parents were shiftless and unsuccessful farm people—his imagination had never really accepted them as his parents at all. The truth was that Jay Gatsby of West Egg, Long Island, sprang from his Platonic conception of himself. He was a son of God—a phrase which, if it means anything, means just that—and he must be about His Father's business,[2] the service of a vast, vulgar, and meretricious beauty.[3] So he invented just the sort of Jay Gatsby that a seventeen-year-old boy would be likely to invent, and to this conception he was faithful to the end.

For over a year he had been beating his way along the south shore of Lake Superior as a clam-digger and a salmon-fisher or in any other capacity that brought him food and bed. His brown, hardening body lived naturally through the half fierce, half lazy work of the bracing days. He knew women early, and since they spoiled him he became contemptuous of them, of young virgins because they were ignorant, of the others because they were hysterical about things which in his overwhelming self-absorption he took for granted.

But his heart was in a constant, turbulent riot. The most grotesque and fantastic conceits haunted him in his bed at night. A universe of ineffable gaudiness spun itself out in his brain while the clock ticked on the wash-stand and the moon soaked with wet light his tangled clothes upon the floor. Each night he added to the pattern of his fancies until drowsiness closed down upon some vivid scene with an oblivious embrace. For a while these reveries provided an outlet for his imagination; they were a satisfactory hint of the unreality of reality, a promise that the rock of the world was founded securely on a fairy's wing.

An instinct toward his future glory had led him, some months before, to the small Lutheran college of St. Olaf's[4] in southern Minnesota. He stayed there two weeks, dismayed at

its ferocious indifference to the drums of his destiny, to destiny itself, and despising the janitor's work with which he was to pay his way through. Then he drifted back to Lake Superior, and he was still searching for something to do on the day that Dan Cody's yacht dropped anchor in the shallows alongshore.

Cody was fifty years old then, a product of the Nevada silver fields, of the Yukon, of every rush for metal since seventy-five. The transactions in Montana copper that made him many times a millionaire found him physically robust but on the verge of soft-mindedness, and, suspecting this, an infinite

Bootleggers being arrested after crashing their car during a police chase, circa 1921.

5 Françoise d'Aubigné (1635–1719), known as Madame de Maintenon, who was secretly married in 1683 to Louis XIV, king of France. She was said to be pious and narrow-minded; she exercised much influence over the king during the last years of his reign.

number of women tried to separate him from his money. The none too savory ramifications by which Ella Kaye, the newspaper woman, played Madame de Maintenon[5] to his weakness and sent him to sea in a yacht, were common property of the turgid journalism of 1902. He had been coasting along all too hospitable shores for five years when he turned up as James Gatz's destiny in Little Girl Bay.

To young Gatz, resting on his oars and looking up at the railed deck, that yacht represented all the beauty and glamour in the world. I suppose he smiled at Cody—he had probably discovered that people liked him when he smiled. At any rate Cody asked him a few questions (one of them elicited the brand new name) and found that he was quick and extravagantly ambitious. A few days later he took him to Duluth and bought him a blue coat, six pair of white duck trousers, and a yachting cap. And when the *Tuolomee* left for the West Indies and the Barbary Coast, Gatsby left too.

He was employed in a vague personal capacity—while he remained with Cody he was in turn steward, mate, skipper, secretary, and even jailor, for Dan Cody sober knew what lavish doings Dan Cody drunk might soon be about, and he provided for such contingencies by reposing more and more trust in Gatsby. The arrangement lasted five years, during which the boat went three times around the Continent. It might have lasted indefinitely except for the fact that Ella Kaye came on board one night in Boston and a week later Dan Cody inhospitably died.

I remember the portrait of him up in Gatsby's bedroom, a gray, florid man with a hard, empty face—the pioneer debauchee, who during one phase of American life brought back to the Eastern seaboard the savage violence of the frontier brothel and saloon. It was indirectly due to Cody that Gatsby drank so little. Sometimes in the course of gay parties women used to rub champagne into his hair; for himself he formed the habit of letting liquor alone.

And it was from Cody that he inherited money—a legacy

of twenty-five thousand dollars. He didn't get it. He never understood the legal device that was used against him, but what remained of the millions went intact to Ella Kaye. He was left with his singularly appropriate education; the vague contour of Jay Gatsby had filled out to the substantiality of a man.

He told me all this very much later,[6] but I've put it down here with the idea of exploding those first wild rumors about his antecedents, which weren't even faintly true. Moreover he told it to me at a time of confusion, when I had reached the point of believing everything and nothing about him. So I take advantage of this short halt, while Gatsby, so to speak, caught his breath, to clear this set of misconceptions away.

It was a halt, too, in my association with his affairs. For several weeks I didn't see him or hear his voice on the phone—mostly I was in New York, trotting around with Jordan and trying to ingratiate myself with her senile aunt—but finally I went over to his house one Sunday afternoon. I hadn't been there two minutes when somebody brought Tom Buchanan in for a drink. I was startled, naturally, but the really surprising thing was that it hadn't happened before.

They were a party of three on horseback—Tom and a man named Sloane and a pretty woman in a brown riding habit, who had been there previously.

"I'm delighted to see you," said Gatsby, standing on his porch. "I'm delighted that you dropped in."

As though they cared!

"Sit right down. Have a cigarette or a cigar." He walked around the room quickly, ringing bells. "I'll have something to drink for you in just a minute."

He was profoundly affected by the fact that Tom was there. But he would be uneasy anyhow until he had given them something, realizing in a vague way that that was all they came

6 Most of the information about Gatsby's past that Nick recounts was positioned later in the narrative in the manuscript and galley proofs. Fitzgerald moved it to Chapter VI in response to Perkins's suggestion, in his letter of November 20, 1924, that some details of Gatsby's background be revealed sooner: "I thought you might find ways to let the truth of some of his claims like 'Oxford' and his army career come out bit by bit in the course of actual narrative," Perkins suggested—rather than withholding nearly all of this information until the end. Perkins's letter is included on pp. 200–203 in this volume.

for. Mr. Sloane wanted nothing. A lemonade? No, thanks. A little champagne? Nothing at all, thanks. . . . I'm sorry——

"Did you have a nice ride?"

"Very good roads around here."

"I suppose the automobiles——"

"Yeah."

Moved by an irresistible impulse, Gatsby turned to Tom, who had accepted the introduction as a stranger.

"I believe we've met somewhere before, Mr. Buchanan."

"Oh, yes," said Tom, gruffly polite, but obviously not remembering. "So we did. I remember very well."

"About two weeks ago."

"That's right. You were with Nick here."

"I know your wife," continued Gatsby, almost aggressively.

"That so?"

Tom turned to me.

"You live near here, Nick?"

"Next door."

"That so?"

Mr. Sloane didn't enter into the conversation, but lounged back haughtily in his chair; the woman said nothing either—until unexpectedly, after two highballs, she became cordial.

"We'll all come over to your next party, Mr. Gatsby," she suggested. "What do you say?"

"Certainly. I'd be delighted to have you."

"Be ver' nice," said Mr. Sloane, without gratitude. "Well— think ought to be starting home."

"Please don't hurry," Gatsby urged them. He had control of himself now, and he wanted to see more of Tom. "Why don't you—why don't you stay for supper? I wouldn't be surprised if some other people dropped in from New York."

"You come to supper with *me*," said the lady enthusiastically. "Both of you."

This included me. Mr. Sloane got to his feet.

"Come along," he said—but to her only.

"I mean it," she insisted. "I'd love to have you. Lots of room."

Gatsby looked at me questioningly. He wanted to go, and he didn't see that Mr. Sloane had determined he shouldn't.

"I'm afraid I won't be able to," I said.

"Well, you come," she urged, concentrating on Gatsby.

Mr. Sloane murmured something close to her ear.

"We won't be late if we start now," she insisted aloud.

"I haven't got a horse," said Gatsby. "I used to ride in the army, but I've never bought a horse. I'll have to follow you in my car. Excuse me for just a minute."

The rest of us walked out on the porch, where Sloane and the lady began an impassioned conversation aside.

"My God, I believe the man's coming," said Tom. "Doesn't he know she doesn't want him?"

"She says she does want him."

"She has a big dinner party and he won't know a soul there." He frowned. "I wonder where in the devil he met Daisy. By God, I may be old-fashioned in my ideas, but women run around too much these days to suit me. They meet all kinds of crazy fish."

Suddenly Mr. Sloane and the lady walked down the steps and mounted their horses.

"Come on," said Mr. Sloane to Tom. "We're late. We've got to go." And then to me: "Tell him we couldn't wait, will you?"

Tom and I shook hands, the rest of us exchanged a cool nod, and they trotted quickly down the drive, disappearing under the August foliage just as Gatsby, with hat and light overcoat in hand, came out the front door.

Tom was evidently perturbed at Daisy's running around alone, for on the following Saturday night he came with her to Gatsby's party.[7] Perhaps his presence gave the evening its peculiar quality of oppressiveness—it stands out in my memory from Gatsby's other parties that summer. There were the same people, or at least the same sort of people, the same profusion of champagne, the same many-colored, many-keyed commotion, but I felt an unpleasantness in the air, a pervading harshness that hadn't been there before. Or perhaps I had

7. In the manuscript and galley proofs, Gatsby's soirée is a masquerade party— appropriately so, because almost everyone in the novel is engaged in some form of disguise. Nick comes to the party dressed as a farmer in overalls; Daisy wears the costume of a Provençal peasant girl. Nick sets the scene: "The party was a little more elaborate than any of the others; there were two orchestras for example—jazz in the gardens and intermittent 'classical stuff' from the veranda above. It was a harvest dance with the immemorial decorations—sheaves of wheat, crossed rakes, and corncobs in geometrical designs. . . . The real bar was outside, under a windmill whose blades, studded with colored lights, revolved slowly through the summer air. . . . Only about a third of the guests were in costume, and this included the orchestra who were dressed as 'village constables.' As most of the others were village constables also the effect was given that the members of the orchestra got up at intervals and danced with the ladies present—an illusion which added to the pleasant confusion of the scene." From *Trimalchio: An Early Version of The Great Gatsby*, ed. James L. W. West III (Cambridge University Press, 2000), pp. 80-81. Fitzgerald removed the element of masquerade when he revised the galleys, perhaps to make the party rougher and less attractive to Daisy.

Dust jacket of the 1934 Modern Library edition of *The Great Gatsby*. Fitzgerald wrote an introduction for the Modern Library Edition that reads in part: "Now that this book is being reissued, the author would like to say that never before did one try to keep his artistic conscience as pure as during the ten months put into doing it. Reading it over one can see how it could have been improved—yet without feeling guilty of any discrepancy from the truth, as far as I saw it; truth or rather the *equivalent* of the truth, the attempt at honesty of imagination" (p. viii).

merely grown used to it, grown to accept West Egg as a world complete in itself, with its own standards and its own great figures, second to nothing because it had no consciousness of being so, and now I was looking at it again, through Daisy's eyes. It is invariably saddening to look through new eyes at things upon which you have expended your own powers of adjustment.

They arrived at twilight, and, as we strolled out among the sparkling hundreds, Daisy's voice was playing murmurous tricks in her throat.

"These things excite me *so*," she whispered. "If you want to kiss me any time during the evening, Nick, just let me know and I'll be glad to arrange it for you. Just mention my name. Or present a green card. I'm giving out green——"

"Look around," suggested Gatsby.

"I'm looking around. I'm having a marvellous——"

"You must see the faces of many people you've heard about."

Tom's arrogant eyes roamed the crowd.

"We don't go around very much," he said. "In fact, I was just thinking I don't know a soul here."

"Perhaps you know that lady." Gatsby indicated a gorgeous, scarcely human orchid of a woman who sat in state under a white-plum tree. Tom and Daisy stared, with that peculiarly unreal feeling that accompanies the recognition of a hitherto ghostly celebrity of the movies.

"She's lovely," said Daisy.

"The man bending over her is her director."

He took them ceremoniously from group to group:

"Mrs. Buchanan . . . and Mr. Buchanan—" After an instant's hesitation he added: "the polo player."

"Oh no," objected Tom quickly, "not me."

But evidently the sound of it pleased Gatsby for Tom remained "the polo player" for the rest of the evening.

"I've never met so many celebrities," Daisy exclaimed. "I liked that man—what was his name?—with the sort of blue nose."

Gatsby identified him, adding that he was a small producer.

"Well, I liked him anyhow."

"I'd a little rather not be the polo player," said Tom pleasantly. "I'd rather look at all these famous people in—in oblivion."

Daisy and Gatsby danced. I remember being surprised by his graceful, conservative fox-trot—I had never seen him dance before. Then they sauntered over to my house and sat on the steps for half an hour, while at her request I remained watchfully in the garden. "In case there's a fire or a flood," she explained, "or any act of God."

Tom appeared from his oblivion as we were sitting down to supper together. "Do you mind if I eat with some people over here?" he said. "A fellow's getting off some funny stuff."

"Go ahead," answered Daisy genially, "and if you want to take down any addresses here's my little gold pencil." . . . She looked around after a moment and told me the girl was "common but pretty," and I knew that except for the half hour she'd been alone with Gatsby she wasn't having a good time.

We were at a particularly tipsy table. That was my fault— Gatsby had been called to the phone, and I'd enjoyed these same people only two weeks before. But what had amused me then turned septic on the air now.

"How do you feel, Miss Baedeker?"

The girl addressed was trying, unsuccessfully, to slump against my shoulder. At this inquiry she sat up and opened her eyes.

"Wha'?"

A massive and lethargic woman, who had been urging Daisy to play golf with her at the local club tomorrow, spoke in Miss Baedeker's defense:

"Oh, she's all right now. When she's had five or six cocktails she always starts screaming like that. I tell her she ought to leave it alone."

"I do leave it alone," affirmed the accused hollowly.

"We heard you yelling, so I said to Doc Civet here: 'There's somebody that needs your help, Doc.'"

"She's much obliged, I'm sure," said another friend, without gratitude, "but you got her dress all wet when you stuck her head in the pool."

"Anything I hate is to get my head stuck in a pool," mumbled Miss Baedeker. "They almost drowned me once over in New Jersey."

"Then you ought to leave it alone," countered Doctor Civet.

"Speak for yourself!" cried Miss Baedeker violently. "Your hand shakes. I wouldn't let you operate on me!"

It was like that. Almost the last thing I remember was standing with Daisy and watching the moving-picture director and his Star. They were still under the white-plum tree and their faces were touching except for a pale, thin ray of moonlight between. It occurred to me that he had been very slowly bending toward her all evening to attain this proximity, and even while I watched I saw him stoop one ultimate degree and kiss at her cheek.

"I like her," said Daisy. "I think she's lovely."

But the rest offended her—and inarguably, because it wasn't a gesture but an emotion. She was appalled by West Egg, this unprecedented "place" that Broadway had begotten upon a Long Island fishing village—appalled by its raw vigor that chafed under the old euphemisms and by the too obtrusive fate that herded its inhabitants along a short-cut from nothing to nothing. She saw something awful in the very simplicity she failed to understand.

I sat on the front steps with them while they waited for their car. It was dark here in front; only the bright door sent ten square feet of light volleying out into the soft black morning. Sometimes a shadow moved against a dressing-room blind above, gave way to another shadow, an indefinite procession of shadows, who rouged and powdered in an invisible glass.

"Who is this Gatsby anyhow?" demanded Tom suddenly. "Some big bootlegger?"

"Where'd you hear that?" I inquired.

"I didn't hear it. I imagined it. A lot of these newly rich people are just big bootleggers, you know."

"Not Gatsby," I said shortly.

He was silent for a moment. The pebbles of the drive crunched under his feet.

"Well, he certainly must have strained himself to get this menagerie together."

A breeze stirred the gray haze of Daisy's fur collar.

"At least they are more interesting than the people we know," she said with an effort.

"You didn't look so interested."

"Well, I was."

Tom laughed and turned to me.

"Did you notice Daisy's face when that girl asked her to put her under a cold shower?"

Daisy began to sing with the music in a husky, rhythmic whisper, bringing out a meaning in each word that it had never had before and would never have again. When the melody rose her voice broke up sweetly, following it, in a way contralto voices have, and each change tipped out a little of her warm human magic upon the air.

Sheet music cover, 1922, for "the
sensational dance hit" "Three O'Clock
in the Morning."

**8** Popular song of the 1920s with music by
Julián Robledo (1887–1940) and lyrics by
Dorothy Terriss (1883–1953). The song was
first performed in the *Greenwich Village
Follies of 1921*. An instrumental version by
Paul Whiteman's orchestra was released on
the Victor label in 1922 and sold more than
three million copies. The words to the song
reflect something of Daisy's inner feelings,
as Nick suggests in the paragraph that follows. Many of Fitzgerald's contemporary
readers would have been familiar with the
lyrics:

> It's three o'clock in the morning,
> We've danced the whole night through;
> And daylight soon will be dawning,
> Just one more waltz with you;
> That melody so entrancing,
> Seems to be made for us two;
> I could just keep on dancing,
> Forever, dear, with you.

"Lots of people come who haven't been invited," she said
suddenly. "That girl hadn't been invited. They simply force
their way in and he's too polite to object."

"I'd like to know who he is and what he does," insisted Tom.
"And I think I'll make a point of finding out."

"I can tell you right now," she answered. "He owned some
drug-stores, a lot of drug-stores. He built them up himself."

The dilatory limousine came rolling up the drive.

"Good night, Nick," said Daisy.

Her glance left me and sought the lighted top of the steps,
where "Three O'Clock in the Morning,"[8] a neat, sad little waltz
of that year, was drifting out the open door. After all, in the
very casualness of Gatsby's party there were romantic possibilities totally absent from her world. What was it up there
in the song that seemed to be calling her back inside? What
would happen now in the dim, incalculable hours? Perhaps
some unbelievable guest would arrive, a person infinitely rare
and to be marvelled at, some authentically radiant young girl
who with one fresh glance at Gatsby, one moment of magical encounter, would blot out those five years of unwavering
devotion.

I stayed late that night. Gatsby asked me to wait until he
was free, and I lingered in the garden until the inevitable swimming party had run up, chilled and exalted, from the black
beach, until the lights were extinguished in the guest-rooms
overhead. When he came down the steps at last the tanned
skin was drawn unusually tight on his face, and his eyes were
bright and tired.

"She didn't like it," he said immediately.

"Of course she did."

"She didn't like it," he insisted. "She didn't have a good time."

He was silent, and I guessed at his unutterable depression.

"I feel far away from her," he said. "It's hard to make her
understand."

"You mean about the dance?"

"The dance?" He dismissed all the dances he had given with a snap of his fingers. "Old sport, the dance is unimportant."

He wanted nothing less of Daisy than that she should go to Tom and say: "I never loved you." After she had obliterated four years with that sentence they could decide upon the more practical measures to be taken. One of them was that, after she was free, they were to go back to Louisville and be married from her house—just as if it were five years ago.

"And she doesn't understand," he said. "She used to be able to understand. We'd sit for hours——"

He broke off and began to walk up and down a desolate path of fruit rinds and discarded favors and crushed flowers.

"I wouldn't ask too much of her," I ventured. "You can't repeat the past."

"Can't repeat the past?" he cried incredulously. "Why of course you can!"

He looked around him wildly, as if the past were lurking here in the shadow of his house, just out of reach of his hand.

"I'm going to fix everything just the way it was before," he said, nodding determinedly. "She'll see."

He talked a lot about the past, and I gathered that he wanted to recover something, some idea of himself perhaps, that had gone into loving Daisy. His life had been confused and disordered since then, but if he could once return to a certain starting place and go over it all slowly, he could find out what that thing was. . . .

. . . One autumn night, five years before, they had been walking down the street when the leaves were falling, and they came to a place where there were no trees and the sidewalk was white with moonlight. They stopped here and turned toward each other. Now it was a cool night with that mysterious excitement in it which comes at the two changes of the year. The quiet lights in the houses were humming out into the darkness and there was a stir and bustle among the stars. Out of the corner of his eye Gatsby saw that the blocks of the

**9** Glossing the two highly lyrical paragraphs that precede, Morris Dickstein writes: "No other modern novelist could have sounded such a note, though romance writers would grasp at tawdry versions of it. The language is evocative and poetic rather than descriptive; the final image comes directly from the poetry and letters of Keats, Fitzgerald's favorite writer. . . . This is the heightened language of desire, the milk of inspiration, that reaches for the infinite only to founder in frustration. . . . [O]nce the object takes flesh and blood, once it is incarnated in another person's 'perishable breath,' it becomes bounded, vulnerable. Gatsby's failure is built into his huge but absurd ambition. This grail can be sought and sighted but never carried home." See Morris Dickstein's introduction to *Critical Insights: The Great Gatsby* (Salem Press, 2010), pp. 3–4.

sidewalks really formed a ladder and mounted to a secret place above the trees—he could climb to it, if he climbed alone, and once there he could suck on the pap of life, gulp down the incomparable milk of wonder.

His heart beat faster and faster as Daisy's white face came up to his own. He knew that when he kissed this girl, and forever wed his unutterable visions to her perishable breath, his mind would never romp again like the mind of God. So he waited, listening for a moment longer to the tuning-fork that had been struck upon a star. Then he kissed her. At his lips' touch she blossomed for him like a flower and the incarnation was complete.[9]

Through all he said, even through his appalling sentimentality, I was reminded of something—an elusive rhythm, a fragment of lost words, that I had heard somewhere a long time ago. For a moment a phrase tried to take shape in my mouth and my lips parted like a dumb man's, as though there was more struggling upon them than a wisp of startled air. But they made no sound, and what I had almost remembered was uncommunicable forever.

# CHAPTER VII

It was when curiosity about Gatsby was at its highest that the lights in his house failed to go on one Saturday night—and, as obscurely as it had begun, his career as Trimalchio[1] was over. Only gradually did I become aware that the automobiles which turned expectantly into his drive stayed for just a minute and then drove sulkily away. Wondering if he were sick I went over to find out—an unfamiliar butler with a villainous face squinted at me suspiciously from the door.

"Is Mr. Gatsby sick?"

"Nope." After a pause he added "sir" in a dilatory, grudging way.

"I hadn't seen him around, and I was rather worried. Tell him Mr. Carraway came over."

"Who?" he demanded rudely.

"Carraway."

"Carraway. All right, I'll tell him."

Abruptly he slammed the door.

My Finn informed me that Gatsby had dismissed every servant in his house a week ago and replaced them with half a dozen others, who never went into West Egg Village to be bribed by the tradesmen, but ordered moderate supplies over the telephone.

The grocery boy reported that the kitchen looked like a pigsty, and the general opinion in the village was that the new people weren't servants at all.

Next day Gatsby called me on the phone.

"Going away?" I inquired.

"No, old sport."

[1] A wealthy freed slave in the *Satyricon*, a Latin fiction likely written by the Roman author Petronius (c. 27–66 CE). Trimalchio appears in a section of the *Satyricon* called "Trimalchio's Feast." He hosts ostentatious parties for his guests, who speak slightingly of him when he is absent from the room and depart without bothering to learn his name. The narrator of the *Satyricon* is a layabout (but a keen observer) named Encolpius, who calls to mind Nick Carraway. "Trimalchio" and "Trimalchio in West Egg" were working titles for *The Great Gatsby*. Fitzgerald dropped the idea of using the character's name in the title when it was pointed out to him that the dust jacket would have to include an explanation of this literary allusion.

2 The novelist Jay McInerney writes: "Fitzgerald had a kind of double agent's consciousness about the tinsel of the jazz age, and about the privileged world of inherited wealth; he couldn't help stopping to admire and glamorise the glittering interiors of which his midwestern heart ultimately disapproved. Gatsby's lavish weekly summer parties are over the top, ridiculous, peopled with drunks and poseurs, and yet we can't help feeling a sense of loss when he suddenly shuts them down after it's clear that Daisy—for whom the whole show was arranged in the first place—doesn't quite approve. We shouldn't approve either, and yet in memory they seem like parties to which we wish we'd been invited." McInerney, "Why Gatsby Is So Great," *The Observer* (June 9, 2012).

3 A sprawling Nabisco plant located on the Lower West Side of Manhattan (today the Chelsea Market). The sign for the factory towered over the surrounding buildings; the noon whistle from the plant could be heard even on passing trains, as Nick reminds us here.

"I hear you fired all your servants."

"I wanted somebody who wouldn't gossip. Daisy comes over quite often—in the afternoons."

So the whole caravansary had fallen in like a card house at the disapproval in her eyes.[2]

"They're some people Wolfshiem wanted to do something for. They're all brothers and sisters. They used to run a small hotel."

"I see."

He was calling up at Daisy's request—would I come to lunch at her house tomorrow? Miss Baker would be there. Half an hour later Daisy herself telephoned and seemed relieved to find that I was coming. Something was up. And yet I couldn't believe that they would choose this occasion for a scene—especially for the rather harrowing scene that Gatsby had outlined in the garden.

The next day was broiling, almost the last, certainly the warmest, of the summer. As my train emerged from the tunnel into sunlight, only the hot whistles of the National Biscuit Company[3] broke the simmering hush at noon. The straw seats of the car hovered on the edge of combustion; the woman next to me perspired delicately for a while into her white shirt-waist, and then, as her newspaper dampened under her fingers, lapsed despairingly into deep heat with a desolate cry. Her pocket-book slapped to the floor.

"Oh, my!" she gasped.

I picked it up with a weary bend and handed it back to her, holding it at arm's length and by the extreme tips of the corners to indicate that I had no designs upon it—but everyone nearby, including the woman, suspected me just the same.

"Hot!" said the conductor to familiar faces. "Some weather! ... Hot! ... Hot! ... Hot! ... Is it hot enough for you? Is it hot? Is it ...?"

My commutation ticket came back to me with a dark stain from his hand. That anyone should care in this heat whose

The 15–16th Street Bakery of the National Biscuit Company, 1898–1958, on the Lower West Side. Oreo Sandwiches, Uneeda Biscuits, and Zu Zu Ginger Snaps were among the baked goods produced there.

flushed lips he kissed, whose head made damp the pajama pocket over his heart!

. . . Through the hall of the Buchanans' house blew a faint wind, carrying the sound of the telephone bell out to Gatsby and me as we waited at the door.

"The master's body!" roared the butler into the mouthpiece. "I'm sorry, madame, but we can't furnish it—it's far too hot to touch this noon!"

What he really said was: "Yes . . . Yes . . . I'll see."

He set down the receiver and came toward us, glistening slightly, to take our stiff straw hats.

"Madame expects you in the salon!" he cried, needlessly indicating the direction. In this heat every extra gesture was an affront to the common store of life.

The room, shadowed well with awnings, was dark and cool. Daisy and Jordan lay upon an enormous couch, like silver idols weighing down their own white dresses against the singing breeze of the fans.

"We can't move," they said together.

Jordan's fingers, powdered white over their tan, rested for a moment in mine.

"And Mr. Thomas Buchanan, the athlete?" I inquired.

Simultaneously I heard his voice, gruff, muffled, husky, at the hall telephone.

Gatsby stood in the center of the crimson carpet and gazed around with fascinated eyes. Daisy watched him and laughed, her sweet, exciting laugh; a tiny gust of powder rose from her bosom into the air.

"The rumor is," whispered Jordan, "that that's Tom's girl on the telephone."

We were silent. The voice in the hall rose high with annoyance: "Very well, then, I won't sell you the car at all. . . . I'm under no obligations to you at all . . . and as for your bothering me about it at lunch-time, I won't stand that at all!"

"Holding down the receiver," said Daisy cynically.

"No, he's not," I assured her. "It's a bona-fide deal. I happen to know about it."

Tom flung open the door, blocked out its space for a moment with his thick body, and hurried into the room.

"Mr. Gatsby!" He put out his broad, flat hand with well-concealed dislike. "I'm glad to see you, sir . . . Nick. . . ."

"Make us a cold drink," cried Daisy.

As he left the room again she got up and went over to Gatsby and pulled his face down, kissing him on the mouth.

"You know I love you," she murmured.

"You forget there's a lady present," said Jordan.

Daisy looked around doubtfully.

"You kiss Nick too."

"What a low, vulgar girl!"

"I don't care!" cried Daisy, and began to clog on the brick fireplace. Then she remembered the heat and sat down guiltily on the couch just as a freshly laundered nurse leading a little girl came into the room.

"Bles-sed pre-cious," she crooned, holding out her arms. "Come to your own mother that loves you."

The child, relinquished by the nurse, rushed across the room and rooted shyly into her mother's dress.

"The bles-sed pre-cious! Did mother get powder on your old yellowy hair? Stand up now, and say—How-de-do."

Gatsby and I in turn leaned down and took the small reluctant hand. Afterward he kept looking at the child with surprise. I don't think he had ever really believed in its existence before.

"I got dressed before luncheon," said the child, turning eagerly to Daisy.

"That's because your mother wanted to show you off." Her face bent into the single wrinkle of the small white neck. "You dream, you. You absolute little dream."

"Yes," admitted the child calmly. "Aunt Jordan's got on a white dress too."

"How do you like mother's friends?" Daisy turned her around so that she faced Gatsby. "Do you think they're pretty?"

"Where's Daddy?"

"She doesn't look like her father," explained Daisy. "She looks like me. She's got my hair and shape of the face."

Daisy sat back upon the couch. The nurse took a step forward and held out her hand.

"Come, Pammy."

"Good-by, sweetheart!"

With a reluctant backward glance the well-disciplined child held to her nurse's hand and was pulled out the door, just as Tom came back, preceding four gin rickeys[4] that clicked full of ice.

Gatsby took up his drink.

"They certainly look cool," he said, with visible tension.

We drank in long, greedy swallows.

"I read somewhere that the sun's getting hotter every year," said Tom genially. "It seems that pretty soon the earth's going to fall into the sun—or wait a minute—it's just the opposite—the sun's getting colder every year.

"Come outside," he suggested to Gatsby. "I'd like you to have a look at the place."

I went with them out to the veranda. On the green Sound,

4 A hot-weather drink made with gin, lime juice, fruit syrup or sugar, and seltzer water. It is served over ice, usually with a wedge of lime, in a lowball glass.

5 Daisy's remark about Gatsby's resemblance to "the advertisement of the man" is probably an allusion to the ubiquitous Arrow Collar advertisements of the period. Created by illustrator J. C. Leyendecker, the Arrow Collar Man was featured in numerous magazine and billboard ads for Arrow collars and shirts, from 1907 to 1931. (Most men's dress shirts during this period had detachable collars. Collars were attached with collar buttons and came in a variety of styles: the Lexicon, Gothic, Standish, Ashby, etc.). By the 1920s the Arrow Collar Man had become an American icon, not unlike the Marlboro Man in the latter part of the century—symbolizing, however, not rugged manliness but urban sophistication and leisure. Gatsby's ease here—like Jay Gatsby himself—is a pretense, a fiction, no more real than the Arrow Collar Man.

stagnant in the heat, one small sail crawled slowly toward the fresher sea. Gatsby's eyes followed it momentarily; he raised his hand and pointed across the bay.

"I'm right across from you."

"So you are."

Our eyes lifted over the rose-beds and the hot lawn and the weedy refuse of the dog-days alongshore. Slowly the white wings of the boat moved against the blue cool limit of the sky. Ahead lay the scalloped ocean and the abounding blessed isles.

"There's sport for you," said Tom, nodding. "I'd like to be out there with him for about an hour."

We had luncheon in the dining-room, darkened too against the heat, and drank down nervous gayety with the cold ale.

"What'll we do with ourselves this afternoon?" cried Daisy. "And the day after that, and the next thirty years?"

"Don't be morbid," Jordan said. "Life starts all over again when it gets crisp in the fall."

"But it's so hot," insisted Daisy, on the verge of tears, "and everything's so confused. Let's all go to town!"

Her voice struggled on through the heat, beating against it, molding its senselessness into forms.

"I've heard of making a garage out of a stable," Tom was saying to Gatsby, "but I'm the first man who ever made a stable out of a garage."

"Who wants to go to town?" demanded Daisy insistently. Gatsby's eyes floated toward her. "Ah," she cried, "you look so cool."

Their eyes met, and they stared together at each other, alone in space. With an effort she glanced down at the table.

"You always look so cool," she repeated.

She had told him that she loved him, and Tom Buchanan saw. He was astounded. His mouth opened a little, and he looked at Gatsby, and then back at Daisy as if he had just recognized her as someone he knew a long time ago.

"You resemble the advertisement of the man,"[5] she went on innocently. "You know the advertisement of the man——"

"All right," broke in Tom quickly, "I'm perfectly willing to go to town. Come on—we're all going to town."

He got up, his eyes still flashing between Gatsby and his wife. No one moved.

"Come on!" His temper cracked a little. "What's the matter, anyhow? If we're going to town, let's start."

His hand, trembling with his effort at self-control, bore to his lips the last of his glass of ale. Daisy's voice got us to our feet and out on to the blazing gravel drive.

"Are we just going to go?" she objected. "Like this? Aren't we going to let anyone smoke a cigarette first?"

"Everybody smoked all through lunch."

"Oh, let's have fun," she begged him. "It's too hot to fuss."

He didn't answer.

"Have it your own way," she said. "Come on, Jordan."

They went upstairs to get ready while we three men stood there shuffling the hot pebbles with our feet. A silver curve of the moon hovered already in the western sky. Gatsby started to speak, changed his mind, but not before Tom wheeled and faced him expectantly.

"Pardon me?"

"Have you got your stables here?" asked Gatsby with an effort.

"About a quarter of a mile down the road."

"Oh."

A pause.

"I don't see the idea of going to town," broke out Tom savagely. "Women get these notions in their heads——"

"Shall we take anything to drink?" called Daisy from an upper window.

"I'll get some whiskey," answered Tom. He went inside.

Gatsby turned to me rigidly:

"I can't say anything in his house, old sport."

"She's got an indiscreet voice," I remarked. "It's full of—" I hesitated.

"Her voice is full of money," he said suddenly.

Advertisement circa 1920 featuring the Arrow Collar Man. One of Amory Blaine's young female admirers in *This Side of Paradise* is conscious of "his intent green eyes [and] his mouth, that to her thirteen-year-old, Arrow-Collar taste was the quintessence of romance." "A generation of college men regarded him as the go-to authority for fashion advice," Deborah Solomon writes. "Leyendecker [who created the character] single-handedly changed advertising by switching the emphasis from text to image and making his pitch in emphatically visual terms. Earlier, in the nineteenth century, most printed advertisements had been crammed with tiny, hard-to-read type imploring you to buy effective or ineffective remedies for your headaches and nerves and itchy skin. The Arrow Collar Man, by contrast, was selling a vision as much as a product. He was selling the notion that any man could acquire instant class by spending twenty cents on a detachable collar." See Deborah Solomon's *American Mirror: The Life and Art of Norman Rockwell* (Farrar, Straus and Giroux, 2013), p. 116.

6 Fitzgerald put this exchange between Nick and Gatsby through three revisions before he was satisfied with it. In the first two versions (in the manuscript and the galley proofs) Gatsby appears suddenly resentful of Daisy's life of privilege and ease—surprised by his own observation about her voice. In the final book version the words come reflexively from his lips, as if the thought had been formulated long ago, during his years of dreaming and fantasizing about Daisy. Fitzgerald's attitude toward the rich was complex: he recognized their coldness and insularity but admired their beauty and style, when he encountered it. For the three versions of the passage, see James L. W. West III, "The Composition and Publication of *The Great Gatsby*," in *Approaches to Teaching Fitzgerald's* The Great Gatsby, ed. Jackson R. Bryer and Nancy P. VanArsdale (MLA, 2009), pp. 23–24.

7 During Prohibition, drugstores were sometimes fronts for bootlegging. Tom's implication is that Gatsby is (or was) a bootlegger. The "indefinable expression" that passes over Gatsby's face indicates that Tom is correct. If the members of the party want to drink privately in the city, they must take their alcohol with them and find a place where they can consume it. This helps to explain why they take a room at the Plaza, though Tom's bottle will remain unopened during the confrontation there.

That was it. I'd never understood before. It was full of money—that was the inexhaustible charm that rose and fell in it, the jingle of it, the cymbals' song of it. . . . High in a white palace the king's daughter, the golden girl. . . .[6]

Tom came out of the house wrapping a quart bottle in a towel, followed by Daisy and Jordan wearing small tight hats of metallic cloth and carrying light capes over their arms.

"Shall we all go in my car?" suggested Gatsby. He felt the hot, green leather of the seat. "I ought to have left it in the shade."

"Is it standard shift?" demanded Tom.

"Yes."

"Well, you take my coupé and let me drive your car to town."

The suggestion was distasteful to Gatsby.

"I don't think there's much gas," he objected.

"Plenty of gas," said Tom boisterously. He looked at the gauge. "And if it runs out I can stop at a drug-store. You can buy anything at a drug-store nowadays."[7]

A pause followed this apparently pointless remark. Daisy looked at Tom frowning, and an indefinable expression, at once definitely unfamiliar and vaguely recognizable, as if I had only heard it described in words, passed over Gatsby's face.

"Come on, Daisy," said Tom, pressing her with his hand toward Gatsby's car. "I'll take you in this circus wagon."

He opened the door, but she moved out from the circle of his arm.

"You take Nick and Jordan. We'll follow you in the coupé."

She walked close to Gatsby, touching his coat with her hand. Jordan and Tom and I got into the front seat of Gatsby's car, Tom pushed the unfamiliar gears tentatively, and we shot off into the oppressive heat, leaving them out of sight behind.

"Did you see that?" demanded Tom.

"See what?"

He looked at me keenly, realizing that Jordan and I must have known all along.

"You think I'm pretty dumb, don't you?" he suggested.

"I have never been able to forgive the rich for being rich," Fitzgerald wrote to his agent Harold Ober, "and it has colored my entire life and works." Fitzgerald to Harold Ober, March 4, 1938, in *As Ever, Scott Fitz: Letters Between F. Scott Fitzgerald and His Literary Agent, Harold Ober, 1919-1940*, ed. Matthew Bruccoli (Lippincott, 1972), p. 357.

"Perhaps I am, but I have a—almost a second sight, sometimes, that tells me what to do. Maybe you don't believe that, but science——"

He paused. The immediate contingency overtook him, pulled him back from the edge of the theoretical abyss.

"I've made a small investigation of this fellow," he continued. "I could have gone deeper if I'd known——"

"Do you mean you've been to a medium?" inquired Jordan humorously.

"What?" Confused, he stared at us as we laughed. "A medium?"

Agents pouring alcohol down a storm drain in the early 1920s.

**8** Scott Donaldson writes: "Gatsby's clothes, his car, his house, his parties—all brand him as newly rich, unschooled in the social graces and casual sense of superiority ingrained in those brought up in an atmosphere of privilege." Richard Chase offers this further, relevant observation about the pink-suited Gatsby: "[W]e have a figure who is from one point of view a hero of romance but from another is related to the gulls and fops of high comedy." See Scott Donaldson's "Gatsby and the American Dream," in *Fitzgerald and the War between the Sexes* (Pennsylvania State University Press, 2022), p. 66; and Richard Chase's *The American Novel and Its Tradition* (Johns Hopkins University Press, 1980), p. 166.

**9** During the 1920s most automobiles were equipped with two mechanisms for stopping: hand brakes, which acted on the rear wheels, and pedal-operated brakes, which acted on the transmission shaft.

"About Gatsby."

"About Gatsby! No, I haven't. I said I'd been making a small investigation of his past."

"And you found he was an Oxford man," said Jordan helpfully.

"An Oxford man!" He was incredulous. "Like hell he is! He wears a pink suit."[8]

"Nevertheless he's an Oxford man."

"Oxford, New Mexico," snorted Tom contemptuously, "or something like that."

"Listen, Tom. If you're such a snob, why did you invite him to lunch?" demanded Jordan crossly.

"Daisy invited him; she knew him before we were married—God knows where!"

We were all irritable now with the fading ale, and aware of it we drove for a while in silence. Then as Doctor T. J. Eckleburg's faded eyes came into sight down the road, I remembered Gatsby's caution about gasoline.

"We've got enough to get us to town," said Tom.

"But there's a garage right here," objected Jordan. "I don't want to get stalled in this baking heat."

Tom threw on both brakes[9] impatiently, and we slid to an

March 1974 illustrated GQ cover of Robert Redford as Gatsby, in his pink suit.

abrupt dusty stop under Wilson's sign. After a moment the proprietor emerged from the interior of his establishment and gazed hollow-eyed at the car.

"Let's have some gas!" cried Tom roughly. "What do you think we stopped for—to admire the view?"

"I'm sick," said Wilson without moving. "Been sick all day."

"What's the matter?"

"I'm all run down."

"Well, shall I help myself?" Tom demanded. "You sounded well enough on the phone."

With an effort Wilson left the shade and support of the doorway and, breathing hard, unscrewed the cap of the tank. In the sunlight his face was green.

"I didn't mean to interrupt your lunch," he said. "But I need money pretty bad, and I was wondering what you were going to do with your old car."

"How do you like this one?" inquired Tom. "I bought it last week."

"It's a nice yellow one," said Wilson, as he strained at the handle.

"Like to buy it?"

"Big chance," Wilson smiled faintly. "No, but I could make some money on the other."

"What do you want money for, all of a sudden?"

"I've been here too long. I want to get away. My wife and I want to go West."

"Your wife does!" exclaimed Tom, startled.

"She's been talking about it for ten years." He rested for a moment against the pump, shading his eyes. "And now she's going whether she wants to or not. I'm going to get her away."

The coupé flashed by us with a flurry of dust and the flash of a waving hand.

"What do I owe you?" demanded Tom harshly.

"I just got wised up to something funny the last two days," remarked Wilson. "That's why I want to get away. That's why I been bothering you about the car."

"What do I owe you?"

"Dollar twenty."

The relentless beating heat was beginning to confuse me and I had a bad moment there before I realized that so far his suspicions hadn't alighted on Tom. He had discovered that Myrtle had some sort of life apart from him in another world, and the shock had made him physically sick. I stared at him and then at Tom, who had made a parallel discovery less than an hour before—and it occurred to me that there was no difference between men, in intelligence or race, so profound as the difference between the sick and the well. Wilson was so sick that he looked guilty, unforgivably guilty—as if he had just got some poor girl with child.

"I'll let you have that car," said Tom. "I'll send it over tomorrow afternoon."

That locality was always vaguely disquieting, even in the broad glare of afternoon, and now I turned my head as though I had been warned of something behind. Over the ashheaps the giant eyes of Doctor T. J. Eckleburg kept their vigil, but I perceived, after a moment, that other eyes were regarding us with peculiar intensity from less than twenty feet away.

In one of the windows over the garage the curtains had been moved aside a little, and Myrtle Wilson was peering down at the car. So engrossed was she that she had no consciousness of being observed, and one emotion after another crept into her face like objects into a slowly developing picture. Her expression was curiously familiar—it was an expression I had often seen on women's faces, but on Myrtle Wilson's face it seemed purposeless and inexplicable until I realized that her eyes, wide with jealous terror, were fixed not on Tom, but on Jordan Baker, whom she took to be his wife.

There is no confusion like the confusion of a simple mind, and as we drove away Tom was feeling the hot whips of panic. His wife and his mistress, until an hour ago secure and inviolate, were slipping precipitately from his control. Instinct made him step on the accelerator with the double purpose of overtaking Daisy and leaving Wilson behind, and we sped along toward Astoria at fifty miles an hour, until, among the spidery girders of the elevated, we came in sight of the easygoing blue coupé.

"Those big movies around Fiftieth Street are cool," suggested Jordan. "I love New York on summer afternoons when everyone's away. There's something very sensuous about it— overripe, as if all sorts of funny fruits were going to fall into your hands."

The word "sensuous" had the effect of further disquieting

Tom, but before he could invent a protest the coupé came to a stop, and Daisy signalled us to draw up alongside.

"Where are we going?" she cried.

"How about the movies?"

"It's so hot," she complained. "You go. We'll ride around and meet you after." With an effort her wit rose faintly. "We'll meet you on some corner. I'll be the man smoking two cigarettes."

"We can't argue about it here," Tom said impatiently, as a truck gave out a cursing whistle behind us. "You follow me to the south side of Central Park, in front of the Plaza."

Several times he turned his head and looked back for their car, and if the traffic delayed them he slowed up until they came into sight. I think he was afraid they would dart down a side street and out of his life forever.

But they didn't. And we all took the less explicable step of engaging the parlor of a suite in the Plaza Hotel.

The prolonged and tumultuous argument that ended by herding us into that room eludes me, though I have a sharp physical memory that, in the course of it, my underwear kept climbing like a damp snake around my legs and intermittent beads of sweat raced cool across my back. The notion originated with Daisy's suggestion that we hire five bathrooms and take cold baths, and then assumed more tangible form as "a place to have a mint julep." Each of us said over and over that it was a "crazy idea"—we all talked at once to a baffled clerk and thought, or pretended to think, that we were being very funny . . .

The room was large and stifling, and, though it was already four o'clock, opening the windows admitted only a gust of hot shrubbery from the Park. Daisy went to the mirror and stood with her back to us, fixing her hair.

"It's a swell suite," whispered Jordan respectfully, and everyone laughed.

"Open another window," commanded Daisy, without turning around.

"There aren't any more."

"Well, we'd better telephone for an axe——"

"The thing to do is to forget about the heat," said Tom impatiently. "You make it ten times worse by crabbing about it."

He unrolled the bottle of whiskey from the towel and put it on the table.

"Why not let her alone, old sport?" remarked Gatsby. "You're the one that wanted to come to town."

There was a moment of silence. The telephone book slipped from its nail and splashed to the floor, whereupon Jordan whispered, "Excuse me"—but this time no one laughed.

"I'll pick it up," I offered.

"I've got it." Gatsby examined the parted string, muttered "Hum!" in an interested way, and tossed the book on a chair.

"That's a great expression of yours, isn't it?" said Tom sharply.

"What is?"

"All this 'old sport' business. Where'd you pick that up?"

"Now see here, Tom," said Daisy, turning around from the mirror, "if you're going to make personal remarks I won't stay here a minute. Call up and order some ice for the mint julep."

As Tom took up the receiver the compressed heat exploded into sound and we were listening to the portentous chords of Mendelssohn's Wedding March[10] from the ballroom below.

"Imagine marrying anybody in this heat!" cried Jordan dismally.

"Still—I was married in the middle of June," Daisy remembered. "Louisville in June! Somebody fainted. Who was it fainted, Tom?"

"Biloxi," he answered shortly.

"A man named Biloxi. 'Blocks' Biloxi, and he made boxes—that's a fact—and he was from Biloxi, Tennessee."[11]

"They carried him into my house," appended Jordan, "because we lived just two doors from the church. And he stayed three weeks, until Daddy told him he had to get out.

10 Nick refers to the march from the incidental music for *A Midsummer Night's Dream* (1842), by Felix Mendelssohn (1809–1847), usually played as a recessional at weddings. The ceremony downstairs appears to be beginning; the music one might expect to hear would be the "Bridal Chorus" ("Here comes the bride . . .") from *Lohengrin*, by Richard Wagner (1813–1883).

11 Biloxi is a city in Harrison County, Mississippi, on the Gulf Coast. Daisy is perhaps confused.

Opposite: Fitzgerald's Plaza Hotel bill, June 1, 1927. Fittingly, the showdown between Gatsby and Tom Buchanan takes place in the Plaza, an emblem of American money and aristocratic pretension in *The Great Gatsby*. The total bill ($267.70) translates to $4,826.66 in 2025.

The day after he left Daddy died." After a moment she added, as if she might have sounded irreverent, "There wasn't any connection."

"I used to know a Bill Biloxi from Memphis," I remarked.

"That was his cousin. I knew his whole family history before he left. He gave me an aluminum putter that I use today."

The music had died down as the ceremony began and now a long cheer floated in at the window, followed by intermittent cries of "Yea—ea—ea!" and finally by a burst of jazz as the dancing began.

"We're getting old," said Daisy. "If we were young we'd rise and dance."

"Remember Biloxi," Jordan warned her. "Where'd you know him, Tom?"

"Biloxi?" He concentrated with an effort. "I didn't know him. He was a friend of Daisy's."

"He was not," she denied. "I'd never seen him before. He came down in the private car."

"Well, he said he knew you. He said he was raised in Louisville. Asa Bird brought him around at the last minute and asked if we had room for him."

Jordan smiled.

"He was probably bumming his way home. He told me he was president of your class at Yale."

Tom and I looked at each other blankly.

"Biloxi?"

"First place, we didn't have any president——"

Gatsby's foot beat a short, restless tattoo and Tom eyed him suddenly.

"By the way, Mr. Gatsby, I understand you're an Oxford man."

"Not exactly."

"Oh, yes, I understand you went to Oxford."

"Yes—I went there."

A pause. Then Tom's voice, incredulous and insulting:

## Communications

### FALSE AND EXTREMELY UNWISE TRADITION

*Graduate Finds Cause for Fear in Advertisement of Erroneous "Sacred Old Football Tradition."*

TO THE EDITOR OF THE PRINCETONIAN:

Sir:—I see that the fact of a lineman being elected Football Captain is still being sent out to the papers as a "sacred old tradition." As the present writer pointed out in the *Alumni Weekly* last winter, there is no such tradition—Ralph Gilroy was Captain-elect in 1922—and the report serves merely to fill two lines of space for unimaginative Press Club members each year. The point is that I believe it directly responsible for the fact that no first class backs have entered Princeton for four years; where Roper used to make tackles out of extra halfbacks he is now compelled to make fullbacks out of guards and quarterbacks out of air. If anyone believes that rival colleges don't make full use of this alleged discrimination in winning over prospective triple threats, he is simply an innocent; for American boys have a pretty highly developed desire for glory.

It will take five years to kill this rumor, but the Athletic Association has obviously done nothing—and no matter what steps are taken now we can scarcely expect any more Slagles, Miles, Wittmers and Caulkins until 1940.

"SEVENTEEN."

Paris, January 24, 1930.

## JAZZ AGE WRITER MAKES HOME HERE

### F. Scott Fitzgerald to Live Near Edge Moor to Finish His Novel.

F. Scott Fitzgerald, novelist and playwright, has made his home in the old Bradford mansion, "Ellerslie," on the banks of the Delaware river, near Edge Moor.

He moves here with his wife and four-year-old daughter, Frances, and will live here for about two years. For the past few years, Mr. Fitzgerald has been "making the grand tour," living in various places in Europe, particularly in France and Italy.

He chose the site near Wilmington, particularly because he is a personal friend of John Biggs, Jr., lawyer, of this city, and because he wanted a quiet place to finish a novel. The new novel will be a picaresque one, different from his others, which have been emphasizing the current jazz age.

The Bradford house is a spacious Colonial building, with an expansive view of the river.

Mr. Fitzgerald left Princeton University in 1917 to join the army as an officer. His first novel was "This Side of Paradise," published in 1920. This was followed by "The Beautiful and Damned," issued in 1921; "Tales of Jazz Age," 1922; "The Great Gatsby," in 1925; "All the Sad Young Men," 1926.

His play, "The Vegetable," written in 1923, had its premier in Wilmington.

---

THE COPLEY-PLAZA,
BOSTON.
THE GREENBRIER,
WHITE SULPHUR SPRINGS, W. VA.

CABLE ADDRESS, "PLAZA, NEW YORK"
TELEPHONE, PLAZA 1740

NEW YORK      JUN 1 – 1927      192

# THE PLAZA

FIFTH AVENUE AT CENTRAL PARK
58TH TO 59TH STREETS

Mr. F. Scott Fitzgerald,

Ellerslie, Edgemoor, Del.

To THE PLAZA Dr.

ROOM NO. 1662

ACCT. NO. E5903   RATE 11.00

FRED. STERRY,
PRESIDENT.      JOHN D. OWEN,
MANAGER.

May 1927

| DATE | ITEM | AMOUNT | TOTAL | DATE | ITEM | AMOUNT | TOTAL |
|---|---|---|---|---|---|---|---|
| 23 | Rooms | 11.00 | | 26 | Telephone | .10 | |
| | Cash Advance | 10.00 | 21.00 | | Hair Dresser | 4.25 | |
| | | | | | Waiter's Fee | .60 | |
| 24 | Rooms | 11.00 | | | Room Service | 4.05 | 9.00 |
| | Telephone | 1.00 | | | | | |
| | Tel. Suburb. | .30 | | | | | 275.70 |
| | Cash Adv. Taxi | 29.60 | | 24 | Cash, Galvin | | 8.00 |
| | Waiter Fee | 3.00 | | | | | |
| | Cash Advance | 25.00 | | | | | 267.70 |
| | | 100.00 | | | | | |
| | Florist | 4.00 | | | | | |
| | Cigars | .20 | | | | | |
| | Restaurant | 16.60 | | | | | |
| | Room Service | 1.50 | 192.40 | | | | |
| 25 | Rooms | 11.00 | | | | | |
| | Telephone | .90 | | | | | |
| | Tel. Long D. | 1.55 | | | | | |
| | Dr Fee | 10.00 | | | | | |
| | News | 2.35 | | | | | |
| | Valet | 6.50 | | | | | |
| | Florist | 4.00 | | | | | |
| | Waiter's Fee | .50 | | | | | |
| | | .60 | | | | | |
| | | .40 | | | | | |
| | | 2.00 | | | | | |
| | Room Service | .45 | | | | | |
| | | 3.35 | | | | | |
| | | 1.85 | | | | | |
| | | 2.20 | | | | | |
| | | 5.65 | 53.30 | | | | |

THE PLAZA

PAID

JUN – 6 1927

TREASURER'S OFFICE

*Gilbuts adress*
*2 Beekman Place*

**12** "For Tom, as for Stoddard," Walter Benn Michaels remarks, "Gatsby (né Gatz, with his Wolfshiem 'gonnegtion') isn't quite white, and Tom's identification of him as in some sense black suggests the power of the expanded notion of the alien. Gatsby's love for Daisy seems to Tom the expression of something like the impulse to miscegenation." Jeffory A. Clymer takes a similar approach, exploring Gatsby's resemblance to "Latin Lover" Rudolph Valentino and white anxieties about the influx of non-Nordic immigrants in the early twentieth century. See Walter Benn Michaels's *Our America: Nativism, Modernism, and Pluralism* (Duke University Press, 1995), p. 25; and Jeffory A. Clymer's "'Mr. Nobody from Nowhere': Rudolph Valentino, Jay Gatsby, and the End of the American Race," *Genre* 29 (1996), pp. 161–92.

"You must have gone there about the time Biloxi went to New Haven."

Another pause. A waiter knocked and came in with crushed mint and ice but the silence was unbroken by his "thank you" and the soft closing of the door. This tremendous detail was to be cleared up at last.

"I told you I went there," said Gatsby.

"I heard you, but I'd like to know when."

"It was in nineteen-nineteen, I only stayed five months. That's why I can't really call myself an Oxford man."

Tom glanced around to see if we mirrored his unbelief. But we were all looking at Gatsby.

"It was an opportunity they gave to some of the officers after the armistice," he continued. "We could go to any of the universities in England or France."

I wanted to get up and slap him on the back. I had one of those renewals of complete faith in him that I'd experienced before.

Daisy rose, smiling faintly, and went to the table.

"Open the whiskey, Tom," she ordered, "and I'll make you a mint julep. Then you won't seem so stupid to yourself. . . . Look at the mint!"

"Wait a minute," snapped Tom. "I want to ask Mr. Gatsby one more question."

"Go on," Gatsby said politely.

"What kind of a row are you trying to cause in my house anyhow?"

They were out in the open at last and Gatsby was content.

"He isn't causing a row." Daisy looked desperately from one to the other. "You're causing a row. Please have a little self-control."

"Self-control!" repeated Tom incredulously. "I suppose the latest thing is to sit back and let Mr. Nobody from Nowhere make love to your wife. Well, if that's the idea you can count me out. . . . Nowadays people begin by sneering at family life and family institutions, and next they'll throw everything over-board and have intermarriage between black and white."

Flushed with his impassioned gibberish, he saw himself standing alone on the last barrier of civilization.

"We're all white here," murmured Jordan.[12]

"I know I'm not very popular. I don't give big parties. I suppose you've got to make your house into a pigsty in order to have any friends—in the modern world."

Angry as I was, as we all were, I was tempted to laugh whenever he opened his mouth. The transition from libertine to prig was so complete.

"I've got something to tell *you*, old sport—" began Gatsby. But Daisy guessed at his intention.

"Please don't!" she interrupted helplessly. "Please let's all go home. Why don't we all go home?"

"That's a good idea." I got up. "Come on, Tom. Nobody wants a drink."

"I want to know what Mr. Gatsby has to tell me."

"Your wife doesn't love you," said Gatsby. "She's never loved you. She loves me."[13]

"You must be crazy!" exclaimed Tom automatically.

Gatsby sprang to his feet, vivid with excitement.

"She never loved you, do you hear?" he cried. "She only married you because I was poor and she was tired of waiting for me. It was a terrible mistake, but in her heart she never loved anyone except me!"

At this point Jordan and I tried to go, but Tom and Gatsby insisted with competitive firmness that we remain—as though neither of them had anything to conceal and it would be a privilege to partake vicariously of their emotions.

"Sit down, Daisy." Tom's voice groped unsuccessfully for the paternal note. "What's been going on? I want to hear all about it."

"I told you what's been going on," said Gatsby. "Going on for five years—and you didn't know."

13 Anne Margaret Daniel observes: "Fitzgerald's command of language propels the narrative straight through our eyes and minds into our hearts. One word he deploys with precision and passion is 'love' (and its corollaries, like 'loved'). In a novel of less than fifty thousand words, he uses the word love and its forms nearly fifty times—with half coming during the short, cataclysmic scene in the Plaza Hotel in Chapter VII. That scene, though, is the denial of love, the end of love, the dismissal of what Gatsby has felt for Daisy: the end of the relationship that is, quite literally, at the heart of the novel." See Daniel's "The Enduring Power of *Gatsby*," in *Princeton Alumni Weekly* (January 13, 2016).

Theatrical poster for *The Great Gatsby*, a 1926 silent film adaptation (now lost), directed by Irish-born American director Herbert Brenon. *Gatsby* has been adapted to the screen in three subsequent Hollywood productions: in 1949, with Alan Ladd as Jay Gatsby; in 1979, with Robert Redford in the role; and most recently in 2013 by Baz Luhrmann, with Leonardo DiCaprio playing the part of the titular character.

Tom turned to Daisy sharply.

"You've been seeing this fellow for five years?"

"Not seeing," said Gatsby. "No, we couldn't meet. But both of us loved each other all that time, old sport, and you didn't know. I used to laugh sometimes"—but there was no laughter in his eyes—"to think that you didn't know."

"Oh—that's all." Tom tapped his thick fingers together like a clergyman and leaned back in his chair.

"You're crazy!" he exploded. "I can't speak about what happened five years ago, because I didn't know Daisy then—and I'll be damned if I see how you got within a mile of her unless you brought the groceries to the back door. But all the rest of that's a God Damned lie. Daisy loved me when she married me and she loves me now."

"No," said Gatsby, shaking his head.

"She does, though. The trouble is that sometimes she gets foolish ideas in her head and doesn't know what she's doing." He nodded sagely. "And what's more, I love Daisy too. Once in a while I go off on a spree and make a fool of myself, but I always come back, and in my heart I love her all the time."

"You're revolting," said Daisy. She turned to me, and her voice, dropping an octave lower, filled the room with thrilling scorn: "Do you know why we left Chicago? I'm surprised that they didn't treat you to the story of that little spree."

Gatsby walked over and stood beside her.

"Daisy, that's all over now," he said earnestly. "It doesn't matter any more. Just tell him the truth—that you never loved him—and it's all wiped out forever."

She looked at him blindly. "Why—how could I love him—possibly?"

"You never loved him."

She hesitated. Her eyes fell on Jordan and me with a sort of appeal, as though she realized at last what she was doing—and as though she had never, all along, intended doing anything at all. But it was done now. It was too late.

"I never loved him," she said, with perceptible reluctance.

"Not at Kapiolani?"[14] demanded Tom suddenly.

"No."

From the ballroom beneath, muffled and suffocating chords were drifting up on hot waves of air.

"Not that day I carried you down from the Punch Bowl[15] to keep your shoes dry?" There was a husky tenderness in his tone. . . . "Daisy?"

"Please don't." Her voice was cold, but the rancor was gone from it. She looked at Gatsby. "There, Jay," she said—but her hand as she tried to light a cigarette was trembling. Suddenly she threw the cigarette and the burning match on the carpet.

"Oh, you want too much!" she cried to Gatsby. "I love you now—isn't that enough? I can't help what's past." She began to sob helplessly. "I did love him once—but I loved you too."

Gatsby's eyes opened and closed.

**14** A three hundred–acre park in Honolulu, Hawaii, where Tom and Daisy went for their honeymoon.

**15** Extinct volcano crater in Honolulu.

**16** In the summer of 1924, while Scott was hard at work on *The Great Gatsby* in Villa Marie, the house the Fitzgeralds had rented on the hillside outside Valescure, France, Zelda became involved with a French naval aviator named Edouard Jozan, whom she met on one of the nearby St. Raphaël beaches. Maureen Corrigan writes: "If Fitz-gerald had written these bitter scenes pre-Jozan, then rereading them and revising them with Zelda's help—as he did with the entire manuscript of *The Great Gatsby* before sending it to Perkins in October—must have been humiliating. And if he wrote all or some of these passages in the aftermath of Zelda's affair with Jozan, that chronology could account for their punch-in-the-gut intensity." See Corrigan's *So We Read On*, p. 170.

"You loved me *too?*"[16] he repeated.

"Even that's a lie," said Tom savagely. "She didn't know you were alive. Why—there're things between Daisy and me that you'll never know, things that neither of us can ever forget."

The words seemed to bite physically into Gatsby.

"I want to speak to Daisy alone," he insisted. "She's all excited now——"

"Even alone I can't say I never loved Tom," she admitted in a pitiful voice. "It wouldn't be true."

"Of course it wouldn't," agreed Tom.

She turned to her husband.

"As if it mattered to you," she said.

"Of course it matters. I'm going to take better care of you from now on."

"You don't understand," said Gatsby, with a touch of panic. "You're not going to take care of her any more."

"I'm not?" Tom opened his eyes wide and laughed. He could afford to control himself now. "Why's that?"

"Daisy's leaving you."

"Nonsense."

"I am, though," she said with a visible effort.

"She's not leaving me!" Tom's words suddenly leaned down over Gatsby. "Certainly not for a common swindler who'd have to steal the ring he put on her finger."

"I won't stand this!" cried Daisy. "Oh, please let's get out."

"Who are you, anyhow?" broke out Tom. "You're one of that bunch that hangs around with Meyer Wolfshiem—that much I happen to know. I've made a little investigation into your affairs—and I'll carry it further tomorrow."

"You can suit yourself about that, old sport," said Gatsby steadily.

"I found out what your 'drug-stores' were." He turned to us and spoke rapidly. "He and this Wolfshiem bought up a lot of side-street drug-stores here and in Chicago and sold grain alcohol over the counter. That's one of his little stunts. I picked him for a bootlegger[17] the first time I saw him, and I wasn't far wrong."

"What about it?" said Gatsby politely. "I guess your friend Walter Chase wasn't too proud to come in on it."

"And you left him in the lurch, didn't you? You let him go to jail for a month over in New Jersey. God! You ought to hear Walter on the subject of *you*."

"He came to us dead broke. He was very glad to pick up some money, old sport."

"Don't you call me 'old sport'!" cried Tom. Gatsby said nothing. "Walter could have you up on the betting laws too, but Wolfshiem scared him into shutting his mouth."

That unfamiliar yet recognizable look was back again in Gatsby's face.

"That drug-store business was just small change," continued Tom slowly, "but you've got something on now that Walter's afraid to tell me about."

I glanced at Daisy, who was staring terrified between Gatsby and her husband, and at Jordan, who had begun to balance an invisible but absorbing object on the tip of her chin. Then I turned back to Gatsby—and was startled at his expression. He looked—and this is said in all contempt for the babbled slander of his garden—as if he had "killed a man." For a moment the set of his face could be described in just that fantastic way.

It passed, and he began to talk excitedly to Daisy, denying everything, defending his name against accusations that had not been made. But with every word she was drawing further and further into herself, so he gave that up, and only the dead dream fought on as the afternoon slipped away, trying to touch what was no longer tangible, struggling unhappily, undespairingly, toward that lost voice across the room.

The voice begged again to go.

"*Please*, Tom! I can't stand this any more."

Her frightened eyes told that whatever intentions, whatever courage she had had, were definitely gone.

17 While people of Tom Buchanan's set continued to procure the brands and varieties of alcohol they had always favored, those lower on the social scale purchased various decoctions, called "hooch," "bathtub gin," "bust head," and other slang names, from bootleggers and moonshiners.

"You two start on home, Daisy," said Tom. "In Mr. Gatsby's car."

She looked at Tom, alarmed now, but he insisted with magnanimous scorn.

"Go on. He won't annoy you. I think he realizes that his presumptuous little flirtation is over."

They were gone, without a word, snapped out, made accidental, isolated, like ghosts, even from our pity.

After a moment Tom got up and began wrapping the unopened bottle of whiskey in the towel.

"Want any of this stuff? Jordan? . . . Nick?"

I didn't answer.

"Nick?" He asked again.

"What?"

"Want any?"

"No . . . I just remembered that today's my birthday."

I was thirty. Before me stretched the portentous, menacing road of a new decade.

It was seven o'clock when we got into the coupé with him and started for Long Island. Tom talked incessantly, exulting and laughing, but his voice was as remote from Jordan and me as the foreign clamor on the sidewalk or the tumult of the elevated overhead. Human sympathy has its limits, and we were content to let all their tragic arguments fade with the city lights behind. Thirty—the promise of a decade of loneliness, a thinning list of single men to know, a thinning brief-case of enthusiasm, thinning hair. But there was Jordan beside me, who, unlike Daisy, was too wise ever to carry well-forgotten dreams from age to age. As we passed over the dark bridge her wan face fell lazily against my coat's shoulder and the formidable stroke of thirty died away with the reassuring pressure of her hand.

So we drove on toward death through the cooling twilight.

The young Greek, Michaelis, who ran the coffee joint beside the ashheaps was the principal witness at the inquest. He had slept through the heat until after five, when he strolled over to the garage, and found George Wilson sick in his office—really sick, pale as his own pale hair and shaking all over. Michaelis advised him to go to bed, but Wilson refused, saying that he'd miss a lot of business if he did. While his neighbor was trying to persuade him a violent racket broke out overhead.

"I've got my wife locked in up there," explained Wilson calmly. "She's going to stay there till the day after tomorrow, and then we're going to move away."

Michaelis was astonished; they had been neighbors for four years, and Wilson had never seemed faintly capable of such a statement. Generally he was one of these worn-out men: when he wasn't working, he sat on a chair in the doorway and stared at the people and the cars that passed along the road. When anyone spoke to him he invariably laughed in an agreeable, colorless way. He was his wife's man and not his own.

So naturally Michaelis tried to find out what had happened, but Wilson wouldn't say a word—instead he began to throw curious, suspicious glances at his visitor and ask him what he'd been doing at certain times on certain days. Just as the latter was getting uneasy, some workmen came past the door bound for his restaurant, and Michaelis took the opportunity to get away, intending to come back later. But he didn't. He supposed he forgot to, that's all. When he came outside again, a little after seven, he was reminded of the conversation because he heard Mrs. Wilson's voice, loud and scolding, downstairs in the garage.

"Beat me!" he heard her cry. "Throw me down and beat me, you dirty little coward!"

A moment later she rushed out into the dusk, waving her hands and shouting—before he could move from his door the business was over.

The "death car," as the newspapers called it, didn't stop; it came out of the gathering darkness, wavered tragically for a moment, and then disappeared around the next bend. Michaelis wasn't even sure of its color—he told the first policeman that it was light green. The other car, the one going toward New York, came to rest a hundred yards beyond, and its driver hurried back to where Myrtle Wilson, her life violently extinguished, knelt in the road and mingled her thick dark blood with the dust.

Michaelis and this man reached her first, but when they had torn open her shirtwaist, still damp with perspiration, they saw that her left breast was swinging loose like a flap, and there was no need to listen for the heart beneath. The mouth was wide open and ripped at the corners, as though she had choked a little in giving up the tremendous vitality she had stored so long.

———

We saw the three or four automobiles and the crowd when we were still some distance away.

"Wreck!" said Tom. "That's good. Wilson'll have a little business at last."

He slowed down, but still without any intention of stopping, until, as we came nearer, the hushed, intent faces of the people at the garage door made him automatically put on the brakes.

"We'll take a look," he said doubtfully, "just a look."

I became aware now of a hollow, wailing sound which issued incessantly from the garage, a sound which as we got out of the coupé and walked toward the door resolved itself into the words "Oh, my God!" uttered over and over in a gasping moan.

"There's some bad trouble here," said Tom excitedly.

He reached up on tiptoes and peered over a circle of heads into the garage, which was lit only by a yellow light in a swinging wire basket overhead. Then he made a harsh sound in his

Here:  Sat Oct 15 3.

throat, and with a violent thrusting movement of his powerful arms pushed his way through.

The circle closed up again with a running murmur of expostulation; it was a minute before I could see anything at all. Then new arrivals disarranged the line, and Jordan and I were pushed suddenly inside.

Myrtle Wilson's body, wrapped in a blanket, and then in another blanket, as though she suffered from a chill in the hot night, lay on a work table by the wall, and Tom, with his back to us, was bending over it, motionless. Next to him stood a motorcycle policeman taking down names with much sweat and correction in a little book. At first I couldn't find the source of the high, groaning words that echoed clamorously through the bare garage—then I saw Wilson standing on the raised threshold of his office, swaying back and forth and holding to

Glass slide from 1926 silent film adaptation of *The Great Gatsby*.

the doorposts with both hands. Some man was talking to him in a low voice and attempting, from time to time, to lay a hand on his shoulder, but Wilson neither heard nor saw. His eyes would drop slowly from the swinging light to the laden table by the wall, and then jerk back to the light again, and he gave out incessantly his high, horrible call:

"Oh, my Ga-od! Oh, my Ga-od! Oh, Ga-od! Oh, my Ga-od!"

Presently Tom lifted his head with a jerk and, after staring around the garage with glazed eyes, addressed a mumbled incoherent remark to the policeman.

"M-a-v—" the policeman was saying, "—o——"

"No, r—" corrected the man, "M-a-v-r-o——"

"Listen to me!" muttered Tom fiercely.

"r—" said the policeman, "o——"

"g——"

"g—" He looked up as Tom's broad hand fell sharply on his shoulder. "What you want, fella?"

"What happened?—that's what I want to know."

"Auto hit her. Ins'antly killed."

"Instantly killed," repeated Tom, staring.

"She ran out ina road. Son-of-a-bitch didn't even stopus car."

"There was two cars," said Michaelis, "one comin', one goin', see?"

"Going where?" asked the policeman keenly.

"One goin' each way. Well, she"—his hand rose toward the blankets but stopped half way and fell to his side—"she ran out there an' the one comin' from N'York knock right into her, goin' thirty or forty miles an hour."

"What's the name of this place here?" demanded the officer.

"Hasn't got any name."

A pale well-dressed negro stepped near.

"It was a yellow car," he said, "big yellow car. New."

"See the accident?" asked the policeman.

"No, but the car passed me down the road, going faster'n forty. Going fifty, sixty."

"Come here and let's have your name. Look out now. I want to get his name."[18]

Some words of this conversation must have reached Wilson, swaying in the office door, for suddenly a new theme found voice among his gasping cries:

"You don't have to tell me what kind of car it was! I know what kind of car it was!"

Watching Tom, I saw the wad of muscle back of his shoulder tighten under his coat. He walked quickly over to Wilson and, standing in front of him, seized him firmly by the upper arms.

"You've got to pull yourself together," he said with soothing gruffness.

Wilson's eyes fell upon Tom; he started up on his tiptoes and then would have collapsed to his knees had not Tom held him upright.

"Listen," said Tom, shaking him a little. "I just got here a minute ago, from New York. I was bringing you that coupé we've been talking about. That yellow car I was driving this afternoon wasn't mine—do you hear? I haven't seen it all afternoon."

Only the negro and I were near enough to hear what he said, but the policeman caught something in the tone and looked over with truculent eyes.

"What's all that?" he demanded.

"I'm a friend of his." Tom turned his head but kept his hands firm on Wilson's body. "He says he knows the car that did it. . . . It was a yellow car."

Some dim impulse moved the policeman to look suspiciously at Tom.

"And what color's your car?"

"It's a blue car, a coupé."

"We've come straight from New York," I said.

Someone who had been driving a little behind us confirmed this, and the policeman turned away.

"Now, if you'll let me have that name again correct——"

18 This exchange between the police officer and the nameless "well-dressed negro" has been largely overlooked by scholars who have explored the novel's concerns with race and ethnicity. Emily Moore Harrison offers this observation: "The black witness claims that he saw the car on the road, and he would have, it seems, been able to give more information about the driver (and passenger), which suggests the possibility of an alternative ending had the man been acknowledged. However, he is silently pushed aside and, subsequently, ignored." See Emily Moore Harrison's "Beyond Black and White: Visualizing Cultural Identity Amidst Racial Anxiety and Nativism in American Modernist Novels," Master's Thesis, University of Tennessee (2017), p. 22.

Picking up Wilson like a doll, Tom carried him into the office, set him down in a chair, and came back.

"If somebody'll come here and sit with him," he snapped authoritatively. He watched while the two men standing closest glanced at each other and went unwillingly into the room. Then Tom shut the door on them and came down the single step, his eyes avoiding the table. As he passed close to me he whispered: "Let's get out."

Self-consciously, with his authoritative arms breaking the way, we pushed through the still gathering crowd, passing a hurried doctor, case in hand, who had been sent for in wild hope half an hour ago.

Tom drove slowly until we were beyond the bend—then his foot came down hard, and the coupé raced along through the night. In a little while I heard a low husky sob, and saw that the tears were overflowing down his face.

"The God Damn coward!" he whimpered. "He didn't even stop his car."

⸻

The Buchanans' house floated suddenly toward us through the dark rustling trees. Tom stopped beside the porch and looked up at the second floor, where two windows bloomed with light among the vines.

"Daisy's home," he said. As we got out of the car he glanced at me and frowned slightly.

"I ought to have dropped you in West Egg, Nick. There's nothing we can do tonight."

A change had come over him, and he spoke gravely, and with decision. As we walked across the moonlit gravel to the porch he disposed of the situation in a few brisk phrases.

"I'll telephone for a taxi to take you home, and while you're waiting you and Jordan better go in the kitchen and have them get you some supper—if you want any." He opened the door. "Come in."

taxi-starters in front of hotels lined up as bookmakers,
squeezing money out of taxi-drivers and ~~that~~ drunks
and the poor ~~that~~ bums hang the streets around. And
every night one of Wolfsheim's men collected the
money, He ~~looked~~ turned to Gatsby ~~disdainfully~~ with a sneer, "Who went
to jail for you when the police stopped that game?"

The ~~peculiar~~ unfamiliar yet recognizable
look that I had seen for the first time three
hours before ~~was~~ was back again into Gatsby's face (?)

"That was just small change," continued Tom
slowly, "~~~~ But you've got something on now that
~~~~ Walter's afraid to tell me about."

Then a peculiar ~~and rather~~ thing
thing happened. I looked at Daisy who was staring ~~~~
terrified between Gatsby and her husband ~~with frightened
eyes~~ and at Jordan who had begun to balance
something, carefully and precisely, leaning back
in her chair. Then I turned back to Gatsby—and found
him looking as if he'd killed a man! His eyes
were wide open and fixed ~~~~
~~~~ fixed as though upon an
absence of deep, an unoccupied human shape that
was conceivably his own shape, with a sort of terrified despair. ~~~~
~~~~ They and now had only derision for the
babbled slander in his garden but the the expression itself
couldn't be described any other way.

Then it passed, and his confidence with
it. The failure was complete. He ~~struggled~~ spoke talked for

"No, thanks. But I'd be glad if you'd order me the taxi. I'll wait outside."

Jordan put her hand on my arm.

"Won't you come in, Nick?"

"No, thanks."

I was feeling a little sick and I wanted to be alone. But Jordan lingered for a moment more.

"It's only half past nine," she said.

I'd be damned if I'd go in; I'd had enough of all of them for one day, and suddenly that included Jordan too. She must have seen something of this in my expression, for she turned abruptly away and ran up the porch steps into the house. I sat down for a few minutes with my head in my hands, until I heard the phone taken up inside and the butler's voice calling a taxi. Then I walked slowly down the drive away from the house, intending to wait by the gate.

I hadn't gone twenty yards when I heard my name and Gatsby stepped from between two bushes into the path. I must have felt pretty weird by that time, because I could think of nothing except the luminosity of his pink suit under the moon.

"What are you doing?" I inquired.

"Just standing here, old sport."

Somehow, that seemed a despicable occupation. For all I knew he was going to rob the house in a moment; I wouldn't have been surprised to see sinister faces, the faces of "Wolfshiem's people," behind him in the dark shrubbery.

"Did you see any trouble on the road?" he asked after a minute.

"Yes."

He hesitated.

"Was she killed?"

"Yes."

"I thought so; I told Daisy I thought so. It's better that the shock should all come at once. She stood it pretty well."

He spoke as if Daisy's reaction was the only thing that mattered.

"I got to West Egg by a side road," he went on, "and left the car in my garage. I don't think anybody saw us, but of course I can't be sure."

I disliked him so much by this time that I didn't find it necessary to tell him he was wrong.

"Who was the woman?" he inquired.

"Her name was Wilson. Her husband owns the garage. How the devil did it happen?"

"Well, I tried to swing the wheel—" He broke off, and suddenly I guessed at the truth.

"Was Daisy driving?"

"Yes," he said after a moment, "but of course I'll say I was. You see, when we left New York she was very nervous and she thought it would steady her to drive—and this woman rushed out at us just as we were passing a car coming the other way. It all happened in a minute, but it seemed to me that she wanted to speak to us, thought we were somebody she knew. Well, first Daisy turned away from the woman toward the other car, and then she lost her nerve and turned back. The second my hand reached the wheel I felt the shock—it must have killed her instantly."

"It ripped her open——"

"Don't tell me, old sport." He winced. "Anyhow—Daisy stepped on it. I tried to make her stop, but she couldn't, so I pulled on the emergency brake. Then she fell over into my lap and I drove on.

"She'll be all right tomorrow," he said presently. "I'm just going to wait here and see if he tries to bother her about that unpleasantness this afternoon. She's locked herself into her room, and if he tries any brutality she's going to turn the light out and on again."

"He won't touch her," I said. "He's not thinking about her."

"I don't trust him, old sport."

"How long are you going to wait?"

"All night, if necessary. Anyhow, till they all go to bed."

A new point of view occurred to me. Suppose Tom found out that Daisy had been driving. He might think he saw a connection in it—he might think anything. I looked at the house; there were two or three bright windows downstairs and the pink glow from Daisy's room on the second floor.

"You wait here," I said. "I'll see if there's any sign of a commotion."

I walked back along the border of the lawn, traversed the gravel softly, and tiptoed up the veranda steps. The drawing-room curtains were open, and I saw that the room was empty. Crossing the porch where we had dined that June night three months before, I came to a small rectangle of light which I guessed was the pantry window. The blind was drawn, but I found a rift at the sill.

Daisy and Tom were sitting opposite each other at the kitchen table, with a plate of cold fried chicken between them, and two bottles of ale. He was talking intently across the table at her, and in his earnestness his hand had fallen upon and covered her own. Once in a while she looked up at him and nodded in agreement.

They weren't happy, and neither of them had touched the chicken or the ale—and yet they weren't unhappy either. There was an unmistakable air of natural intimacy about the picture, and anybody would have said that they were conspiring together.

As I tiptoed from the porch I heard my taxi feeling its way along the dark road toward the house. Gatsby was waiting where I had left him in the drive.

"Is it all quiet up there?" he asked anxiously.

"Yes, it's all quiet." I hesitated. "You'd better come home and get some sleep."

He shook his head.

"I want to wait here till Daisy goes to bed. Good night, old sport."

He put his hands in his coat pockets and turned back eagerly to his scrutiny of the house, as though my presence marred the sacredness of the vigil. So I walked away and left him standing there in the moonlight—watching over nothing.

Page from Fitzgerald's photo album, with snapshot of Empire State Building and inscription "HOME AGAIN." During his years in Europe, from the mid-1920s until the early 1930s, Fitzgerald lost touch with New York. When he returned after the crash, the city seemed to him "an echoing tomb." Viewing Manhattan from the top of the recently completed Empire State Building, he experienced an epiphany of sorts: "I had discovered the crowning error of the city, its Pandora's box. Full of vaunting pride, the New Yorker had climbed here and seen with dismay what he had never suspected, that the city was not the endless succession of canyons that he had supposed but that it had limits—from the tallest structure he saw for the first time that it faded out into country on all sides, into an expanse of green and blue that alone was limitless. And with that awful realization that New York was a city after all and not a universe, the whole edifice that he had reared in his imagination came crashing to the ground." See "My Lost City," in *The Crack-Up*, p. 32.

# CHAPTER VIII

I couldn't sleep all night; a fog-horn was groaning incessantly on the Sound, and I tossed half sick between grotesque reality and savage, frightening dreams. Toward dawn I heard a taxi go up Gatsby's drive, and immediately I jumped out of bed and began to dress—I felt that I had something to tell him, something to warn him about, and morning would be too late.

Crossing his lawn, I saw that his front door was still open and he was leaning against a table in the hall, heavy with dejection or sleep.

"Nothing happened," he said wanly. "I waited, and about four o'clock she came to the window and stood there for a minute and then turned out the light."

His house had never seemed so enormous to me as it did that night when we hunted through the great rooms for cigarettes. We pushed aside curtains that were like pavilions, and felt over innumerable feet of dark wall for electric light switches—once I tumbled with a sort of splash upon the keys of a ghostly piano. There was an inexplicable amount of dust everywhere, and the rooms were musty, as though they hadn't been aired for many days. I found the humidor on an unfamiliar table, with two stale, dry cigarettes inside. Throwing open the French windows of the drawing-room, we sat smoking out into the darkness.

"You ought to go away," I said. "It's pretty certain they'll trace your car."

"Go away *now*, old sport?"

"Go to Atlantic City for a week, or up to Montreal."

He wouldn't consider it. He couldn't possibly leave Daisy

1 An earlier but readily recognizable version of this passage appears in the magazine text of Fitzgerald's story "Winter Dreams," published in *Metropolitan Magazine* (December 1922). Like many writers, Fitzgerald was a magpie: he often took material from his stories and reused it in his novels, but he was careful to delete or rewrite a passage when the story was later included in one of his collections, as he did here, eliminating the passage from the version of "Winter Dreams" that appears in *All the Sad Young Men* (1926). In a letter of early June 1925 to Maxwell Perkins, Fitzgerald refers to "Winter Dreams" as "A sort of 1st draft of the Gatsby idea." Bryant Mangum writes: "The more closely one looks at the *Metropolitan* version of 'Winter Dreams' the more obvious becomes its importance as perhaps the earliest stage in Fitzgerald's conceptualizing of *The Great Gatsby* and his use of 'Winter Dreams' as a springboard into the holograph manuscript." See Mangum's "*Metropolitan*'s 'Winter Dreams' and *The Great Gatsby*," *F. Scott Fitzgerald Review* 19 (2021), pp. 54–66. The *Metropolitan* text of "Winter Dreams" is available in James L. W. West III's *The Perfect Hour*, pp. 156–91.

until he knew what she was going to do. He was clutching at some last hope and I couldn't bear to shake him free.

It was this night that he told me the strange story of his youth with Dan Cody—told it to me because "Jay Gatsby" had broken up like glass against Tom's hard malice, and the long secret extravaganza was played out. I think that he would have acknowledged anything now, without reserve, but he wanted to talk about Daisy.

She was the first "nice" girl he had ever known. In various unrevealed capacities he had come in contact with such people, but always with indiscernible barbed wire between. He found her excitingly desirable. He went to her house, at first with other officers from Camp Taylor, then alone. It amazed him—he had never been in such a beautiful house before. But what gave it an air of breathless intensity was that Daisy lived there—it was as casual a thing to her as his tent out at camp was to him. There was a ripe mystery about it, a hint of bedrooms upstairs more beautiful and cool than other bedrooms, of gay and radiant activities taking place through its corridors, and of romances that were not musty and laid away already in lavender but fresh and breathing and redolent of this year's shining motor-cars and of dances whose flowers were scarcely withered. It excited him, too, that many men had already loved Daisy—it increased her value in his eyes. He felt their presence all about the house, pervading the air with the shades and echoes of still vibrant emotions.[1]

But he knew that he was in Daisy's house by a colossal accident. However glorious might be his future as Jay Gatsby, he was at present a penniless young man without a past, and at any moment the invisible cloak of his uniform might slip from his shoulders. So he made the most of his time. He took what he could get, ravenously and unscrupulously—eventually he took Daisy one still October night, took her because he had no real right to touch her hand.

He might have despised himself, for he had certainly taken

her under false pretenses. I don't mean that he had traded on his phantom millions, but he had deliberately given Daisy a sense of security; he let her believe that he was a person from much the same strata as herself—that he was fully able to take care of her. As a matter of fact, he had no such facilities—he had no comfortable family standing behind him, and he was liable at the whim of an impersonal government to be blown anywhere about the world.

But he didn't despise himself and it didn't turn out as he had imagined. He had intended, probably, to take what he could and go—but now he found that he had committed himself to the following of a grail. He knew that Daisy was extraordinary, but he didn't realize just how extraordinary a "nice" girl could be. She vanished into her rich house, into her rich, full life, leaving Gatsby—nothing. He felt married to her, that was all.

When they met again, two days later, it was Gatsby who was breathless, who was, somehow, betrayed. Her porch was bright with the bought luxury of star-shine; the wicker of the settee squeaked fashionably as she turned toward him and he kissed her curious and lovely mouth. She had caught a cold, and it made her voice huskier and more charming than ever, and Gatsby was overwhelmingly aware of the youth and mystery that wealth imprisons and preserves, of the freshness of many clothes, and of Daisy, gleaming like silver, safe and proud above the hot struggles of the poor.

⚬════⚬

"I can't describe to you how surprised I was to find out I loved her, old sport. I even hoped for a while that she'd throw me over, but she didn't, because she was in love with me too. She thought I knew a lot because I knew different things from her . . . Well, there I was, way off my ambitions, getting deeper in love every minute, and all of a sudden I didn't care. What was the use of doing great things if I could have a better time telling her what I was going to do?"

**2** Early blues tune by American songwriter and pianist W. C. Handy (1873–1958), first published in 1917. A sampling of the lyrics:

If Beale Street could talk, if Beale Street
  could talk,
Married men would have to take their
  beds and walk,
Except one or two who never drink
  booze
And the blind man on the corner singing
  "Beale Street Blues!"

I'd rather be there than any place I know
I'd rather be there than any place I know
It's gonna take a sergeant for to make
  me go!

I'm goin' to the river, maybe by and by,
Yes, I'm goin' to the river, maybe by and
  by,
Because the river's wet, and Beale
  Street's done gone dry!

On the last afternoon before he went abroad, he sat with Daisy in his arms for a long, silent time. It was a cold fall day, with fire in the room and her cheeks flushed. Now and then she moved and he changed his arm a little, and once he kissed her dark shining hair. The afternoon had made them tranquil for a while, as if to give them a deep memory for the long parting the next day promised. They had never been closer in their month of love, nor communicated more profoundly one with another, than when she brushed silent lips against his coat's shoulder or when he touched the end of her finger, gently, as though she were asleep.

He did extraordinarily well in the war. He was a captain before he went to the front, and following the Argonne battles he got his majority and the command of the divisional machine-guns. After the armistice he tried frantically to get home, but some complication or misunderstanding sent him to Oxford instead. He was worried now—there was a quality of nervous despair in Daisy's letters. She didn't see why he couldn't come. She was feeling the pressure of the world outside, and she wanted to see him and feel his presence beside her and be reassured that she was doing the right thing after all.

For Daisy was young and her artificial world was redolent of orchids and pleasant, cheerful snobbery and orchestras which set the rhythm of the year, summing up the sadness and suggestiveness of life in new tunes. All night the saxophones wailed the hopeless comment of the "Beale Street Blues"[2] while a hundred pairs of golden and silver slippers shuffled the shining dust. At the gray tea hour there were always rooms that throbbed incessantly with this low, sweet fever, while fresh faces drifted here and there like rose petals blown by the sad horns around the floor.

Through this twilight universe Daisy began to move again with the season; suddenly she was again keeping half a dozen dates a day with half a dozen men, and drowsing asleep at dawn with the beads and chiffon of an evening dress tangled among dying orchids on the floor beside her bed. And all the time something within her was crying for a decision. She wanted her life shaped now, immediately—and the decision must be made by some force—of love, of money, of unquestionable practicality—that was close at hand.

That force took shape in the middle of spring with the arrival of Tom Buchanan. There was a wholesome bulkiness about his person and his position, and Daisy was flattered. Doubtless there was a certain struggle and a certain relief. The letter reached Gatsby while he was still at Oxford.

⌒══⌒

It was dawn now on Long Island and we went about opening the rest of the windows downstairs, filling the house with gray-turning, gold-turning light. The shadow of a tree fell abruptly across the dew and ghostly birds began to sing among the blue leaves. There was a slow, pleasant movement in the air, scarcely a wind, promising a cool, lovely day.

"I don't think she ever loved him." Gatsby turned around from a window and looked at me challengingly. "You must remember, old sport, she was very excited this afternoon. He told her those things in a way that frightened her—that made it look as if I was some kind of cheap sharper. And the result was she hardly knew what she was saying."

He sat down gloomily.

"Of course she might have loved him just for a minute, when they were first married—and loved me more even then, do you see?"

Suddenly he came out with a curious remark.

"In any case," he said, "it was just personal."[3]

What could you make of that, except to suspect some intensity in his conception of the affair that couldn't be measured?

He came back from France when Tom and Daisy were still

3 Lionel Trilling calls Gatsby's odd remark "overwhelming in its intellectual audacity. . . . With that sentence [Gatsby] achieves an insane greatness, convincing us that he really is a Platonic conception of himself, really some sort of Son of God." Trilling, "F. Scott Fitzgerald," in *The Liberal Imagination*, p. 252.

on their wedding trip, and made a miserable but irresistible journey to Louisville on the last of his army pay. He stayed there a week, walking the streets where their footsteps had clicked together through the November night and revisiting the out-of-the-way places to which they had driven in her white car. Just as Daisy's house had always seemed to him more mysterious and gay than other houses, so his idea of the city itself, even though she was gone from it, was pervaded with a melancholy beauty.

He left feeling that if he had searched harder, he might have found her—that he was leaving her behind. The day- coach—he was penniless now—was hot. He went out to the open vestibule and sat down on a folding chair, and the station slid away and the backs of unfamiliar buildings moved by. Then out into the spring fields, where a yellow trolley raced them for a minute with people in it who might once have seen the pale magic of her face along the casual street.

The track curved and now it was going away from the sun, which, as it sank lower, seemed to spread itself in benediction over the vanishing city where she had drawn her breath. He stretched out his hand desperately as if to snatch only a wisp of air, to save a fragment of the spot that she had made lovely for him. But it was all going by too fast now for his blurred eyes and he knew that he had lost that part of it, the freshest and the best, forever.

It was nine o'clock when we finished breakfast and went out on the porch. The night had made a sharp difference in the weather and there was an autumn flavor in the air. The gardener, the last one of Gatsby's former servants, came to the foot of the steps.

"I'm going to drain the pool today, Mr. Gatsby. Leaves'll start falling pretty soon, and then there's always trouble with the pipes."

"Don't do it today," Gatsby answered. He turned to me apologetically. "You know, old sport, I've never used that pool all summer?"

I looked at my watch and stood up.

"Twelve minutes to my train."

I didn't want to go to the city. I wasn't worth a decent stroke of work, but it was more than that—I didn't want to leave Gatsby. I missed that train, and then another, before I could get myself away.

"I'll call you up," I said finally.

"Do, old sport."

"I'll call you about noon."

We walked slowly down the steps.

"I suppose Daisy'll call too." He looked at me anxiously, as if he hoped I'd corroborate this.

"I suppose so."

"Well, good-by."

We shook hands and I started away. Just before I reached the hedge I remembered something and turned around.

"They're a rotten crowd," I shouted across the lawn. "You're worth the whole damn bunch put together."

I've always been glad I said that. It was the only compliment I ever gave him, because I disapproved of him from beginning to end. First he nodded politely, and then his face broke into that radiant and understanding smile, as if we'd been in ecstatic cahoots on that fact all the time. His gorgeous pink rag of a suit made a bright spot of color against the white steps, and I thought of the night when I first came to his ancestral home, three months before. The lawn and drive had been crowded with the faces of those who guessed at his corruption—and he had stood on those steps, concealing his incorruptible dream, as he waved them good-by.

I thanked him for his hospitality. We were always thanking him for that—I and the others.

"Good-by," I called. "I enjoyed breakfast, Gatsby."

4 During the early 1920s most telephones were not equipped with mechanisms for dialing. (Rotary dialing was first offered to American consumers only in 1919.) One gave the number to an operator at a "Central" office who placed the call through a switchboard. For long-distance calls (Gatsby receives several in the novel) the line had to be cleared in advance through several interchanges, even for rotary dial phones.

Up in the city, I tried for a while to list the quotations on an interminable amount of stock, then I fell asleep in my swivel chair. Just before noon the phone woke me, and I started up with sweat breaking out on my forehead. It was Jordan Baker; she often called me up at this hour because the uncertainty of her own movements between hotels and clubs and private houses made her hard to find in any other way. Usually her voice came over the wire as something fresh and cool, as if a divot from a green golf-links had come sailing in at the office window, but this morning it seemed harsh and dry.

"I've left Daisy's house," she said. "I'm at Hempstead, and I'm going down to Southampton this afternoon."

Probably it had been tactful to leave Daisy's house, but the act annoyed me, and her next remark made me rigid.

"You weren't so nice to me last night."

"How could it have mattered then?"

Silence for a moment. Then:

"However—I want to see you."

"I want to see you, too."

"Suppose I don't go to Southampton, and come into town this afternoon?"

"No—I don't think this afternoon."

"Very well."

"It's impossible this afternoon. Various——"

We talked like that for a while, and then abruptly we weren't talking any longer. I don't know which of us hung up with a sharp click, but I know I didn't care. I couldn't have talked to her across a tea-table that day if I never talked to her again in this world.

I called Gatsby's house a few minutes later, but the line was busy. I tried four times; finally an exasperated Central[4] told me the wire was being kept open for Long Distance from Detroit. Taking out my time-table, I drew a small circle around the

Operators working a switchboard in New York, circa 1929. By the late nineteenth century, most "Central" operators were women. The job required manual dexterity, concentration, and the ability to speak quickly and clearly.

three-fifty train. Then I leaned back in my chair and tried to think. It was just noon.

⌐————⌐

When I passed the ashheaps on the train that morning I had crossed deliberately to the other side of the car. I supposed there'd be a curious crowd around there all day with little boys searching for dark spots in the dust, and some garrulous man telling over and over what had happened, until it became less and less real even to him and he could tell it no longer, and Myrtle Wilson's tragic achievement was forgotten. Now I want to go back a little and tell what happened at the garage after we left there the night before.

They had difficulty in locating the sister, Catherine. She must have broken her rule against drinking that night, for when she arrived she was stupid with liquor and unable to understand that the ambulance had already gone to Flushing. When they convinced her of this, she immediately fainted, as if that was the intolerable part of the affair. Someone, kind or curious, took her in his car and drove her in the wake of her sister's body.

Until long after midnight a changing crowd lapped up against the front of the garage, while George Wilson rocked himself back and forth on the couch inside. For a while the door of the office was open, and everyone who came into the garage glanced irresistibly through it. Finally someone said it was a shame, and closed the door. Michaelis and several other men were with him; first, four or five men, later two or three men. Still later Michaelis had to ask the last stranger to wait there fifteen minutes longer, while he went back to his own place and made a pot of coffee. After that, he stayed there alone with Wilson until dawn.

About three o'clock the quality of Wilson's incoherent muttering changed—he grew quieter and began to talk about the yellow car. He announced that he had a way of finding out whom the yellow car belonged to, and then he blurted out that a couple of months ago his wife had come from the city with her face bruised and her nose swollen.

But when he heard himself say this, he flinched and began to cry "Oh, my God!" again in his groaning voice. Michaelis made a clumsy attempt to distract him.

"How long have you been married, George? Come on there, try and sit still a minute and answer my question. How long have you been married?"

"Twelve years."

"Ever had any children? Come on, George, sit still—I asked you a question. Did you ever have any children?"

The hard brown beetles kept thudding against the dull light, and whenever Michaelis heard a car go tearing along the road outside it sounded to him like the car that hadn't stopped a few hours before. He didn't like to go into the garage, because the work bench was stained where the body had been lying, so he moved uncomfortably around the office—he knew every object in it before morning—and from time to time sat down beside Wilson trying to keep him more quiet.

"Have you got a church you go to sometimes, George? Maybe even if you haven't been there for a long time? Maybe I could call up the church and get a priest to come over and he could talk to you, see?"

"Don't belong to any."

"You ought to have a church, George, for times like this. You must have gone to church once. Didn't you get married in a church? Listen, George, listen to me. Didn't you get married in a church?"

"That was a long time ago."

The effort of answering broke the rhythm of his rocking— for a moment he was silent. Then the same half knowing, half bewildered look came back into his faded eyes.

"Look in the drawer there," he said, pointing at the desk.

"Which drawer?"

"That drawer—that one."

Michaelis opened the drawer nearest his hand. There was nothing in it but a small, expensive dog-leash, made of leather and braided silver. It was apparently new.

"This?" he inquired, holding it up.

Wilson stared and nodded.

"I found it yesterday afternoon. She tried to tell me about it, but I knew it was something funny."

"You mean your wife bought it?"

"She had it wrapped in tissue paper on her bureau."

Michaelis didn't see anything odd in that, and he gave Wilson a dozen reasons why his wife might have bought the dog-leash. But conceivably Wilson had heard some of these same explanations before, from Myrtle, because he began saying "Oh, my God!" again in a whisper—his comforter left several explanations in the air.

"Then he killed her," said Wilson. His mouth dropped open suddenly.

"Who did?"

"I have a way of finding out."

"You're morbid, George," said his friend. "This has been a

strain to you and you don't know what you're saying. You'd better try and sit quiet till morning."

"He murdered her."

"It was an accident, George."

Wilson shook his head. His eyes narrowed and his mouth widened slightly with the ghost of a superior "Hm!"

"I know," he said definitely. "I'm one of these trusting fellas and I don't think any harm to *no*body, but when I get to know a thing I know it. It was the man in that car. She ran out to speak to him and he wouldn't stop."

Michaelis had seen this too, but it hadn't occurred to him that there was any special significance in it. He believed that Mrs. Wilson had been running away from her husband, rather than trying to stop any particular car.

"How could she of been like that?"

"She's a deep one," said Wilson, as if that answered the question. "Ah-h-h——"

He began to rock again, and Michaelis stood twisting the leash in his hand.

"Maybe you got some friend that I could telephone for, George?"

This was a forlorn hope—he was almost sure that Wilson had no friend: there was not enough of him for his wife. He was glad a little later when he noticed a change in the room, a blue quickening by the window, and realized that dawn wasn't far off. About five o'clock it was blue enough outside to snap off the light.

Wilson's glazed eyes turned out to the ashheaps, where small gray clouds took on fantastic shapes and scurried here and there in the faint dawn wind.

"I spoke to her," he muttered, after a long silence. "I told her she might fool me but she couldn't fool God. I took her to the window"—with an effort he got up and walked to the rear window and leaned with his face pressed against it—"and I said 'God knows what you've been doing, everything you've been doing. You may fool me, but you can't fool God!'"

Standing behind him, Michaelis saw with a shock that he was looking at the eyes of Doctor T. J. Eckleburg, which had just emerged, pale and enormous, from the dissolving night.

"God sees everything," repeated Wilson.

"That's an advertisement,"[5] Michaelis assured him. Something made him turn away from the window and look back into the room. But Wilson stood there a long time, his face close to the window pane, nodding into the twilight.

By six o'clock Michaelis was worn out, and grateful for the sound of a car stopping outside. It was one of the watchers of the night before who had promised to come back, so he cooked breakfast for three, which he and the other man ate together. Wilson was quieter now, and Michaelis went home to sleep; when he awoke four hours later and hurried back to the garage, Wilson was gone.

His movements—he was on foot all the time—were afterward traced to Port Roosevelt and then to Gad's Hill, where he bought a sandwich that he didn't eat, and a cup of coffee. He must have been tired and walking slowly, for he didn't reach Gad's Hill until noon. Thus far there was no difficulty

Billboard sign for Dr. T. J. Eckleburg, still from Baz Luhrmann's *The Great Gatsby* (2013).

5 The short story writer James Alan McPherson's observation is relevant here: "It must be remembered that after Princeton, Fitzgerald worked in advertising, at the Barron Collier agency in New York. His most famous [ad slogan] was 'We keep you clean in Muscatine.'" (The slogan was developed for a steam laundry in Muscatine, Iowa.) McPherson goes on to point out that Fitzgerald had witnessed the transition from a culture based on morality and religion to a secular one based on commerce. See James Alan McPherson in *F. Scott Fitzgerald at 100*, ed. Jackson Bryer, (Quill & Brush, 1996).

in accounting for his time—there were boys who had seen a man "acting sort of crazy," and motorists at whom he stared oddly from the side of the road. Then for three hours he disappeared from view. The police, on the strength of what he said to Michaelis, that he "had a way of finding out," supposed that he spent that time going from garage to garage thereabouts, inquiring for a yellow car. On the other hand, no garage man who had seen him ever came forward, and perhaps he had an easier, surer way of finding out what he wanted to know. By half past two he was in West Egg, where he asked someone the way to Gatsby's house. So by that time he knew Gatsby's name.

At two o'clock Gatsby put on his bathing suit and left word with the butler that if anyone phoned word was to be brought to him at the pool. He stopped at the garage for a pneumatic mattress that had amused his guests during the summer, and the chauffeur helped him pump it up. Then he gave instructions that the open car wasn't to be taken out under any circumstances—and this was strange, because the front right fender needed repair.

Gatsby shouldered the mattress and started for the pool. Once he stopped and shifted it a little, and the chauffeur asked him if he needed help, but he shook his head and in a moment disappeared among the yellowing trees.

No telephone message arrived, but the butler went without his sleep and waited for it until four o'clock—until long after there was anyone to give it to if it came. I have an idea that Gatsby himself didn't believe it would come, and perhaps he no longer cared. If that was true he must have felt that he had lost the old warm world, paid a high price for living too long with a single dream. He must have looked up at an unfamiliar sky through frightening leaves and shivered as he found what a grotesque thing a rose is and how raw the sunlight was

upon the scarcely created grass. A new world, material without being real, where poor ghosts, breathing dreams like air,
drifted fortuitously about . . . like that ashen, fantastic figure
gliding toward him through the amorphous trees.

The chauffeur—he was one of Wolfshiem's protégés—
heard the shots—afterward he could only say that he hadn't
thought anything much about them. I drove from the station
directly to Gatsby's house and my rushing anxiously up the
front steps was the first thing that alarmed anyone. But they
knew then, I firmly believe. With scarcely a word said, four of
us, the chauffeur, butler, gardener, and I, hurried down to the
pool.

There was a faint, barely perceptible movement of the water
as the fresh flow from one end urged its way toward the drain
at the other. With little ripples that were hardly the shadows
of waves, the laden mattress moved irregularly down the pool.
A small gust of wind that scarcely corrugated the surface was
enough to disturb its accidental course with its accidental burden. The touch of a cluster of leaves revolved it slowly, tracing,
like the leg of a compass, a thin red circle in the water.

It was after we started with Gatsby toward the house that
the gardener saw Wilson's body a little way off in the grass,
and the holocaust was complete.

Francis Cugat's sketch of the valley of
ashes, for the dust jacket of *The Great
Gatsby*. Charcoal with pen-and-ink,
watercolor, and gouache on paper. See
other Cugat sketches for the dust jacket
on p. 197.

# CHAPTER IX

After two years I remember the rest of that day, and that night and the next day, only as an endless drill of police and photographers and newspaper men in and out of Gatsby's front door. A rope stretched across the main gate and a policeman by it kept out the curious, but little boys soon discovered that they could enter through my yard, and there were always a few of them clustered open-mouthed about the pool. Someone with a positive manner, perhaps a detective, used the expression "madman" as he bent over Wilson's body that afternoon, and the adventitious authority of his voice set the key for the newspaper reports next morning.

Most of those reports were a nightmare—grotesque, circumstantial, eager, and untrue. When Michaelis's testimony at the inquest brought to light Wilson's suspicions of his wife I thought the whole tale would shortly be served up in racy pasquinade—but Catherine, who might have said anything, didn't say a word. She showed a surprising amount of character about it too—looked at the coroner with determined eyes under that corrected brow of hers, and swore that her sister had never seen Gatsby, that her sister was completely happy with her husband, that her sister had been into no mischief whatever. She convinced herself of it, and cried into her handkerchief, as if the very suggestion was more than she could endure. So Wilson was reduced to a man "deranged by grief" in order that the case might remain in its simplest form. And it rested there.

But all this part of it seemed remote and unessential. I found myself on Gatsby's side, and alone. From the moment I telephoned news of the catastrophe to West Egg Village, every surmise about him, and every practical question, was referred to me. At first I was surprised and confused; then, as he lay in his house and didn't move or breathe or speak, hour upon hour, it grew upon me that I was responsible, because no one else was interested—interested, I mean, with that intense personal interest to which everyone has some vague right at the end.

I called up Daisy half an hour after we found him, called her instinctively and without hesitation. But she and Tom had gone away early that afternoon, and taken baggage with them.

"Left no address?"

"No."

"Say when they'd be back?"

"No."

"Any idea where they are? How I could reach them?"

"I don't know. Can't say."

I wanted to get somebody for him. I wanted to go into the room where he lay and reassure him: "I'll get somebody for you, Gatsby. Don't worry. Just trust me and I'll get somebody for you——"

Meyer Wolfshiem's name wasn't in the phone book. The butler gave me his office address on Broadway, and I called Information, but by the time I had the number it was long after five, and no one answered the phone.

"Will you ring again?"

"I've rung them three times."

"It's very important."

"Sorry. I'm afraid no one's there."

I went back to the drawing-room and thought for an instant that they were chance visitors, all these official people who suddenly filled it. But, as they drew back the sheet and looked at Gatsby with unmoved eyes, his protest continued in my brain:

"Look here, old sport, you've got to get somebody for me. You've got to try hard. I can't go through this alone."

Someone started to ask me questions, but I broke away and

going upstairs looked hastily through the unlocked parts of his desk—he'd never told me definitely that his parents were dead. But there was nothing—only the picture of Dan Cody, a token of forgotten violence, staring down from the wall.

Next morning I sent the butler to New York with a letter to Wolfshiem, which asked for information and urged him to come out on the next train. That request seemed superfluous when I wrote it. I was sure he'd start when he saw the newspapers, just as I was sure there'd be a wire from Daisy before noon—but neither a wire nor Mr. Wolfshiem arrived; no one arrived except more police and photographers and newspaper men. When the butler brought back Wolfshiem's answer I began to have a feeling of defiance, of scornful solidarity between Gatsby and me against them all.

> Dear Mr. Carraway. This has been one of the most terrible shocks of my life to me I hardly can believe it that it is true at all. Such a mad act as that man did should make us all think. I cannot come down now as I am tied up in some very important business and cannot get mixed up in this thing now. If there is anything I can do a little later let me know in a letter by Edgar. I hardly know where I am when I hear about a thing like this and am completely knocked down and out.
>
> Yours truly
>
> MEYER WOLFSHIEM

and then hasty addenda beneath:

> Let me know about the funeral etc do not know his family at all.

When the phone rang that afternoon and Long Distance said Chicago was calling I thought this would be Daisy at last. But the connection came through as a man's voice, very thin and far away.

"This is Slagle speaking . . ."

"Yes?" The name was unfamiliar.

"Hell of a note, isn't it? Get my wire?"

"There haven't been any wires."

"Young Parke's in trouble," he said rapidly. "They picked him up when he handed the bonds over the counter. They got a circular from New York giving 'em the numbers just five minutes before. What d'you know about that, hey? You never can tell in these hick towns———"

"Hello!" I interrupted breathlessly. "Look here—this isn't Mr. Gatsby. Mr. Gatsby's dead."

There was a long silence on the other end of the wire, followed by an exclamation . . . then a quick squawk as the connection was broken.

———

I think it was on the third day that a telegram signed Henry C. Gatz arrived from a town in Minnesota. It said only that the sender was leaving immediately and to postpone the funeral until he came.

It was Gatsby's father, a solemn old man, very helpless and dismayed, bundled up in a long cheap ulster against the warm September day. His eyes leaked continuously with excitement, and when I took the bag and umbrella from his hands he began to pull so incessantly at his sparse gray beard that I had difficulty in getting off his coat. He was on the point of collapse, so I took him into the music-room and made him sit down while I sent for something to eat. But he wouldn't eat, and the glass of milk spilled from his trembling hand.

"I saw it in the Chicago newspaper," he said. "It was all in the Chicago newspaper. I started right away."

"I didn't know how to reach you."

His eyes, seeing nothing, moved ceaselessly about the room.

"It was a madman," he said. "He must have been mad."

"Wouldn't you like some coffee?" I urged him.

"I don't want anything. I'm all right now, Mr.——"

"Carraway."

"Well, I'm all right now. Where have they got Jimmy?"

I took him into the drawing-room, where his son lay, and left him there. Some little boys had come up on the steps and were looking into the hall; when I told them who had arrived, they went reluctantly away.

After a little while Mr. Gatz opened the door and came out, his mouth ajar, his face flushed slightly, his eyes leaking isolated and unpunctual tears. He had reached an age where death no longer has the quality of ghastly surprise, and when he looked around him now for the first time and saw the height and splendor of the hall and the great rooms opening out from it into other rooms, his grief began to be mixed with an awed pride. I helped him to a bedroom upstairs; while he took off his coat and vest I told him that all arrangements had been deferred until he came.

"I didn't know what you'd want, Mr. Gatsby——"

"Gatz is my name."

"——Mr. Gatz. I thought you might want to take the body West."

He shook his head.

"Jimmy always liked it better down East. He rose up to his position in the East. Were you a friend of my boy's, Mr.——?"

"We were close friends."

"He had a big future before him, you know. He was only a young man, but he had a lot of brain power here."

He touched his head impressively, and I nodded.

"If he'd of lived, he'd of been a great man. A man like James J. Hill.[1] He'd of helped build up the country."

"That's true," I said, uncomfortably.

He fumbled at the embroidered coverlet, trying to take it from the bed, and lay down stiffly—was instantly asleep.

That night an obviously frightened person called up, and demanded to know who I was before he would give his name.

"This is Mr. Carraway," I said.

[1] A Canadian American railroad executive and financier (1838–1916) whose base of operations was in Fitzgerald's hometown of St. Paul, Minnesota. Hill, a self-made man, was a hero to many midwestern boys. His thirty-two-room mansion, which contains a ballroom and an art gallery, still stands on Summit Avenue in St. Paul.

Gilded Age mansion of railroad tycoon James J. Hill, on Summit Avenue in St. Paul.

"Oh!" He sounded relieved. "This is Klipspringer."

I was relieved too, for that seemed to promise another friend at Gatsby's grave. I didn't want it to be in the papers and draw a sightseeing crowd, so I'd been calling up a few people myself. They were hard to find.

"The funeral's tomorrow," I said. "Three o'clock, here at the house. I wish you'd tell anybody who'd be interested."

"Oh, I will," he broke out hastily. "Of course I'm not likely to see anybody, but if I do."

His tone made me suspicious.

"Of course you'll be there yourself."

"Well, I'll certainly try. What I called up about is——"

"Wait a minute," I interrupted. "How about saying you'll come?"

"Well, the fact is—the truth of the matter is that I'm

staying with some people up here in Greenwich, and they rather expect me to be with them tomorrow. In fact, there's a sort of picnic or something. Of course I'll do my very best to get away."

I ejaculated an unrestrained "Huh!" and he must have heard me, for he went on nervously:

"What I called up about was a pair of shoes I left there. I wonder if it'd be too much trouble to have the butler send them on. You see, they're tennis shoes, and I'm sort of helpless without them. My address is care of B. F.——"

I didn't hear the rest of the name, because I hung up the receiver.

After that I felt a certain shame for Gatsby—one gentleman to whom I telephoned implied that he had got what he deserved. However, that was my fault, for he was one of those who used to sneer most bitterly at Gatsby on the courage of Gatsby's liquor, and I should have known better than to call him.

The morning of the funeral I went up to New York to see Meyer Wolfshiem; I couldn't seem to reach him any other way. The door that I pushed open, on the advice of an elevator boy, was marked "The Swastika Holding Company,"[2] and at first there didn't seem to be anyone inside. But when I'd shouted "hello" several times in vain, an argument broke out behind a partition, and presently a lovely Jewess appeared at an interior door and scrutinized me with black hostile eyes.

"Nobody's in," she said. "Mr. Wolfshiem's gone to Chicago."

The first part of this was obviously untrue, for someone had begun to whistle "The Rosary,"[3] tunelessly, inside.

"Please say that Mr. Carraway wants to see him."

"I can't get him back from Chicago, can I?"

At this moment a voice, unmistakably Wolfshiem's, called "Stella!" from the other side of the door.

"Leave your name on the desk," she said quickly. "I'll give it to him when he gets back."

"But I know he's there."

[2] Wolfshiem's cover name for his shady business dealings would have resonated differently with readers in 1925, almost a decade before the Nazi party came to power, than it does for us today. What strikes us as prophetic and morbid would have been, then, merely ironic—perhaps little more ironic than Wolfshiem's whistling "The Rosary"—supposing readers made any connection at all between the swastika and the Nazis. While the swastika was adopted as an antisemitic emblem by the Nazis in 1920, it had associations with many cultures and was a familiar, non-threatening design element used in advertisements and logos in the early twentieth century. The Danish brewer Carlsberg, for example, used the swastika on its beer labels until the mid-thirties; and, as Sarah Churchwell has pointed out, the emblem appeared emblazoned on the doors of the Manhattan-based Fay Cab Company in the early twenties. For discussion of Fitzgerald's use of the swastika see Churchwell's *Careless People*, pp. 155–58; and Alan Margolies's "The Maturing of F. Scott Fitzgerald," in *Twentieth Century Literature* 43.1 (1997), pp. 75–93.

[3] Popular sentimental tune written by American composer and pianist Ethelbert Nevin (1862–1901), with lyrics by Robert Cameron Rogers (1862–1912): "The hours I spent with thee, dear heart, / Are as a string of pearls to me; / I count them over, every one apart, / My rosary, my rosary!"

4 The young Jay Gatsby seems to have adapted quickly to his new criminal life. Maureen Corrigan, reflecting on Gatsby's name, observes: "A *gat* is twenties slang for a gun. Certainly, Gatsby must have been packing, at least in the early years of his rise in Meyer Wolfshiem's employ." Corrigan offers a reading of *Gatsby* that is attentive to the novel's "gonnegtions" to the emerging genre of hard-boiled detective fiction: "[T]here's something hard-boiled about [*The Great Gatsby*], an aspect to his poetic masterpiece that derives from the very same urban American sources that inspired the gals-guts-and-guns school of fiction that evolved into the pulp magazines of the early to mid-1920s." One might think, for example, of the shadowy criminal under-world *Gatsby* represents, the scenes of violent death, the novel's obsession with the past, and its sense of fatedness. See Corrigan's *So We Read On*, p. 128.

She took a step toward me and began to slide her hands indignantly up and down her hips.

"You young men think you can force your way in here any time," she scolded. "We're getting sickantired of it. When I say he's in Chicago, he's in Chicago."

I mentioned Gatsby.

"Oh-h!" She looked at me all over again. "Will you just— What was your name?"

She vanished. In a moment Meyer Wolfshiem stood solemnly in the doorway, holding out both hands. He drew me into his office, remarking in a reverent voice that it was a sad time for all of us, and offered me a cigar.

"My memory goes back to when first I met him," he said. "A young major just out of the army and covered over with medals he got in the war. He was so hard up he had to keep on wearing his uniform because he couldn't buy some regular clothes. First time I saw him was when he come into Winebrenner's poolroom at Forty-third Street and asked for a job. He hadn't eat anything for a couple of days. 'Come on have some lunch with me,' I sid. He ate more than four dollars' worth of food in half an hour."4

"Did you start him in business?" I inquired.

"Start him! I made him."

"Oh."

"I raised him up out of nothing, right out of the gutter. I saw right away he was a fine-appearing, gentlemanly young man, and when he told me he was an Oggsford I knew I could use him good. I got him to join up in the American Legion and he used to stand high there. Right off he did some work for a client of mine up to Albany. We were so thick like that in everything"—he held up two bulbous fingers— "always together."

I wondered if this partnership had included the World's Series transaction in 1919.

"Now he's dead," I said after a moment. "You were his

closest friend, so I know you'll want to come to his funeral this afternoon."

"I'd like to come."

"Well, come then."

The hair in his nostrils quivered slightly, and as he shook his head his eyes filled with tears.

"I can't do it—I can't get mixed up in it," he said.

"There's nothing to get mixed up in. It's all over now."

"When a man gets killed I never like to get mixed up in it in any way. I keep out. When I was a young man it was different—if a friend of mine died, no matter how, I stuck with them to the end. You may think that's sentimental, but I mean it—to the bitter end."

I saw that for some reason of his own he was determined not to come, so I stood up.

"Are you a college man?" he inquired suddenly.

For a moment I thought he was going to suggest a "gonnegtion," but he only nodded and shook my hand.

"Let us learn to show our friendship for a man when he is alive and not after he is dead," he suggested. "After that my own rule is to let everything alone."[5]

When I left his office the sky had turned dark and I got back to West Egg in a drizzle. After changing my clothes I went next door and found Mr. Gatz walking up and down excitedly in the hall. His pride in his son and in his son's possessions was continually increasing and now he had something to show me.

"Jimmy sent me this picture." He took out his wallet with trembling fingers. "Look there."

It was a photograph of the house, cracked in the corners and dirty with many hands. He pointed out every detail to me eagerly. "Look there!" and then sought admiration from my eyes. He had shown it so often that I think it was more real to him now than the house itself.

"Jimmy sent it to me. I think it's a very pretty picture. It shows up well."

5 Glossing Wolfshiem's remark, Harold Bloom writes: "Edith Wharton rather nastily praised Fitzgerald for having created the 'perfect Jew' in the gambler Meyer Wolfshiem. Had she peered closer, she might have seen the irony of her patrician prejudice reversed in the ancient Jewish wisdom that even Wolfshiem is [here] made to express. . . . Whether Nick Carraway is capable of apprehending this as wisdom is disputable, but Fitzgerald evidently could, since Wolfshiem is not wholly devoid of the dignity of grief." See Bloom's *The American Canon*, p. 236.

**6** One in a series of novels and stories by American writer Clarence E. Mulford (1883–1956) that featured a rough-talking cowboy hero of the same name. Jimmy Gatz's list is dated September 12, 1906. This mention of the novel, not published until 1910, is anachronistic but appropriate. By placing Jimmy's schedule of self-improvement in his copy of *Hopalong Cassidy*, Fitzgerald allows us to see the particularly potent confection of elements that worked on the boy's imagination: the romance of the West, the creed of American individualism, and the dream of upward social and economic mobility.

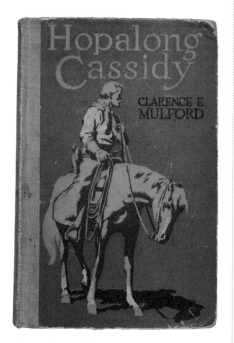

First edition of *Hopalong Cassidy* (1910), the book in which Jimmy Gatz recorded his schedule of self-improvement.

"Very well. Had you seen him lately?"

"He come out to see me two years ago and bought me the house I live in now. Of course we was broke up when he run off from home, but I see now there was a reason for it. He knew he had a big future in front of him. And ever since he made a success he was very generous with me."

He seemed reluctant to put away the picture, held it for another minute, lingeringly, before my eyes. Then he returned the wallet and pulled from his pocket a ragged old copy of a book called "Hopalong Cassidy."[6]

"Look here, this is a book he had when he was a boy. It just shows you."

He opened it at the back cover and turned it around for me to see. On the last fly-leaf was printed the word SCHEDULE, and the date September 12, 1906. And underneath:[7]

| | | |
|---|---|---|
| Rise from bed | 6.00 | A.M. |
| Dumbbell exercise and wall-scaling | 6.15–6.30 | " |
| Study electricity, etc. | 7.15–8.15 | " |
| Work | 8.30–4.30 | P.M. |
| Baseball and sports | 4.30–5.00 | " |
| Practice elocution, poise and how to attain it | 5.00–6.00 | " |
| Study needed inventions | 7.00–9.00 | " |

### GENERAL RESOLVES

No wasting time at Shafters or [a name, indecipherable]

No more smoking or chewing.

Bath every other day

Read one improving book or magazine per week

Save $5.00 [crossed out] $3.00 per week

Be better to parents

"I come across this book by accident," said the old man. "It just shows you, don't it?"

"It just shows you."

"Jimmy was bound to get ahead. He always had some resolves like this or something. Do you notice what he's got about improving his mind? He was always great for that. He told me I et like a hog once, and I beat him for it."

He was reluctant to close the book, reading each item aloud and then looking eagerly at me. I think he rather expected me to copy down the list for my own use.

A little before three the Lutheran minister arrived from Flushing, and I began to look involuntarily out the windows for other cars. So did Gatsby's father. And as the time passed and the servants came in and stood waiting in the hall, his eyes began to blink anxiously, and he spoke of the rain in a worried, uncertain way. The minister glanced several times at his watch, so I took him aside and asked him to wait for half an hour. But it wasn't any use. Nobody came.

About five o'clock our procession of three cars reached the cemetery and stopped in a thick drizzle beside the gate—first a motor-hearse, horribly black and wet, then Mr. Gatz and the minister and I in the limousine, and a little later four or five servants and the postman from West Egg, in Gatsby's station wagon, all wet to the skin. As we started through the gate into the cemetery I heard a car stop and then the sound of someone splashing after us over the soggy ground. I looked around. It was the man with owl-eyed glasses whom I had found marvelling over Gatsby's books in the library one night three months before.

I'd never seen him since then. I don't know how he knew about the funeral, or even his name. The rain poured down his thick glasses, and he took them off and wiped them to see the protecting canvas unrolled from Gatsby's grave.

7 Jimmy's schedule mimics young Benjamin Franklin's "scheme of employment for the twenty-four hours of a natural day" in Part Two of *The Autobiography* but tellingly omits Franklin's emphasis on the attainment of virtue: See *Franklin: Autobiography, Poor Richard, and Later Writings* (New York: Library of America), p. 649.

SCHEME.

| | Hours. | |
|---|---|---|
| *Morning.* | 5 | Rise, wash, and address |
| The Ques. | 6 | *Powerful Goodness!* |
| What good shall | 7 | Contrive day's business, |
| I do this day? | | and take the resolution of the day; prosecute the present study, and breakfast. |
| | 8 | |
| | 9 | |
| | 10 | Work. |
| | 11 | |
| *Noon.* | 12 | Read, or look over my |
| | 1 | accounts and dine. |
| | 2 | |
| *Afternoon.* | 3 | Work. |
| | 4 | |
| | 5 | |
| *Evening.* | 6 | Put things in their places. |
| The Ques. | 7 | Supper, Music or diversion, |
| What good have | 8 | or conversation. Examination |
| I done to day? | 9 | of the day. |
| | 10 | |
| | 11 | |
| *Night.* | 12 | Sleep. |
| | 1 | |
| | 2 | |
| | 3 | |
| | 4 | |

8 Paraphrase of a line from "Rain" (1916), by the British war poet Edward Thomas (1878–1917), killed on the Western Front during World War I. This is a soldier's poem, appropriate for Gatsby.

Rain

Rain, midnight rain, nothing but the
   wild rain
On this bleak hut, and solitude, and me
Remembering again that I shall die
And neither hear the rain nor give it
   thanks
For washing me cleaner than I have been
Since I was born into this solitude.
Blessed are the dead that the rain rains
   upon:
But here I pray that none whom once I
   loved
Is dying tonight or lying still awake
Solitary, listening to the rain,
Either in pain or thus in sympathy
Helpless among the living and the dead,
Like a cold water among broken reeds,
Myriads of broken reeds all still and stiff,
Like me who have no love which this
   wild rain
Has not dissolved except the love of
   death,
If love it be towards what is perfect and
Cannot, the tempest tells me, disappoint.

I tried to think about Gatsby then for a moment, but he was already too far away, and I could only remember, without resentment, that Daisy hadn't sent a message or a flower. Dimly I heard someone murmur "Blessed are the dead that the rain falls on,"[8] and then the owl-eyed man said "Amen to that," in a brave voice.

We straggled down quickly through the rain to the cars. Owl Eyes spoke to me by the gate.

"I couldn't get to the house," he remarked.

"Neither could anybody else."

"Go on!" He started. "Why, my God! they used to go there by the hundreds."

He took off his glasses and wiped them again, outside and in.

"The poor son-of-a-bitch," he said.

One of my most vivid memories is of coming back West from prep school and later from college at Christmas time. Those who went farther than Chicago would gather in the old dim Union Station at six o'clock of a December evening, with a few Chicago friends, already caught up into their own holiday gayeties, to bid them a hasty good-by. I remember the fur coats of the girls returning from Miss This-or-That's and the chatter of frozen breath and the hands waving overhead as we caught sight of old acquaintances, and the matchings of invitations: "Are you going to the Ordways'? the Herseys'? the Schultzes'?" and the long green tickets clasped tight in our gloved hands. And last the murky yellow cars of the Chicago, Milwaukee & St. Paul railroad looking cheerful as Christmas itself on the tracks beside the gate.

When we pulled out into the winter night and the real snow, our snow, began to stretch out beside us and twinkle against the windows, and the dim lights of small Wisconsin stations moved by, a sharp wild brace came suddenly into the

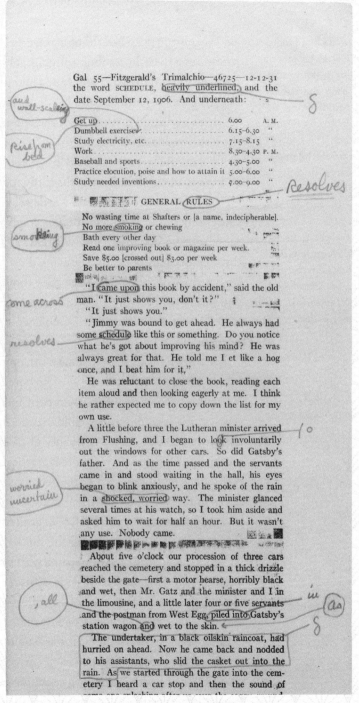

Gal 55—Fitzgerald's Trimalchio—46725—12-12-31
the word SCHEDULE, heavily underlined, and the
date September 12, 1906. And underneath:

*(margin, left: and wall-scaling)*
*(margin, right: §)*

Get up ....................................... 6.00    A. M.
Dumbbell exercise ............................ 6.15-6.30    "
Study electricity, etc. ....................... 7.15-8.15    "
Work ....................................... 8.30-4.30    P. M.
Baseball and sports .......................... 4.30-5.00    "
Practice elocution, poise and how to attain it  5.00-6.00    "
Study needed inventions ...................... 7.00-9.00    "

*(margin, left: Rise from bed)*
*(margin, right: Resolves)*

GENERAL RULES

No wasting time at Shafters or [a name, indecipherable].
No more smoking or chewing
Bath every other day
Read one improving book or magazine per week
Save $5.00 [crossed out] $3.00 per week
Be better to parents

*(margin, left: smoking)*

"I came upon this book by accident," said the old
man. "It just shows you, don't it?"
    "It just shows you."

*(margin, left: come across)*

    "Jimmy was bound to get ahead. He always had
some schedule like this or something. Do you notice
what he's got about improving his mind? He was
always great for that. He told me I et like a hog
once, and I beat him for it."

*(margin, left: resolves)*

    He was reluctant to close the book, reading each
item aloud and then looking eagerly at me. I think
he rather expected me to copy down the list for my
own use.

    A little before three the Lutheran minister arrived
from Flushing, and I began to look involuntarily
out the windows for other cars. So did Gatsby's
father. And as the time passed and the servants
came in and stood waiting in the hall, his eyes
began to blink anxiously, and he spoke of the rain
in a shocked, worried way. The minister glanced
several times at his watch, so I took him aside and
asked him to wait for half an hour. But it wasn't
any use. Nobody came.

*(margin, right: o)*
*(margin, left: worried uncertain)*

    About five o'clock our procession of three cars
reached the cemetery and stopped in a thick drizzle
beside the gate—first a motor hearse, horribly black
and wet, then Mr. Gatz and the minister and I in
the limousine, and a little later four or five servants
and the postman from West Egg, piled into Gatsby's
station wagon and wet to the skin.

*(margin, left: , all)*
*(margin, right: in    as    §)*

    The undertaker, in a black oilskin raincoat, had
hurried on ahead. Now he came back and nodded
to his assistants, who slid the casket out into the
rain. As we started through the gate into the cemetery I heard a car stop and then the sound of

Detail from galley 55 of *Trimalchio*. Fitzgerald revises Jimmy Gatz's
"GENERAL RESOLVES." Princeton University Library.

9 Arthur Mizener, Fitzgerald's first biographer, writes: "*The Great Gatsby* becomes a kind of tragic pastoral, with the East exemplifying urban sophistication and culture and corruption, and the Middle West, 'the bored, sprawling, swollen towns beyond the Ohio,' the simple virtues. This contrast is summed up in the title to which Fitzgerald came with such reluctance. In so far as Gatsby represents the simplicity of heart Fitzgerald associated with the Middle West, he is really a great man. . . . Out of Gatsby's ignorance of his real greatness and his misunderstanding of his notoriety, Fitzgerald gets most of the book's direct irony." See Arthur Mizener's *The Far Side of Paradise: A Biography of F. Scott Fitzgerald*, rev. ed. (Houghton Mifflin, 1965), p. 190.

air. We drew in deep breaths of it as we walked back from dinner through the cold vestibules, unutterably aware of our identity with this country for one strange hour, before we melted indistinguishably into it again.

That's my Middle West—not the wheat or the prairies or the lost Swede towns, but the thrilling returning trains of my youth, and the street lamps and sleigh bells in the frosty dark and the shadows of holly wreaths thrown by lighted windows on the snow. I am part of that, a little solemn with the feel of those long winters, a little complacent from growing up in the Carraway house in a city where dwellings are still called through decades by a family's name. I see now that this has been a story of the West,[9] after all—Tom and Gatsby, Daisy and Jordan and I, were all Westerners, and perhaps we possessed some deficiency in common which made us subtly unadaptable to Eastern life.

Even when the East excited me most, even when I was most keenly aware of its superiority to the bored, sprawling, swollen towns beyond the Ohio, with their interminable inquisitions which spared only the children and the very old—even then it had always for me a quality of distortion. West Egg, especially, still figures in my more fantastic dreams. I see it as a night scene by El Greco:[10] a hundred houses, at once conventional and grotesque, crouching under a sullen, overhanging sky and a lustreless moon. In the foreground four solemn men in dress suits are walking along the sidewalk with a stretcher on which lies a drunken woman in a white evening dress. Her hand, which dangles over the side, sparkles cold with jewels. Gravely the men turn in at a house—the wrong house. But no one knows the woman's name, and no one cares.

After Gatsby's death the East was haunted for me like that, distorted beyond my eyes' power of correction. So when the blue smoke of brittle leaves was in the air and the wind blew the wet laundry stiff on the line I decided to come back home.

There was one thing to be done before I left, an awkward, unpleasant thing that perhaps had better have been let alone.

**10** Doménikos Theotokópoulos (1541–1614), a Greek painter and sculptor. Fitzgerald likely has in mind El Greco's *View of Toledo*. Charles A. Nicholas observes that "the world of El Greco's landscapes is also a green one, not the green of the pastoral paradise but a lurid and ghastly green not unlike the green which appears on the face of George Wilson as he plots his murder." See Charles A. Nicholas's "The G-G-Great Gatsby," in *CEA Critic* 38.2 (1976), pp. 8–10.

*View of Toledo* (c. 1599–1600) by El Greco.

But I wanted to leave things in order and not just trust that obliging and indifferent sea to sweep my refuse away. I saw Jordan Baker and talked over and around what had happened to us together, and what had happened afterward to me, and she lay perfectly still, listening, in a big chair.

She was dressed to play golf, and I remember thinking she looked like a good illustration, her chin raised a little jauntily, her hair the color of an autumn leaf, her face the same brown tint as the fingerless glove on her knee. When I had finished she told me without comment that she was engaged to another man. I doubted that, though there were several she could have married at a nod of her head, but I pretended to be surprised. For just a minute I wondered if I wasn't making a mistake, then I thought it all over again quickly and got up to say good-by.

"Nevertheless you did throw me over," said Jordan suddenly. "You threw me over on the telephone. I don't give a damn about you now, but it was a new experience for me, and I felt a little dizzy for a while."

We shook hands.

"Oh, and do you remember"—she added—"a conversation we had once about driving a car?"

"Why—not exactly."

"You said a bad driver was only safe until she met another bad driver? Well, I met another bad driver, didn't I? I mean it was careless of me to make such a wrong guess. I thought you were rather an honest, straightforward person. I thought it was your secret pride."

"I'm thirty," I said. "I'm five years too old to lie to myself and call it honor."

She didn't answer. Angry, and half in love with her, and tremendously sorry, I turned away.

One afternoon late in October I saw Tom Buchanan. He was walking ahead of me along Fifth Avenue in his alert, aggressive way, his hands out a little from his body as if to fight off interference, his head moving sharply here and there, adapting itself to his restless eyes. Just as I slowed up to avoid overtaking him he stopped and began frowning into the windows of a jewelry store. Suddenly he saw me and walked back, holding out his hand.

"What's the matter, Nick? Do you object to shaking hands with me?"

"Yes. You know what I think of you."

"You're crazy, Nick," he said quickly. "Crazy as hell. I don't know what's the matter with you."

"Tom," I inquired, "what did you say to Wilson that afternoon?"

He stared at me without a word, and I knew I had guessed right about those missing hours. I started to turn away, but he took a step after me and grabbed my arm.

"I told him the truth," he said. "He came to the door while we were getting ready to leave, and when I sent down word that we weren't in he tried to force his way upstairs. He was crazy enough to kill me if I hadn't told him who owned the car. His hand was on a revolver in his pocket every minute he was in the house—" He broke off defiantly. "What if I did tell him? That fellow had it coming to him. He threw dust into your eyes just like he did in Daisy's, but he was a tough one. He ran over Myrtle like you'd run over a dog and never even stopped his car."[11]

There was nothing I could say, except the one unutterable fact that it wasn't true.

"And if you think I didn't have my share of suffering—look here, when I went to give up that flat and saw that damn box of dog biscuits sitting there on the sideboard, I sat down and cried like a baby. By God it was awful——"

I couldn't forgive him or like him, but I saw that what he had done was, to him, entirely justified. It was all very careless and confused. They were careless people, Tom and Daisy—they smashed up things and creatures and then retreated back into their money or their vast carelessness, or whatever it was that kept them together, and let other people clean up the mess they had made....

I shook hands with him; it seemed silly not to, for I felt suddenly as though I were talking to a child. Then he went into the jewelry store to buy a pearl necklace—or perhaps only a pair of cuff buttons—rid of my provincial squeamishness forever.

———

Gatsby's house was still empty when I left—the grass on his lawn had grown as long as mine. One of the taxi drivers in the village never took a fare past the entrance gate without stopping for a minute and pointing inside; perhaps it was he who drove Daisy and Gatsby over to East Egg the night of the accident, and

11 Possibly, Daisy has lied to Tom about who ran over Myrtle Wilson—or Tom is lying now to protect Daisy. Fitzgerald leaves the matter unclear. Either way, the Buchanans share blame for Gatsby's murder: "They were careless people, Tom and Daisy—they smashed up things and creatures and then retreated back into their money or their vast carelessness, or whatever it was that kept them together, and let other people clean up the mess they had made...."

**12** Sarah Churchwell writes of this passage: "The trees are long gone, replaced by vulgar mansions and the wasteland of ash heaps next to which poor George and Myrtle Wilson live, 'contiguous to absolutely nothing.' What is left is what was always there—the imagination. But even this Fitzgerald undercuts: pandering, after all, is ministering to mere gratification. The idea that America panders to our fantasies is the precise opposite of the American dream. We are forever chasing the green light, a chimera, a false promise of self-empowerment in which we are desperate to believe. And yet although it is a lie, we can't survive without it, for we always need something commensurate to our capacity for wonder, even if it compels us into a contemplation we neither understand nor desire." From Churchwell's "What Makes *The Great Gatsby* Great?" *The Observer* (May 3, 2013).

perhaps he had made a story about it all his own. I didn't want to hear it and I avoided him when I got off the train.

I spent my Saturday nights in New York because those gleaming, dazzling parties of his were with me so vividly that I could still hear the music and the laughter, faint and incessant, from his garden, and the cars going up and down his drive. One night I did hear a material car there, and saw its lights stop at his front steps. But I didn't investigate. Probably it was some final guest who had been away at the ends of the earth and didn't know that the party was over.

On the last night, with my trunk packed and my car sold to the grocer, I went over and looked at that huge incoherent failure of a house once more. On the white steps an obscene word, scrawled by some boy with a piece of brick, stood out clearly in the moonlight, and I erased it, drawing my shoe raspingly along the stone. Then I wandered down to the beach and sprawled out on the sand.

Most of the big shore places were closed now and there were hardly any lights except the shadowy, moving glow of a ferryboat across the Sound. And as the moon rose higher the inessential houses began to melt away until gradually I became aware of the old island here that flowered once for Dutch sailors' eyes—a fresh, green breast of the new world. Its vanished trees, the trees that had made way for Gatsby's house, had once pandered in whispers to the last and greatest of all human dreams; for a transitory enchanted moment man must have held his breath in the presence of this continent, compelled into an æsthetic contemplation he neither understood nor desired, face to face for the last time in history with something commensurate to his capacity for wonder.[12]

And as I sat there brooding on the old, unknown world, I thought of Gatsby's wonder when he first picked out the green light at the end of Daisy's dock. He had come a long way to this blue lawn, and his dream must have seemed so close that he could hardly fail to grasp it. He did not know that it was already behind him, somewhere back in that vast obscurity beyond the city, where the dark fields of the republic rolled on under the night.

Gatsby believed in the green light, the orgastic future that year by year recedes before us. It eluded us then, but that's no matter—tomorrow we will run faster, stretch out our arms farther. . . . And one fine morning——

So we beat on, boats against the current, borne back ceaselessly into the past.

The green light at the end of Daisy's dock, still from Baz Luhrmann's *The Great Gatsby* (2013).

(45)

And as I sat there, brooding on the old unknown
world I thought of Gatsby ~~wonder~~ when he picked
out the green light at the end of Daisy's dock.
He had come a long way to this blue lawn but
now his dream must have seemed so close that
he could hardly fail to grasp it. He did not know
that ~~he had left it behind him, before, It lay~~
~~somew~~ it was all behind him, ~~his~~ ~~somew~~,
back in that vast obscurity on the other side
of the city, where the dark fields of the republic
rolled on under the night.

He believed in the green glimmer, in the orgastic
future that year by year recedes before us. It eluded
us then but never mind — tomorrow we will run
faster, stretch out our arms farther, And one
fine morning —

So we beat on, a boat against the current,
borne back ceaselessly into the past.

The final manuscript page of *The Great Gatsby*. Here Jay Gatsby believes in "the green glimmer." In the first edition, he believes in "the green light."

# LETTERS

Maxwell Perkins, circa 1920, Fitzgerald's editor at Scribner's. He started his career working in the firm's advertising department.

*TO: Maxwell Perkins*[1]
*c. April 10, 1924*                              *Long Island, New York*
                                                                *Great Neck.*

Dear Max:

A few words more relative to our conversation this afternoon. While I have every hope + plan of finishing my novel in June you know how those things often come out. And even it takes me 10 times that long I cannot let it go out unless it has the very best I'm capable of in it or even as I feel sometimes, something better than I'm capable of. Much of what I wrote last summer was good but it was so interrupted that it was ragged + in approaching it from a new angle I've had to discard a lot of it—in one case 18,000 words (part of which will appear in the Mercury as a short story).[2] It is only in the last four months that I've realized how much I've— well, almost <u>deteriorated</u> in the three years since I finished the Beautiful and Damned.[3] The last four months of course I've worked but in the two years—over two years—before that, I produced exactly <u>one</u> play, <u>half a dozen</u> short stories and three or four articles—an average of about <u>one</u> <u>hundred</u> words a day. If I'd spent this time reading or travelling or doing anything— even staying healthy—it'd be different but I spent it uselessly, niether in study nor in contemplation but only in drinking and raising hell generally. If I'd written the B. & D. at the rate of 100 words a day it would have taken me <u>4 years</u> so you can imagine the moral effect the whole chasm had on me.

What I'm trying to say is just that I'll have to ask you to have patience about the book and trust me that at last, or at least for the 1st time in years, I'm doing the best I can. I've gotten in dozens of bad habits that I'm trying to get rid of

1. Laziness
2. Referring everything to Zelda—a terrible habit, nothing ought to be referred to anybody until its finished

1 Perkins (1884–1947), one of the most important American editors of the twentieth century, was employed by Scribner's for the entirety of his career, editing the writings of a wide range of the firm's most important authors, including Ernest Hemingway, Thomas Wolfe, Marjorie Kinnan Rawlings, Younghill Kang, John P. Marquand, Erskine Caldwell, James Boyd, Alan Payton, Marguerite Young, and S. S. Van Dine. Fitzgerald was Perkins's first discovery. He guided Fitzgerald's debut novel, *This Side of Paradise* (1920), into print and remained his editor until the author's death in 1940. Though conservative by temperament, Perkins was open to experiments in language, form, and subject matter. See the two-part profile by Malcolm Cowley, "Unshaken Friend," *The New Yorker*, March 24 and April 1, 1944; and the biography by A. Scott Berg, *Max Perkins: Editor of Genius* (Dutton, 1978). The letters between Fitzgerald and Perkins have been published in *Dear Scott/Dear Max: The Fitzgerald–Perkins Correspondence*, ed. John Kuehl and Jackson R. Bryer (Scribner's, 1971).

2 "Absolution," first published in *The American Mercury* 2 (June 1924) and collected in *All the Sad Young Men* (1926).

3 Fitzgerald's second novel, published by Scribner's in March 1922, after having been serialized, in a cut and bowdlerized text, in *Metropolitan Magazine*.

4 *David Copperfield* (1850) by Charles Dickens (1812–1870), and *Pendennis* (1849–50) by W. M. Thackeray (1811–1863).

3.   Word consciousness—self doubt

ect. ect. ect. ect.

I feel I have an enormous power in me now, more than I've ever had in a way but it works so fitfully and with so many bogeys because I've <u>talked so much</u> and not lived enough within myself to delelop the nessessary self reliance. Also I don't know anyone who has used up so [torn]sonel experience as I have at 27. Copperfield + Pendennis[4] were written at past forty while This Side of Paradise was three books + the B. + D. was two. So in my new novel I'm thrown directly on purely creative work—not trashy imaginings as in my stories but the sustained imagination of a sincere and yet radiant world. So I tread slowly and carefully + at times in considerable distress. This book will be a consciously artistic achievment + must depend on that as the 1st books did not.

If I ever win the right to any liesure again I will assuredly not waste it as I wasted this past time. Please believe me when I say that now I'm doing the best I can.

Yours Ever

Scott F———

TO: *Maxwell Perkins*
*c. August 27, 1924*

Villa Marie, Valescure
St Raphael, France

Dear Max:

(1) The novel will be done next week. That doesn't mean however that it'll reach America before October 1st. as Zelda + I are contemplating a careful revision after a weeks complete rest.

(2) The clippings have never arrived.

(3) Seldes[5] has been with me and he thinks "For the Grimalkins" is a wonderful title for Rings book. Also I've got great ideas about "My Life and Loves"[6] which I'll tell Ring when comes over in September.

(4) How many copies has his short stories sold?

(5) Your bookkeeper never did send me my royalty report for Aug 1st.

(6) For Christs sake don't give anyone that jacket you're saving for me. I've written it into the book.[7]

(7) I think my novel is about the best American novel ever written. It is rough stuff in places, runs only to about 50,000 words, and I hope you won't shy at it

(8) Its been a fair summer. I've been unhappy but my work hasn't suffered from it. I am grown at last.

(9) What books are being talked about? I don't mean best sellers. Hergeshiemers[8] novel in the Post seems vile to me.

(10) I hope you're reading Gertrude Stiens novel in The Transatlantic Review.[9]

(11) Raymond Radiguets last book (he is the young man who wrote "Le deable au Corps" at sixteen [untranslatable]) is a great hit here. He wrote it at 18. Its called "Le Bal de Compte Orgel" + though I'm only half through it I'd get an opinion on it if I were you. Its cosmopolitan rather than French and my

5 Gilbert Seldes (1893–1970) was an editor, book reviewer, and cultural critic. He published two reviews of *The Great Gatsby*, both highly favorable: "New York Chronicle," *New Criterion* 4 (January 1926); and "Spring Flight," *The Dial* 79 (August 1925). Ring Lardner (1885–1933), a humorist, playwright, and short-story writer, eventually settled on *What of It?* as the title of his 1925 collection of stories.

6 Sexually explicit memoir by Irish American writer Frank Harris (1856–1931), published privately from 1922 to 1927.

7 Before departing with his wife and daughter for an extended stay in Europe, Fitzgerald had seen in the Scribner's offices the eventual dust-jacket art for *Gatsby*, a gouache on paper by the Cuban American artist Francis Cugat (1893–1981). Whether Fitzgerald saw the final painting or several preliminary sketches is impossible to know. The consensus is that Fitzgerald is referring to Dr. T. J. Eckleburg's eyes when he says that he has "written [the jacket] into the book." It is also possible that Fitzgerald has in mind this passage in Chapter IV: "Unlike Gatsby and Tom Buchanan, I had no girl whose disembodied face floated along the dark cornices and blinding signs." See also pp. iv and 197 in this volume.

8 *Basiland* (1924) by American novelist Joseph Hergesheimer (1880–1954). First serialized in *The Saturday Evening Post*, it would soon be published in book form by Alfred A. Knopf.

9 Excerpts from *The Making of Americans*—a novel of encyclopedic scope by Gertrude Stein (1874–1946)—began appearing in 1924 in Ford Madox Ford's *The Transatlantic Review*. In 1925, a limited

edition of the novel would be published in Paris by Contact Press.

10 During his brief literary career, French writer Raymond Radiguet (1903–1923) wrote two novels. *Le Diable au corps* (1923), about a married woman who has an affair with a sixteen-year-old boy while her husband is away fighting the Germans on the Western Front, was a *succès de scandale*. *Le bal du Comte d'Orgel* (1924) appeared after the author's death from typhoid fever; its preface was supplied by his friend and mentor Jean Cocteau (1889–1963).

11 *The Dance of Life* (1923), by the English physician, writer, and eugenicist Havelock Ellis (1859–1939), advocates self-development through a variety of activities, including meditation, writing, and dance.

12 Maxwell Struthers Burt (1882–1954), American poet and fiction writer, was a fellow Princetonian and a friend of Fitzgerald. Burt's first novel, *The Interpreter's House*, was published by Scribner's in 1924.

instinct tells me that in a good translation it might make an enormous hit in America where everyone is yearning for Paris. Do look it up + get at least one opinion of it. The preface is by the da-dist Jean Cocteau but the book is not da-da at all.[10]

(12)   Did you get hold of Rings other books?

(13)   We're liable to leave here by Oct 1st so after the 15th of Sept I wish you'd send everything care of Guarantee Trust Co. Paris

(14)   Please ask the bookstore, if you have time, to send me Havelock Ellis "Dance of Life"[11] + charge to my account

(15)   I asked Struthers Burt[12] to dinner but his baby was sick.

(16)   Be <u>sure</u> and answer <u>every</u> question, Max.

I miss seeing you like the devil.

Scott

Ring Lardner and his wife, Ellis, 1923. From fall 1922 to spring 1924, Fitzgerald and Lardner were neighbors in Great Neck, where their friendship flourished. In an appreciation of Lardner published after his friend's death, Fitzgerald recalls: "Frequently he was the melancholy Jaques, and sad company indeed, but under any conditions a noble dignity flowed from him, so that time in his presence always seemed well spent." Characteristically generous to friends, Fitzgerald was instrumental in bringing the older, established writer to Scribner's. See Fitzgerald's "Ring," in *The Crack-Up*, pp. 34–40.

Early sketches for Francis Cugat's gouache painting *Celestial Eyes*, which was used on the front panel of the original dust jacket for *The Great Gatsby*. See p. xviii for the final cover illustration.

**13** American novelist and short-story writer Ernest Hemingway (1899–1961) had moved to Paris in 1921 with his wife, Hadley Richardson Hemingway. At the time Fitzgerald wrote to Perkins about Hemingway ("the real thing"), Hemingway was the author of only two small-press books, both printed in Paris: *Three Stories and Ten Poems* (1923) and *in our time* (1924). The two writers met for the first time seven months later, in April 1925, at the Dingo Bar in Montparnasse, two weeks after the publication of *The Great Gatsby*. Their friendship prospered for a time; both were competitive and forthright in their criticism of each other's work. Hemingway's unflattering portrait of Fitzgerald in his posthumously published memoir *A Moveable Feast* (1964) is a thinly veiled attack on a literary rival. See Scott Donaldson's *Hemingway vs. Fitzgerald: The Rise and Fall of a Literary Friendship* (Overlook Press, 1999).

**14** The autobiographical novel *Plumes* (1924), by the American author Lawrence Stallings (1894–1968), depicts the physical and mental anguish of a wounded World War I veteran. The book was the basis for King Vidor's 1925 film *The Big Parade*.

Ernest Hemingway, 1923 passport photograph. Fitzgerald helped to guide Hemingway to Scribner's and offered crucial, timely suggestions for cutting the opening of *The Sun Also Rises* (1926), when Hemingway's novel was already in galleys.

TO: *Maxwell Perkins*
*c. October 10, 1924*

Villa Marie,
Valescure
St Raphael, France

Dear Max:

The royalty was better than I'd expected. This is to tell you about a young man named Ernest Hemmingway, who lives in Paris, (an American) writes for the transatlantic Review + has a brilliant future. Ezra Pount published a a collection of his short pieces in Paris, at some place like the Egotist Press. I havn't it hear now but its remarkable + I'd look him up right away. He's the real thing.[13]

My novel goes to you with a long letter within five days. Ring arrives in a week. This is just a hurried scrawl as I'm working like a dog. I thought Stalling's book was disappointingly rotten. It takes a genius to whine appealingly.[14] Have tried to see Struthers Burt but he's been on the move. More later.

Scott
. . . .

*TO: Maxwell Perkins*

October 27th, 1924
Villa Marie, Valescure
St. Raphael, France
(After Nov. 3d Care of
American Express Co, Rome Italy)

Dear Max:

Under separate cover I'm sending you my third novel:

### The Great Gatsby

(I think that at last I've done something really my own), but how good "my own" is remains to be seen.

I should suggest the following contract.

15% up to 50,000

20% after 50,000

The book is only a little over fifty thousand words long but I believe, as you know, that Whitney Darrow[15] has the wrong psychology about prices (and about what class constitute the bookbuying public now that the lowbrows go to the movies) and I'm anxious to charge two dollars for it and have it a <u>full size book</u>.

Of course I want the binding to be absolutely uniform with my other books—the stamping too—and the jacket we discussed before. This time I don't want any signed blurbs on the jacket—not Mencken's or Lewis' or Howard's[16] or

15 Head of the sales department at Scribner's.

16 H. L. Mencken (1880–1956), American journalist and critic; Sinclair Lewis (1885–1951), American novelist; Sidney Howard (1891–1939), American playwright and screenwriter.

The Dingo American Bar and Restaurant, at 10 rue Delambre, in Montparnasse. The Dingo was a relatively new establishment when Fitzgerald and Hemingway met there in late April 1925.

200    LETTERS

**17** In January 1923 Fitzgerald signed a contract with the Hearst organization giving them an option on all the short stories he would produce that year. The contract also granted Hearst first refusal on the serial rights for Fitzgerald's next novel. Ray Long (1878–1935) was the editor of *Metropolitan*, the Hearst magazine in which *The Beautiful and Damned* had been serialized, from September 1921 to March 1922.

**18** An American weekly illustrated magazine, founded earlier in 1924, that competed with *The Saturday Evening Post*. It was promoted as "A Weekly for Everybody."

**19** Paul Revere Reynolds (1864–1944), head of Paul R. Reynolds and Son, the literary agency that handled Fitzgerald's magazine fiction until 1929, when Fitzgerald followed Harold Ober after he left Reynolds to open his own agency.

*Liberty* magazine, June 21, 1924.

anyone's. I'm tired of being the author of <u>This Side of Paradise</u> and I want to start over.

About serialization. I am bound under contract to show it to Hearsts but I am asking a prohibitive price, Long[17] hates me and its not a very serialized book. If they should take it— they won't—it would put of publication in the fall. Otherwise you can publish it in the spring. When Hearst turns it down I'm going to offer it to Liberty[18] for $15,000 on condition that they'll publish it in ten weekly installments before April 15th. If they don't want it I shan't serialize. <u>I am absolutely positive Long won't want it</u>.

I have an alternative title:

<u>Gold-hatted Gatsby</u>

After you've read the book let me know what you think about the title. Naturally I won't get a nights sleep until I hear from you but do tell me the absolute truth, <u>your first impression of the book</u> + tell me anything that bothers you in it.

As Ever
Scott

I'd rather you wouldn't call Reynolds[19] as he might try to act as my agent. Would you send me the N.Y. World with accounts of Harvard-Princeton and Yale-Princeton games?

FROM: *Maxwell Perkins*

Nov. 18, 1924

Dear Scott:

I think the novel is a wonder. I'm taking it home to read again and shall then write my impressions in full;—but it has vitality to an extraordinary degree, and <u>glamour</u>, and a great deal of underlying thought of unusual quality. It has a kind of mystic atmosphere at times that you infused into parts of "Paradise"[20] and have not since used. It is a marvelous fusion, into a unity of presentation, of the extraordinary incongruities of life today. And as for sheer writing, it's astonishing.

Now deal with this question: various gentlemen here don't like the title,—in fact none like it but me. To me, the strange incongruity of the words in it sound the note of the book. But the objectors are more practical men than I. Consider as quickly as you can the question of a change.

But if you do not change, you will have to leave that note off the wrap.[21] Its presence would injure it too much;—and good as the wrap always seemed, it now seems a masterpiece for this book. So judge of the value of the title when it stands alone and write or cable your decision the instant you can.

With congratulations, I am,
Yours,
[Max]

[20] *This Side of Paradise* (1920).

[21] Perkins refers to "Trimalchio in West Egg," one of several provisional titles for *The Great Gatsby*. Perkins's colleagues at Scribner's—or perhaps in truth Perkins himself—wished to discourage the title. See also the marginal note on p. 119 in this volume.

*FROM: Maxwell Perkins*

November 20, 1924

Dear Scott:

I think you have every kind of right to be proud of this book. It is an extraordinary book, suggestive of all sorts of thoughts and moods. You adopted exactly the right method of telling it, that of employing a narrator who is more of a spectator than an actor: this puts the reader upon a point of observation on a higher level than that on which the characters stand and at a distance that gives perspective. In no other way could your irony have been so immensely effective, nor the reader have been enabled so strongly to feel at times the strangeness of human circumstance in a vast heedless universe. In the eyes of Dr. Eckleberg various readers will see different significances; but their presence gives a superb touch to the whole thing: great unblinking eyes, expressionless, looking down upon the human scene. It's magnificent!

I could go on praising the book and speculating on its various elements, and meanings, but points of criticism are more important now. I think you are right in feeling a certain slight sagging in chapters six and seven, and I don't know how to suggest a remedy. I hardly doubt that you will find one and I am only writing to say that I think it does need something to hold up here to the pace set, and ensuing. I have only two actual criticisms:—

One is that among a set of characters marvelously palpable and vital—I would know Tom Buchanan if I met him on the street and would avoid him—Gatsby is somewhat vague. The reader's eyes can never quite focus upon him, his outlines are dim. Now everything about Gatsby is more or less a mystery i.e. more or less vague, and this may be somewhat of an artistic intention, but I think it is mistaken. Couldn't <u>he</u> be physically described as distinctly as the others, and couldn't you add one or two characteristics like the use of that phrase "old sport",—not verbal, but physical ones, perhaps. I think that for some reason or other a reader—this was true of Mr. Scribner and

The Charles Scribner's Sons Building, 597 Fifth Avenue, between 48th and 49th Streets, circa 1925. It was built in 1912–13 to house the company's publishing offices and the Scribner's Bookstore.

22 Charles Scribner II (1854–1930), president of the publishing firm bearing his father's name, and Louise Saunders Perkins (1887–1965), wife of Maxwell Perkins.

of Louise[22]—gets an idea that Gatsby is a much older man than he is, although you have the writer say that he is little older than himself. But this would be avoided if on his first appearance he was seen as vividly as Daisy and Tom are, for instance;—and I do not think your scheme would be impaired if you made him so.

The other point is also about Gatsby: his career must remain mysterious, of course. But in the end you make it pretty clear that his wealth came through his connection with Wolfshiem. You also suggest this much earlier. Now almost all readers numerically are going to be puzzled by his having all this wealth and are going to feel entitled to an explanation. To give a distinct and definite one would be, of course, utterly absurd. It did occur to me though, that you might here and there interpolate some phrases, and possibly incidents, little touches of various kinds, that would suggest that he was in some active way mysteriously engaged. You do have him called on the telephone, but couldn't he be seen once or twice consulting at his parties with people of some sort of mysterious significance, from the political, the gambling, the sporting world, or whatever it may be. I know I am floundering, but that fact may help you to see what I mean. The <u>total</u> lack of an explanation through so large a part of the story does seem to me a defect;—or not of an explanation, but of the suggestion of an explanation. I wish you were here so I could talk about it to you for then I know I could at least make you understand what I mean. What Gatsby did ought never to be definitely imparted, even if it could be. Whether he was an innocent tool in the hands of somebody else, or to what degree he was this, ought not to be explained. But if some sort of business activity of his were simply adumbrated, it would lend further probability to that part of the story.

There is one other point: in giving deliberately Gatsby's biography when he gives it to the narrator you do depart from the method of the narrative in some degree, for otherwise almost everything is told, and beautifully told, in the regular flow of it,—in the succession of events or in accompaniment with them. But you can't avoid the biography altogether. I thought you might find ways to let the truth of some of his claims like "Oxford" and his army career come out bit by bit in the course of actual narrative. I mention the point anyway for consideration in this interval before I send the proofs.

The general brilliant quality of the book makes me ashamed to make even these criticisms. The amount of meaning you get into a sentence, the dimensions and intensity of the impression you make a paragraph carry, are most extraordinary. The manuscript is full of phrases which make a scene blaze with life. If one enjoyed a rapid railroad journey I would compare the number and vividness of pictures your living words suggest, to the living scenes disclosed in that way. It seems in reading a much shorter book than it is, but it carries the mind through a series of experiences that one would think would require a book of three times its length.

The presentation of Tom, his place, Daisy and Jordan, and the unfolding of their characters is unequalled so far as I know. The description of the valley of ashes adjacent to the lovely country, the conversation and the action in Myrtle's apartment, the marvelous catalogue of those who came to Gatsby's house,—these are such things as make a man famous. And all these things, the whole pathetic episode, you have given a place in time and space, for with the help of T. J. Eckleberg and by an occasional glance at the sky, or the sea, or the city, you have imparted a sort of sense of eternity. You once told me you were not a <u>natural</u> writer—my God! You have plainly mastered the craft, of course; but you needed far more than craftsmanship for this.

As ever,<br>
[Max]

P.S. Why do you ask for a lower royalty on this than you had on the last book where it changed from 15% to 17½% after 20,000 and to 20% after 40,000? Did you do it in order to give us a better margin for advertising? We shall advertise very energetically anyhow and if you stick to the old terms you will sooner overcome the advance. Naturally we should like the ones you suggest better, but there is no reason you should get less on this than you did on the other.[23]

23 The eventual contract between Fitzgerald and Scribner's for *The Great Gatsby*, dated December 22, 1924, gave the author a royalty of 15 percent of the retail price for the first 40,000 copies sold and 20 percent thereafter. No mention is made in the contract of subsidiary rights; by custom these were divided equally between author and publisher.

**24** *Cowboys North and South* (1924) by Canadian American writer Will James (1892–1942). This was the first of many books by James about the American West that Scribner's would publish.

**25** See the relevant notes on pages 36 and 37 of this volume.

**26** Nickname for Fitzgerald's Princeton friend Edmund Wilson (1895–1972), already a notable journalist and book critic at this early point in his career. At Fitzgerald's request, Wilson had read the manuscript of *The Beautiful and Damned* and had given advice about language and style in the novel. Fitzgerald and Wilson remained friends for the rest of Fitzgerald's life, though the relationship was complicated. In his 1936 essay "Pasting It Together," Fitzgerald called Wilson his "intellectual conscience." Wilson edited the posthumously published *The Last Tycoon* (1941), the Hollywood novel that Fitzgerald was writing at the time of his death. Wilson also published an anthology of Fitzgerald's autobiographical essays and other writings titled *The Crack-Up* (1945), a book that helped to revive Fitzgerald's literary reputation in the late 1940s and in the decades that followed.

*TO: Maxwell Perkins*
*c. December 1, 1924*

Hotel des Princes
Piazza di Spagna
Rome, Italy

Dear Max:

Your wire + your letters made me feel like a million dollars—I'm sorry I could make no better response than a telegram whining for money. But the long siege of the novel winded me a little + I've been slow on starting the stories on which I must live.

I think all your critisisms are true

(a)   About the title. I'll try my best but I don't know what I can do. Maybe simply "Trimalchio" or "Gatsby." In the former case I don't see why the note shouldn't go on the back.

(b)   Chapters VI + VII I know how to fix

(c)   Gatsby's business affairs I can fix. I get your point about them.

(d)   His vagueness I can repair by <u>making more pointed</u>—this doesn't sound good but wait and see. It'll make him clear

(e)   But his long narrative in Chap VIII will be difficult to split up. Zelda also thought I was a little out of key but it is good writing and I don't think I could bear to sacrifice any of it

(f)   I have 1000 minor corrections which I will make on the proof + several more large ones which you didn't mention.

Your critisisms were excellent + most helpful + you picked out all my favorite spots in the book to praise as high spots. Except you didn't mention my favorite of all—the chapter where Gatsby + Daisy meet.

Two more things. Zelda's been reading me the cowboy book[24] aloud to spare my mind + I love it—tho I think he learned the American language from Ring rather than from his own ear.

Another point—in Chap. II of my book when Tom + Myrte go into the bedroom while Carraway reads Simon called Peter[25]—is that raw? Let me know. I think its pretty nessesary.

I made the royalty smaller because I wanted to make up for all the money you've advanced these two years by letting it pay a sort of interest on it. But I see by calculating I made it too small—a difference of 2000 dollars. Let us call it 15% up to 40,000 and 20% after that. That's a good fair contract all around.

[ .... ]

Anyhow thanks + thanks + thanks for your letters. I'd rather have you + Bunny[26] like it than anyone I know. And I'd rather have you like it than Bunny. If its as good as you say, when I finish with the proof it'll be perfect.

Remember, by the way, to put by some cloth for the cover uniform with my other books.

As soon as I can think about the title I'll write or wire a decision. Thank Louise for me, for liking it. Best Regards to Mr. Scribner. Tell him Galsworthy[27] is here in Rome.

As Ever,
Scott

Edmund Wilson, in 1929. "I know I'll wake some morning and find that the debutantes have made me famous overnight," Fitzgerald wrote to his college friend, soon after finishing "The Romantic Egotist," his first attempt at a novel. FSF to Wilson, Jan. 10, 1917, in *F. Scott Fitzgerald: A Life in Letters*, ed. Matthew J. Bruccoli (Scribner's, 1994), p. 17.

**27** John Galsworthy (1867–1933), English novelist whose books were published in the U.S. by Scribner's. Fitzgerald and Zelda had met Galsworthy in the spring of 1921 on their first trip to England.

**28** Fitzgerald would begin work in the spring of 1925 on a novel of matricide, set on the French Riviera. Among his working titles: "Our Type," "The Boy Who Shot His Mother," and "The World's Fair." The novel would eventually be published by Scribner's in 1934 as *Tender Is the Night*.

**29** Fitzgerald refers to his advance against royalties for *The Great Gatsby*.

**30** Gustave Flaubert (1821–1880) was a compulsive reviser of his own writing. His revisions in proof for *Madame Bovary* (1857) were especially heavy. Fitzgerald did in fact make major revisions to *The Great Gatsby* in galley proofs.

**31** Fitzgerald refers to Ring Lardner's *How to Write Short Stories* (1924), Thomas Boyd's *Through the Wheat* (1923), Willa Cather's *A Lost Lady* (1923), Edna Ferber's *So Big* (1924), and Sinclair Lewis's *Babbitt* (1922).

**32** Fitzgerald often used details from the lives of people he knew or had read about when he created his characters. The man Fitzgerald "had in mind" is possibly newspaperman Herbert Bayard Swope (1882–1958), who was living on East Shore Road in Great Neck, next to Ring Lardner's residence, during the period in which Fitzgerald and his wife, Zelda, were living on Long Island—and Fitzgerald was working on the early chapters of *The Great Gatsby*. Fitzgerald attended several parties at Swope's house.

It is also possible that Fitzgerald refers to Max von Gerlach, a German by birth who came to America as a nine-year-old orphan. He served in the U.S. Army during World War I and, after the war, seems to have engaged in bootlegging and other criminal activities. He was friendly with

*TO: Maxwell Perkins*
*c. December 20, 1924*

Hotel des Princes, Piazza de Spagna, Rome.

Dear Max:

I'm a bit (not very—not dangerously) stewed tonight + I'll probably write you a long letter. We're living in a small, unfashionable but most comfortable hotel at $525.00 a month including tips, meals ect. Rome does <u>not</u> particularly interest me but its a big year here, and early in the spring we're going to Paris. There's no use telling you my plans because they're usually just about as unsuccessful as to work as a religious prognosticaters are as to the End of the World. I've got a new novel[28] to write—title and all, that'll take about a year. Meanwhile, I don't want to start it until this is out + meanwhile I'll do short stories for money (I now get $2000.00 a story but I hate worse than hell to do them) and there's the never dying lure of another play.

Now! Thanks enormously for making up the $5000.00. I know I don't technically deserve it considering I've had $3000.00 or $4000.00 for as long as I can remember. But since you force it on me (inexecrable [or is it execrable] joke) I will accept it. I hope to Christ you get 10 times it back on Gatsby[29]——and I think perhaps you will.

For:

I can now make it perfect but the proof (I will soon get the immemorial letter with the statement "We now have the book in hand and will soon begin to send you proof" [what is 'in hand'—I have a vague picture of everyone in the office holding the book in the right and and reading it]) will be one of the most expensive affairs since Madame Bovary.[30] <u>Please</u> charge it to my account. If its possible to send a second proof over here I'd love to have it. Count on 12 days each way—four days here on first proof + two on the second. I hope there are other good books in the spring because I think now the public interest in <u>books</u> per se rises when there seems to be a group of them as in 1920 (spring + fall), 1921 (fall), 1922 (spring). Ring's + Tom's (first) books, Willa Cathers <u>Lost Lady</u> + in an inferior, cheap way Edna Ferber's are the only American fiction in over two years that had a really excellent press (say, since Babbit).[31]

With the aid you've given me I can make "Gatsby" perfect. The chapter VII (the hotel scene) will never quite be up to mark—I've worried about it too long + I can't quite place Daisy's reaction. But I can improve it a lot. It isn't imaginative energy thats lacking—its because I'm automaticly prevented from thinking it out over again <u>because I must get all those characters to New York</u> in order to have the catastrophe on the road going back + I must have it pretty much that way. So there's no chance of bringing the freshness to it that a new free conception sometimes gives.

The rest is easy and I see my way so clear that I even see the mental quirks that queered it before. Strange to say my notion of Gatsby's vagueness was O.K. What you and Louise + Mr. Charles Scribner found wanting was that:

<u>I myself didn't know what Gatsby looked like or was engaged in</u> + you felt it. If I'd known + kept it from you you'd have been <u>too</u> <u>impressed with my knowledge to protest</u>. This is a complicated idea but I'm sure you'll understand. But I know now—and as a penalty for not having known first, in other words to make sure I'm going to tell more.

It seems of almost mystical significance to me that you thot he was older—the man I had in mind,[32] half unconsciously, <u>was</u> older (a specific individual) and evidently, without so much as a definate word, I conveyed the fact.—or rather, I must qualify this Shaw-Desmond-trash by saying, that I conveyed it without a word that I can at present and for the life of me, trace. (I think Shaw Desmond was one of your bad bets[33]—I was the other)

Anyhow after careful searching of the files (of a man's mind here) for the Fuller Magee case[34] + after having had Zelda draw pictures until her fingers ache I know Gatsby better

the Fitzgeralds; he clipped a photograph of Scott and Zelda from a newspaper in 1923 and sent it to them with this inscription: "How are you and the family old sport?" For details see Horst H. Kruse's "Max von Gerlach, the Man behind Jay Gatsby," in Kruse's collection *F. Scott Fitzgerald at Work: The Making of "The Great Gatsby"* (University of Alabama Press, 2014), pp. 4–73.

Joseph G. Robin, né Rabinovitch (ca. 1876–1929), represents yet a third candidate for "the man I had in mind": he was a Russian-born immigrant who amassed a fortune in banking, built a mansion on Long Island, and held "automobile parties" to attract the newly wealthy. Eventually, Robin came to ruin: in 1912 he was convicted of bribery and embezzlement and served a one-year sentence in jail. Theodore Dreiser published a profile of Robin, with whom he was friendly, under the title "'Vanity, Vanity,' Saith the Preacher," in his collection *Twelve Men* (Liveright, 1919)—a book with which Fitzgerald was familiar. See Thomas P. Riggio's "Dreiser, Fitzgerald, and the Question of Influence," in *Theodore Dreiser and American Culture: New Readings*, ed. Yoshinobu Hakutani (University of Delaware Press, 2000), pp. 234–47.

Whomever Fitzgerald had in mind, Gatsby is a fictional creation, and ultimately a composite, since he also bears some resemblance to his creator. While living in Edgemoor, Delaware, in 1927, Fitzgerald inscribed a copy of *The Great Gatsby* to Charles T. Scott: "Gatsby was never quite real to me. His original served for a good enough exterior until about the middle of the book he grew thin and I began to fill him with my own emotional life." The inscription on the flyleaf of Scott's copy is reproduced as the frontispiece to

*Trimalchio: An Early Version of The Great Gatsby*, ed. James L. W. West III (Cambridge University Press, 2000), p. ii.

**33** The Irish novelist and playwright Shaw Desmond (1887–1960) was a proponent of spiritualism and a student of fairy lore and the occult. Scribner's published Desmond's *The Drama of Sinn Féin* in 1923.

**34** High-profile criminal trial of 1923 in which the New York stockbrokers Edward W. Fuller and William F. McGee pled guilty to using their firm as a "bucket shop"—a brokerage that permits gambling on the rise and fall of stocks without purchasing or selling any shares. The racketeer Arnold Rothstein (1882–1928), the model for Meyer Wolfshiem in *The Great Gatsby*, was believed to have been involved in the machinations.

**35** Leslie Wagstaff, half brother to Griffith Adams, in *Salt; or the Education of Griffith Adams* (1919), by Charles G. Norris (1881–1945), and George Hurstwood in *Sister Carrie* (1900), by Theodore Dreiser (1871–1945).

**36** Cummings (1899–1984), golfer, Chicago socialite, and friend of Ginevra King, Fitzgerald's first serious sweetheart. See also p. 25 in this volume.

**37** Fitzgerald's satirical play *The Vegetable: or from President to Postman*, which he wrote in 1921 and 1922, opened in Atlantic City on November 19, 1923. The play was a flop. It never made it to Broadway and left Fitzgerald in serious debt. Scribner's published *The Vegetable* in book form in 1923.

**38** Medal for civil and military merit, awarded by Montenegro since 1853. In Chapter IV of *The Great Gatsby*, Gatsby shows this medal to Nick Carraway (see p. 73 in this volume).

than I know my own child. My first instinct after your letter was to let him go + have Tom Buchanan dominate the book (I suppose he's the best character I've ever done—I think he and the brother in "Salt" + Hurstwood in "Sister Carrie"[35] are the three best characters in American fiction in the last twenty years, perhaps and perhaps not) but Gatsby sticks in my heart. I had him for awhile then lost him + now I know I have him again. I'm sorry Myrtle is better than Daisy. Jordan of course was a great idea (perhaps you know its Edith Cummings)[36] but she fades out. Its Chap VII thats the trouble with Daisy + it may hurt the book's popularity that its a man's book.

Anyhow I think (for the first time since The Vegetable failed)[37] that I'm a wonderful writer + its your always wonderful letters that help me to go on believing in myself.

Now some practical, very important questions. Please answer every one.

1. Montenegro has an order called The Order of Danilo.[38] Is there any possible way you could find out for me there what it would look like—whether a courtesy decoration given to an American would bear an English inscription—or anything to give versimilitude to the medal which sounds horribly amateurish.

2. Please have no blurbs of any kind on the jacket!!! No Mencken or Lewis or Sid Howard or anything. I don't believe in them one bit any more.

3. Don't forget to change name of book in list of works

4. Please shift exclamation point from end of 3d line to end of 4th line in title page. Please! Important!

5. I thought that the whole episode (2 paragraphs) about their playing the Jazz History of the world at Gatsby's first party was rotten. Did you? Tell me frank reaction—personal. Don't think! We can all think!

[ . . . . ]

I still owe the store almost $700 on my Encyclopedia[39] but I'll pay them on about Jan 10th—all in a lump as I expect my finances will then be on a firm footing. Will you ask them to send me Ernest Boyd's book?[40] Unless it has about my drinking in it that would reach my family. However, I guess it'd worry me more if I hadn't seen it than if I had. If my book is a big success or a great failure (financial—no other sort can be imagined, I hope) I don't want to publish stories in the fall. If it goes between 25,000 and 50,000 I have an excellent collection for you. This is the longest letter I've written in three or four years. Please thank Mr. Scribner for me for his exceeding kindness.

> Always yours
> Scott Fitz——

Front panel of the original cover for Fitzgerald's *The Vegetable* (1923). "I feel old. . . . I have ever since the failure of my play a year ago," Fitzgerald wrote to his Princeton friend Ludlow Fowler in August 1924. "Thats the whole burden of [*The Great Gatsby*]—the loss of those illusions that give such color to the world so that you don't care whether things are true or false as long as they partake of the magical glory." See *Correspondence of F. Scott Fitzgerald* (Random House, 1980), p. 145.

**39** Scribner's was the American publisher of the *Encyclopedia Britannica*. Fitzgerald had purchased the multivolume set from his publisher on credit.

**40** Fitzgerald is asking for a copy of *Portraits: Real and Imaginary* (1924) by the Irish journalist and literary critic Ernest Boyd (1887–1946). Published in the U.S. by Doran, the book contains a personality sketch of Fitzgerald.

41 See note 24 on p. 206 of this volume.

*TO: Maxwell Perkins*
*c. January 15, 1925*

American Express Co.
Rome.

Dear Max:

Proof hasn't arrived yet. Have been in bed for a week with grippe but I'm ready to attack it violently. Here are two important things.

1.  In the scene in Myrtes appartment—in the place where <u>Tom + Myrtle dissapear for awhile</u> noticeably raw. Does it stick out enough so that the censor might get it. Its the only place in the book I'm in doubt about on that score. Please let me know right away

2.  Please have <u>no quotations from any critics whatsoever on the jacket</u>—simply your own blurb on the back and don't give away too much of the idea— especially don't connect Daisy + Gatsby (I need the quality of surprise there) Please be <u>very general</u>.

These points are both very important. Do drop me a line about them. Wish I could see your new house. I havn't your faith in Will James[41]—I feel its old material without too much feeling or too new a touch.

As Ever,
Scott

FROM: *Maxwell Perkins*

Jan. 20, 1925

Dear Scott:

I am terribly rushed for time so I am answering your letter as briefly and rapidly as I can,—but I will have a chance to write to tell you the news, etc. etc., soon.

First as to the jazz history of the world:—that did jar on me unfavorably. And yet in a way it pleased me as a tour de force, but one not completely successful. Upon the whole, I should probably have objected to it in the first place except that I felt you needed something there in the way of incident, something special. But if you have something else, I would take it out.[42]

You are beginning to get me worried about the scene in Myrtle's apartment for you have spoken of it several times. It never occurred to me to think there was any objection to it. I am sure there is none. No censor could make an issue on that,—nor I think on anything else in the book.

I will be sure not to use any quotations and I will make it very general indeed, because I realize that not much ought to be said about the story. I have not thought what to say, but we might say something very brief which gave the impression that nothing need any longer be said.

I certainly hope the proofs have got to you and that you have been at work on them for some time. If not you had better cable. They were sent first-class mail. The first lot on December 27th and the second lot on December 30th.

Yours,

[Max]

P.S. The mysterious hand referred to in the immemorial phrase is that of the typesetter.[43]

42 Perkins refers to a passage in the typescript of the novel that Fitzgerald had submitted to Scribner's in October 1924. Fitzgerald cut Nick's account of the "Jazz History of the World" in the proofs. The passage, reproduced in the Cambridge edition of *Trimalchio* (2000), reads in part: "It started out with a weird, spinning sound, mostly from the cornets. Then there would be a series of interruptive notes which colored everything that came after them until before you knew it they became the theme and new discords were opposed outside. But just as you'd get used to the new discord one of the old themes would drop back in, this time as a discord, until you'd get a weird sense that it was a preposterous cycle after all. Long after the piece was over it went on and on in my head—whenever I think of that summer I can hear it yet" (p. 42).

43 Perkins refers to Fitzgerald's query about his manuscript being "in hand," this from Fitzgerald's letter c. December 20, 1924. See p. 208 in this volume.

*TO: Maxwell Perkins*

Hotel des Princes
Rome, Italy
January 24. 1925
(But address the American Express Co.
because its damn cold here and we may leave any day.

Dear Max:

This is a most important letter so I'm having it typed. Guard it as your life.

1) Under a separate cover I'm sending the first part of the proof. While I agreed with the general suggestions in your first letters I differ with you in others. I <u>want</u> Myrtle Wilson's breast ripped off—its exactly the thing, I think, and I don't want to chop up the good scenes by too much tinkering. When Wolfshiem says "sid" for "said", it's deliberate. "Orgastic" is the adjective from "orgasm" and it expresses exactly the intended ecstasy. It's not a bit dirty. I'm much more worried about the disappearance of Tom and Myrtle on galley 9—I think it's all right but I'm not sure. If it isn't please wire and I'll send correction.

2) Now about the page proof—under certain conditions never mind sending them (unless, of course, there's loads of time, which I suppose there isn't. I'm keen for late March or early April publication)

<u>The conditions are two</u>.

a) That someone reads it <u>very carefully twice</u> to see that every one of my inserts are put in correctly. There are so many of them that I'm in terror of a mistake.

b) That no changes <u>whatsoever</u> are made in it except in the case of a misprint so glaring as to be certain, and that only by you.

If there's some time left but not enough for the double mail send them to me and I'll simply wire O.K. which will save two weeks. However don't postpone for that. In any case send me the page proof as usual just to see.

3) Now, many thanks for the deposit. Two days after wiring you I had a cable from Reynolds[44] that he'd sold two stories of mine for a total of $3,750. but before that I was in debt to him and after turning down the ten thousand dollars from College Humor[45] I was afraid to borrow more from him until he'd made a sale. I won't ask for any more from you until the book has earned it. My guess is that it will sell about 80,000 copies but I may be wrong. Please thank Mr. Charles Scribner for me. I bet he thinks he's caught another John Fox now for sure. Thank God for John Fox. It would have been awful to have had no predecessor.[46]

4) This is very important. Be sure not to give away <u>any</u> of my plot in the blurb. Don't give away that Gatsby <u>dies</u> or is a <u>parvenu</u> or <u>crook</u> or anything. It's a part of the suspense of the book that all these things are in doubt until the end. You'll watch this won't you? And remember about having no quotations from critics on the jacket—<u>not even about my</u> other books!

5) This is just a list of small things.
   a) What's Ring's title for his spring book?[47]
   b) Did O'Brien star my story Absolution or any of my others on his trash-album?[48]
   c) I wish your bookkeeping department would send me an account on Feb. 1st. Not that it gives me pleasure to see how much in debt I am but that I like to keep a yearly record of the sales of all my books.

44 See note 19 on p. 200 in this volume.

45 Fitzgerald had rejected an offer from *College Humor* for serial rights to *The Great Gatsby*. He feared that the appearance of the novel in a magazine of light humor and satire would damage his literary reputation and have a negative effect on the reception of the book.

46 American journalist and novelist John Fox Jr. (1862–1919) published several novels with Scribner's, including the best sellers *The Little Shepherd of Kingdom Come* (1903) and *The Trail of the Lonesome Pine* (1908), historical romances set in the Appalachian Mountains of Kentucky and Virginia. Fox borrowed large sums of money from Scribner's during his career.

47 Forthcoming from Scribner's in the spring of 1925, Lardner's short story collection was titled *What of It?*

48 Fitzgerald refers to the annual Best Short Stories series, edited by anthologist Edward J. O'Brien (1890–1941). Each year O'Brien made his selections from American periodicals, having previously chosen Fitzgerald's "Two for a Cent" for the 1922 volume ("Babylon Revisited" would be reprinted in the 1931 volume). At the back of each volume, O'Brien awarded stars to worthy stories not included in his roundup. "Absolution" received three stars in *The Best Short Stories of 1923*. Though Fitzgerald was disdainful of the series, he made a note in his personal ledger whenever one of his stories was starred.

Do answer every question and keep this letter until the proof comes. Let me know how you like the changes. I miss seeing you, Max, more than I can say.

As ever,

Scott

P.S. I'm returning the proof of the title page ect. It's O.K. but my heart tells me I should have named it <u>Trimalchio</u>. However against all the advice I suppose it would have been stupid and stubborn of me. <u>Trimalchio in West Egg</u> was only a compromise. <u>Gatsby</u> is too much like Babbit and <u>The Great Gatsby</u> is weak because there's no emphasis even ironically on his greatness or lack of it. However let it pass.

*TO: Maxwell Perkins*
*c. February 18, 1925*

New Address $\left\{\begin{array}{l}\text{Hotel Tiberio}\\\text{Capri}\end{array}\right.$

Dear Max:

After six weeks of uninterrupted work the proof is finished and the last of it goes to you this afternoon. On the whole its been very successful labor

(1.)  I've brought Gatsby to life
(2.)  I've accounted for his money
(3.)  I've fixed up the two weak chapers (VI and VII)
(4.)  I've improved his first party
(5.)  I've broken up his long narrative in Chap. VIII

This morning I wired you to <u>hold up the galley of Chap 40</u>. The correction—and God! its important because in my other revision I made Gatsby look too mean—is enclosed herewith. Also some corrections for the page proof.

We're moving to Capri. We hate Rome, I'm behind financially and have to write three short stories. Then I try another play, and by June, I hope, begin my new novel.

Had long interesting letters from Ring and John Bishop.[49] Do tell me if all corrections have been recieved. I'm worried

Scott

I hope you're setting publication date at first possible moment.

**49** John Peale Bishop (1892–1944), American poet, novelist, and critic. Fitzgerald met Bishop at Princeton. See also note 2 on p. 2 in this volume.

**50** Charles Dunn and Roger Burlingame, members of the editorial department at Scribner's. Burlingame later wrote a house history on the occasion of the firm's centenary: *Of Making Many Books: A Hundred Years of Reading, Writing and Publishing* (Scribner's, 1946).

**51** In 1925 Scribner's reissued *You Know Me Al*, *The Big Town*, and *Gullible's Travels*—previously published by other firms—as part of a five-volume set of Lardner's writings that included *What of It?* and *How to Write Short Stories*.

**52** Perkins refers to Ring Lardner's article "General Symptoms of Being 35—Which Is What I Am," published in *American Magazine* (May 1921). The article would later be included in an augmented third printing of *What of It?*

**53** Perkins refers to Hemingway's *in our time* (1924), published in Paris in a limited edition by William Bird's Three Mountains Press. The book would have been difficult for Perkins to find: approximately 130 copies of the 300-copy print run were spoiled by the printer, leaving only about 170 copies for sale. The expanded *In Our Time* (1925), Hemingway's first commercial book, was published in October 1925 by Boni & Liveright.

*FROM: Maxwell Perkins*

Feb. 24, 1925

Dear Scott:

I congratulate you on resisting the $10,000. I don't see how you managed it. But it delighted us, for otherwise book publication would have been deferred until too late in the spring. . . . Those [changes] you have made do wonders for Gatsby,—in making him visible and palpable. You're right about the danger of meddling with the high spots—instinct is the best guide there. I'll have the proofs read twice, once by Dunn and once by Roger,[50] and shall allow no change unless it is certain the printer has blundered. I know the whole book so well myself that I could hardly decide wrongly. But I won't decide anything if there is ground for doubt.

Ring Lardner came back last week from Nassau looking brown and well, with the page proof of his new book—"What of It". I'll send you a copy soon. That and "How to Write Short Stories," "Alibi Ike," "The Big Town," and "Gullible's Travels," with new prefaces, constitute the set.[51] I simply could not get Ring to pay enough attention to it to reorganize the material as we might have done. I tried to work out a book to contain "Symptoms of Being 35"[52] and some of the shorter things; but without the war material—which, good as it was, seems dreadfully old now—there was not enough. And the subscription agents wanted to retain the familiar titles for their canvassing. "How to Write Short Stories" has sold 16,500 copies and it continues steadily to sell: the new book and the old books in new forms and wrappers, in the trade, will give it new impetus. We'll have a wonderful Ring Lardner window when we get all these books out.

As for Hemingway: I finally got his "In our time"[53] which accumulates a fearful effect through a series of brief episodes, presented with economy, strength and vitality. A remarkable, tight, complete expression of the scene, in our time, as it looks to Hemingway. I have written him that we wish he would write us about his plans and if possible send a ms.; but I must say I have little hope that he will get the letter,—so hard was it for me to get his book. Do you know his address?

[ .... ]

As ever,
[Max]

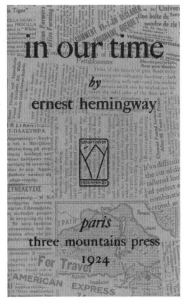

Front panel of the cover for the 1924 *in our time*, published by Three Mountains Press as part of Ezra Pound's "Inquest" series (an "Inquest into the state of contemporary English prose"). Like Pound, Fitzgerald had a keen eye for spotting new talent.

# CHRONOLOGY

1896    Born September 24 at his parents' home at 481 Laurel Avenue, in St. Paul, Minnesota, first surviving child of Mollie McQuillan Fitzgerald and Edward Fitzgerald. Named Francis Scott Key Fitzgerald after the author of "The Star-Spangled Banner," his father's second cousin three times removed. Mother, born 1860 in St. Paul, is the eldest of five children of successful grocery wholesaler who at his death in 1877 left an estate of more than $250,000 and a large Victorian home on Summit Avenue, St. Paul's most fashionable street. Father, born in 1853 in Rockville, Maryland, is a furniture manufacturer. They had two daughters who died, aged three and one, earlier in 1896.

1898    When furniture business fails, family moves to Buffalo, New York, where father takes a job as a wholesale grocery salesman for Procter & Gamble.

1901    Father transferred by Procter & Gamble to Syracuse, New York, and family moves in January. Sister Annabel born in July.

1902    Enrolls in Miss Goodyear's School in September.

1903    Family moves back to Buffalo. Attends school at Holy Angels Convent.

1905    Transfers to Miss Nardin's private Catholic school. Reads *The Scottish Chiefs*, *Ivanhoe*, and the adventure novels of G. A. Henty.

1908    Father loses his job at Procter & Gamble in March and in July family moves back to St. Paul, where at first they live with the McQuillans and then in a series of rented homes, eventually settling at 599 Summit Avenue. Enters St. Paul Academy in September.

1909    Publishes first story, "The Mystery of the Raymond Mortgage," in *Now and Then*, the St. Paul Academy school paper, in October.

1910    Publishes two more stories in *Now and Then*, "Reade, Substitute Right Half" (February) and "A Debt of Honor" (March).

1911    Publishes story "The Room with the Green Blinds" in the June *Now and Then*. In August, writes and plays the lead in a play, *The Girl from Lazy J*, for the Elizabethan Dramatic Club, local amateur theatrical group. Because of poor grades at St. Paul Academy, is sent in September to boarding school at the Newman School in Hackensack, New Jersey, where his personality makes him unpopular. Takes frequent trips to New York City and attends theater often, seeing Ina Claire in *The Quaker Girl* and Gertrude

Bryant in *Little Boy Blue*. Publishes poem "Football" in Christmas issue of the school magazine, the *Newman News*.

1912–13    Writes another play, *The Captured Shadow*, which is produced by the Elizabethan Dramatic Club in the summer of 1912. Publishes three stories in the *Newman News* during the 1912–13 school year. Meets Father Cyril Sigourney Webster Fay, prominent Catholic priest, who becomes a mentor. During a visit to Father Fay in Washington, meets Henry Adams and Anglo-Irish writer Shane Leslie. Despite failing four courses in two years at the Newman School, Fitzgerald takes entrance examination for Princeton University in May 1913. Writes play *Coward* for Elizabethan Dramatic Club in July. Grandmother McQuillan dies in August, leaving his mother enough money for his college tuition. Enters Princeton in September as member of Class of 1917.

1914    Meets John Peale Bishop and Edmund Wilson, fellow students at Princeton. In January his book and lyrics for *Fie! Fie! Fi-Fi!* win the competition for the 1914–15 Triangle Club show. Contributes to the *Princeton Tiger*, the college humor magazine. Reads and admires the social reform writings of H. G. Wells and George Bernard Shaw and Compton Mackenzie's novel *Sinister Street*. Writes fourth and last play for the Elizabethan Dramatic Club, *Assorted Spirits*, during summer. Returns to Princeton in September but is ineligible for extracurricular activities because of poor grades and cannot act in *Fie! Fie! Fi-Fi!* during the fall semester.

1915    Meets Ginevra King, sixteen-year-old from socially prominent Lake Forest, Illinois, family, while home for Christmas vacation. Falls in love with her and writes to her almost daily after he returns to Princeton. Elected secretary of the Triangle Club in February after his grades improve; later in the term is selected for the Cottage Club and for the editorial board of the *Tiger*. Story "Shadow Laurels" is published in the *Nassau Literary Magazine* (the *Lit*) in April, followed in June by "The Ordeal." Writes the lyrics (Edmund Wilson writes the book) for *The Evil Eye*, the 1915–16 Triangle Club show. Takes Ginevra King to the Princeton prom in June. In the fall, his low grades again make him ineligible for campus activities. Takes French literature course taught by Christian Gauss and begins lifelong friendship with Gauss, who later becomes Dean of the College. Continues to write for the *Tiger*. In November, falls ill and leaves college for the remainder of the semester to recuperate (illness is diagnosed as malaria, but may have been mild case of tuberculosis).

1916    Spends the spring in St. Paul on a leave of absence from Princeton; publishes poem "To My Unused Greek Book" in the *Lit*. Continues courtship of Ginevra King, whom he visits in Lake Forest in August. Returns to Princeton in September to repeat his junior year and writes the lyrics for the Triangle Club show, *Safety First*, in which he is again ineligible to perform. Attends Princeton–Yale football game with King in November.

1917    Courtship of Ginevra King ends in January. Publishes play "The Debutante," whose title character is modeled on King, in the *Lit*. During spring semester, his writing appears another twelve times in the *Lit* (four stories, three poems, and five reviews of books by Shane Leslie, E. F. Benson, H. G. Wells, and Booth Tarkington). In May, a month after the U.S. enters World War I, signs up for three weeks of intensive military training and takes exam for infantry commission. During summer in St. Paul, reads William James, Schopenhauer, and Bergson. While waiting for his commission, returns to Princeton in September and rooms with John Biggs, Jr., editor of the *Tiger*, and continues to contribute to both the *Tiger* and the *Lit*. Receives commission as second lieutenant in the infantry and in November reports for training to Fort Leavenworth, Kansas. Expecting that he will eventually be killed in combat, begins writing a novel.

1918    On leave from the army in February, finishes novel, "The Romantic Egotist," at the Cottage Club in Princeton and sends it to Shane Leslie, who has agreed to recommend it to his publisher, Charles Scribner's Sons. Reports in March to 45th Infantry Regiment at Camp Zachary Taylor, near Louisville; in April, regiment is transferred to Camp Gordon in Georgia, and in June, to Camp Sheridan, outside Montgomery, Alabama. In July, at a dance at the Country Club of Montgomery, meets Zelda Sayre, eighteen-year-old daughter of a justice of the Alabama Supreme Court. Scribner's rejects "The Romantic Egotist" in August; Fitzgerald submits a revised version, which is rejected in October. War ends on November 11, as Fitzgerald is waiting to embark for France with his regiment. Continues courtship of Zelda Sayre, who is reluctant to commit to marriage because of his lack of income and prospects.

1919    Father Fay dies on January 10. Fitzgerald is discharged from the army, moves to New York in February, and takes job at Barron Collier advertising agency writing trolley-car ads. Writes fiction and poetry at night, accumulating 112 rejection slips. *The Smart Set* accepts "Babes in the Woods," revised version of story published in 1917 issue of the *Lit*, paying him $30 (story appears in September). Sends Zelda his mother's engagement ring in March, but cannot convince her to marry him during visits to Montgomery, April–June. During his last visit, Zelda breaks off the engagement. Quits job and returns to parents' house in St. Paul, determined to rewrite novel and have it accepted for publication. Sends novel, now titled *This Side of Paradise*, to editor Maxwell Perkins at Scribner's in September. Perkins writes on September 16 that the firm has accepted it: "The book is so different that it is hard to prophesy how it will sell but we are all for taking a chance and supporting it with vigor." Revises several of his rejected stories; four are accepted by *The Smart Set*, two by *Scribner's Magazine*, and one by *The Saturday Evening Post*. Earns $879 from his writing by the end of the year. During a trip to New York in November, engages Harold Ober as his agent. Visits Zelda in Montgomery.

1920    With Harold Ober's assistance, begins to sell stories regularly to *The Saturday Evening Post*, which pays $400 each for them; by February, they have bought six. Reads

Samuel Butler's *Note-Books* and H. L. Mencken's essays. Spends January in New Orleans writing stories and reading proofs of his novel, then moves back to New York in February. Sells story "Head and Shoulders" to Metro Films for $2,500. *This Side of Paradise* is published March 26; it sells three thousand copies in three days, and makes its author a celebrity. Marries Zelda in vestry of New York's St. Patrick's Cathedral on April 3. Develops friendships with Mencken and George Jean Nathan, editors of *The Smart Set*. Reads Mark Twain. In May, *Metropolitan Magazine* takes option on his stories at $900 per story and, eventually, publishes four. Rents house in Westport, Connecticut, and in July takes car trip to Montgomery. Scribner's publishes *Flappers and Philosophers*, collection of eight stories, September 10. Rents apartment on West 59th Street in New York in October and works on second novel.

1921    Zelda discovers she is pregnant in February. In May, they sail for Europe, visiting England (where they have tea with John Galsworthy), Paris, Venice, Florence, and Rome, returning in July to the U.S., where they live in St. Paul. Second novel, *The Beautiful and Damned*, begins to run serially in *Metropolitan Magazine* in September. Daughter Frances Scott (Scottie) Fitzgerald is born on October 26.

1922    *The Beautiful and Damned* published by Scribner's March 4; it receives mixed reviews and sells forty thousand copies in a year. Begins work on play. Moves to Great Neck, Long Island, where he begins close friendships with Ring Lardner and John Dos Passos. *Tales of the Jazz Age*, short-story collection, published by Scribner's on September 22. Reads Dostoevsky and Dickens.

1923    Sells first option on his stories to Hearst organization for $1,500 per story. Receives $10,000 for film rights to *This Side of Paradise*. Play *The Vegetable* is published by Scribner's on April 27. Begins work on third novel. *The Vegetable* opens for pre-Broadway tryout in Atlantic City, New Jersey, on November 19, is received badly, and closes almost immediately, leaving its author in debt. Starts selling stories to *The Saturday Evening Post* for $1,250 each. Earns $28,759.78 from his writing for the year, but spends more.

1924    Sails for France in May to complete novel, settling on the Riviera. Zelda becomes romantically involved with French naval aviator Edouard Jozan in July; although the relationship ends quickly, Fitzgerald later writes, "I knew something had happened that could never be repaired." Meets Gerald and Sara Murphy during the summer. In October, recommends the work of Ernest Hemingway to Perkins and Scribner's. After sending manuscript of new novel to Scribner's in late October, goes to Rome and Capri for winter. Drinks heavily and quarrels constantly with Zelda.

1925    Extensively revises novel in galley proof in January and February, changing title to *The Great Gatsby*. Moves to Paris in April. *The Great Gatsby* is published by Scribner's on April 10, receives mostly favorable reviews, but sales are disappointing. Meets Hemingway for first time at the Dingo bar in Montparnasse and subsequently takes trip

Wealthy American expatriates Gerald and Sara Murphy, 1923, on the beach at Cap d'Antibes. After the Fitzgeralds arrived on the Riviera in the summer of 1924, they became friendly with the Murphys, who were older than Scott and Zelda and felt protective toward them. The Murphys introduced the Fitzgeralds to a circle of European avant-garde writers and artists, including Cocteau, Picasso, Satie, and Tristan Tsara. Gerald Murphy's self-discipline, social poise, and philosophy of living were particularly appealing to Scott.

to Lyon with him. Has tea with Edith Wharton at her home outside Paris in July. Through Hemingway, meets Gertrude Stein, Robert McAlmon (founder of Contact Editions publishers), and Sylvia Beach (owner of Shakespeare & Co. bookstore in Paris). Spends part of summer ("1000 parties and no work") on the Riviera, where his friends include writers Dos Passos, Max Eastman, Archibald MacLeish, and Floyd Dell and movie star Rudolph Valentino. Returns to Paris in September and spends a great deal of time with Hemingway.

1926    *All the Sad Young Men*, short-story collection, is published by Scribner's on February 26. Returns to the Riviera in March and begins work on new novel. Encourages Scribner's to publish Hemingway's novels *The Torrents of Spring* and *The Sun Also Rises*. Reads draft of *The Sun Also Rises* in July and convinces Hemingway to eliminate the first two chapters. Returns to U.S. in December, spending Christmas in Montgomery.

1927    Spends first two months of year in Hollywood, under contract to United Artists to write flapper comedy for Constance Talmadge; script, "Lipstick," is eventually rejected.

Meets and is infatuated with seventeen-year-old Hollywood starlet Lois Moran; also meets producer Irving Thalberg, Lillian Gish, John Barrymore, and Richard Barthelmess. With help of Princeton roommate John Biggs, Jr., rents Ellerslie, Greek Revival–style mansion outside Wilmington, Delaware. Zelda begins ballet lessons with director of Philadelphia Opera Ballet and also writes magazine articles. Fitzgerald's income from writing for year totals $29,757.87, a new high.

1928    Goes to Paris for the summer in April. Zelda continues ballet studies there with Lubov Egorova. Writes nine Basil Duke Lee stories for *The Saturday Evening Post*, which earn him $31,500. Meets James Joyce at dinner given by Sylvia Beach in June. Later in summer, meets Thornton Wilder and heavyweight boxing champion Gene Tunney, who are on a walking tour of Europe together. Returns to U.S. in October and resumes work on novel. Attends Princeton–Yale football game in Princeton on November 19 with Hemingway and his wife, Pauline.

1929    Gives up lease on Ellerslie in spring and returns to Europe, renting apartment in Paris in April. Zelda resumes ballet lessons with Egorova and also publishes series of short stories in *College Humor*. Fitzgerald reads typescript of Hemingway's novel *A Farewell to Arms* in June and offers suggestions for revisions, all of which Hemingway ridicules but some of which he takes. Rents villa in Cannes from July to September. Now is paid $4,000 per story by *The Saturday Evening Post*. Returns to Paris in October and lives in rented apartment. Works on novel, while Zelda continues her ballet lessons and writing.

1930    Travels with Zelda to North Africa in February. Her behavior shows signs of extreme stress, and on April 23, she enters Malmaison clinic outside Paris. Discharges herself on May 11 to resume ballet lessons, then attempts suicide and enters Val-Mont clinic in Glion, Switzerland, on May 22. After being diagnosed as schizophrenic by Dr. Oscar Forel, she is transferred in June to Forel's Les Rives de Prangins clinic on Lake Geneva. Fitzgerald spends summer traveling between Paris and Switzerland. Meets Thomas Wolfe in Paris and later spends time with him in Switzerland. In order to pay for Zelda's treatment, writes and sells stories to *The Saturday Evening Post*, earning $32,000 for the year from eight stories, among them "Babylon Revisited," published in December. Spends fall at Hotel de la Paix in Lausanne and has brief affair with Englishwoman Bijou O'Conor.

1931    Father dies in January in Washington and Fitzgerald goes home for funeral. After visits to Montgomery and New York, returns to Europe and finds Zelda's condition improved; she becomes an outpatient and is allowed to take trips to Paris and the Austrian Tyrol, then is discharged from Prangins on September 15. Sails for U.S. with Zelda on September 19, and settles in Montgomery. Goes to Hollywood in November after being offered $1,200 a week by M-G-M to work on a Jean Harlow movie, leaving Zelda in Montgomery to be with her ailing father, who dies on November 17. Returns to Montgomery for Christmas.

1932    Takes Zelda in January on vacation to Florida and she works on a novel. Zelda has relapse on trip back to Montgomery, and enters Henry Phipps Psychiatric Clinic in Baltimore on February 12. Fitzgerald remains in Montgomery to work on his novel. Zelda finishes her novel while at the Phipps Clinic and, after Fitzgerald comes to Baltimore to help her revise it, Scribner's accepts it. Rents La Paix, Victorian-style house on the Turnbull estate in Towson, just outside Baltimore, in May. Zelda is discharged from Phipps on June 26. In August, Fitzgerald spends time at Johns Hopkins Hospital with what is diagnosed as typhoid fever (will eventually be hospitalized there eight more times from 1933 to 1937 for alcoholism and chronic inactive fibroid tuberculosis). Zelda's novel *Save Me the Waltz* is published October 7; it receives bad reviews and sells very poorly. Resumes serious work on his novel, while Zelda paints and writes play, *Scandalabra*.

1933    *Scandalabra* is produced by the Junior Vagabonds, Baltimore amateur little theater, in the spring. In September, Ring Lardner dies and Fitzgerald writes tribute for *The New Republic*. Sends new novel, *Tender Is the Night*, to Scribner's in late October.

1934    *Tender Is the Night* serialized in *Scribner's Magazine*, January–April, and is published on April 12, receiving largely favorable reviews and selling well. While working on revising the book in New York in January and February, spends time with John O'Hara and with Dorothy Parker. Zelda reenters Phipps Clinic on February 12 and later is transferred to Craig House in Beacon, New York ("I left my capacity for hoping on the little roads that led to Zelda's sanitarium"). Fitzgerald arranges showing of her paintings at art gallery in New York in March and April, and she is permitted to attend opening. When her condition deteriorates, Zelda is admitted to the Sheppard and Enoch Pratt Hospital outside Baltimore on May 19. Fitzgerald begins to sell stories and articles to recently established magazine *Esquire*, which pays $250 per piece.

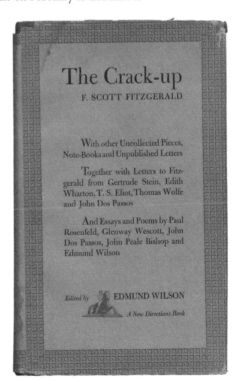

"The Crack-Up"—the first of three successive *Esquire* essays about Fitzgerald's physical and mental collapse—appeared in the magazine's February 1936 issue. Believing the essays would be injurious to Fitzgerald's reputation, Maxwell Perkins at Scribner's declined Edmund Wilson's proposal for a posthumous collection of his friend's writings that would bring the three essays together with other of Fitzgerald's autobiographical writings. *The Crack-Up* (1945) was published instead by New Directions.

1935    Travels to Tryon, North Carolina, in February in attempt to improve his health. *Taps at Reveille*, short-story collection, published by Scribner's on March 10. Spends summer in Asheville, North Carolina, at the Grove Park Inn, where he has affair with Beatrice Dance, who is married. Returns to Baltimore in September and lives in rented apartment. Spends winter in Hendersonville, North Carolina.

1936    Writes three confessional articles, "The Crack-Up," "Pasting It Together," and "Handle With Care," which appear in *Esquire*, February–April, and arouse considerable consternation among his friends. Zelda is transferred to Highland Hospital in Asheville on April 6, and Fitzgerald spends summer at Grove Park Inn to be near her. Mother dies in August, but Fitzgerald is unable to attend funeral. Daughter enters Ethel Walker School in Simsbury, Connecticut, in September. On his fortieth birthday in September is interviewed by Michel Mok of the New York *Post*. Subsequent article is headlined "Scott Fitzgerald, 40, Engulfed in Despair"; after it appears, Fitzgerald attempts suicide with overdose of morphine. Through Perkins, meets Marjorie Kinnan Rawlings when she comes to Asheville. Spends Christmas holidays in Johns Hopkins Hospital recovering from influenza and heavy drinking.

1937    Spends first months of year at Oak Hall Hotel in Tryon, North Carolina. Has great difficulty selling stories; his debts exceed $40,000, with $12,000 owed to his agent, Harold Ober. Hired as a screenwriter by M-G-M in July for six months at $1,000 per week. Rents small apartment at Garden of Allah, 8152 Sunset Boulevard, in Hollywood. Meets Sheilah Graham, twenty-eight-year-old Englishwoman who writes a Hollywood gossip column, at a party soon after his arrival, and they begin an affair. Works on film adaptation of Erich Maria Remarque's novel *Three Comrades*. Though it is extensively altered by producer Joseph Mankiewicz, his work on it contributes to renewal of his M-G-M contract (will be only screenplay for which he receives on-screen credit).

Fitzgerald in Hollywood, June 1937. "I wish now I'd *never* relaxed or looked back—but said at the end of *The Great Gatsby*: 'I've found my line—from now on this comes first. This is my immediate duty—without this I am nothing.'"—Fitzgerald, in a letter to Scottie, June 12, 1940. *The Letters of F. Scott Fitzgerald*, p. 79.

1938    Visits Zelda in January and takes her to Florida and Montgomery. Returns to Hollywood, and works from February to May on "Infidelity," movie for Joan Crawford, which is never produced. During daughter's spring vacation, takes her and Zelda to Virginia

Beach and Norfolk, Virginia, but gets drunk and behaves badly. Moves to house at 114 Malibu Beach in April. Daughter is accepted at Vassar College. Fitzgerald works from May to October on screenplay of Claire Boothe Luce's play *The Women* but is eventually replaced. Moves to Encino in November and rents small house on Belly Acres estate of actor Edward Everett Horton. Hires Frances Kroll as his secretary. Plans educational curriculum, "College of One," for Sheilah Graham, a two-year course in the arts and humanities that he participates in by tutoring her as well as assigning readings. Begins work in November on *Madame Curie*, film for Greta Garbo.

1939    Plans for *Madame Curie* are shelved in January, and after he is loaned to David O. Selznick to work very briefly on *Gone With the Wind*, Fitzgerald learns that M-G-M is dropping its option after eighteen months. Becomes freelance screenwriter and socializes in Hollywood with, among others, Nathanael West and S. J. Perelman. Hired by producer Walter Wanger of United Artists to collaborate with recent Dartmouth graduate Budd Schulberg on screenplay of *Winter Carnival*; they take a disastrous trip to Dartmouth College in February, during which Fitzgerald is drunk the entire time, and they are both fired. Goes on trip to Cuba with Zelda in April, and is so drunk and ill that she has to take him to New York, where he is hospitalized before returning to California. Begins work on a novel about Hollywood, with main character, Monroe Stahr, based on Irving Thalberg (never completed, it is edited by Edmund Wilson and published posthumously in 1941 as *The Last Tycoon*). Receives intermittent but brief screenwriting assignments but falls deeper in debt, eventually severing ties with longtime agent Harold Ober because Ober refuses to lend him any more money; becomes his own agent.

The Armed Services Edition of *The Great Gatsby* has often been credited with aiding the novel's postwar rise to canonical status. Some 155,000 ASE copies of *Gatsby* were distributed to members of the armed forces during World War II. From 1925 to 1942, Scribner's printed only 25,000 copies of the novel.

1940 Begins to publish series of stories in *Esquire* about Pat Hobby, a hack Hollywood writer, for which he receives $250 per story; ultimately, *Esquire* publishes seventeen Pat Hobby stories, one in each monthly number from January 1940 to July 1941. Writes "Cosmopolitan," screen adaptation of his story "Babylon Revisited," but it is never used. Moves in May to apartment at 1403 Laurel Avenue in Hollywood, a block from Sheilah Graham's apartment, and works intensively on his novel through the summer and fall. Suffers heart attack in late November and is ordered to rest in bed. Moves to Sheilah Graham's apartment, where he dies, apparently of a second heart attack, on December 21. With Zelda's approval, decision is made to bury Fitzgerald with his father's family in Rockville, Maryland, but he is refused burial at St. Mary's Church cemetery because he was not a practicing Catholic at his death. Buried December 27 at Rockville Union Cemetery.

# TEXTUAL NOTE

The text of this Library of America edition of *The Great Gatsby* is based on the first printing of the first edition. This text has been collated against the surviving manuscript, the revised galley proofs, and several subsequent editions and printings. Six plate alterations from the second Scribner's printing have been admitted into the text, along with one correction from the duplicate electrotype plates employed by the British publisher Chatto & Windus for its 1926 printing. The revisions marked by Fitzgerald into his personal copy have been included. Typographical errors and other obvious mistakes have been corrected; punctuation and capitalization have been regularized. No attempt has been made to correct factual errors. Fitzgerald was a romantic fabulist, not a realist; his writings need not conform precisely to reality. Fitzgerald's preferred American spellings have been restored: the Scribner's 1925 text was typeset in a quasi-British house style that employed such spellings as "centre," "to-day," "defence," and "criticising"—all contrary to Fitzgerald's usual practice in his manuscripts. The result, in this Library of America edition, is a text that captures Fitzgerald's intentions as nearly as bibliographical labor and editorial imagination can bring it.

The letters between Fitzgerald and Perkins selected for this volume are printed in *F. Scott Fitzgerald: A Life in Letters* (Scribner's, 1994), edited by Matthew Bruccoli, with the following three exceptions. Fitzgerald's letter of January 15, 1925, to Perkins, and Perkins's letters of January 20, 1925, and February 24, 1925, to Fitzgerald have been newly transcribed by James L. W. West. Misspellings and other irregularities are preserved in all the selections. In a handful of stipulated cases, words dropped from the letters have been supplied in brackets. Some material not concerning *The Great Gatsby* has been omitted from the present volume; these omissions are signaled in the texts by four ellipsis points.

# SELECTED SOURCES

## PRIMARY EDITIONS

*The Great Gatsby.* New York: Charles Scribner's Sons, 1925. The first edition.

*The Last Tycoon, An Unfinished Novel … Together with The Great Gatsby and Selected Stories.* Edited by Edmund Wilson. New York: Charles Scribner's Sons, 1941. The first posthumous edition.

*The Great Gatsby: A Variorum Edition.* Edited by James L. W. West III. Cambridge and New York: Cambridge University Press, 2019. Scholarly edition, with illustrations and apparatus.

*The Great Gatsby and Related Stories.* Edited by James L. W. West III. New York: Library of America, 2023. The Library of America corrected text, with four short stories and Fitzgerald's correspondence with Maxwell Perkins.

## OTHER EDITIONS AND SOURCE MATERIALS

Full-color digital reproductions of the manuscript and the revised galley proofs of *The Great Gatsby* are available on the Special Collections website, Princeton University Library.

*The Great Gatsby: The Revised and Rewritten Galleys.* Edited by Matthew J. Bruccoli. New York and London: Garland Publishing, Inc., 1990. Facsimile of the revised galley proofs.

*The Great Gatsby.* New York: Collectors Reprints/First Edition Library, 1991. Photo-facsimile of the first-printing text. Green cloth, enclosed in a facsimile of the first-edition dust jacket.

*The Great Gatsby.* Cambremer, France: Éditions des Saints Pères, 2017. Facsimile of the manuscript, from the original at Princeton.

*Trimalchio: An Early Version of The Great Gatsby.* Edited by James L. W. West III. Cambridge and New York: Cambridge University Press, 2000. The text of the unrevised galley proofs, with editorial emendations.

*The Great Gatsby: An Edition of the Manuscript.* Edited by James L. W. West III and Don C. Skemer. Cambridge and New York: Cambridge University Press, 2018. The unemended manuscript text.

*The Great Gatsby: The 1926 Broadway Script.* By Owen Davis, based upon the novel by F. Scott Fitzgerald. Edited by Anne Margaret Daniel and James L. W. West III. Cambridge and New York: Cambridge University Press, 2024. The first dramatization of the novel.

*Dear Scott/Dear Max: The Fitzgerald–Perkins Correspondence.* Edited by John Kuehl and Jackson R. Bryer. New York: Charles Scribner's Sons, 1971. Letters between the author and editor.

*F. Scott Fitzgerald: A Life in Letters.* Edited by Matthew J. Bruccoli. New York: Charles Scribner's Sons, 1994. Letters to family, friends, and publishing professionals.

# ILLUSTRATION CREDITS

*Celestial Eyes* by Francis Cugat, cover art for the dust jacket for the first edition of *The Great Gatsby*. Courtesy of Princeton University Library.   *iv*

Page from Fitzgerald's scrapbook, reviews and dust jacket of *The Great Gatsby*. Illustration by Francis Cugat. The Great Gatsby, to Silent-Film Version of Gatsby; F. Scott Fitzgerald Papers, C0187, Manuscripts Division, Department of Special Collections. Courtesy of Princeton University Library.   *xviii*

Profile sketch of F. Scott Fitzgerald by Gordon Bryant. First published in *Shadowland* magazine in 1921.   *xxi*

Page from Fitzgerald's scrapbook, reviews of *The Great Gatsby*. The Great Gatsby, to Silent-Film Version of Gatsby; F. Scott Fitzgerald Papers, C0187, Manuscripts Division, Department of Special Collections. Courtesy of Princeton University Library.   *xxv*

Page from Fitzgerald's scrapbook, photograph of F. Scott Fitzgerald and daughter, Scottie, in Rome. The Great Gatsby, to Silent-Film Version of Gatsby; F. Scott Fitzgerald Papers, C0187, Manuscripts Division, Department of Special Collections. Courtesy of Princeton University Library.   *xxx*

Photograph of Zelda Fitzgerald. This Side of Paradise; F. Scott Fitzgerald Papers, C0187, Manuscripts Division, Department of Special Collections. Courtesy of Princeton University Library.   *4*

Photograph of Scott and Zelda Fitzgerald by Alfred Cheney Johnston. First published in *Hearst's International*, May 1923.   *6*

Joseph Conrad on the cover of *TIME*, April 7, 1923. Illustration by Gordon Stevenson.   *8*

1915 Dodge Brothers Touring Car, photographed by Tom Burnside. Courtesy of Science Photo Library.   *10*

Photograph of F. Scott Fitzgerald in military uniform (1917). Courtesy of ARCHIVIO GBB/ Alamy Stock Photo.   *11*

Drawing of F. Scott Fitzgerald by James Montgomery Flagg, undated. F. Scott Fitzgerald Papers, C0187, Manuscripts Division, Department of Special Collections, Courtesy of Princeton University Library.   *12*

Ginevra King on the cover of *Town & Country*, July 1918. Photograph by Arnold Genthe.   *14*

Cover of the 1920 first edition of Lothrop Stoddard's *The Rising Tide of Color*.   *18*

Postcard of the ocean liner RMS "Aquitania." Courtesy of World History Archive/Alamy Stock Photo.   *21*

Cover of *Saturday Evening Post*, May 1, 1922. Illustration by Norman Rockwell. Courtesy of Curtis Licensing.   *24*

Photograph of Edith Cummings (c. 1918). Courtesy of The Collection of the History Center of Lake Forest–Lake Bluff.   *25*

Cover of the 1920 first edition of *This Side of Paradise*. Illustration by W. E. Hill. Courtesy of Facsimile Dust Jackets LLC.    *26*

Cover of the 1922 first edition of *Tales of the Jazz Age*. Illustration by John Held, Jr. Courtesy of Facsimile Dust Jackets LLC.    *27*

Cover of the 1920 first edition of *Flappers and Philosophers*. Illustration by W. E. Hill.    *27*

Sketch of cover for *The Beautiful and Damned*, by Zelda Fitzgerald. The Beautiful and Damned—Drawing by Zelda Fitzgerald; F. Scott Fitzgerald Papers, C0187, Manuscripts Division, Department of Special Collections. Courtesy of Princeton University Library.    *28*

Cover of the 1922 first edition of *The Beautiful and Damned*. Illustration by W. E. Hill.    *28*

Map of Great Neck, published in *The New Yorker*, 1927. By John Held Jr., The New Yorker, © Condé Nast.    *30*

Cover of the 1922 first edition of *The Waste Land* by T. S. Eliot. Courtesy of Facsimile Dust Jackets LLC.    *32*

Photograph of sanitation workers at the Corona Ash Dump in Queens (c. 1920s). New York Department of Sanitation Museum Project, Faculty Digital Archive. New York University Libraries.    *33*

Photograph of John D. Rockefeller (1922). Cleveland Memory Project, Cleveland State University Library Special Collections.    *35*

Cover of the 1921 British edition of *Simon Called Peter* by Robert Keable.    *37*

Publicity photograph of F. Scott Fitzgerald posing at desk (c. 1920). Courtesy of Pictorial Press Ltd./Alamy Stock Photo.    *40*

Photograph of F. Scott Fitzgerald and Zelda Fitzgerald in Antibes, France. © Estate of Honoria Murphy Donnelly/Licensed by VAGA at Artists Rights Society (ARS), New York.    *43*

Joe Frisco doing the "Frisco Dance." Printed in *The New York Clipper*, May 26, 1920, p. 7.    *48*

Theatrical poster of Gilda Gray. Library of Congress, Prints and Photographs Division. Holly Press, Allied Printing, Portland, Oregon. Courtesy of Library of Congress.    *49*

*The Great Gatsby*, Trimalchio Galleys, Galley #13. The Great Gatsby—Trimalchio Galleys; F. Scott Fitzgerald Papers, C0187, Manuscripts Division, Department of Special Collections. Courtesy of Princeton University Library.    *51*

"Be Your Age" bookplate cartoon by Herb Roth. First published in *The New Yorker*, September 26, 1925.    *61*

Photograph of interior of the Murray Hill Hotel (c. 1905–15). Detroit Publishing Company photograph collection. Courtesy of Library of Congress.    *65*

Propaganda poster (1916) by Louis Raemaekers for *Century Magazine*. Courtesy of Library of Congress.    *72*

The Order of Danilo medal. Courtesy of eMedals Inc.    *73*

View of Midtown Manhattan skyline from Queensboro bridge (c. 1930). By Irving Browning. Photography © New-York Historical Society.    *75*

Photograph of Rathskeller in the Hotel Metropole at Broadway and 42nd Street (1915). Byron Company, New York, NY. Museum of the City of New York.    *77*

Photograph of "Lefty Louie" Rosenberg and "Gyp the Blood" Horowitz and their captors (1912). Bain News Service photograph collection. Courtesy of Library of Congress.    *78*

Photograph of Arnold Rothstein exiting a car in Chicago (1919).    *80*

Photograph of the 1919 Chicago White Sox team.    *81*

Photograph of Plaza Hotel, Fifth Avenue, New York City (c. 1927), by William J. Roege. Photography © New-York Historical Society.    *83*

Rudolph Valentino in a publicity scene from the film *The Sheik* (1921). Bettmann via Getty Images.    *86*

Jordan Motor Car Company advertisement, published in the June 23, 1923, issue of *The Saturday Evening Post*. Illustration by Fred Cole. Courtesy of Curtis Licensing.    *88*

Line drawing titled *View from Kant's Window*. Courtesy of the Bumers family wing of Friedrich Lahrs.    *95*

Scene from the stage production *The Great Gatsby* (1926). Billy Rose Theatre Division, The New York Public Library. New York Public Library Digital Collections.    *100*

Page from Fitzgerald's scrapbook, reviews of *The Great Gatsby* stage production. The Great Gatsby, to Silent-Film Version of Gatsby; F. Scott Fitzgerald Papers, C0187, Manuscripts Division, Department of Special Collections. Courtesy of Princeton University Library.    *104*

Photograph of bootleggers carted off to prison after their car was wrecked in a police chase (c. 1921). Buyenlarge/Archive Photos via Getty Images.    *107*

Cover of the 1935 Modern Library Edition of *The Great Gatsby* by F. Scott Fitzgerald. Courtesy of Facsimile Dust Jackets LLC.    *112*

Cover of sheet music for "Three O'Clock in the Morning" (1922).    *116*

Photograph of the National Biscuit Company building, at 15th Street and 10th Avenue (c. 1913), taken by Irving Underhill. Courtesy of the Library of Congress.    *121*

"Arrow Collars & Shirts" advertising poster by Joseph Christian Leyendecker. Library of Congress/Corbis Historical via Getty Images.    *125*

Publicity photograph of F. Scott Fitzgerald (1925). Courtesy of Ian Dagnall Computing/Alamy Stock Photo.    *127*

Photograph of men dumping alcohol during Prohibition (1918). Courtesy of Süddeutsche Zeitung Photo/Alamy Stock Photo.    *128*

Cover of GQ Magazine, March 1974. By Richard Amsel, GQ, © Condé Nast.    *129*

Page from Fitzgerald's scrapbook, showing a receipt from The Plaza Hotel. The Great Gatsby, to Silent-Film Version of Gatsby; F. Scott Fitzgerald Papers, C0187, Manuscripts Division, Department of Special Collections. Courtesy of Princeton University Library.    *135*

Theatrical poster for *The Great Gatsby* silent film (1926).    *138*

Glass slide from the 1926 silent film of *The Great Gatsby*. Courtesy of the Matthew J. and Arlyn Bruccoli Collection of F. Scott Fitzgerald, University of South Carolina Libraries, Columbia, SC.    *145*

*The Great Gatsby*, Autograph Manuscript, chapter VII, leaf 17. The Great Gatsby—Autograph Manuscript; F. Scott Fitzgerald Papers, C0187, Manuscripts Division, Department of Special Collections. Courtesy of Princeton University Library.    *149*

Page from Fitzgerald's photograph album bearing the title "Home Again." Matthew J. and Arlyn Bruccoli Collection of F. Scott Fitzgerald, University of South Carolina Libraries, Columbia, SC.    *154*

Photograph of switchboard operators in New York City (1929). Bettmann via Getty Images.    *163*

Still from Baz Luhrmann's *The Great Gatsby*, Eckleburg's eyes. Warner Bros., 2013.    *167*

Sketch by Francis Cugat for dust jacket of *The Great Gatsby*. Courtesy of Jay McInerney.    *169*

Photograph of the James J. Hill House, Saint Paul, Minnesota (2020), by Ben R Cooper. Courtesy of Ben Cooper.    *176*

Cover of the 1910 first edition of Clarence E. Mulford's *Hopalong Cassidy*.    *180*

*The Great Gatsby*, Trimalchio Galleys, Galley #55. The Great Gatsby—Trimalchio Galleys; F. Scott Fitzgerald Papers, C0187, Manuscripts Division, Department of Special Collections. Courtesy of Princeton University Library.    *183*

*View of Toledo* (oil on canvas) by El Greco (1541–1614). The Metropolitan Museum of Art, New York, H. O. Havemeyer Collection, Bequest of Mrs. H. O. Havemeyer, 1929. www.metmuseum.org.    *185*

Still from Baz Luhrmann's *The Great Gatsby*, green light from Gatsby's dock. *The Great Gatsby*. Warner Bros., 2013.    *189*

Handwritten final page of *The Great Gatsby* manuscript, chapter VIII, leaf 45. The Great Gatsby—Autograph Manuscript; F. Scott Fitzgerald Papers, C0187, Manuscripts Division, Department of Special Collections. Courtesy of Princeton University Library.    *190*

Photograph of Maxwell Perkins (c. 1920). Courtesy of ARCHIVIO GBB/Alamy Stock Photo.    *192*

Photograph of Ring Lardner with his wife on the boardwalk of Atlantic City (1923). Bettmann via Getty Images.    *196*

Preliminary sketches of Francis Cugat's *Celestial Eyes*, jacket art for *The Great Gatsby*. Courtesy of Jay McInerney.    *197*

Ernest Hemingway's passport photograph (1923). Courtesy of the John F. Kennedy Presidential Library and Museum.    *198*

Photograph of the Dingo American Bar and Restaurant.    *199*

Front cover of *Liberty Magazine*, June 21, 1924. Illustration by Coles Phillips.    *200*

Photograph of Fifth Avenue–47th Street, showing the Charles Scribner's Building (1925). Courtesy of Milstein Division, The New York Public Library.    *203*

Photograph of Edmund Wilson (1922). Edmund Wilson Papers. Yale Collection of American Literature, Beinecke Rare Book and Manuscript Library.    *207*

Cover of the 1923 first edition of *The Vegetable* by F. Scott Fitzgerald. Illustration by John Held, Jr.    *211*

Cover of the 1924 Three Mountains Press edition of Ernest Hemingway's *in our time*.    *219*

Photograph of Gerald and Sara Murphy on a beach in Antibes (1923). © Estate of Honoria Murphy Donnelly/Licensed by VAGA at Artists Rights Society (ARS), New York.    *225*

Cover of the 1945 first edition of *The Crack-Up*. Reprinted by permission of New Directions Publishing Corp.    *227*

Photograph of F. Scott Fitzgerald in Hollywood (1937). Library of Congress, Prints & Photographs Division, Carl Van Vechten Collection.    *228*

Cover of the Armed Services Edition of *The Great Gatsby*. Courtesy of the Rare Book and Special Collections Division of the Library of Congress, Washington, DC.    *229*

The text and notes for *The Annotated Great Gatsby* are set in Adobe Jenson, a serif typeface created by award-winning designer Robert Slimbach and released in 1996. Distinguished by its low "x" height, the lettering is based on a typeface cut in Venice in the 1470s by Nicolas Jenson, a book printer still celebrated for perfecting the form of roman type. The italics are inspired by a style designed in Rome a half century later by Ludovico Vicentino degli Arrighi, a papal scribe whose legacy is a series of italic typefaces modeled after chancery script.

The captions and running heads are set in Neutra Text, a sans-serif typeface created in 2002 by Christian Schwartz, who was inspired by the early-twentieth-century design principles of Austrian American architect Richard Neutra.

Text design and composition by Gopa & Ted2, Inc. Albuquerque, NM. Printing and binding by Versa Press, Inc., East Peoria, Il. The jacket was printed by Phoenix Color, A Division of Lakeside Book Company. The paper is acid-free and exceeds the requirements for permanence established by the American National Standards Institute.